The military aide to the President of the United States returned to the room. Major Felter realized that there must be a
hidden button somewhere that the President had pressed to
summon him.

'Major Felter's volunteered to go, Charley,' the President
said. 'Get the show on the road.'

'Yes, Mr. President.'

The President sat down at a table and took a sheet of
notepaper and quickly scrawled something on it.

'This may come in handy, Major,' he said, handing it to
him. Major Felter read it.

'Yes, sir, I'm sure it will.'

'Every soldier's ultimate ambition, Felter,' the President
chuckled. 'Commander in Chief.' He put out his hand. 'Go
with God, Major,' he said.

Also in Arrow by W.E.B. Griffin

BROTHERHOOD OF WAR

Book I: The Lieutenants
Book II: The Captains

The Majors

BROTHERHOOD OF WAR

BOOK III

by W.E.B. Griffin

ARROW BOOKS

Arrow Books Limited
62-65 Chandos Place, London WC2N 4NW

An imprint of Century Hutchinson Limited

London Melbourne Sydney Auckland
Johannesburg and agencies throughout
the world

First published in Great Britain by Century 1989
Arrow edition 1989

Printed and bound in Great Britain by
Courier International Ltd, Tiptree, Essex

ISBN 0 09 961430 8

For Uncle Charley and The Bull
RIP October 1979

And for Donn.
Who would have ever believed four *stars?*

I

(One)
Washington, D.C.
10 March 1954

The black, four-door Buick Roadmaster carried Virginia license plates. Attached to the plates was a strip of metal on which was stamped ALEXANDRIA 1954, as proof the owner had paid his 1954 Alexandria city automobile tax. The car showed none of the other decalomania, however, that many of the cars in the Washington, D.C., area showed, thus identifying them as military personnel attached to the Military District of Washington, or as employees of the federal government authorized to park in Section B, Parking Lot III, of the Department of Labor, or so on.

There was nothing about the car, in other words, that made it appear to be anything but the car of someone who lived in Alexandria, Virginia. But when it turned off Pennsylvania Avenue, the normally closed gates of 1600 Pennsylvania Avenue were open, and the two guards on duty touched their caps in salute and waved it through without stopping it either to ex-

1

amine the driver's identification or to telephone to see if he was expected, though it was late at night.

The driver proceeded to the entrance nearest the Executive Office Building, the ornate old Army-Navy-State Department Building. Two marines, in dress blues, came out to the car before it had stopped.

"I'll park it for you, sir," one of them said to the driver.

"If you'll come with me, sir," the other one said.

The man who emerged from the car was a small, prematurely bald, rather skinny man wearing a baggy suit, white shirt, nondescript necktie, and black shoes. He was the antithesis of memorable.

When the marine headed away from the elevator that went to the Command Operations Room, the small man asked him where they were going.

"To the quarters, sir.".

The small man did not reply.

When he got off the elevator which opened on the wide entrance corridor of the living quarters, the Secret Service agent on duty nodded to him.

"You're to go right in," he said.

"Thank you," the small man said politely, as he passed through the double door the agent held open for him.

There were two men in the room. One of them, a brigadier general whose tunic was adorned with the heavy golden cord, the *fourragère*, identifying the military aide-de-camp to the President of the United States, was bending over the back of a fragile, gilt chair. In the chair sat a balding, bespectacled man wearing a tattered sweater. On the sweater was sewn a large "A."

"That was quick," the President of the United States said.

"There's not much traffic this time of night, sir."

"We're drinking," the President said, indicating a silver tray on which whiskey bottles sat. "Will you have something? Or coffee?"

"Coffee, please, sir, black," the small man said.

The military aide walked out of the room.

"I spoke with John an hour or so ago," the President said. "He sends his regards."

"Thank you, sir."

"I only recently learned that you were classmates and friends," the President said.

"Acquaintances, sir," the small man said. "And he is '44. I would have been '46."

The President nodded, and then smiled. "He leads me to believe it can get a little chilly in Korea."

"The troops call it 'Frozen Chosen,' sir," the small man said.

A black man, a U.S. Navy chief steward, wearing a starched white jacket, came into the room with a silver pot of coffee and two cups and saucers. He left, closing the door behind him. The aide did not return.

The President poured coffee into one of the two white china cups, and then said, "I think I'll have a little of that myself," and poured the second cup full. "Reinforced, of course," he said, splashing bourbon into the cup. He held the bottle over the second cup and looked at the small man.

"Please," the small man said.

"Help yourself, Major," the President said, and went to a table and opened a folder. He took from it a stapled document, the cover sheet of which was stamped, top and bottom, with TOP SECRET in inch-high red letters. Red stripes ran diagonally across the cover sheet.

He waited until the small man had seated himself, rather awkwardly, on a low, red leather couch and then he handed it to him. The small man put his cup and saucer down, held the cover sheet out of the way, and carefully read what the President had given him.

COPY *1* of *3*

DUPLICATION
FORBIDDEN

TOP SECRET

(QUINCY)

THE JOINT CHIEFS OF STAFF

THE PENTAGON

WASHINGTON 25, D.C.

8 March 1954

EYES ONLY

VIA FIELD-GRADE OFFICER COURIER

TO: Commander in Chief
       U.S. Forces, Far East
       The Dai Ichi Building, Tokyo, Japan

INFO: The President
       The White House
       Washington, D.C.

By direction of the Chairman of the Joint Chiefs of Staff, the President concurring, you are authorized and directed to appoint Lieutenant General E. Z. Black, USA, as your representative to meet with the Commander in Chief, French forces in French Indo-China at Hanoi, as soon as possible. The purpose of the meeting is to determine if augmentation of French forces by American forces no longer required for operations in Korea would permit the French, in the immediate future, to sustain their operations at Dien Bien Phu, and ultimately to suppress Viet Minh/Communist insurgent forces currently threatening French control of Indo-China.

It is emphasized that General Black's mission is solely to evaluate the present military situation. He is *NOT* authorized to commit U.S. forces, of any type, for any purpose.

For planning purposes only, it is contemplated that the following U.S. forces might be made available for service in French Indo-China, should United States intervention be determined to be feasible and desirable:

Elements, Eighth U.S. Army, as follows:
    1st U.S. Cavalry Division (Dismounted)
    40th U.S. Infantry Division
    187th Infantry Regimental Combat Team (Airborne)
    8058th Mobile Army Surgical Hospital

555th Artillery Group
Command and Support units to be determined

Elements, 20th U.S. Air Force, as follows:
433rd Air Transport Group
2055th Air Control Squadron
2057th Meteorological Squadron
271st Fighter Wing
107th Fighter Bomber Squadron
707th Bomber Squadron (Augmented)
Command and Support units to be determined

Elements, Pacific Fleet, as follows:
Four attack transports
Fleet oiler
Task force, elements to be determined, but including:
Aircraft carrier with three fighter squadrons and
one fighter-bomber squadron aboard
Escort vessels
Ships of the line to be determined

Inasmuch as it is anticipated that should American augmentation of French forces occur, General Black would be placed in command, you are authorized and directed to designate such general or flag officers as General Black may desire, representing the forces named above, to accompany him to Hanoi, or such other place as he may deem necessary.

In view of the politically sensitive nature of General Black's mission, it is directed that his party travel in civilian clothing by chartered civilian aircraft. This letter constitutes authority for the expenditure of whatever discretionary funds are necessary. Waiver of normal passport and visa requirements has been received from the French Colonial Administration.

General Black will make a daily report, to be encrypted in French Indo-China, and transmitted via officer courier to Tokyo for radio teletype transmittal to the Chairman of the Joint Chiefs of Staff. 20th Air Force has been directed to make courier aircraft available.

On completion of his discussions with the French authorities, General Black will prepare a report, to be encrypted in French Indo-China, and transmitted in like manner. *NO*, repeat *NO*, copies of this report are to be retained in the Far East, and all notes and other material used in its preparation are to be destroyed.

General Black may select whatever staff he desires to accompany him.

FOR THE CHAIRMAN, THE JOINT CHIEFS:
Edmund C. Williams
Major General, USMC
Secretary of The Joint Chiefs of Staff

"Yes, sir?" the small man asked, when he had finished reading.

"You read that pretty carefully," the President said.

"Yes, sir."

"I was led to believe you wrote it."

"I drafted it, sir, for the Joint Chiefs. They might have changed it."

"Did they?"

"Not significantly, sir."

"How's your health, Felter?" the President asked.

"Fine, sir."

"I mean, really. Not officially. Are you fully recovered?"

"Yes, sir."

"I understand the only way you can get into Dien Bien Phu is by parachute. You feel up to that?"

"Yes, sir,"

"I want you to go to Indo-China with General Black." the President said, "and then detach yourself, quietly, from the official party, go to Dien Bien Phu, see what shape they're in, positions, supplies, morale, the whole business, and then come back here and tell me what you find."

"Yes, sir."

"I want you to take someone with you, sort of a backup. A soldier, preferably. Do you know someone like that?"

Major Felter thought a moment.

"Yes, sir, I know just the man. He's at Fort Knox."

"Tell me about him."

"Major, Armor," Felter said. "He had five combat jumps in World War II as a pathfinder. And was given the Medal. He wasn't wounded in World War II."

"MacMillan?" the President asked. "He was with you when you had your misfortune in Korea, wasn't he?"

"Yes, sir."

The military aide to the President of the United States returned to the room. Major Felter realized that there must be a hidden button somewhere that the President had pressed to summon him.

"Major Felter's volunteered to go, Charley," the President said. "Get the show on the road."

"Yes, Mr. President."

The President sat down at a table and took a sheet of notepaper and quickly scrawled something on it.

"This may come in handy, Major," he said, handing it to him. Major Felter read it.

"Yes, sir, I'm sure it will."

"Every soldier's ultimate ambition, Felter," the President chuckled. "Commander in Chief." He put out his hand. "Go with God, Major," he said.

(Two)
Hq XIX U.S. Corps (Group)
Kwandae-Ri, North Korea
12 March 1954

The air force C-47 gooney bird which touched down daily at the XIX Corps (Group) airstrip had six passenger seats. They were up front in the cabin just behind the bulkhead separating the cabin from the cockpit. The rest of the cabin was given to cargo transportation, and sometimes the sick, on litters. Not the wounded; they passed their way through a Mobile Army Surgical Hospital (MASH) on their way to more complete medical facilities via a separate aerial evacuation system.

The gooney bird carried mail bags, and priority air freight, and milk. Fresh milk, from a herd of dairy cattle in Japan whose output had been contracted for by the U.S. Army Veterinary Corps, and was dispensed by the U.S. Army Quartermaster Corps at the direction of the U.S. Army Medical Corps to pregnant dependent women, dependent children under the age of five, and those soldiers whose gastrointestinal difficulties indicated a daily ingestion of fresh milk.

There were two means of aerial travel from XIX Corps (Group) in North Korea to Eighth U. S. Army Headquarters in Seoul, South Korea. One was by light army aircraft; Cessna L-19s, observation and liaison aircraft which would carry one passenger; and DeHavilland L-20s, "Beavers," of Teeny-Weeny Airlines, which carried six passengers. In addition, there were two North American "Navions" at XIX Corps (Group), but these were generally reserved for the corps commander, Lieutenant General E. Z. Black, or one of the other five general officers assigned to the corps.

The second means of aerial transportation was the milk-run gooney bird, which stopped at XIX Corps (Group) as its last stop on a round-robin flight from K16 (Kimpo) in Seoul to the three corps (I, IX, and X) and one corps (group) (XIX) on the front lines.

The C-47 gooney bird was faster and more comfortable than the light army aircraft and thus popular with senior officers. Officers at I, IX, and X Corps, however, which were closer to Seoul, sometimes found that if they tried to get to Seoul on the milk-run gooney bird, they got no further than XIX Corps (Group) where they were bumped (Rank Hath Its Priviliges) by senior XIX Corps (Group) officers and left to get to Seoul the best way they could. This was because XIX Corps (Group) was, in everything but name, an army, with an army-sized complement of senior officers. Consequently, the low man in a milk-run passenger seat was seldom any more junior than a lieutenant colonel.

There were three full bull colonels and three light birds in the seats of the milk-run gooney bird when it touched down at the XIX Corps (Group) airstrip. A young lieutenant, who looked as if he was torn between pleasure and worry about brass-hat wrath, climbed up the folding step to make his announcement.

"Gentlemen," he said. "I'm sorry. You've been bumped."

There was some grumbling, and after a moment, a full bull

colonel in his late fifties asked incredulously, "Certainly, Lieutenant, not all of us?"

"Yes, sir," the lieutenant said. "All of you."

When they had collected their gear and climbed back out of the gooney bird, the three full colonels stood by the wing. They had each separately concluded that it was highly unlikely that there were six full colonels, each of them senior in grade to themselves.

A jeep, top down, drove up to where the gooney bird sat at the extreme end of the narrow dirt runway. The jeep held four passengers, all enlisted men, one more passenger than regulations prescribed. In addition, there was a motley collection of luggage, some GI barracks bags, some canvas Valv-Paks, and three civilian suitcases. While authorities generally looked the other way at Valv-Paks, regulations proscribed civilian suitcases in Korea. They were supposed to be entrusted to the Quartermaster Corps in Japan for safekeeping.

The enlisted men—a middle-aged master sergeant, a sorrowful-faced technical sergeant, a baby-faced staff sergeant, and a buck sergeant—got out of the jeep, and with the driver, formed a human chain to load the luggage onto the aircraft. Buried under the personal luggage were several GI equipment cases. When all the luggage was on board, the enlisted men climbed onto the airplane.

When they did not emerge after sufficient time for them to have stowed and tied down the luggage and equipment cases, one of the colonels, curiosity aroused, went to the aircraft door and looked inside. The enlisted men were seated in the seats the brass had just been ordered to vacate.

The colonel climbed aboard the C-47 and went to the middle-aged master sergeant.

"What the hell is going on here, Sergeant?" he demanded.

"Sergeant Greer is in charge, sir," the middle-aged master sergeant said, nodding his head at the baby-faced staff sergeant, who, having taken off his stiff-crowned "Ridgeway hat" (after Gen. Matthew Ridgeway, who had found the issue fatigue cap unmilitary and stiffened his with cardboard), looked even younger.

The colonel went to Staff Sergeant Greer, whom he now

remembered having seen around the general's office.

"You're in charge, Sergeant?" the colonel demanded. "Is that correct?"

"For the moment, sir, yes, sir," Staff Sergeant Greer replied.

"Presumably you're on orders?"

"Yes, sir."

"May I see them, please?"

"No, sir."

"What do you mean, 'No, sir'?" the colonel demanded, furiously.

"We ready to go, Greer?" a voice called out. The colonel saw a full colonel, one he recognized, Colonel Carson Newburgh, officially the XIX Corps (Group) headquarters commandant, the man in charge of housekeeping. The colonel was also aware that Carson Newburgh was a good deal more influential than military housekeepers usually are. He was a reserve officer, a Texan, an Aggie, an oil millionaire. He had gone across Africa and Europe with E. Z. Black. E. Z. Black had gone into combat in North Africa with the "Hell's Circus" Armored Division as a major. When Eisenhower had stopped Hell's Circus on the banks of the Elbe, twenty-four hours—no more—from Berlin, E. Z. Black had been a major general, commanding. Carson Newburgh had been with him there, too, as a light bird. And he'd come back on active duty when Black had been given XIX Corps (Group) in Korea.

He was the only man in Korea who dared to call Ezakiah Zachariah Black "E. Z." to his face.

"You got the boss's bags," baby-faced Staff Sergeant Greer called back, "then we're ready."

The colonel made his way back down the cabin of the gooney bird. Colonel Carson Newburgh gave him a faint smile and a curious look. The colonel had hoped to avoid meeting General Black. He did not.

General Black got on the airplane, and then turned around. Leaning out the door, he pointed a finger at another master sergeant, this one enormous, black, and sad-faced. "Goddamn-it," Lieutenant General E. Z. Black said, "I told you why you can't go."

"Yes, sir," the master sergeant said.

"Take a goddamned R&R," General Black said. "That's an

order, Wesley, goddamnit, not a suggestion."

"Yes, sir," the master sergeant said.

"Greer, goddamnit, speaks French, and you don't," General Black concluded. "You'd be excess baggage."

"Yes, sir," the master sergeant said. "I understand I'd be excess baggage, sir."

"Oh, shit," General Black said. "Get on the goddamned airplane."

"Yes, sir," the master sergeant said, and with surprising grace for his bulk, climbed aboard.

General Black's eyes fell on the colonel. They were icy cold.

"Just debarking, sir," the colonel said.

General Black met the eyes of Colonel Newburgh.

"Wesley's been with me longer than you have," General Black said, defensively.

"Yes, sir," Colonel Newburgh said, smiling broadly.

"That will be twenty dollars, thank you kindly, Colonel Newburgh, sir," baby-faced Staff Sergeant Greer said.

"Goddamnit, Greer, did you actually bet I'd bring him along?" General Black asked. "Am I that goddamned predictable?"

"To those of us who know and love you so well, sir," Staff Sergeant Greer said, unctuously.

"Go to hell, Greer," General Black said. "Well, what are we waiting for? Let's get the show on the road."

The enormous black master sergeant was waiting impatiently at the door for the colonel to get off the aircraft. When he did, he effortlessly pulled the heavy door closed and then settled himself on the floor for the takeoff.

(Three)
K16 Air Base
Seoul, South Korea
12 March 1954

The milk-run gooney bird from XIX Corps (Group) came in low over the Han River bridge, which had been dropped into the river in the early days of the police action and which the engineers had subsequently repaired so that it was partially usable, and touched down at K16. The pilot contacted ground control. Instead of being ordered to proceed down the taxiway to the terminal, he was ordered on a roundabout trip around the airfield, up and down taxiways and across runways, and finally ordered to stop before an unmarked hangar on the civilian side of the field.

"What the fuck are they doing?" he asked of his copilot. The copilot didn't reply. Instead, he pointed out the windshield to a man in a light gray flight suit who was making the standard arm signals (a finger pointing, and a hand making a cutting motion across his throat) ordering him to shut down the port (passenger door side) engine.

Unless the pilot's eyes were failing him, the man performing this buck-sergeant, ground-handler operation wore the star of a brigadier general and the wings of a master aviator.

The pilot cut the port engine.

Lt. General E. Z. Black and his party debarked the aircraft and disappeared through a small door in the huge hangar door. The buck general ground handler made a get-it-out-of-here signal with his hand.

"Air Force 879," ground control said in the pilot's earphones. "Take taxiway eleven to base operations."

Inside the hangar was a China Air Transport (CAT) DC-4. The pilots, standing by the wheels, were American. General Black was not surprised. CAT was an offspring of American involvement with Chiang Kai-shek's China, starting with the American Volunteer Group (the Flying Tigers) before the United States was officially involved in World War II.

The air force brigadier general came in from outside and walked to General Black and saluted. Black shook his hand.

"We about ready to get this show on the road?" General Black asked.

"No, sir," the air force brigadier said. He handed General Black a sheet of yellow teletype paper.

URGENT

HQ USAF WASH DC

TO: CG K16 AFB

DELAY DEPARTURE CAT SEOUL-HANOI CHARTER FOR TWO AD-
DITIONAL PASSENGERS ENROUTE VIA MIL AIR. AUTH: WILLIAMS,
MAJ GEN USMC JCS.

"Jesus H. Christ!" General Black exploded. "I should have
known goddamned well those bastards would send somebody
from the Pentagon, or the goddamned State Department, to
snoop."

"I don't have anything else, General," the air force brigadier
said. "No names. Not even an ETA." (Estimated Time of
Arrival.)

"What the hell," Black said. "I don't have anything better
to do anyway than sit around a goddamned hangar with my
finger up my ass."

"Would the general like a little belt?" the brigadier asked.

"The general would dearly love a little belt," Black replied.
"But I don't think this is the time or place."

The enormous black master sergeant whom Black had taken
along at the last minute came up.

"General," he reported, "I've got your civvies unpacked.
They're kind of messed up."

"Isn't everything?" General Black replied. "Where are they,
Wes?"

"On the airplane," the sergeant replied.

"Everybody else is here?" Black asked the air force brigadier.

"Yes, sir," he replied. "Here and in civvies." He pulled the
full-length zipper of his flight suit down, revealing a shirt and
tie and brown tweed sports coat.

"I will change clothes," General Black announced. "And if
the goddamned snoops haven't shown up by the time I'm finished, then I *will* have a little belt."

General Black boarded the DC-4 and walked up the aisle
to the front, where his orderly had unpacked a footlocker rushed
priority air freight from the United States. Two suits, both of
them mussed and creased from long storage, and an equally
mussed trio of shirts had been laid across one of the seats.

He picked the least mussed of the suits, and changed out
of his uniform. He understood the necessity of wearing civilian

clothing—the shit would really hit the fan if the press found out the Americans were thinking of saving the French's ass in Indo-China—but he didn't like it. Particularly since his civvies were mussed up.

When he was finished, he stepped into the aisle.

"Gentlemen," he said, "may I have your attention, please?"

There were five army officers, four generals and the colonel commanding the 187th Regimental Combat Team; four air force generals, two admirals, and a dozen others, officers or enlisted technicians.

The middle-aged master sergeant in General Black's party was a cryptographer; the technical sergeant was a cartographer familiar with French military maps; the buck sergeant was a court stenographer Black had brought along to take precise notes; the baby-faced staff sergeant fit no precise military description. Black had often told Colonel Carson Newburgh that S/Sgt Greer was the official court jester. But he was more than that. He had been a buck sergeant with the 223rd Infantry Regiment when he had been sent to XIX Corps to function as a court reporter in a personnel hassle. Carson Newburgh had kept him on for his clerical skills, and somehow he had become part of the inner circle, gradually assuming greater and greater responsibilities and discharging them without fault. He had earned the jealous ire of his enlisted seniors. There had been a choice of getting rid of him, or keeping him and giving him the stripes commensurate with his responsibility, and despite his youth and length of service. They had kept him, and made him a staff sergeant, and Black had never regretted the decision.

A wall of faces filled the aisle. General Black's eye fell on S/Sgt Greer.

"Sergeant Greer," he said, "is there any reason why you're still wearing your uniform?"

"Sir," Greer replied immediately, "I thought that I would wait until we got where we're going, and *then* I'd muss my civvies up."

General Black was not the only senior officer in a storage-mussed uniform, and the remark was met first with a muted chuckle, and then a couple of snorts, and finally outright laughter.

"Gentlemen," General Black said. "You have just met Ser-

geant Greer. Unless there are objections, he'll handle all enlisted arrangements and problems. As you may have sensed,
Greer is a past master at taking care of Number One. Colonel
Newburgh will handle the officers. I don't think we'll have
any problems. The French can be quite charming when they
want something. I really hate to bring this up, but the situation
is delicate, and I think I have to. This whole affair is very
secret for what should be obvious reasons. I have to tell you,
and this is an order, that you are not to tell anyone, wives,
superiors, anyone, where we are, have been, or what we did
while we were there. This is just as important as a situation
where an air force major general, in London, found himself a
lieutenant colonel the next morning after he talked too much.

"Item Two: No one, myself included, is authorized to prom-
ise, or even suggest, anything to the French. We're there to
assess the situation and that's all.

"Item Three: We are about to be joined by two VIPs. That's
why we're sitting here. I don't know who they are, or what
they want. When I find out, I'll tell you."

"General?" the air force brigadier who had met the gooney
bird interrupted.

"Go," General Black said.

"A jet bomber that nobody expected is about to land from
Honolulu. They asked that I be informed. It's probably our
VIPs."

"Thank you."

Ten minutes later, the hangar doors began to creak open.
A tug hitched itself to the nosewheel of the DC-4 and it was
pulled outside. A jeep, painted in a black-and-white checkerboard pattern and with a huge checkerboard flag flying from
its rear came across the field. Two men in flight suits got out
of it, each carrying a canvas Valv-Pak. General Black saw
them out the window.

"I'll be goddamned!" he said.

The two newcomers got aboard. The pilot of the DC-4
immediately started his engines, and the transport lumbered
down the taxiway. Then, after a brief pause to test the engines,
the plane turned onto the runway, gathered speed, and took
off.

When they had reached altitude, the newcomers made their

way forward, to where General Black was seated alone. Colonel Newburgh and the air force brigadier came with them.

Both men were army officers, both majors, one a muscular, ruggedly handsome Scot, the second a slight, bespectacled Jew.

"Well, Felter," General Black said, "I see they put you back together again."

"Yes, sir," the little Jew said. "Nearly as good as new. You know how grateful I am."

"And where the hell did you find that?" General Black said, pointing to the Scot. "I thought I was rid of him, once and for all."

"Colonel Bellmon said he didn't care what I did, or where I went, General," the Scot said, "just so long as I stayed out of trouble. So here I am."

"And what are you going to do here?" General Black asked, innocently.

"We're going to very quietly go have a look at Dien Bien Phu," Major Felter said.

"That's not on the program," the air force brigadier said flatly, confirming what Black had suspected, that the brigadier was his counterpart even though he was outranked by the air force major general aboard.

"Yes, sir," Major Felter said. "I know."

"You can't visit Dien Bien Phu without General Black's permission," the air force brigadier said. "And I would strongly suggest he not give it."

Felter looked at Black and the air force brigadier. Then he reached into his pocket and handed Black a squarish white envelope. Black read it, and nodded, and then handed it to the air force brigadier general. It was a handwritten note on engraved stationery.

THE WHITE HOUSE
WASHINGTON

10 March 54

Major Felter is traveling at my request. He is to be given whatever assistance he requires.

DDE

"And does Mac have friends in very high places, too, Felter?" General Black inquired.

"Well, sir," Major Felter said, "he knows you and me."

"Goddamnit, Mac," General Black said. "I know I shouldn't be, but I'm glad to see you." He grabbed MacMillan's hand in both of his own.

II

Including the smell, which was so foul he was really afraid that he might throw up, there was a hell of a lot about this escapade that was very familiar to Major Rudolph G. "Mac" MacMillan.

The airplane was American, a good old faithful Douglas C-47 gooney bird. The frogs had been using it to evacuate their wounded. That's where the stink came from, from blood and piss and rotting flesh and shit. The first thing a body did when it was dead was crap its pants, when the sphincter muscles relaxed. The frogs were evacuating only their badly wounded.

The chutes, main and reserve, were American, but Mac MacMillan wasn't at all sure they could be trusted. He suspected that the frogs who had packed them had not paid as much attention to the fine points of packing or to the condition of the chutes themselves as the riggers in an American airborne

19

outfit would have. The uniforms the frogs were wearing were American, too: GI fatigues and web equipment, weapons, everything but the boots. The boots were native frog boots.

The kid didn't even have boots. He wasn't even a parachutist, so obviously he didn't have jump boots. He was going to jump in regular Class "A" uniform oxfords, the kind the army called "low quarters." The kid was apparently a gutsy little bastard, but he was scared, and Mac knew it. Mac had had a lot of experience over the years with scared people.

The kid was some kind of superclerk for General Black, and when Black had learned that they were going to Dien Bien Phu, he had sent the kid along.

"If you think you could learn something, Greer," was the way Black had put it. "For all I care, you can go along."

For a young sergeant working for Lieutenant General E. Z. Black, that was the same thing as a direct order. So the kid had come along on this little excursion thinking that he was going to be flown in and out. When the frogs said they would have to jump in, he'd said OK, he'd jump. He said he'd always wanted to try it anyhow. That was so much bullshit. The kid was scared shitless. But there was nothing anybody could do about that. Anything that anybody said to him would only make it worse. What was going to happen would happen, and he couldn't do a damn thing for him.

Mac MacMillan's boots were standard American jump boots, not GI but Corcoran's. It was accepted as an article of faith among parachutists that Corcoran jump boots not only took a higher polish than GI jump boots, but that you stood much less chance of breaking your ankles when you landed. MacMillan had started wearing Corcoran's when there had been no GI jump boots, when somebody in the Quartermaster Corps had done something right for once and had asked the Massachusetts shoe manufacturer to come up with a pair of boots that would be suitable for crazy people who were planning to jump out of airplanes.

The first order had been issued to the members of the battalion of the 82nd Infantry Division that had been designated as a Test Battalion (Parachute). Mac MacMillan, recent All-Philippines boxing champion, had joined up because they were going to pay him another fifty bucks a month to jump out of airplanes. He had just gotten married and needed the money.

He hadn't had those boots a month when some thieving sonofabitch slit his duffel bag at Benning and stole them. When he went to the supply room and looked at the non-Corcoran jump boots they wanted to issue him, he remembered hearing that the "good" boots were being sold in the PX. Every pair of jump boots he had ever owned since then he had bought either at the PX or direct from Corcoran in Massachusetts.

He thought that if anybody had told him a month ago when he bought the pair he was wearing now that he would be jumping in them into some frog outpost in some asshole corner of nowhere, with Sandy Felter, some kid sergeant making his first jump, and a dozen frogs, he would have told him he was out of his fucking gourd.

"Something on your mind, Mac?" Felter asked him, sticking his head so close because of the noise that MacMillan could smell his toothpaste.

"Geronimo! You little bastard," MacMillan said.

"Geronimo!" was what John Wayne had shouted as he went out the door in a war movie about paratroops. Everybody knew about that. MacMillan, who had been a parachutist since 1940, and on whose wings there was barely room for the five stars he had earned, one a time, on five jumps into combat, had never heard anybody else yell "Geronimo!"

Felter smiled.

"You didn't tell me this is what you had in mind," MacMillan said, gesturing around the airplane. "You said 'inspection trip,' shitface."

"You love it," Felter said.

"You may love it, you little prick," MacMillan said. "I've been here before."

"That's why I brought you along," Felter said.

"I'm going to get you for this, Sandy," MacMillan said.

Major Sandy Felter was one of the few people for whom Major MacMillan felt both affection and admiration. Felter had been responsible for one of MacMillan's very few philosophical observations: *You can't tell what a warrior looks like*.

Felter was even a West Pointer, though he rarely wore his

ring. He was Class of '46, but he hadn't been there when the rest of the Class of '46 had thrown their hats into the air on graduation day. He'd resigned from the Corps of Cadets to take a direct commission as a linguist. As a POW interrogation officer with Major General "Porky" Waterford's "Hell's Circus" Armored Division, he had learned the location of a group of American officer prisoners-of-war being moved on foot away from the advancing Russians.

Task Force Parker (Colonel Philip Sheridan Parker III) had been formed to go get them, and Felter had gone with them. By the time his classmates were admiring themselves in their brand-new second lieutenant suits, Felter had been a first lieutenant with a Bronze Star for the Task Force Parker operation, and the admiration of Porky Waterford, whose son-in-law, Lt. Col. Bob Bellmon, had been one of the rescued American officers.

MacMillan had been in the stalag with Bellmon, as a technical sergeant, the senior NCO of the American enlisted men imprisoned with the officers. That had been before he had learned that his behavior in Operation Market-Basket, where he had been captured, had earned him both a battlefield promotion to second lieutenant and the Medal.

Just after the Germans marched the officers off to the west, leaving the enlisted men to fend as well as they could, MacMillan had led an escape in an odyssey across Poland that had earned him the Distinguished Service Cross to go with the Medal. He'd heard about Felter when he and Bellmon had got together in the States.

And he'd heard about Felter's activities with the U.S. Army Advisory Group to Greece from another old buddy, Lt. Col. Red Hanrahan, who had been with Mac at Benning, jumping out of airplanes before there had been an 82nd Airborne Division. Felter had been sent to Greece as a Russian language linguist, and had wound up commanding a relief column that had stopped a major Albanian border-crossing operation. Hanrahan had refused to confirm the rumor that it had been necessary for Felter to blow away the American officer in charge, who'd turned yellow and wanted to run. So far as MacMillan was concerned, if the story wasn't true, Hanrahan would have said so.

And MacMillan had personal experience with the little Jew.
In Korea, MacMillan had run an irregular outfit, Task Force
Able, and Felter had dropped in one day with orders from
above that Task Force Able was now in the spy business, and
would take its orders from Felter. Felter wasn't expected to do
anything more than sit behind a desk and run the show. But
he was a warrior, and he'd spent as much time behind North
Korean lines as any of the agents, and he'd damned near got
himself blown away when one operation went sour.

He'd taken a nasty wound in the knee, that damned near
cost him his leg, and had shown a lot of guts in dragging
himself off the beach and back into the water, willing to drown
rather than be captured; he knew too much to be captured.

Sandy Felter was MacMillan's kind of man. He was a warrior.

The jumpmaster came down the aisle and hesitantly gestured
to MacMillan.

"Talk to him, prick," MacMillan said. "You speak frog."

Felter spoke to the jumpmaster in French, then switched to
German. The eyes of the jumpmaster half smiled.

"He wants to know if you have jumped before," Felter said,
smiling.

"Oh, Jesus, that's all I need, a kraut jumpmaster in the frog
airborne!"

"Somebody's going to understand English, Mac, for God's
sake!" Felter said, torn between amusement and genuine concern.

"Find somebody who does, and tell him I want to go home,"
MacMillan said. Then he looked up and met the jumpmaster's
eyes and said, in not bad German: *"Ja, ich war ein Fall-
schirmjäger im zweiten Weltkrieg."*

The jumpmaster didn't seem surprised that MacMillan had
been a paratrooper in War II. *"Und der Bub?"* he asked.

MacMillan replied that *"der Bub,"* the boy, was a virgin,
but that he would take care of him.

The jumpmaster nodded.

"Ungefähr fünf Minuten," he announced. He wore the stripes
of a company sergeant major and the unit insignia of the Third
Parachute Regiment of the French Foreign Legion.

The jumpmaster gave the commands in French, but they

were still all very familiar to MacMillan.

"Stand up," the jumpmaster said. And the parachutists—the legionnaires and Felter, MacMillan, and Greer—got up out of their aluminum and nylon sheeting benches and stood up, fastening the chin harnesses of their helmets, checking the position of their scrotums relative to the straps that ran between their legs, and making whatever adjustments were necessary.

"Check your equipment," the jumpmaster ordered. The buddy system. Major Rudolph G. MacMillan, Armor, USA, checked the harness and other equipment of Staff Sergeant Greer, trying not to make a big deal of it, and then checked Felter. Finally, Felter checked MacMillan.

"Hook up!" They snapped the hooks of their static lines around the stainless steel cable running along the roof of the cabin, and tugged on it to make sure it was secure and that the spring-lock opening had closed as it was supposed to.

"Stand in the door!"

The jumpmaster put Felter and MacMillan second and third on line, and Greer after them. MacMillan changed that. He unhooked his static line and put it behind the kid's, and then got in the line behind Felter and Greer. It would be better to have the kid in the middle.

First man in the stick was a Foreign Legion corporal. He was a Frenchman, a foreigner in his own army (no Frenchman can serve in the Foreign Legion) because he had believed that National Socialism was the wave of the future and had gone off with ten thousand other Frenchmen into the Charlemagne Legion of the Waffen SS. The Charlemagne Legion fought with distinction in Russia, and died in the battle of Berlin, but Unterfeldwebel Francois Ferrer had been one of the lucky ones. He hadn't died, and he had made his way west and gone into French captivity, but as a German with a Waffen SS paybook. Being in the SS was bad, but not as bad as being a member of the Charlemagne Legion. Once the war was over, there was a rebirth of fervent patriotism in France.

One day they had taken him from the POW enclosure and carried him to Marseilles, and he had thought he had been found out and would be tried as a traitor. He had been found out, but what they did was drop him off without a word before the recruiting office of the Foreign Legion.

He was a corporal again. The Legion carried him on their rolls as Franz Ferrer, and in 1957, when he'd done his twelve year hitch, he would be eligible for French citizenship. The Legion didn't care where you came from. If you gave the Legion twelve years, and lived through it, and wanted to try Civvie Street, they would see to it that you got the proper papers.

The legionnaire did not feel sorry for himself. He had enlisted in the Charlemagne Legion of the Waffen SS to fight communists, and that's what he was doing now.

The gooney bird's pilot throttled the engines back and lowered the flaps. They were six or seven hundred feet over thickly forested mountains, approaching a valley.

There came a sound, a dull, metallic pinging, like a full garbage can being kicked. The gooney bird lifted its left wing and started to bank to the right. A faint trail of smoke began to flow off the left wing. It grew larger, darker.

"Oh, *shit!*" Major Mac MacMillan said.

The dense cloud of dark smoke began to glow, then burst into orange. There were flames now, furious flames.

MacMillan let go of the stainless steel static line cable and with both hands pushed Corporal Franz Ferrer out of the door. He didn't have to push Felter. Felter had figured out what was happening. He went out the door a split second after the legionnaire.

MacMillan grabbed Staff Sergeant Greer's shoulders and shoved him, with a mighty heave, through the door.

MacMillan felt himself falling backward into the gooney bird as the door side of the airplane went high. He managed to get one hand on the leading edge of the door; otherwise he would have fallen across the cabin. The C-47 was in a steep diving bank to the right. MacMillan pulled himself closer to the door; got both hands on it; and finally, using all his strength, pulled himself through it.

His static line caught momentarily on the doorsill, then slid to the rear. MacMillan thought he would slam into the tail assembly. But it passed a foot from his face. A moment later, he felt the barely perceptible tug as the static line pulled first the cover off and then the pilot chute from his main chute. Soon he felt the chute deploying, sensed that it was out of the bag, that it was opening. At the moment when his experience taught him to expect the opening shock, he felt it.

He had spun around and around, and when the canopy filled and the risers grew taut, he was facing in the direction where he could see the C-47. In a gentle, graceful curve, the left engine nacelle an orange ball of fire, it flew into the forest canopy, disappeared for a moment, and then exploded. No one else got out.

MacMillan twisted his head to see what had happened to Felter and the kid and the frog corporal. There was only one parachute canopy still in the air. That was Felter. He had gone out before the kid, but soaking wet the little bastard didn't weigh 130 pounds. He would take a little longer getting down.

MacMillan saw the frog corporal's canopy and the kid's hanging from treetops. Then he saw Felter's canopy lose its fullness. Felter was down in the trees, too.

MacMillan looked between his feet, put them together, and bent his knees to protect his balls. In that instant he hit the first upper branches. He closed his eyes and put his arm over them as protection against a branch getting him in the eyes.

And then, amid the sounds of breaking branches, recoiling from painful slaps and punches at his head and legs and body, he was down. He opened his eyes. He was thirty feet up in a tree, maybe forty.

It was very, very quiet.

He got himself swinging, hoping the chute wouldn't rip free and he wouldn't suddenly find himself dropping to the ground, and in time was able to grab a branch he thought would hold his weight. He climbed on it, hit the quick release on his harness, and stood there for a moment, hanging on to the tree trunk with both arms.

He heard movement, fifty yards away, a hundred, who knows. The thing to do was get out of the goddamned tree.

He climbed to within twenty feet of the ground, beneath which there were no branches. He hung from the lowest branch and dropped. The landing was surprisingly soft; the ground was covered with rotting vegetation. It smelled like a septic tank.

He sat a moment and considered his position. This wasn't his goddamned war. Personally, he wasn't all that fond of the French, and he didn't give a shit if they owned Indo-China or not. He was a neutral. The Viet Minh, Sandy had told him, were run by a guy named Ho Chi Minh. All during War II, the United States had had an OSS detachment with Ho Chi Minh. Ho Chi Minh might hate the frogs, but he might like Americans.

If Ho Chi Minh's people saw him in this frog jump suit, they would naturally decide that he was a frog. MacMillan unzipped the jump suit and climbed out of it. Beneath it, he wore a Class "A" (less tunic) summer uniform. Including decorations. Sandy Felter had told him to wear his decorations. Frogs were big on medals, and Mac had the big medal, the Medal of Honor. The reason they were all in goddamned Class "A" tropicals was that they were sort of sneaking into Dien Bien Phu. If it had come to the attention of some of the big frog brass that they were going to take a look at Dien Bien Phu for themselves, instead of relying on the word of *le Général* that everything was peachy keen, he more than likely would have tried to stop them. So they had had breakfast in the Cercle Sportif in their Class "A" tropical worsteds, so the frogs could count noses, and then they had sneaked off to the airport, where Felter, somehow, had it fixed for them to get on the gooney bird bound for Dien Bien Phu.

He started walking in the direction of the noise he thought he had heard. He kept sinking into the rotting vegetation and cursed, thinking he had ruined what were damned near new jump boots.

He heard voices after a while, and they damned sure weren't American or French. Sort of sing-songy. He moved quietly, with a skill learned stalking deer and an occasional bear in the woods around Mauch Chuck, Pennsylvania, and honed as a pathfinder in North Africa and Sicily and France and Germany. Then he dropped to his hands and knees and scurried across the ground like an insect. Finally, he dropped flat on his belly and crawled. He thought he was fucking up a nearly new set of TWs, too.

There were three Chinks, or whatever they were, dressed in black pajamas, and they had the frog, the one he'd pushed out the door. The gooks were armed with Chink submachine guns and one GI carbine, and knives. They had the frog tied to a tree, spread-eagled, and what they were doing was working on him with the knives.

They had slit his cheeks and his chest, and he was covered with blood. The reason he wasn't screaming was because they had his mouth stuffed full of the rotting shit from the jungle floor.

Then they pulled his pants off. He tried to scream, and almost made it, when he realized what the gooks were going to do now.

MacMillan had thought the stories they had been told in Hanoi about the Viet Minh cutting people's cocks off and stuffing them in their mouths was so much bullshit.

MacMillan reached in the back pocket of his trousers and took out a Colt .32 ACP pistol. Very carefully, he took the clip out and checked it, and then he silently replaced it and very carefully worked the action, chambering a cartridge.

Shit, a lousy .32 automatic against three guys with submachine guns and a carbine!

He inched himself around the trunk of a large tree. Two of the Viet Minh guys were working on the frog, the dirty bastards really enjoying themselves, and the third was looking vaguely in MacMillan's direction. Fifteen yards away. Maybe even less. But the vegetation was so thick!

MacMillan rested his left arm against the tree trunk, held the pistol in both hands, and aimed right at the gook's nose. It hardly made any noise going off, the sound swallowed by the dense, moist vegetation. The gook, for a moment, seemed surprised. Then blood gushed out of his right eye, and he sank to the ground. MacMillan turned the pistol on the other two, got off a hasty shot, and then another, and then he rolled back, so the tree trunk would give him protection.

There came expected bursts of fire from the Chink submachine gun. Two bursts. Two guns? Or one burst from two guns?

Then something else. Two shots, evenly spaced. *Boom! Boom!*

Loud shots. Certainly not a pistol. Nor a rifle. It sounded more like a shotgun. What the hell were the Chinks, or whatever they were, armed with? All he'd seen were the Chink sub-machine guns. Were there more gooks than he'd seen? A couple of perimeter guards, maybe?

"It's OK, Major," the kid called out. "They're all down."

MacMillan very cautiously edged around the tree. The kid was untying the frog.

MacMillan stood up, and walked over and looked at the dead, holding the little .32 automatic out in front of him. He felt a little foolish when he got close enough for a good look. One of the Chinks had half of his head blown off, and the other one's entire midsection was a mass of bloody pulp.

It was a shotgun; no other weapon would have made a wound like that. He looked at the kid. He had the frog loose now, and was picking something up from the ground. A sawed-off shotgun.

The frog, blood streaming all over him, bent over and picked up one of the submachine guns. He walked to the body of one of the Viet Minh and emptied the magazine into his crotch.

MacMillan walked over to the kid and took the sawed-off shotgun from him. It was really a sawed-off people killer, not just what was left after somebody took a hacksaw to a 12-gauge Winchester Model 12. Even the magazine tube and the mechanism to work the action had been cut down. Instead of five in the magazine and one in the chamber, this wouldn't hold more than two shells in the magazine. The stock behind the pistol grip had been cut off. What was left wasn't a hell of a lot bigger than a .45.

"Very nice," MacMillan said.

"I was an infantryman before I was a dog robber," the kid said.

"What the hell did you shoot the first one with?" the kid asked. MacMillan held out the little .32 Colt.

"Don't knock it, it worked," he said. And then he thought of something else and grew angry. "Especially when you're supposed to be unarmed."

"Yeah," the kid said.

"Where did you have that?" MacMillan asked. "I didn't see it."

The kid didn't answer. There was a sound in the forest. The kid dropped to his knees, holding the sawed-off people killer in front of him. MacMillan, holding the .32 out, realized that the kid had only one shell left.

"Hold your fire," Felter called out, from somewhere in the thick vegetation. "It's me."

He came into sight a moment later, tucking a .45 automatic into his belt at the small of his back under his tropical worsted tunic.

"You miserable little prick!" MacMillan said, as Felter walked into the small natural clearing. "God*damn* you!"

Felter ignored him and knelt before the Frenchman, who was now sitting down, resting his back against a tree.

"He's going to bleed some more," he said. "What happened to him?"

"The Chinks were about to feed him his own cock," MacMillan said.

"*Viet Minh*, Mac," Felter corrected him. "Are you all right, Sergeant?"

"Yes, sir," Staff Sergeant Greer said.

"He saved our ass with his shotgun," MacMillan said. "You owe us one big fucking apology, Felter."

"Because of the gun, you mean?" Felter asked, smiling.

"You're goddamned right," MacMillan said. "'No guns, Mac. Not even that little Colt of yours. We're neutral observers.'"

"I didn't think for a minute that you'd pay a bit of attention to me," Felter said. "That was for the record."

"Bullshit!" MacMillan said.

"Off the record, Sergeant," Felter said, "I'm glad you misunderstood my instructions."

"He must have had that thing stuck inside his pants," MacMillan said. "Take a look at it."

Staff Sergeant Greer handed over the sawed-off shotgun.

"That's very nice," Felter said. "*Very* nice. Where'd you get it?"

"I made it," Greer said.

"When we get out of this," Felter said, "I'd like you to make one for me."

"Are we going to get out of this?" Sergeant Greer asked.

"At this point, Sergeant," Felter said, "we place ou
in the capable hands of Major MacMillan. He's actually
good at dealing with situations like ours."

"Fuck you, Sandy," MacMillan said. He walked over and
had a look at the frog, to see if he was up to doing what they
would have to do to keep alive.

(Two)
Hanoi, French Indo-China
17 March 1954

Les cocktails were served by *le Général Commandant de
les Forces Francaise de Indo-Chine* and his staff, to Lieutenant
General E. Z. Black, USA, and his staff in the Cercle Sportif's
upstairs lounge. The cocktails were served by soldiers, enormous, jet-black Senegalese in French service, who wore white
jackets, billowing trousers, and red hats, soft, but something
on the order of a fez. Following cocktails, *le dîner* would be
served in the main dining room.

The French officers were in full uniform, despite the civilian
clothing the Americans wore in the now obviously absurd notion that by so doing they might conceal their presence in Hanoi.

General Black was not in a good mood. What the goddamned French actually were having the gall to ask for was
troops, and airplanes, and ships, but mostly troops, infantry
troops, to fight their goddamned colonial war under French
officers. They had the experience in dealing with communist
insurgents, they said, and the Americans didn't, and Indo-
China *was* part of France.

Black had slipped a note to Newburgh at the conference
table:

"Take a list of names, so we'll know where we can find
experienced officers the next time we need to lose a war."

He had, of course, behaved himself during the conference.
He had been the soul of military charm and tact, and tried to
explain the difficulty that General Eisenhower, *President* Ei-
senhower, would have in getting Congress to agree to send
American troops to Indo-China at all, much less to serve under
French officers.

He had made it through lunch without incident, and through

the afternoon session, but here, with a couple of drinks in him, Colonel Newburgh was just a little worried about Black. He had encountered him at the urinals.

"I have just figured out what all those medals the frogs are wearing are," Black had said to him. "The brass one with the naked lady on the horse is for the Phony War. The one with the massed flags is for losing the battle of the Maginot Line, and the one with the triple-barred cross is for shelling the Americans when we came ashore at Casablanca..."

"Take it easy, E. Z.," Newburgh said, sternly. "It'll be over soon."

"You know when I was happiest, Carson?" Black said, zipping his fly. "When I was a full bull colonel, hoping for a buck general's star to retire on in the by and by, and had nothing to worry about but commanding Combat Command A. Just a soldier, none of this smiling bullshit."

"I suppose George Washington felt the same way about the French and Indian Wars when he was asking Congress for money and troops."

"French and Indian Wars? Goddamn right. *He* knew who the enemy was."

"Prepare to smile," Newburgh said, chuckling. "Smile!"

"I'll go charm the sonsofbitches, Colonel," Black said. "A good soldier goes where he is told to go, and does what he is told to do, and he smiles." He leered insanely at Colonel Newburgh. "Smile satisfactory, Colonel?"

"Try to hide the fangs a little more," Newburgh said.

It was very difficult.

A major general waited outside in the lounge to tell General Black that while he was sure *le Général* didn't remember him, he remembered *le Général* from the glorious days when *le Général* had Combat Command A of Hell's Circus, and had "assisted" *le Général* LeClerc's 2nd (French) Armored Division in their preparations to liberate Paris.

It was Lieutenant General E. Z. Black's professional opinion that (a) there had been no military requirement whatever to take Paris in the first place; it could have been easily bypassed, and Von Choltitz, the German commandant, had been perfectly willing to declare it an open city if they had bypassed it; and (b) that if it was in the best interests of the United States to take the goddamned place, they should have permitted Hell's Circus to take it. Combat Command "A" of Hell's Circus (which he just coincidentally happened to command) had been poised on the outskirts of Paris, ready to roll around or through (whichever was ordered) when the radio had come from SHAEF ordering him to stand in place and let LeClerc pass through him.

General E. Z. Black's smile was rather strained when a French colonel came to the French major general and spoke into his ear in what he thought was a whisper.

The C-47 on which the two American officers and the American sergeant had been trying to get into Dien Bien Phu had been shot down. There were no survivors.

The French major general was obviously torn between telling General Black what he had just heard, or passing this sad responsibility to *le Général Commandant*.

"General," General Black said, in his fluent French, "please be so good as to offer my apologies to *le Général Commandant*. The men lost to your enemy were all personal friends of mine, and I must see about informing their families of this tragedy."

Lieutenant General E. Z. Black and Colonel Carson Newburgh left the Cercle Sportif in the Rolls-Royce the French had assigned for his use. They went to the American Consulate on the Rue General Marneaux, got the cryptographer, and sent the URGENT radio to the Joint Chiefs of Staff reporting that Majors Sanford T. Felter and Rudolph G. MacMillan and S/Sgt Edward C. Greer had been aboard a French C-47, trying to get to Dien Bien Phu, had been shot down, and were presumed dead.

Then General Black and Colonel Newburgh went to the villa they had been assigned by *le Général Commandant*, and they drank all of one, and part of a second, quart bottle of Haig and Haig scotch whiskey.

(Three)
Dien Bien Phu
French Indo-China
21 March 1954

"What we're betting on," MacMillan said, "is that they're soldiers."

"Blooded troops, is what you mean," Felter said.

It was six in the morning and they were in the jungle, overlooking one of the outposts of the French garrison at Dien Bien Phu. They were in what in World War I would have been called "no-man's-land." The French emplacements were two hundred yards ahead of them, across a relatively open area strung with barbed wire, and probably mined, and torn up by literally a hundred thousand artillery and mortar shells. The Viet Minh emplacements were behind them, over the crest of a line of hills, out of sight and safe from direct, line-of-sight rifle and machine-gun fire from the French.

They had spent the last four nights crawling through the Viet Minh lines on their bellies, literally inches at a time. They had made it—although privately none of them thought they would—but it hadn't solved their problem. They were within two hundred yards of French protection, but it might as well have been two hundred miles.

So far as the French were concerned, anybody out there in the jungle was Viet Minh. The moment the French saw movement out there, they would bring the area under fire. From the shot-down trees, and the countless craters in the ground, a generous expenditure of ammunition to repel a ground attack was the standard French tactic.

The problem, then, was to let the French know that they were out there, and friendly, without having the French blow them away.

MacMillan's solution to the problem was unusual, but neither Felter nor Greer could think of a better idea.

They would start a fire, using dried leaves, twigs, and limbs from the shot-down trees. The French would naturally bring this under fire. So the fire would have to be started slowly, in order for them to get away before the firing started. The fire would be large. It would continue to attract French attention. After they had brought the fire site under enough small arms and mortar fire to have blown away anybody close to it, they would crawl back to it, stand up, put their hands over their heads, wave their arms, and walk slowly toward the French lines.

They would either be permitted to enter the French lines, or they would be blown away.

If they stayed where they were, they would be blown away by the Viet Minh, probably after the Viet Minh had cut their cheeks open and fed them their cocks.

"Fuck it," S/Sgt Greer said, "let's do it. Light the sonofabitch."

"'Light the sonofabitch, please, sir,' Sergeant," Major MacMillan said.

"With all respect," Greer replied, as he started to crawl away, "fuck you, Major."

It went almost exactly as planned. The fire was lit; the fire site was brought under fire by the French; the mortar fire was lifted; they crawled back to the fire site; then gathered their courage and stood up.

They held their arms over their heads and walked, waving their arms toward the French positions. The French did not open fire on them. They had walked perhaps fifty yards when the French opened up.

They dove to the ground, and spent ninety seconds, which under some circumstances can be a very long time, trying to make themselves as thin and flat as possible. And then they realized that the machine-gun and rifle fire was ten feet in the air, and that the mortars were arcing down to the ground and exploding between them and the Viet Minh positions. The frogs' fire was covering them!

They got up and ran toward the French emplacements, and made it unhurt, except for Greer, who caught a piece of mortar shrapnel on his right leg, outside, about ten inches from his crotch.

(Four)

The Dien Bien Phu hospital was, of course, underground. Despite the fact that everybody knew it was impossible, the Viet Minh had manhandled American 105 mm howitzers, captured in the early days of the Korean War, up into positions overlooking the French positions, and kept them under a steady barrage of fire. Sometimes one shell every ten minutes, sometimes fifty shells in one minute.

The French were living underground, and their hospital was underground.

The piece of shrapnel which had caught Ed Greer had sliced his skin open like a jagged knife, but had not stayed in his body. The wound had been sutured shut, and he had been given, by injection and orally, medicine to resist infection and pain. The doctor who had treated him, after professing astonishment and joy that the American spoke French, told him that the greatest risk of infection was not from the shrapnel wound, but from the leech and other insect bites, and that "after you're out of here, take a lot of baths with antibacteriological soap."

He was put to bed for the night in a private room, a small cubicle equipped with a U.S. Army hospital bed, an American Coleman gasoline lantern, two canteens of water and a glass, and copies of months-old French and Indo-Chinese newspapers.

Felter and MacMillan came to see him. MacMillan explained the situation precisely, if not with overwhelming tact.

"We're going to party with the officers," he said. "That leaves you out. You can party with the troops, if you like, but if you're smart, you'll stay where you are in the clean bed. The troops here sleep on the ground. They're going to try to get us out of here in the morning, or the next day."

"I'll stay here," Greer said.

"Got you some clothes," Felter said. He hung a set of Foreign Legion jungle pattern camouflage fatigues on a nail driven into one of the white-painted tree trunks which supported the hospital bunker roof.

"You want something to drink?" MacMillan asked.

"Please," Greer said.

"I'll see what I can do."

Ten minutes later, the legionnaire the Viet Minh had tied to the tree came into his room accompanied by two other very drunk legionnaires. Greer was sure that one of them was an American, although he denied it and said he was a Belgian. He was either American, or he'd lived in the States long enough to acquire a perfect command of Chicago English. He was a sergeant, and he had been brought along to translate by the company sergeant major, who didn't know that Greer spoke French.

"Franz told us what you did for him," the "Belgian" legionnaire said. "And the sergeant major says that now that you nearly got yourself killed in this sewer, and jumped into here, you are now one of us."

They sat him up in bed, put the camouflage fatigue jacket on him, pinned parachutist's wings on it, the company sergeant major kissed him on both cheeks, they both saluted him, helped him out of the jacket, handed him two unlabeled bottles of red wine, and left, staggering.

Greer drank about half a bottle of wine, from the neck, while reading *Paris Match* and *Le Figaro* by the hissing light of the Coleman lantern. Then he turned it off and went to sleep, naked under the damp sheet.

He woke up when he sensed the nurse's flashlight probing the room, but didn't move until he heard the hiss of the Coleman as she lit it. Then he turned his head and looked up at her.

A blond, her hair was parted in the middle and drawn tight against her skull. She wore the legionnaire's jungle fatigues. Thirty, Greer judged. Maybe not that old. A woman would turn old quick here.

"I will bathe your leech bites," she said, in English.

"Je parle français, Mademoiselle," Greer said.

She asked him how he came to speak French, and he told her that he had been with a carnival, and there had been some French acrobats. She asked him what he had done with the carnival, and he lied and told her his father had owned it.

And all the time, she dabbed at the leech bites and the insect bites on his backside with cotton-soaked alcohol, pulling the sheet off him when it was necessary to work below his waist. He smelled the alcohol, of course, but it was overwhelmed by the smell of her perfume.

By the time she had worked her way down to his calves and ankles, he had a prize-winning erection.

"Roll over," she said.

"That would be very embarrassing for both of us, just now," Greer said.

She laughed, and handed him a towel.

He told himself that he was embarrassed, and that it would go down naturally under the circumstances, which were, after all, nurse-patient, rather than romantic.

She found a bite they hadn't noticed before under his armpit, and worked on that, and then she worked her way down his body. The hard-on did not go down. She worked around it, down his legs. She rebandaged the sutured shrapnel wound.

"You still have it hard," she said, level voiced.

He blushed. She chuckled, deep in her throat.

"It is nothing to embarrass," she said.

Her hand was on his stomach, an inch or so above the tent his erection was making of the towel.

"There are thirty-nine women here," she said. *"French* women. Five of them are married, three to officers and two to sergeants. That means thirty-four women for several thousand of mens."

"Those are pretty good odds," he said.

"We have enough with the Viet Minh without fighting among ourselves over men," she said. "And we are not whores."

He had no idea what she was leading up to.

"I only once in a while wish a man," she said. "But if I were to have to do with a man here, it would cause difficulty."

He nodded.

"You understand?" she asked.

He met her eyes.

She slid her hand under the towel, held him, chuckled appreciatively. She picked the towel off him with the other hand, and hung it over the rail at the foot of the bed.

"No move," she said, and let go of him, and got out of her Foreign Legion fatigue pants, and climbed onto the bed and straddled him and guided him into her.

He had never had anybody do that to him before, and he never forgot it.

The plane that came to get them out the next day crashed on landing, and then there was fog the day after that, and no plane; so it was the third day before they ran out to a gooney bird in the midst of an artillery barrage, got in it, and were soaked with the clammy sweat of fear until it got down the runway and into the air out of range of the Viet Minh's heavy .50s.

(Five)
The Embassy of the United States of America
Taipei, Formosa
25 March 1954

Lt. General E. Z. Black returned from dinner with the ambassador as soon as he could without giving offense. He had declined the offer of the VIP guest house and had been assigned quarters in the main Embassy building instead.

When the marine guard saluted him, even though he was in civilian clothing, Black asked him if he had happened to see Sergeant Greer.

"Yes, sir," the guard said. "He's in the attaché's office, sir."

"What's he doing there?" Black wondered out loud.

"Sir," the guard said, "he told the officer of the day that he was acting under your orders."

"Yes, of course," General Black said. "That's on the third floor, right?"

"Yes, sir," the marine said.

He had inquired of Greer's whereabouts out of some vestigial (perhaps parental?) concern that Greer would celebrate his safe return with whiskey and wild, wild women. What he had hoped to learn was that Greer hadn't left the Embassy, not that he had invoked his name and was up to God alone knows what in the attaché's office.

It wasn't hard to find the attaché's office. Its door was the only one in the long corridor from which light spilled into the corridor.

There was a soldier from the Embassy, a technical sergeant in his late thirties, perhaps even his early forties, in the outer office. Greer had installed himself at the secretary's desk, and was furiously pounding her IBM electric typewriter.

The Embassy sergeant came to attention the instant he saw General Black. Sergeant Greer glanced up at him, and then resumed his typing, finishing the line or the paragraph or whatever, before finally standing up.

Greer was in a new khaki uniform. When they thought he was dead, they had packed up his personal gear and his uniforms and sent them home. When MacMillan, Felter, and Greer finally returned from Dien Bien Phu, the three had been wearing French Foreign Legion jungle fatigues. The khakis had probably come from the military attaché's supply room here.

Greer's sleeves now held chevrons with one more stripe. He has just as many stripes, General Black thought, as the sergeant who has been sent to keep an eye on him, a man twice his age. Greer was also wearing a set of French parachutist's wings, and pinned to the epaulets of his khaki shirt was the regimental badge of the *3ième Régiment Parachutiste de la Légion Étranger*. He could probably get away with wearing the jump wings, General Black thought, but the Foreign Legion regimental crest had to go. But now, he decided, was not the time to tell him so.

"You about finished, Greer?" General Black asked, when Greer had finally found time to come to attention.

"Another half a page, General," Greer said. He picked up a stack of paper from the secretary's IN basket and handed them to General Black. Then he sat down, put a sheet of paper in the typewriter, and resumed his furious typing. He was finished, tearing the page from the typewriter with a reckless flourish, before General Black had read what Greer had given him.

"This would have waited until morning," General Black said, as he read. It was his final report on the Hanoi Conference. He corrected himself. Not exactly. His nineteen-year-old technical sergeant, fresh from vanquishing the enemy on the field of battle, had taken it upon himself to "improve" the draft Col. Carson Newburgh had written, and which he had just about decided to transmit.

I should jump all over his ass, Black thought, but the truth was that the boy had cleaned it up, removed what could have been ambiguities.

"I had planned to be hung over in the morning, General," Greer said. He had had his tie pulled down. He was now standing in front of a mirror, adjusting it in place.

Devotion to duty, General Black thought, wryly, may be defined as correcting your general's sloppy English before you go out and get drunk.

"Do you know what 'hoist on your own petard' means, Greer?"

"I'm afraid to ask."

General Black turned to the Embassy sergeant. "Can you get Colonel Newburgh on the horn for me?" he asked.

"Carson," he said when Newburgh came on the line, "Greer has made certain improvements to our document. Do you feel up to having a look at them now?"

Sergeant Wallace, the court reporter, was summoned, and the sergeant from the Embassy dismissed. It took more than an hour to make still further changes, until Colonel Carson W. Newburgh announced: "That ought to do it. We can sit around here from now on, just moving commas around. It looks good to me, E. Z."

"All right, Sergeant," General Black said. "Please retype it and have it encrypted and sent off. URGENT, I think. I don't think PRIORITY will hack it."

"It doesn't have to be retyped," Sergeant Greer said. Black glowered at him. "We're going to burn the goddamned original anyway," Greer said.

"Encrypt it the way it is, Sergeant Wallace," General Black said.

"We don't have a title for it, sir," Sergeant Wallace Black said.

"'Report of Lieutenant General E. Z. Black to the Joint Chiefs of Staff,'" Sergeant Greer answered for him. "'Subject: An Evaluation of the French Military Position in Indo-China, with Emphasis on the French Garrison at Dien Bien Phu.'"

Black thought a minute, and then nodded his head.

Sergeant Wallace took the report and went in search of the cryptographer.

"Your head is so large now, Greer, that I say this reluctantly," General Black said. "But you did a good job, and I appreciate it."

"And may the sergeant say, general, that the sergeant is delighted with the manner the general has chosen to show his appreciation?" He fondly patted his new chevrons.

"That's in lieu of a medal," Black said. "You deserve them."

"When I get the medal, do I have to give it back?"

"What medal?"

"Croix de guerre," Greer said. "For preserving that Frenchman's most important possession. It'll probably say for valor, or some such bullshit, but that's what it'll be for. I thought you knew about it."

"The Pentagon won't let you accept it, Greer," Carson Newburgh said. "It would be embarrassing politically."

"Christ, and I always wanted to be a certified hero," Greer said.

"And those Foreign Legion regimental crests have to go, too," General Black said. "Have them put on a cigarette lighter, or something, but get them off your uniform."

Greer started to take them off.

"What about the wings?" he asked.

"I think he can keep those, can't he, Carson? As a qualification badge?" Newburgh nodded. "If anybody asks, say you took the French parachute course."

"I did, I did," Greer laughed. "The *quick* course."

"You know what we mean, Greer," Colonel Newburgh said.

"I'm sorry about the Croix de guerre, Greer," General Black said. "The French pass out medals like samples, but they're generally pretty choosy about the Croix de guerre."

"They also parade magnificently," Newburgh said, sarcastically.

"I thought about that," Greer said. "Maybe we're too quick to make fun of them. They need that bullshit. We don't."

"I don't follow you, Greer," Colonel Newburgh said.

"We haven't lost a war, yet," Greer replied. "They have."

Black looked at him intently. The same thought had occurred to him during the four days of the conference. It was not the sort of observation you expected from a sergeant. A nineteen-year-old sergeant.

"Now what, Greer?" Black said.

"Sir?"

"What are you going to do now?"

"Well, sir, the sergeant hoped that the general could see his way clear to placing the sergeant on, say, five days' TDY right here in Taipei. To tidy up loose ends, so to speak."

"That would obviously explain those gorgeous wings you're wearing," Colonel Newburgh said.

"I am solemnly informed they work wonders with the ladies."

"You can have the TDY," General Black said. "But that's not what I was asking."

"I wanted to talk about that, too," Greer said. "But I didn't think this was the time or place."

"You want to stay in? You want to go to West Point?"

"Yes, sir, I want to stay in," Sergeant Greer said. "No, sir, I don't want to go to West Point."

"Why not?" General Black asked, somewhat sharply.

"Being a plebe would be a hell of a comedown after I've been a hero of the French Foreign Legion," Greer said, laughing.

Col. Carson Newburgh laughed. "Is that it? You think you're too good to be a plebe?"

"I don't think I'd last very long, Colonel," Greer said.

"How about Norwich?" Black asked. "I think I can get you a scholarship."

"Or A&M," Newburgh said. "I have some influence there." He was, in fact, a trustee and former president of the Alumni Association.

"How about a direct commission?" Greer asked. "As a first john?"

Newburgh looked at Black, who took a long moment to collect his thoughts before replying.

"If you had come to work for me as a lieutenant, Greer, I would write an efficiency report on you that would, unless you really fucked up, get your career on the right tracks."

"But?" Greer replied.

"You didn't. You're an enlisted man."

"I get your point," Colonel Newburgh said.

"Forgive me, sir," Greer said, disappointment evident in his voice. "I don't."

"You haven't had your card punched, Son," Newburgh said. "You've got to play the game by the rules. You shouldn't even be a tech sergeant."

"Sir, I was under the impression I was earning my keep."

"Technical sergeants are supposed to be thirty years old," General Black said. "Lieutenants, at least those who will have responsible careers, are supposed to come out of the Point, or A&M, or Norwich, or the Citadel. I can get you a commission,

Greer, and you'd probably get to be a captain before somebody stuck a knife in your back. What we're talking about here is making you into a responsible senior officer, not somebody who puts in twenty years and retires."

"I couldn't put up with that West Point bullshit," Greer said.

"No," Black said, "I don't think you could, either. But you're going to have to get a college degree somehow, Greer. Or you might as well get out."

"Which brings us back to A&M," Colonel Newburgh said. "I can arrange a full scholarship, Greer, if it's a question of money."

"Thank you," Greer said, but from the tone of his voice, both Newburgh and Black knew that it was thanks for the offer, but not an acceptance of it.

"You tell me what you want," General Black said. "And you can have it. The commission, too, against my better judgment."

"I wipe out correspondence courses," Greer said. "Getting a degree isn't going to be a problem."

"There's a hurry-up program at A&M," Newburgh said. "Get your degree in three years. And a regular commission."

"Or, I can go to helicopter school," Greer said.

"Helicopter school?" Black asked, surprised. That was the first time that had been mentioned.

"Which means I get a warrant in six months. Then I go to the University of Chicago, which gives college credit for military experience, including flight school, and take some correspondence courses. Then I apply for a reserve commission, and a competitive tour for a regular commission."

"You'd have to take the Series 10 courses," Newburgh replied. Series 10 courses were correspondence courses offered to enlisted men. If successfully completed, the noncommissioned officer was then eligible to apply for a reserve commission.

"I already have," Greer said.

"How'd you do?"

"Three decimal nine," Greer said. Four decimal zero was perfect.

"Then what's this warrant officer helicopter pilot business?" Black asked.

"That's where the action's going to be," Greer said. "And the establishment is going to keep it for themselves. If I was a pilot before I took a commission, I'd be in already. Otherwise, I'm not sure I could get in."

"Then what's this bullshit about wanting me to commission you?"

"I was hoping I could get both out of you," Greer admitted. "A commission and flight school."

Carson Newburgh laughed.

"*L'audace, l'audace, toujours l'audace,*" he said.

"*Mais certainement, mon Colonel,*" Sergeant Greer said.

"I think you ought to shrink that oversized head of yours, Greer, and I think you're making a serious, perhaps fatal mistake in not going to either the Point, or A&M, or Norwich. But if the helicopter school is what you want, I'll see that you get it."

The middle-aged general and the teen-aged sergeant looked at each other.

"Thanks," Sergeant Greer said. There was more respect, and affection, in the one word than either General Black or Colonel Newburgh had ever before heard from Sergeant Greer.

"Take off, Greer," General Black said. "And five days is spelled Eff Eye Vee Eee. Not six, not seven, not even five and a half."

"The sergeant assures the general he will report as required, where required, and when required," Greer said. He saluted crisply, and then he left the room.

"If that little sonofabitch doesn't wind up either in the stockade or in the hospital with a terminal case of social disease," General Black said, "I think he'll do very well."

III

(One)
Ozark, Alabama
26 March 1954

Thirty minutes out of Atlanta, Southern Airways Flight 117, a Super DC-3, landed at Columbus, Georgia. Six of the twenty-one passengers who had filled the seats got off, and no one got on. Howard Dutton took advantage of the opportunity to take both of his heavy, bulging, worn briefcases from beneath the seats and put them on the empty seat beside him.

He was a stocky, square-faced man wearing rimless spectacles, a starched white shirt already well wilted, and a suit that seemed a half size too small for his body. He was always uncomfortable when his briefcases were out of his sight, for they, rather than the turn-of-the-century safe in his office, were really his private and confidential files. His wife, who was his secretary, had the combination to the safe in the office. She had orders, which he believed she followed faithfully, never to mess around in his briefcases.

His briefcases were rarely out of his sight, even at night,

47

when he kept them at the side of his bed in his frame house on Broad Street. They contained his secrets. He now had the biggest, most important secret of his life in the double-strap briefcase.

There were two briefcases. The first he had had since he graduated from the University of Alabama. It closed with one strap. He had carried his books in the single-strapper through the University of Alabama Law School. He had bought the double-strapper after the war, when he had been in Washington as administrative assistant to the Hon. Bascomb J. Henry (D–Fifth District, Ala.), and the single-strapper just hadn't been big enough to hold all that he had to carry around.

He resisted the temptation to open the double-strapper and take out the papers which made the secret official. But he rested his hand, casually, on the double-strapper, while he smiled a no-thanks to the stewardess's offer of a Coke-or-coffee and a bag of peanuts.

Thirty minutes out of Columbus, the Super DC-3 landed again, at Dothan, Alabama, and taxied to the one-floor frame terminal building. From Dothan it would go to Panama City, Florida, and from Panama City to Fort Walton Beach, eighty miles down the coast, where the flight would terminate.

Three people got off at Dothan, two of them standing by the Super DC-3 while a ground crewman opened the door in the fuselage and removed their luggage. Howard Dutton had no luggage besides the briefcases. The single-strapper held two soiled white shirts, identical to the one he was wearing, a soiled sleeveless undershirt, soiled boxer shorts, and a soiled pair of black nylon socks.

Howard Dutton had gone from Ozark, Alabama, to the nation's capital, to the halls of Congress, to the seat of power, to deal with some of the most powerful men in the nation, with a change of underwear and two extra shirts, and he had returned victorious.

A warm feeling swept through him, instantly replaced by one of annoyance, concern, and a little anger. He had seen his daughter, Melody, standing inside the plate glass doors of the terminal. Howard Dutton dearly loved his daughter Melody, who was seventeen, and a senior at Ozark High School, and had been touched that she had driven all the way here from Ozark to meet her daddy.

But then he had noticed how Melody was dressed. Melody was wearing a white T-shirt, through which the brassiere restraining her pert young breasts was clearly visible, and a pair of blue shorts that were so short they reminded Howard, to his immediate shame, of the shorts worn by a whore in a Birmingham brothel he had gone to one drunken weekend when he was at the university.

That was a hell of a thing for a father to think about his own seventeen-year-old daughter, he thought, but the cold facts were that that's how the whore had been dressed. Melody, of course, was simply blind to what she looked like. She had never seen a whore, as far as he knew, and probably wasn't sure what one did. It was hot, and, still a child, she did what she had done when she had been a child. She took off as many clothes as she could.

Howard mentally cursed his wife. Wives were supposed to see about that sort of thing, make sure their daughters looked respectable when they went in public.

Melody ran out of the building and gave him a hug and a wet kiss.

"How's my favorite daddy?" she asked.

If it was anyone's fault that she was running around in public looking like a fancy lady in a Birmingham whorehouse, Howard Dutton decided, it damned sure wasn't this innocent child's.

"You shouldn't have come all the way here in this heat," he said. "You should have sent Clem." Clem was the janitor at the bank, an amiable elderly black man who sometimes drove the car.

"I was *bored* out of my *gourd*, Daddy," Melody said.

"That's the only reason, you were bored?"

"And I missed my favorite daddy," she said. She hugged him again. One of the other debarking passengers happened to be male, happened to see Melody hugging her daddy, and happened to appreciatively notice Melody's pink buttocks, about half of which were visible below the blue shorts.

Goddamned pervert! Howard Dutton thought. *Looking at an innocent young girl like that!*

He walked Melody around, rather than through, the Dothan Municipal Airport Terminal Building, to where she had parked the car, its nose against a cable strung between creosoted six-by-sixes stuck in the reddish clay. He set the double-strapper on the ground and opened the door of the 1951 Ford Super Deluxe. He tossed the single-strapper onto the back seat, and then picked up the double-strapper and tossed that onto the floor in the back.

"You want me to drive, Melody, honey?" he asked.

"No, I don't," she said. "You are one of the world's worst drivers."

He had been afraid of that, and would really have preferred to drive, but he knew that you had to force yourself to let them grow up, and driving cars was part of growing up.

He took off his suit jacket, its inner pockets sagging with the weight of still more paper, and carefully laid it on the seat back so that it wouldn't slide off the slippery plastic upholstery.

The senator had sent one of his assistants to take him to Washington National from the Capitol. In a 1953 Mercury four door. With an air conditioner. That air conditioner had really been nice in the muggy heat of Washington, and the muggy heat of Washington wasn't anything like the muggy heat here. He really wished he could have an air conditioner.

The 1951 Ford Super Deluxe belonged to the Farmers and Planters Bank of Ozark, of which Howard Dutton was president and chairman of the board. While the bank could well afford, financially, an air-conditioned Mercury for its president and chairman of the board, Howard Dutton could not afford, socially, to drive anything that suggested the bank was getting rich on the sweat of its depositors. Howard's father had taught him that. Depositors were just looking for some excuse to bad-mouth their bankers.

Maybe soon. Not right away, but soon, when everybody had a little more money, because of what he was doing for them, he could at least get a car with a goddamned air conditioner.

He decided that they would go home the long way. Indulge himself. For one thing, Prissy (for Priscilla, Mrs. Howard Dutton) had told him on the phone that Tom Zoghby had dropped dead. One moment, Tom had been talking with somebody (Dudley Claxton, he thought Prissy said) and the next moment he was dead on the floor. Right on the sidewalk in front of Zoghby's Emporium.

The minute he got home, of course, he would be expected to go see the widow and young Tom and the girls. There was no getting away from that, even if he had wanted to, but at the same time it wasn't the sort of thing you liked to do. That he liked to do. There were a lot of people who really got their pleasure rushing to console a widow and a bereaved family.

Tom had probably left his family well fixed, which was something. But still, there might be a need for some cash money, and he would have to have a word with young Tom (he wouldn't want to bother the widow) about maybe selling some of that land along County Highway 53.

He was suddenly shamed with the thought. That would be dishonest and unethical, now that he had the secret. He was surprised with himself; he wasn't, no matter what people thought, the kind of banker that went around taking advantage of widows and heirs. After a moment, he was able to convince himself that he had thought about buying the Zoghby land along Highway 53 without thinking about the secret. The secret was so new, that he just hadn't thought about it. He really hadn't been trying to take advantage of Tom's boy.

"Go up 84 toward Enterprise," he told Melody.

There were two ways to get from Dothan to Ozark. The short way was to turn left when leaving the airport, and then left again, and up US 231. The long way was to turn right when leaving the airport, and then right again, on US 84, toward Enterprise, and then, fifteen miles along, turn right again and cut through the Camp Rucker Reservation.

He was entitled, as a reward, both not to rush home to see the Widow Zoghby and to take a look at Camp Rucker. He was a banker and a lawyer, and he knew he didn't own Camp Rucker. But at the same time, he had a special relationship with it that nobody else could claim, not even Congressman Henry (May He Rest in Peace).

In 1934, under Roosevelt's Rural Reclamation Administration, the government had bought from Congressman Henry (and other people) 125,000 acres of worked-out cotton land, after they'd sent experts in who had decided the soil was so poor that nothing man could do was going to make it productive again for at least a generation.

Goddamned fools had cottoned the land, and just worked it to death, destroying the topsoil, so it blew away, and then, when the rains came, gullied it, so that it wasn't worth a damn for anything. Congressman Henry was as guilty as any of them, so you couldn't just say the dumb rednecks were getting what they deserved, reaping what they had sowed.

So the goverment had come in and bought it up, paying ten dollars an acre for land that was worth maybe a dollar, a dollar and a half, and they'd sent in the CCC, and stopped what they could of the worst gullying and planted it in loblolly pine, and said that in maybe fifty years they would think of clearing it again for planting. Maybe by that time they would have come up with some way to make topsoil or do something to clay that would make it grow things; and in the meantime they could timber it, twice, and get something out of it.

And then, six years after that, when the pines were head-high, World War II had come along (or was coming along, and everybody could see it coming) and the military was looking for places to build training bases.

The land was transferred to the War Department in late 1939, but it wasn't until late 1941, right before the Japs bombed Pearl Harbor, when Howard Dutton had been in his last year in the law school at Alabama, that they announced plans to make it a base. And it was nearly a year after that, November 1942, before they did anything.

Once they started, of course, they really got in high gear. When Howard Dutton left the Basic Officer's Course in Miami, in the Air Corps, all there was on what was still called "the Reclamation Land" was some surveyors' tapes and markers, but when he came back on leave three months later, there was Camp Rucker, named for General Rucker, who'd been a Confederate general.

In ninety days they'd built a military post, everything from barracks to a laundry to rifle ranges. All Howard Dutton had seen around Courthouse Square on his leave, before going over to the China-Burma-India theater as an Air Corps lawyer, was khaki uniforms. And, oh, how the money had rolled in!

Two divisions, eleven, twelve thousand men each, plus the support troops, had trained at Camp Rucker, and after they had gone off to war, they had changed it into a POW camp, and the place had held more than twenty thousand Italian prisoners from North Africa. They'd been lucky there, the Eyeties were glad to be out of the war, and they'd caused no trouble at all. They'd worked the farms. Hell, they'd even made out with the women, but nobody talked about that. There was something unpatriotic about the women doing that, with their own men off to war on the other side. But it happened, even if no one talked about it.

Right after the war, the place had closed down again, and where there had been twenty thousand soldiers, there was maybe a dozen enlisted men and a couple of officers, just watching the place, to make sure people didn't steal the place blind.

It had opened again for the Korean War, not the way it had been (they had trained a National Guard regiment from Wisconsin, not a division) and not for as long. It had closed down again in 1953, last year, with the Korean War still going.

And when the soldiers went, so had all that government money. When the camp was open, even with the Eyetie prisoners, they'd had to buy all sorts of things, mostly services, from Ozark and Enterprise and even Dothan. There were jobs, that was the thing, jobs ranging from fireman to barber, all kinds of clerks, people to work in the post exchange, fix the telephones, all the things the army needs and can't do for itself. The best kind of jobs, to a banker's way of thinking, ones that brought money into a community and took nothing out. If a factory opens, that means jobs, sure, but it also means you (the city) have to pay for firemen, and policemen, and sewers, and everything else people expect. But a military post either doesn't need that sort of thing or pays for it itself.

There was all kinds of idiotic talk going around about what to do with the post, when it closed down. Turn it into a university. Get industry to relocate on it. Even, when things got desperate, turn it into a prison. After all, they'd had all those Eyeties out there, so you knew that worked.

But those weren't answers and Howard Dutton knew they weren't. He had seen it from the beginning, from the day he'd come home from the war. War or not, the thing to do with Camp Rucker was keep it Camp Rucker, keep it filled with soldiers.

That was the reason Howard had gone to work on the congressman, gone off to Washington, instead of taking over from his father at the bank or opening a law practice. He had learned in the Air Corps that if there is a system, you can figure out how the system works, and then make it work for you.

That was his secret. He had made the system work the day he wanted it to work.

He didn't think of himself as a hypocrite. What he had done was going to make a lot of people rich around town, be good for the whole county. But it was also, and he knew this, and was not embarrassed by it, going to make him a rich man, too. Richer than he ever would have gotten at the bank. Much richer.

God helps those who help themselves. Say what you like. It was true.

US Highway 84 was a two-lane macadam road, nearly straight, running through gently rolling land between farms and untended land. Fifteen miles from Dothan, Howard Dutton told Melody to take the right turn at a fork. This was the "new road," built when they built Camp Rucker in ninety days from the time the first nail was driven. It cut across large patches of what the Rural Reclamation Administration had called "submarginal farm land" to Daleville, one of the oldest communities in the county.

Daleville was a ghost town when Melody drove her Daddy through it, in the Ford Super Deluxe. When the camp was open, Daleville was just outside the gate, and the single street was lined with cheap frame buildings that used to house laundries and dry cleaners and Army-Navy stores and hamburger stands and used car lots.

No bars or saloons. Dale County (named after the same Dale who had set up a store at the crossroads and named it Daleville) was Baptist dry. That's not dry, that means that there are no bars, and you can't get a drink in a restaurant or beer at the grocery store. You generally get your own beer when you're out of town in a wet county, and you get your whiskey in pint bottles from a bootlegger. But there are no public places to drink, where people can go and ruin their lives with the Devil's Brew.

A small general store was still open, and the one-room post office next door, and there were half a dozen worn-out pickups and as many battered old Fords and Chevvies on the weed-grown lot of one of the used car places, but everything else was closed down and boarded up and falling down. There were no soldiers and there was no business.

There was a sign at the deserted gate, where once MPs in white leggings and pistol belts had stood waving people through and saluting officers in their cars. The sign said, "MILITARY RESERVATION—DO NOT LEAVE MARKED ROUTE."

What that meant was that you were supposed to follow the one road, which ran on the fringes of the built-up area, and which led to the other side, to the road to Ozark. They didn't want people running around loose in the built-up area, where they could help themselves to toilets and wire and pipe and even the barracks themselves because they were just sitting there asking to be stolen.

Howard Dutton gestured with his arm.

"Drive around the sawhorses, Melody," he said. "I want to have a look around."

"Are we looking for anything in particular?" she asked.

"Just drive around the area behind post headquarters," he said.

To their left were enormous wooden garages, where once the rolling stock of infantry divisions, trucks and tanks and cannon, had been repaired. He knew, although he couldn't see it, that beyond the garages was a 2,000 bed hospital. A hundred or more single-story frame buildings connected with walkways to keep the patients out of the sun and rain as they were wheeled between the buildings.

A flag still fluttered from the flagpole in front of post headquarters, for the caretakers had taken over that one building for their headquarters and living quarters. The last contract issued for more than a thousand dollars by the purchasing office before it had closed was to bring electricity from Dale County Rural Electrification Agency lines to the post headquarters. The coal-fired generators which had provided electricity to the post when it was open were still there, and ready to run, but it was cheaper with just a dozen men on the post to string a line and buy electricity from REA.

The grass was cut right in front of post headquarters, but the parade ground in front was grown waist high with grass, and there was grass that high between the endless rows of barracks.

Melody drove past post headquarters to the field house, and around it, and down crumbling macadam streets through regimental areas. The barracks looked in good shape, except for flaking paint and broken windows here and there. Beside each of the two-story wooden buildings, there was even a supply of coal for their furnaces in small concrete-block caches. There were even lights in the fixtures over the doors, and hanging from lamppoles every block.

And then up ahead he saw an Army pickup truck blocking the road.

Melody stopped the Ford with its nose a foot from the pickup's fender and Howard Dutton got out of the car, a smile on his face.

"Oh, it's you, Mayor," the major driving the pickup truck said. He waved his hand. "Hi, Melody!"

Melody got out of the car and walked over to them. Howard Dutton wished she hadn't done that, with half of her bottom hanging out that way.

Howard Dutton was on his second term as mayor of Ozark. He had decided it was really easier to be mayor himself than to pick somebody for the job, and then have to watch every move he made.

"Hot enough for you, Major?" Howard Dutton said, extending his hand. He was always very charming to Major Feeler, the post commander, even though he thought Feeler was a fool, and sometimes wondered what Feeler had done to find himself with an idiot job like this.

"I was so hot," Major Feeler said, "that I went down to the pool at the officer's club. Dirty or not, I was going to have a swim."

"And you did?" Melody asked.

"Would you believe there was three snakes in that pool?" the major said, and they laughed together.

Melody said "Oook" and made a face.

"Anytime you want a swim, you should come to Ozark," Howard Dutton said.

There was a community swimming pool at the community house.

"I just may do that," the major said. "I saw the car driving past headquarters. If I'd known it was you, I wouldn't have chased you."

"I guess I'm violating the law," Howard Dutton said. "But I had a few minutes, and I wanted to get a last look at the place before they start tearing it down."

Major Feeler, very obviously, made up his mind before speaking.

"Maybe I shouldn't be talking out of school, Mayor Dutton," he said. "And I wouldn't want you to quote me."

"I appreciate your confidence, Major," Dutton said.

"I just heard from Third Army in Atlanta that there's a hold on the awarding of the demolition contract."

"Cancelled, you mean?" Dutton asked.

"No, sir. Just a hold."

"Isn't that interesting?" Dutton replied. "What do you suppose that means?"

"I don't know," the major said. "Maybe they figured it would just be cheaper to let it all fall down than to pay to have it torn down."

"You may well be right," Dutton said, seriously. "If you hear anything, I'd appreciate learning about it."

"I'll tell you anything I can, Mayor," the major said. "You know that."

The Farmers and Planters Bank of Ozark, at Dutton's direction, never pressed Major Feeler hard when he was late with his car payment.

"I appreciate that," Dutton said, and shook Major Feeler's hand. "I truly do. And now, I think, we've seen enough. Next time you get to town, you come and have a cup of coffee with me, you hear?"

"I'll do that," Major Feeler said. He got back in his GI pickup truck and drove off, waving as he did.

Dumb ass, Howard Dutton thought.

But he was smiling. Even that had gone well. The demolition contract was on "hold." That happened all the time, for any number of reasons.

The secret, the secret that Camp Rucker was not going to be torn down at all, but reactivated, was still a secret. There were still several days, maybe as much as a week, to do things before the word got out.

"Let's go home, honey," he said to Melody.

He was going to make enough money so that when Melody went off to college, she would really have a good time, without having to worry about what things cost, the way he had had to, when he was at the university. Maybe he'd get her a car, a convertible. Pretty girls like Melody deserved to ride around in convertibles.

(Two)
Fort Knox, Kentucky
26 March 1954

"So there I was," Major Rudolph G. MacMillan said to Colonel Robert F. Bellmon, Assistant G-3 (Plans and Training), Headquarters, the United States Army Armor School and Fort Knox, Kentucky, "surrounded by howling savages, low on water, about out of ammunition, when, far away, I heard the faint sound of a trumpet sounding 'Charge.'"

Then he lowered his head, addressed the ball, and sank a thirty-two-foot putt on the eleventh hole of the Fort Knox officer's open mess golf course. He then raised his head and smiled warmly at Colonel Bellmon.

"So there I was," Colonel Bellmon said, "standing before the general, who had just handed me an URGENT radio, saying you were down and presumed dead, and the general said, 'You better tell Roxie.'"

Their eyes met.

"So I figured I'd wait until morning," Bellmon went on. "That wasn't the first time the Pride of Mauch Chuck had been reported presumed dead."

"I owe you," MacMillan said. "Some dumb sonofabitch from the CIA went and got Sharon Felter out of bed at three o'clock in the morning and told her. Complete routine, even a goddamned rabbi and a doctor."

"I know," Bellmon said. "I've talked to Felter."

"And what did Felter have to say?"

"He said he knew how close you and I are," Bellmon said.

Their eyes met for a long moment. Then Bellmon walked to his ball, wiggled into putting position, and stroked it. It hit the lip of the hole, half circled it, and then rolled two feet back toward Bellmon.

"You going to give me that?" Bellmon asked. MacMillan shook his head. "No." Bellmon shrugged, and then sank his putt. They walked to their clubs, mounted in two-wheel carts, and dragged them to the 12th tee.

There was a Coke machine there, inside a small gazebo. MacMillan fed it dimes, handed a Coke to Bellmon, and leaned on one of the pillars supporting the roof.

"We went over there nonstop in a bomber," MacMillan said. "From Andrews Air Force Base in Washington."

"Nonstop?" Bellmon asked.

"They refueled us in the air twice," MacMillan said. "Once over the West Coast, and again over Hawaii, or near Hawaii. Scared the shit out of me. What they do is fly up under the tanker, and then the tanker extends a probe, got little wings on the end of it to guide it. And then it meshes with a thing on the front of the bomber. We're going six hundred miles an hour, you understand. Very hairy."

"So you went where?" Bellmon asked.

"Seoul. K16. They were holding a civilian transport for us. CAT. You know, from Formosa. A DC-4. Everybody's there, in civilian clothing. E. Z. Black's in charge. Had an air force brigadier who was very unhappy when Felter told him we were going into Dien Bien Phu. Felter had a note from Eisenhower. That shut up the air force."

"I thought you said General Black was in charge."

"Black's people were told to stay away from Dien Bien Phu, and to wear civilian clothes," MacMillan said. "Jesus, that was funny."

"Funny?" Colonel Bellmon asked. "How funny?"

"Well, the whole operation is a big damned secret, see, very hush-hush. They even hid the CAT DC-4 in a hangar in Seoul, for Christ's sake, so nobody would see it. So we arrive in Hanoi. Only Felter and me are in uniform. Everybody else is in civvies. And there's half of the French Army out there, honest to God, Bob, a battalion of troops and a brass band. Cymbals, trumpets with flags hanging down from them, bass drums. Even a couple of goats with gold-painted horns. Full dress reception. Frog brass in dress uniforms. Our brass in mussed civvies, looking like they've been sleeping in their clothes. Except for a couple of the enlisted men. You know that big black orderly of Black's?"

"Sergeant Wesley," Bellmon said.

"Yeah. He must weigh three hundred pounds. Well, Black brought him along. And he's got this kid who works for him, a guy named Greer. He reminds me of Craig Lowell in the old days, except this kid knows what he's doing. Black sends him along to keep an eye on us. About as subtle as a Honolulu whorehouse madam. Well, the first thing the frogs tell us is that we can't land, we have to jump. And the kid is no jumper. But he says he's going even if he has to jump. And he does."

"Lowell, by the way," Bellmon said in a level tone, "just graduated from flight school. He and Parker."

Major Craig W. Lowell and Captain Philip Sheridan Parker IV bothered Lieutenant Colonel Robert F. Bellmon. But he was honest enough to admit to himself that it was probably because he couldn't simply dismiss them as a pair of wise-asses.

Parker was establishment, the fourth soldier to bear the name. The first Philip Sheridan Parker had been the son of a master sergeant who rode in the Indian Wars with General

Philip Sheridan. His son, Colonel Philip Sheridan Parker, Jr., had been the senior "colored" tank officer in World War I. Colonel Philip Sheridan Parker III, of General Porky Waterford's "Hell's Circus" Armored Division, had commanded Task Force Parker that had saved Bellmon from whatever plans besides instant repatriation the Russians had for two hundred "liberated" American prisoners.

Lowell, if not antiestablishment, was certainly not *of* it. He came from a wealthy family, but had entered the army as a draftee after having been kicked out of Harvard. He had turned up in Bellmon's life, when MacMillan, serving at Bellmon's recommendation as aide-de-camp to General Waterford, had been ordered to produce a polo team from personnel assigned to the Constabulary in occupied Germany. And Craig W. Lowell was a three-goal polo player. There are not many three-goal polo players anywhere, and there had been none in the Constabulary except Lowell.

The idea of having the best polo team possible was General Waterford's obsession. General Waterford had graduated, in 1937, from the French cavalry school at Samur. Now he wished to play the French, both for personal reasons, and, Bellmon was sure, for reasons involving the prestige of the U.S. Army. If he was going to win playing the French, he was going to have to have PFC Craig Lowell playing as his number two.

French officers, however, do not play with enlisted men.

So General Waterford delegated the problem to Captain MacMillan. MacMillan arranged for Lowell to be temporarily commissioned as a second lieutenant in the Finance Corps. He would play polo, and then be released from active duty for the convenience of all concerned.

But on the day of the polo game against the French, Porky Waterford suffered a heart attack, dying in a way which would have met his approval: in the saddle, at the gallop, almost at the opposition's goal and about to score.

That left the problem of what to do with 2nd Lt Craig W. Lowell. He was not discharged, but instead swept under the rug. He was sent to Greece, where, it was believed, if he wasn't killed, at least he would be out of sight.

Forced into it, Craig W. Lowell took to soldiering as if he

had been born to be a warrior. He came home from Greece with the second highest decoration for valor the Greek throne bestowed, the highest being reserved for Greek nationals. As Bellmon had heard from Red Hanrahan, Lowell had assumed command of a Greek Mountain Division company after the officers had been killed, and despite several serious wounds, repulsed a communist attack, personally killing more than a dozen of the enemy himself.

After that, Lowell got out of the army, and settled into his new home in Washington Mews with his wife Ilse, a girl he had met in Germany. But then was recalled for Korea. In Korea, he had commanded Task Force Lowell, which spearheaded the breakout from Pusan, earning himself a Distinguished Service Cross and a major's golden leaf. But at the moment of his greatest glory, he learned of the death of his wife in Germany.

Choosing to stay in the army, Lowell had a distinguished military career ahead of him. But the following year, he threw it away, first by cavorting with a visiting movie star in a way unbefitting an officer and a gentleman, and then by defending Philip Sheridan Parker IV, who was court-martialed for having found it necessary to shoot an officer who had lost control on the battlefield.

Bellmon genuinely believed that both Phil Parker and Craig Lowell should have resigned from the service. They had not. They had volunteered for army aviation, which Bellmon (and most other members of the establishment) regarded as a dumping ground for misfits and ne'er-do-wells.

"I heard about that," MacMillan said. "Where'd they send them?"

"Lowell went to Germany, Parker to Alaska. We seem to have gotten away from Hanoi."

"Yeah. OK. Well, this kid sergeant is a real sharp operator. He had just come back from leave in Hong Kong. Where he's bought civilian clothes. He's wearing a plaid suit with a suede vest, and he's bought clothes for Wesley too. Pin-striped, double-breasted suit. Looks like a nigger undertaker. So what we have here is Black's colored orderly and this kid who works for him looking like an advertisement in *Esquire,* and here's all the brass looking like a bunch of bums. So they play the

Marseillaise and the Star Spangled Banner, and Black, in a tweed suit, troops the colors. And then they load everybody into limousines—a Rolls-Royce for Black, and old Packards and old Cadillacs from before War II for everybody else—and sirens screaming, they take us into town in a convoy.

"If Ho Chi Minh didn't know the Americans were coming, the frogs sure arranged for him to find out. Black gets taken to a frog VIP villa, him and Carson Newburgh, and the other generals are spread around among the other frog generals. The rest of us are taken to the Cercle Sportif, which is sort of a golf club, with a place where the frogs jump horses over fences. What do you call it?"

"Steeplechase?"

"I don't think so. But something like that. Anyway, it's pretty first class. So there's going to be cocktails at five o'clock and then dinner. And then the frogs find out that Wesley and the kid who works for Black, and the other technicians, the cryptographer, the map guys, are enlisted men. And the shit hits the fan. Christ, there are fifteen frogs running around flapping their arms and chattering like whores in a cathouse raid. *Enlisted men* in the Cercle Sportif! Napoleon will spin in his grave!"

"I thought you said they were in civvies?" Bellmon asked.

"They were. And they were all high-class troops, too. They weren't about to piss in the potted palms. But anyway, even Black gets involved in this. And he was pissed, too, let me tell you. They finally move them into a hotel in town, which means that they have to lay on transportation for them, to get everybody back and forth . . ."

"Tell me about the meeting," Bellmon said.

"I didn't get to go to the meeting," MacMillan said. "First thing in the morning, Felter takes my ass out to the airport. We're going to fly to Dien Bien Phu. We did. We just didn't land."

"No landing strip?"

"Oh, yeah. Under 105 and mortar fire. The only time they land is to evacuate people. The rest of the supplies go in by being kicked out the door. They don't even put the landing gear down. You know about Air America?"

"Something."

"They've got a bunch of ex-air force guys, and some Flying Boxcars, and they supply the place. Parachutist replacements jump in. It's safer."

"You got hit," Bellmon said.

"They got .50s on the hilltops. And some 20 mm stuff, too. I think they got us with .50s. It didn't blow up when it hit us, just set the goddamned engine on fire."

"So you went out the door?"

"There was a French Foreign Legion guy, a frog, which is unusual, in the door. I pushed him out, and then this Greer kid, and then I went out."

"Where was Felter?"

"You know Felter," MacMillan said. "He knows how to take care of Number One. He was out the door like a shot."

"But nobody else got out?"

"If we hadn't been standing in the door, we wouldn't have gotten out," MacMillan said. "It was hairy."

"Then what?"

"So we land in the trees. Smashed my goddamned watch. So I started sneaking around in the bushes, and I see that the Viet Minh, the communists, have caught the frog, and, honest to God, Bob, they're about to cut off his dick and feed it to him. So I shot one of them . . ."

"With what? You were specifically ordered to go unarmed."

"I shot them with that .32 Colt you gave me in the stalag," MacMillan said. "A goddamned good thing I had it, too. And then I ducked behind a tree, to kiss my ass good-bye, because the slopes I don't blow away had Chink submachine guns. And then, all of a sudden, *Boom! Boom!*"

"What was that?"

"That's this Greer kid. He's got a sawed-off Winchester Model 12, loaded with single ought buckshot. He blew one slope's head half off, and a hole right through the other one. No shit, right *through* him. You could put your fist in the hole."

"Where was Felter?"

"After it's all over, the little bastard walks up, calm as shit, out of the jungle. He told me not to take a gun, but *he* had that goddamned .45 he always carries."

"And then you walked into Dien Bien Phu?"

"Walked is not the word. It took us four days. We crawled. We ran. We climbed trees. But we did very little walking. The legionnaire, who had been there before, made us hide all day, and move at night. Very hairy. The woods were full of gooks looking for us. We hid in trees. Got eaten alive by bugs. And then, and this was the hairy part, we had to get into Dien Bien Phu. They got a major base and a couple of outposts, separated, and as far as they're concerned, anybody out there in the woods is a bad guy. If it moves, shoot it."

"But you made it."

"Yeah."

"The French didn't see anybody get out of the C-47," Bellmon said. "That's when they sent the casualty cables."

"Anyway, we got there. You wouldn't believe that place, Bob. It's like what France in War I must have been. Everything underground. The gooks lay in harassing and intermittent all the time, and then, every once in a while, they shoot boom boom boom, twenty-four hours a day. So the officers stay half drunk, and the troops stay mostly drunk."

"Can they hold it?"

"No way," MacMillan said. "After we kept the gooks from cutting off his dick, the legionnaire told us whatever we wanted to know. I don't know how the hell they're doing it, but the communists are moving 105 howitzers . . . ours, incidentally, ones the First Cav lost in Korea . . . over those goddamned mountains by hand. And ammunition for them. More and more all the time. There's no way the frogs can hold Dien Bien Phu. The legionnaire told me that there's a couple of more cannon every day. Sooner or later, that's it."

"You didn't go to the meetings in Hanoi at all?"

"No, but Sandy got a report from Black, and I was there when he told him."

"Well?"

"The frogs are crazy. They want the First Cav, all right, and they want the 187th RCT, right now, but they want it under

French command. They want to run the show."

"How did you get out of Dien Bien Phu?" Colonel Bellmon asked, half idle curiosity, half because he wanted to consider the ramifications of MacMillan's last remark.

"On an ambulance plane," MacMillan said. "Once you go into Dien Bien Phu, you stay there. Which is why they're not putting any more women in there. The only way to get out is on an ambulance plane. The gooks use the Red Crosses as aiming points."

"You say Colonel Black told Felter the French wanted command of American troops?"

"That's what he said," MacMillan replied. "That's when he started talking French. He told them that there was absolutely no way the American people would stand still for putting American troops under French command, even if, which he doubted they would, they would stand still for Americans being sent there at all."

"And their response?"

"They would rather have their dicks cut off with dignity than admit that they had to have the Americans bail their ass out again."

"So what's going to happen, Mac?" Bellmon asked.

"Dien Bien Phu is going to fall," MacMillan said. "If we sent in a couple of divisions, maybe, just maybe, we could have it. Otherwise, it goes."

"What do you mean, 'it'?"

"All of it, the whole goddamned colony."

Bellmon didn't say anything for a long time.

"You want to play golf, Mac?" he said, finally.

"One more thing," MacMillan said.

"What?"

"Thanks for not running right over to Roxie when the cable came," MacMillan said.

"I figured you'd turn up," Bellmon said. "God takes care of fools and drunks and you qualify on both counts."

They locked eyes for a moment.

"So Lowell got through flight school?" MacMillan said, closing the subject.

"Not without difficulty, I understand, between us," Bellmon said. "He is not a natural-born aviator."

"The Duke generally hires people to do dirty jobs like that," MacMillan said. "They sent him to Seventh Army, huh?"

"Yeah, for a year. Basic utilization tour. Major Lowell will spend the next year being told what to do by lieutenants and captains."

"At least they'll be older than he is," MacMillan said, and then he walked out of the gazebo and thumbed a tee into the ground.

IV

(One)
Broadlawns
Glen Cove, Long Island, N.Y.
12 April 1954

Only a few of the house's chimneys, and only if you knew where to look for them, could be seen from any point along the fence which enclosed Broadlawns. The fence, which enclosed 640 acres, more or less (a square mile, as nearly as they bothered to survey in 1768), marched around the property from the low waterline of Long Island Sound, up and down the rocks and boulders and the flat places and the hollows, and was broken only once, at the gate.

The fence was made of brick pillars, eight feel tall, between which were suspended two iron strips. Every eight inches along the iron strips was a steel pole, pointed at the upper end. The fence and the gate and the gatehouse had been erected as hastily as possible in the early days of the Civil War when one of

Broadlawns's mistresses had been concerned that the draft riots in New York City, fifteen miles away, might spread to the country. She was in the family way at the time and had to be indulged.

There was one gatepost, to which a bronze sign reading BROADLAWNS was affixed. The other side of the gate was tied to the gatehouse, which was built of granite blocks, and made large enough to house ten or a dozen men and feed them, in case the draft riots did get out of hand, and it was necessary to protect the place in the country, as the family thought of it, with private policemen.

A policeman lived in the gatehouse now. He had been brought to the gatehouse as a baby, when his father had been in charge of the gate. He had grown up and gone to high school, and to Fordham University for two years; and then he had become a New York state trooper, and had risen to sergeant in twenty-eight years of service. He had retired to the gatehouse, and now his son was a state trooper lieutenant.

The retired state trooper sergeant had taken over the responsibilities of groundskeeper when the groundskeeper had died. He supervised the men who tended the grounds and the mechanic who kept the lawn mowers and other equipment running, and was responsible for just about everything on the place outside the house. Inside the house was the responsibility of the butler.

The retired state trooper and his son had been very helpful to the present owner of the house when he had been a young man with access to automobiles easily capable of exceeding the speed limits of the state of New York. There was only one arrest on the records, that for a 105-mile-per-hour chase by seven police cars, the arrest coming only when the car had blown a tire and rolled over. There was a limit to the sergeant's influence with his peers.

The house was visible from Long Island Sound, but it was so far back from the water, across broad lawns, that it appeared from the water to be smaller than it was. Even up close, standing in the drive, it wasn't very imposing. It was only when one was inside that the size and complexity of the house became apparent. It had begun as a farmhouse; and additions had been made to it, the most recent in 1919. There were now seven bedrooms, a library, a morning room, a drawing room, a living room, a bar, a small dining room, a large dining room, and a breakfast room.

Many people believed that Broadlawns was a private mental hospital, and others thought it belonged to the Roman Catholic Archdiocese of New York and was used as a retreat for clergy who had problems with alcohol or were otherwise mentally disturbed.

Developers, over the years, studying plats of the land, had often thought it would be a very desirable piece of property to turn into really classy, half-acre, maybe even three-quarters of an acre, plots. They had been informed the property was not for sale. The persistent ones, who believed that everything had its price, were advised by their bankers not to make nuisances of themselves. The people who had owned Broadlawns since 1768 did not wish to be disturbed, and since they were deeply involved in the real estate business around New York, they were not the sort of people small-potatoes developers could afford to antagonize.

Most of the property around Wall Street which was not owned by Trinity Episcopal Church was owned by the people who owned Broadlawns. And they had other property as well.

Broadlawns's butler was a West Indian, a tall, light-brown man with sharp facial features and graying hair. He wore a gray cotton jacket over gray striped trousers. When he walked into the bar to announce a call for Major Craig W. Lowell, his pronunciation was Oxford perfect, and somehow a bit funny.

"I beg your pardon, Major. The firm is on the line. They wish to transfer a call. Is the major at home?"

Major Craig W. Lowell, who was a little drunk, looked at him in annoyance.

"Did they say who?" he asked.

"No, sir," the butler said.

"Shit," Major Lowell said. He was a very large man, who wore his blond hair in a short, barely partable crew cut. He was blue-eyed, although his eyes turned icy sometimes when he was annoyed, as they did now and made him look older than his twenty-six years.

He unfolded himself from the leather armchair in which he had been slumped, his feet on a matching footstool, a cognac snifter cradled in his hands, and walked to the telephone on the bar. The butler beat him to it, pushed a button on the base of the telephone, and then picked up the handset and held it out to him.

"Thank you," Lowell said, and then to the telephone: "This is Major Lowell."

"I have a Major Felter on the line, Major," a voice Lowell recognized to be that of his cousin's, Porter Craig's, secretary said. "May I transfer it?"

"By all means," Lowell said.

He heard her say, "One moment, Major Felter, I have Major Lowell for you."

"Mouse, you little bastard!" Major Lowell said.

"I'm at LaGuardia," Major Felter said. "Where are you?"

"What the hell are you doing at LaGuardia?"

"I came to see you off," Major Felter said.

"Hold on, Mouse," Major Lowell said. He covered the mouthpiece with his hand and turned to face the other man in the room, his "stepfather," Andre Pretier. "Can I use your car?"

"Yes, of course."

"Mouse, go to the Pan American counter and give them my name," Lowell said. "Tell them I'm going to meet you."

"They have taxicabs," Major Felter said.

"Go to the goddamned lounge," Lowell said. "I'll be there in twenty minutes." He hung up before Felter could protest further.

"The chap they thought had been killed?" Andre Pretier asked.

"Uh huh," Lowell said. "He came to see me off."

"Will you see that we can take care of the major's guest?" Andre Pretier said to the butler.

The butler dipped his head, and walked silently out of the room.

"You want some more of this, Andre?" Lowell asked, holding up the bottle of cognac. Andre Pretier shook his head, "no."

"But help yourself," he said, and then he said: "Sorry, Craig.

I seem to be unable to remember this is your house."

"Shit," Lowell said, and then he chuckled. "Sorry, Andre, I seem to be unable to remember one doesn't say 'shit' in polite company."

Andre Pretier smiled and raised his snifter in salute.

"May I make a suggestion?" Pretier asked.

"Yes, of course."

"You've had a bit of that," he said. "Are you all right to drive?"

The eyes turned icy again. But then Major Lowell said, "No, of course I'm not." He pushed a button, and in a moment, the butler reappeared.

"Would you ask Thomas to go to the Pan American VIP lounge at LaGuardia," Andre Pretier ordered, "and pick up a ..."

"Major Sanford T. Felter," Lowell supplied.

"Yes, sir," the butler said.

The butler returned to the bar forty minutes later.

"Major Felter, Major Lowell," he announced.

Felter, wearing a baggy, ill-fitting suit, walked into the room. Lowell jumped out of his chair, hesitated awkwardly, then gave in to the emotion. He went quickly to the slight man, wrapped his arms around him, and lifted him off the ground.

"For God's sake, Craig!" Felter protested. Lowell set him down.

"I'm glad to see you, you little shit," Lowell said. "I thought you were pushing up daisies."

Andre Pretier got to his feet.

"Mouse, this is my stepfather," Lowell said. "Andre Pretier. Andre, Sandy Felter."

"A genuine pleasure, Major Felter," Pretier said.

"How do you do, sir?" Felter said, shaking his hand.

"What do you want to drink, Mouse?" Lowell asked.

"Have you got a Coke? Or ginger ale?"

"Can you imagine this teetotaling little bastard jumping into Dien Bien Phu, Andre?"

"For God's sake, Craig!" Felter protested again.

"The Mouse is a spook, Andre," Lowell said. "He sees Russian spies hiding behind every set of drapes."

"What are you celebrating?" Felter asked, coldly. He had seen that Lowell was drunk.

"Craig was in Hartford," Andre Pretier said. "Visiting his mother."

"How is she?" Felter asked.

"'Progressing nicely' is the phrase they used," Lowell said.

"I'm glad to hear that," Felter said, politely.

"What that means is that she hasn't gone any further over the edge," Lowell said. He looked at Andre Pretier. "I have no secrets from the Mouse, Andre," he said. "But if that was out of line, I'm sorry."

"Not at all," Pretier said. "What we're doing for my wife, and Craig's mother, Major, is trying to get her the best help we can. It doesn't seem to be working as well as we had hoped."

"I'm sorry," Felter said.

"To get off that unpleasant subject, Mouse," Lowell said, "what brings you to Sodom on Hudson?"

"I wanted to see you off," Felter said. "I wanted to thank you for going to see Sharon."

"Shit," Lowell said. He smiled a little drunkenly at Andre Pretier. "There I go again, Ol' Sewer Mouth."

"Sharon told me what you did, Craig," Felter said.

"Christ, I hope not. You mean she told you I proposed?" Felter shook his head resignedly.

"When are you going?" he asked.

"Half past ten," Lowell said. "Pan American has a sleeper flight to Paris. And then I'll catch the Main-Seiner to Frankfurt."

"Then I'm glad I decided to come today," Felter said. "If I had waited until tomorrow, you would have gone without calling. Exactly as you left the house an hour before I got there."

"Well, since you were still alive, I realized that Sharon wasn't going to marry me," Lowell said. "So there was no point in my staying for your great 'here I am home, straight from the mouth of death' scene."

"How did you find out, Craig?" Felter asked. "Sharon said you got there an hour after the notification team."

"Actually, it was closer to two hours," Lowell said. "I had

a little trouble finding an air-taxi."

"And you're not going to tell me who told you?"

"So you can turn him in for breaking security?" Lowell asked. "No way, Mouse."

"OK, let it go," Felter said. "Tell me about flight school."

"There I was, ten thousand feet up, with nothing between me and the earth but a thin blond . . . "

"How much have you had to drink?" Felter asked.

"A bunch," Lowell said. "I wasn't prepared for Hartford."

"I tried to tell him, Major, that she probably wouldn't recognize him," Andre Pretier said. "But he insisted on going."

"Tell me about Dien Bien Phu," Lowell said. "What the hell were you and Mac doing there in the first place?"

"You know more than you should already, Craig," Felter said.

"I want to hear about you and MacMillan running around in the jungle," Lowell insisted. "After bailing out of a gloriously aflame airplane."

"I'm beginning to suspect who you talked to," Felter said.

"What happened, for Christ's sake?"

"Perhaps," Andre Pretier said, "it would be better if I excused myself."

Felter looked at him a moment.

"There's no need . . ."

"Excuse me," Andre Pretier said, and got up and walked out of the room.

"I'm not supposed to talk about this," Felter said. "And you know it. And I feel badly about asking him to leave his own living room."

"This is the bar," Lowell said, "not the living room. And it's mine, not his."

"God, you're impossible. You know what I mean."

"That's so much bullshit," Lowell said. "If you can't tell me, Mouse, who can you tell?"

"Maybe I will have a drink," Felter said. "Can I trust you to keep your mouth shut?" He answered his own question. "No, of course, I can't," he said. "But every spook has to have one weakness. You're mine."

He related what had happened at Dien Bien Phu, painting

a picture of himself as a rear echelon chair-warmer being led to safety through the Indo-China forest by a French Foreign Legion corporal, one of the Army's most decorated parachutists, and a nineteen-year-old sergeant with a sawed-off shotgun.

Lowell automatically added Felter's role to their exploits. In his judgment, Major Sanford Felter was quite as accomplished a close combat warrior as MacMillan or anyone else Lowell had ever met in the service. He had seen Felter in action; in fact, he owed his life to Felter, who had blown away an officer who had stood in the way of a reinforcement column coming to Lowell's rescue during counterinsurgency operations in Greece.

A mental picture came into Lowell's mind of Felter in Indo-China in his tropical worsted uniform, the large .45 automatic he was never without held in front of him with both hands. He literally wasn't large enough, or his thin wrists strong enough, to fire the .45 with one hand. With two hands, firing slowly and deliberately, he seldom missed. He was literally a dead shot.

"So, with appropriate pomp and ceremony," Felter concluded, "during a barrage of 105 mm fire, cannon and ammo courtesy of the First Cavalry, we were formally inducted as honorary members of the *3ième Régiment Parachutiste* of the French Foreign Legion."

"Christ," Lowell said, "I wish I had been there." He wondered if he really meant that. He knew that his saying so had pleased Felter, for Felter had long had the notion (Lowell considered it unfounded) that Lowell was a natural-born combat soldier.

"They tried to give us the Croix de guerre," Felter said. "Naturally, since we weren't supposed to be there in the first place, there's no way we'll be allowed to accept it."

"Christ, and what I've been doing, at enormous expense, is learning how to fly a whirlybird," Lowell said.

"Tell me about it," Felter said.

"Nothing to tell," Lowell said. "It's just as idiotic, having a major fly a helicopter, as I thought it would be. Like assigning a major as a jeep driver. I felt like a goddamned fool, when, with the band playing and flags flying, they pinned our wings on us."

"You don't believe that," Felter said, firmly.

"I don't know if I do or not, Mouse," Lowell said, drunk-serious. "I have to be periodically rebrainwashed; my faith wavers."

Felter glanced out the window and saw Andre Pretier walking on the wide lawn which stretched from the house down to the water's edge. He opened the French doors and walked out to him.

"I seem to have run you out of your own house," he said. "But I'm through talking about what I shouldn't have talked about, if you'd like to come back in."

"I understand," Pretier said. Felter led him back into the house.

"What we're talking about now is the importance of aviation to the army," Felter said. "I'm afraid it's not all that interesting."

"I don't even know what you're talking about," Andre Pretier said. "Craig, frankly, hasn't talked much about what he's been doing."

"He's been becoming an army aviator," Felter said.

"My ignorance is total," Pretier said. "I didn't know the army even had aviators."

"When the air force became autonomous, Andre," Felter began, and Andre Pretier sensed that Felter was relieved to have found a safe subject for conversation, "they began to devote most of their effort toward bombers and high-speed fighters, and to rockets. The army needs light aircraft, right on the battlefield. Since the air force was unable to provide them, the army was given authority to develop its own air service—army aviation. Craig is in on the ground floor."

"There are a few wild-eyed madmen around, Andre," Lowell said, wryly, "who envision entire divisions being airlifted by helicopters."

"I see," Pretier said. "And you saw, or see, enough merit in this theory to leave tanks? As Guderian saw enough merit in the blitzkrieg to change over to the German tank corps from signals as a colonel?"

"Would that it were so," Lowell said. "The cold truth, Andre, is that my last efficiency report in Korea was so bad that I had the choice between going to army aviation or turning in my soldier suit."

Pretier looked in surprise at Felter, saw the pained look on his face, and knew that Lowell was telling the truth.

"It wasn't quite that bad, Craig," Felter said.

"You know better than that, Mouse," Lowell said. "Cut the bullshit."

"But you were decorated in Korea," Pretier said, genuinely surprised. "Several times decorated. And promoted."

"That was before I fucked up," Lowell said, helping himself to more cognac.

"What did you do?"

"You are looking, Andre," Lowell said, making a mock bow, "at one of the few, perhaps the only, soldier in Korea who got into a sexual scandal with a white woman."

"I am *not* surprised," Pretier said, trying to make a joke of it.

"The establishment was almost as pissed about that as they were when I stood up in a court-martial and announced, under oath, that I could see a situation in combat where an officer has the duty to blow away another officer who is not doing his duty."

Andre Pretier looked at Sanford Felter again, and again got confirmation from the pained look on his face that Lowell was telling the truth.

"Who was the woman?" Pretier asked, choosing, he hoped, the least delicate of the two subjects.

"Georgia Paige," Lowell said.

"The actress?" Pretier asked. "The one who..."

"Goes without a bra?" Lowell filled in for him. "Yes, indeed, *that* Georgia Paige."

"And that is what you were doing in Los Angeles when you first came back?" Pretier asked.

"It didn't take long," Lowell said, bitterly, "for it to become painfully apparent that Georgia and I, to coin a phrase, were simply ships that had passed in the night."

"What happened, Craig?" Felter asked, and it was a demand

for information from a friend that could not be denied.

Lowell didn't reply immediately. Felter wondered if he was thinking over his reply, or deciding whether or not to reply at all.

"We hit it off pretty good in Korea," Lowell said.

"How did you arrange that? In Korea, I mean?" Felter asked.

"I think she was carried away with the warrior image," Lowell said. "I showed her my tank, and that seemed to excite her."

"Come on!"

"Scout's honor, Mouse. That's where it happened. Some of the 'immature judgment' my efficiency report talks about was taking her up to the line, to my old outfit."

"That *was* immature," Felter said. "Also stupid."

"Be that as it may, it excited the lady," Lowell said. "And true and undying passion burst into flower. And I returned to the ZI full of youthful dreams. I would pick her up in L.A., and I would fly off to romantic Germany with her, where she would instantly form a fond attachment to my son. We would thereupon start looking for a small house by the side of the road, where we could be friends to man and start making babies."

"What happened?"

"For one thing, she was making a movie and couldn't get away for six weeks, and then when the subject of Peter-Paul came up, she said, 'Oh, yeah. Your kid. I forgot about that.'"

"Oh," Sandy Felter said, sympathetically.

"I began to wonder if she would really make the loving stepmother I believed she would," Lowell said. "Ah, shit, what's the difference?"

"Did she know you're rich?" Felter asked.

"We rich say 'well off,' Mouse," Lowell said.

Felter decided he was onto something.

"She wanted you to get out of the army, and you wouldn't do it?" he asked.

"We didn't get that far," Lowell said.

"But she knew you were 'well-off'?"

"I don't really know. She knew, of course, that I had some clout out there in movieland. The firm, by an interesting coincidence, was financing her movie. If we hadn't been, I don't think I would have been allowed near her. Christ, I had to pull in all the clout I had to get in touch with her. But that wasn't it, one way or the other. What it was was that I was such a goddamned fool that I mistook a marvelous piece of tail for love."

"I'm sorry, Craig," Felter said.

"I thought all my problems were over when Bellmon called me . . . oops, that slipped out, didn't it? . . . and told me you had gone to a hero's grave in far-off Indo-China. After a suitable period, as short as possible, I would marry Sharon, and all of my problems would be solved."

"I'm sorry to disappoint you," Felter said.

"Next time, don't get my hopes up," Lowell said. "Next time, stay dead."

"Somebody will come along, Craig," Felter said. "Aside from your morals, you're every maiden's dream."

"I know, I know," Lowell said. "But it embarrasses me so when they get on their knees and start kissing my hand."

"He's right, Craig," Andre Pretier said. "You'll find someone."

"I don't really think I want to," Lowell said. And then, quickly: "For Christ's sake. Let's start telling dirty jokes or something."

(Two)
Aviation Detachment
Headquarters, Seventh United States Army
Augsburg, Germany
15 April 1954

Lieutenant Colonel Ford W. Davis, Commanding, Aviation Detachment, Headquarters, Seventh Army, happened to be in the outer office of the detachment when the civilian walked in. He was curious to the point of being annoyed. He didn't like what he saw.

The civilian was dressed in a mussed sports coat, and gray

flannel slacks, a civilian-model trench coat hung over his shoulders. There was a silk foulard in the open collar of his white button-down-collar shirt.

A reporter, Colonel Davis decided. Probably an American, probably from the *Munich American,* a tabloid published by a bunch of wise-ass ex-GIs, catering to the enlisted men, a bunch of goddamned troublemakers always looking for a story that made the army generally, and the officer corps specifically, look bad.

Colonel Davis laid the file he had been reading on top of the file cabinet and walked over to where the civilian was talking to the sergeant major.

"What's going on?" Colonel Davis asked.

"This officer is reporting in early from delay-en-route leave, Colonel."

Davis looked at him. Colonel Davis was suspicious of tall, handsome men, particularly the kind that wore scarves around their necks and trench coats over their shoulders. The officer came to something like attention.

"Actually, sir," the handsome young man in the movie actor costume said, "I'm not coming off leave. I'd hoped to be able to get a PX card."

"When are you due off leave?"

"My orders call for me to report to Camp Kilmer 20 April, sir," he said.

"Then what are you doing here now?"

"I was married to a German, sir," the officer said. "I have a son here."

"How'd you get here?"

"I came commercial, sir."

Davis put everything together. As a general rule of thumb, only German whores married Americans. Officers did not marry whores. Not officers with any smarts. So what this young buck had done was marry a kraut whore, and he was smart enough to realize that meant he had ruined his career. What officers who fucked up their careers in their branch of service did was apply for flight school.

Colonel Davis was a career soldier, out of Texas A&M into

the artillery. He had gone to flight school as an artilleryman in War II, when the primary function of army aviation was artillery fire direction, using Piper Cubs as airborne forward observation posts. In those days, there had been an "L" superimposed on pilot's wings, to differentiate between "liaison" pilots flying Cubs and "real pilots." Colonel Davis had been a liaison pilot in those days.

He'd stayed an army aviator, not because he was a fuck-up, but because he and a tiny clique of others saw the future role of light aircraft in the army. The air force, when it had become a separate branch of the armed services, had made it clear they weren't going to bother giving the army what aerial services it would need. They were going to fight the next war with nuclear weapons dropped from 40,000 feet; with fighter planes flying at twice the speed of sound; with rockets, for Christ's sake, from space. They were not going to waste their time fucking around with the guys in the mud on the ground.

The army was going to have to have its own aerial capability, not only artillery direction and liaison—messenger—flights, but medical evacuation, probably by helicopter (Korea had proved that theory) and, eventually, an aerial transport capability in the fifty miles behind the front lines. What the army really needed was its own close support aircraft, low and slow and near the ground. They were a long way from that, but Colonel Davis believed that, too, would come in time.

He had stayed in army aviation because he believed in it.

And because he was a professional soldier, he had looked for and found the weaknesses in army aviation. If you don't know what's wrong, you can't fix it. He was sure he had found the greatest weakness in army aviation, but he had no idea how to fix it.

The weakness could be described simply: the officer corps of army aviation, like Ivory soap, was 99 44/100 percent pure incompetents, malcontents, ne'er-do-wells, and fuck-ups. Instead of throwing the incompetents out of the army, they were allowed to go to flight school. There was no question, looking at Handsome Harry standing here before him with a goddamned silk scarf wrapped around his throat, trying to look like Errol Flynn, that he was about to get one more fuck-up that nobody else in the army wanted, an officer so goddamned dumb that he had married a kraut whore.

"I don't know what you expected to find here," Colonel Davis said, icily. "But this is a military organization, and we expect that when newly assigned officers report for duty, they do so in keeping with the customs of the service. That is to say, in uniform."

"Yes, sir," Handsome Harry said.

"The sergeant here will sign you in," Colonel Davis said. "And see that you're installed in the bachelor officer's quarters. I did hear you use the past tense in reference to your marriage, didn't I?"

"Yes, sir."

"And then you will present yourself here in uniform and report for duty. Clear?"

"Yes, sir."

"You've given the sergeant major a copy of your orders?"

"Yes, sir."

"When you're through with them, Morgan, bring them in to me," Colonel Davis said, and then he turned away and walked into his office.

As he closed the door, he heard Handsome Harry say, his voice amused, "That, Sergeant, is what is known as starting off on the wrong foot."

Wise-ass prick thought it was funny, did he? He'd straighten his ass out in a hurry.

The first occasion Colonel Davis had to consider that perhaps he had made an error in his snap judgment of Handsome Harry was when the sergeant major came into his office a few minutes later and laid a battered, creased copy of Handsome Harry's orders on his desk. Colonel Davis glanced at them quickly, and then looked more closely.

"A *major?*" he said. "A *regular army* major? He doesn't look old enough to be a captain. And regular army?"

"No, sir," the sergeant major agreed. "He doesn't."

"Do we have his service record?"

"No, sir. It must be on the way. He wasn't due to report to Camp Kilmer until 20 April."

Colonel Davis looked at Handsome Harry's orders again, reading them carefully this time, to see what they could tell him.

HEADQUARTERS
THE U.S. ARMY ARTILLERY SCHOOL
FORT SILL, OKLAHOMA

SPECIAL ORDERS:

NUMBER 87: 20 March 1954

E X T R A C T

****

31. MAJ Craig W. LOWELL, 0439067, ARMOR Student Off Det, Avn Sec, The Arty Sch, having successfully completed the prescribed course of instruction, and having graduated from Rotary Wing Aviator's Course 54-6, The Arty Sch, is designated an army aviator, effective 20 Mar 54. (H-13 and H-23 aircraft only).

32. MAJ Craig W. LOWELL, 0439067, ARMOR, is awarded Primary MOS 1707 (Army Aviator, Rotary Wing only) eff 20 Mar 54.

33. MAJ Craig W. LOWELL, 0439067, ARMOR MOS 1707 Stu Off Det, Avn Sec, The Arty Sch, is relvd prsnt asgmt, trfd and WP Hq US 7th Army APO 709 c/o Postmaster, NY,NY, for further asgmt with Avn Sec ARMY SEVEN as RW Aviator. Auth: TWX Hq DA Subj: Initial utilization assgmt newly designated RW Aviators dtd 3 Jan 54. Off will report in uniform NLT 2330 hrs 20 Apr 54 to USA Personnel Cntr, Cp Kilmer, NJ, for further shpmnt to US Army Europe via mil sea transport. Off auth thirty (30) Days Delay En Route Lv. Home of Record: Broadlawns, Glen Cove, Long Island, NY. Off auth trans of household goods and personal auto at Govt expense. Permanent Change of Station. Effective date change Morning Report 20 Apr 54. Tvl & mvmnt household goods and personal auto deemed nec in govt interest. Approp: S-99-999-9999.

****

E X T R A C T

	BY COMMAND OF
OFFICIAL:	MAJ GEN YEAGER:
Peter O. Romano	Jerome T. Waller
Captain, AGC	Colonel, AGC
Asst Adjutant	Adjutant General

All that Major Lowell's orders told Lieutenant Colonel Davis was that Lowell was a just-graduated chopper pilot. But between the lines, Davis could read that he was a fuck-up. Majors didn't go to army aviation unless they had fucked up by the numbers. What piqued Davis's curiosity was Lowell's rank, and his regular army status. He didn't seem old enough to be a major, and Davis would have given odds that he wasn't West Point, or one of the other trade schools, A&M, the Citadel, VMI. Maybe Norwich. Probably Norwich. He was Armor, and Norwich turned out large numbers of RA tankers.

Two hours later, the sergeant major announced Major Lowell.

"Send him in," Davis said.

Major Lowell marched into Lieutenant Colonel Davis's office. He stopped three feet from Davis's desk, raised his hand in a crisp salute, and announced:

"Major C. W. Lowell reporting for duty, sir."

Lieutenant Colonel Davis returned the salute.

"Stand at ease, Major," he said. Lowell assumed a position closer to "parade rest" than "at ease." He met Davis's eyes. At "parade rest" he would have looked six inches over Davis's head.

He was in a Class "A" uniform, "pinks and greens," a green tunic and pink trousers. The uniform, Davis saw, had not come off a rack in an officer's sales store. The fit was impeccable. Obviously tailor-made. Obviously expensive. But what impressed Lt. Col. Davis was the fruit salad.

Above Major Lowell's breast pocket was an Expert Combat Infantry Badge, a silver flintlock on a blue background, with wreath. A star between the open ends of the wreath indicated the second award of the CIB. Major Lowell had been to war, twice. Davis decided that he was obviously a good deal older than he looked, some freak skin and muscle condition that made him look twenty-four, twenty-five years old. Sewn to one shoulder of his tunic was the insignia of the Artillery School. Sewn to the other was a triangular Armored Force patch with the numerals 73. There was no armored division numbered as high as 73, so it must be one of the separate battalions. Davis recalled that a separate armored battalion had made the breakout from Pusan in the opening months of the Korean War.

That tied in with some of the fruit salad: UN Service Medal; Korean Service Medal, with three campaign stars; and the Korean (as well as American) Presidential Unit Citations worn over the other tunic pocket.

Immediately below the CIB were aviator's wings, obviously brand new. Below the wings were his medals. Distinguished Service Cross. That was the nation's second highest award for gallantry in action. He also had the Distinguished Service Medal. And the Silver Star with an oak leaf cluster signifying a second award. And a Bronze Star with "V" device, signifying that it had been awarded for valor. Two oak leaves on that. Did that mean he had four Bronze Stars or just three? Davis wasn't sure if they gave second "V" devices for second valorous awards. Purple Heart with three clusters. Wounded four times. Then there were ribbons signifying foreign decorations, four of those, and then the World War II Victory Medal (which didn't mean he had actually been in World War II: that hadn't been declared over until late in 1946, and if you were in the service then, you got the medal) and the Army of Occupation Medal (Germany).

They were very careful about how they passed out the DSC.

"I don't recognize some of those, Major," Lt. Col. Davis said.

Major Lowell said nothing.

"What are the foreign decorations, Major?" Davis asked, a somewhat menacing tone in his voice. "Korean?"

"Three of them are, sir."

"Tell me about them," Davis said.

Lowell bent his head and pointed to the medals. "This is the Order of St. George and St. Andrew," he said.

"Korean?" Lt. Col. Davis asked, a challenge.

"Greek, sir," Lowell said. "And this is the Korean Distinguished Service Cross, the Korean Military Medal, and the Tae Guk, which is the same as our DSM."

"If it was your intention, Major," Lt. Col. Davis said, "to dazzle me with your fruit salad, you have succeeded."

"Sir, regulations stipulate that decorations will be worn when reporting for duty in garrison."

"I didn't know that," Davis said, coldly. Lowell did not reply.

"How do you plan to handle it, Major," Davis asked, "when Camp Kilmer reports you AWOL as of 20 April?"

"Sir, I spoke with the AC of S, Personnel, a Colonel Gray, who informed me that a TWX from my receiving organization would clear that up."

"And you expect to be reimbursed for your commercial travel here?"

"No, sir."

"And you hoped to be continued on leave here in Germany, is that it?"

"Yes, sir."

"You made a mistake reporting in, Major," Lt. Colonel Davis said. "I'm very short of chopper pilots, even ones fresh from flight school. I am going to have to put you right to work."

"Yes, sir," Major Lowell said, immediately. That was the first thing Major Lowell had done of which Lt. Col. Davis approved. He had expected at the very least a delay while Lowell thought that over, and at worst a recitation of tragic facts that made his being on leave a humanitarian necessity. Lowell hadn't blinked an eye.

"You were with the 73rd Armor in Korea?"

"73rd Heavy Tank," Lowell said, making the correction. "Yes, sir."

"They were involved in the breakout from the Pusan perimeter?"

"Yes, sir."

"Were you with them, then?"

"Yes, sir."

"Tell me something, Major," Lt. Col. Davis asked, with deceptive innocence, "what is a regular army Major with nearly as much fruit salad as George Patton doing flying a chopper?"

Lowell met his eyes, and there was a pause before he replied.

"I came to the conclusion, sir, that my future as an armor officer was going to be less than I hoped."

"Fucked up, did you?"

"Yes, sir."

"And it was reflected on your efficiency report?"

"Yes, sir."

"And it was either into army aviation or out of the army?"

"Very nearly, sir."

"How much service do you have? Until you have your twenty years, I mean?"

"I've got five years and some months of active duty service, sir."

"You made major in five years?" Davis asked, disbelievingly.

"I was out for two years, sir. From 1948 until 1950. I was recalled for the Korean War."

"How old are you, Lowell?" Davis asked.

"Twenty-six, sir."

"And at twenty-six, you have had time to make major and then fuck up by the numbers?"

"That would seem to sum it up nicely, yes, sir."

"You say you have a son?"

"Yes, sir."

"Living with his mother here in Germany?"

"His mother is dead, sir. He lives with his mother's family."

"Do you think your responsibility toward your son is going to interfere with the performance of your duties here?"

"No, sir."

"See that it doesn't," Davis said. "I am one of those old-fashioned soldiers who believes that an officer's primary responsibility is to his duty. Those with personal problems which interfere with their duties should get out of the army."

"Yes, sir."

"You understand your position here, Major?" Davis asked, and went on without waiting for a reply. "You're on an initial utilization tour. The primary purpose of such a tour is to build up your flying time. By and large, you will be treated exactly as if you were a warrant officer or a second lieutenant. Your rank, during your initial utilization tour, is not going to buy you any privileges. You understand that?"

"Yes, sir."

"I'm going to send you down to Lieutenant Colonel Withers, who has the Rotary Wing Special Missions Branch," Colonel Davis said. "Read VIP."

"Yes, sir."

"Colonel Withers will teach you how to fly our way," Davis went on. "And after a long while, he might even let you fly passengers. Unimportant ones. Not the brass. The aides."

Lowell smiled and said, "Yes, sir."

"There is one thing you fuck-ups get when you come to army aviation," Colonel Davis said. "A clean slate. So far as I'm concerned, Major Lowell, your slate is clean. But the other side of that coin is that I dislike people who come to aviation because it's their last chance."

"Yes, sir," Lowell said.

"I'll certainly see you around, Lowell," Davis said. He got up and put out his hand. "You may consider yourself officially welcomed to the Seventh Army Flight Detachment."

"Yes, sir. Thank you, sir."

"You're dismissed, Major."

Lowell looked askance at him.

"Something?"

"It would help, sir, if I knew where to report to Colonel Withers."

Davis had forgotten the little ploy he'd made about needing chopper pilots so badly that Lowell would not get the rest of his leave.

"How much time, minimum, would you require to get your personal affairs straightened out?" he asked.

"My son is in Marburg, sir," Lowell said. "A day up there, a day there, and a day back. Three days."

"Take it as VOCO," Davis said. "Then it won't be charged

as leave. And while you're gone, I'll speak to Colonel Withers. Maybe after we get you checked out in the local area, we can work a week or ten days' leave in."

"Thank you, sir," Lowell said. He saluted, did an about-face, and walked out of the office.

Davis wondered for a moment what Lowell had done to fuck up, and then put him out of his mind. He would make up his mind whether he was a Class "A" fuck-up (unsalvageable), or a Class "B" (just another mediocrity who had a bad efficiency report), or a Class "C" (salvageable and of potential use to army aviation in the future), after he'd read his service record and made some inquiries on his own.

It was not necessary for Colonel Davis to do the latter. The day after Major Lowell had reported for duty, Colonel Davis got a letter from the man recognized by the small group of professional soldiers in army aviation as the President.

The tiny nucleus of army aviators who were interested in more than getting their twenty years in for retirement were generally regarded with disdain by the others. They called them the Cincinnati Flying Club, a derogatory reference to the Society of the Cincinnati, membership in which was limited to descendants of officers who had served under George Washington in the Revolution. Lt. Colonel William R. Roberts, USMA '40, a graduate of the first class of liaison pilots ever trained. ("The Class Before One") was known, affectionately or disparagingly, depending on who was talking, as "the President of the Cincinnati Flying Club."

PO Box 334
Fort Sill, Okla.
20 March 1954

Dear Ford:

I have arranged to have sent to you one Major Craig W. Lowell, who graduated, barely (he is not a natural pilot) from RW 54-6 today. I personally don't like him, but in our present personnel situation, and because of considerable pressure applied to me by, among others, Bob Bellmon, I decided he's worth the risk.

In the opening days of the Korean War, Lowell, then a recalled National Guard captain, led the breakout from Pusan after the Inchon invasion. He's the Lowell of Task Force Lowell. It got him a major's leaf at twenty-two, and he subsequently covered himself with glory and medals in the dash to the Yalu and the withdrawal from Hamhung. Paul Jiggs, who commanded the 73rd, and who was last week given his first star, swears he is a splendid combat commander, and the best plans and training man—and oh, God, how we need them—he has ever known.

The bad news is that he has, Bellmon informs me, an efficiency report as bad as he's ever seen. He is on the s——tlist for two things: not recommended for combat command and lack of judgment.

The first thing that has him in trouble was standing up in a court-martial and announcing that he could see nothing wrong with an officer executing on the spot another officer who didn't measure up in combat. The accused in the trial was a young, Negro, Norwich-type captain who was accused of murdering an allegedly cowardly-in-the-face-of-the-enemy officer in the Pusan perimeter, and then turning his own tank cannon on another yellow one during the move up the peninsula. The connection becomes involved because he's Norwich, and because his father, Colonel Philip Sheridan Parker III, retired, commanded the task force from Porky Waterford's Hell's Circus which snatched Bellmon back from the Russians in the closing days of World War II.

Young Parker, incidentally, "volunteered" for aviation the same day Lowell did, and graduated with him. He has been assigned to Alaska, which is as far apart as I could arrange to have them separated.

The second thing that has Lowell on the spot is the scandal he caused by taking Georgia Paige (the actress who doesn't wear a brassiere) up to the front when she was here with a USO troupe. Photos got out. The story is that Lowell was carrying on with her whenever they could find a horizontal place.

In any event, Lowell was assigned as an assistant professor of military science at Bordentown Military School, and Parker was assistant housing officer at Fort Devens. These are the sort of people from whom we must recruit.

One more thing about Lowell: he is obscenely rich, by inheritance, and has considerable influence in the Congress.

Further interconnection: Bellmon believes that the reason he is not at this moment among the missing in Siberia is because of the decent behavior, at considerable risk to himself, of the officer commanding the stalag. Our man Lowell, when he was in Germany early-on, married a German lady who turned out to be the daughter of Colonel Count Peter-Paul von Greiffenberg, who was at the time cutting down trees for the Russians in Siberia.

The count was released by the Russians in 1950, just in time to meet Lowell before he was sent to Korea. Lowell was in Korea about four months when a drunken quartermaster major (U.S.) ran into her car near Giessen and killed her. The boy is being raised by his grandfather. Grandfather is now Generalmajor von Greiffenberg of the Bundeswehr. Deputy Chief of Intelligence.

All of these details, Ford, so that you'll be aware of what we have in Lowell (and to a lesser degree in Parker). The potential to do us enormous good is there, but so is the potential for damage. My gut feeling is that if the trouble he's just been through hasn't taught him his lesson, we should get rid of him quickly and permanently, even if this enrages the armor establishment. It puts a heavy burden on you, and I'm sorry, but that's the way it is.

It will be announced in the next week or so that Camp Rucker, in Alabama, will be reactivated and designated the Army Aviation School. I have been there. There is one dirt strip, last used during War II as an auxiliary field by the air force. Whatever we need we'll have to build ourselves, which means begging for money. *But at least we have our own base!*

What we need are some senior people, for the next couple of years. I try hard, but evangelism doesn't seem down my alley.

Helen sends love to you and Betty.

Always, Old Buddy,
Bill.

PS: In case you didn't notice, I was #34 (of 36) on the last colonel's list. I think that it should come through (in eight or nine months) in time so that the eagle will qualify me to take over the Aviation Board, which will be among the first activities opened at Camp Rucker.

Lieutenant Colonel Davis had indeed noticed the name of Lt. Col. William Roberts on the colonel's promotion list. His own name had been conspicuously absent. The fact that Bill Roberts was on it might be significant. And it might not. Roberts was West Point. His promotion might be because of the West Point Protective Association, which took care of its own, even the mad-eyed radicals of army aviation. But it *might* be because somebody in the Pentagon appreciated what he had done in the past, and what he might do in the future.

Davis wished that he had known about Lowell before he had assigned him to Withers. Withers had been a horse's ass even before he had discovered Jesus Christ as his personal savior at age forty-four, and what he was now was a religious fanatic. It would have been better to have kept Lowell closer to home, where he could be watched, and perhaps, if he turned out, taught something, perhaps even converted to the One True Faith. But it was too late now. And maybe what Lowell needed was a CO washed in the blood of the lamb.

(Three)
Marburg an der Lahn, West Germany
15 April 1954

The major domo at Schloss Greiffenberg (it was more of a villa than a castle, having been built in 1818, after improvements in the tools of warfare had rendered battlements and moats obsolete; but a Graf doesn't live in a villa, he lives in a Schloss) was new and didn't know Lowell, and was unimpressed when Lowell told him who he was. He left him outside, with the door closed in his face, with the announcement he would "make inquiries."

A woman opened the door. An attractive, prematurely grayhaired woman who smiled and put out her hand, and spoke to him in English.

"My dear Major Lowell, you will have to forgive us. All Peter-Paul's man said was that 'there was an American at the door.' Please come in."

"Thank you," he said.

"Peter-Paul didn't expect you until next month," she said, and then she raised her voice, and called in German, "Liebchen, your Papa is here!"

Her voice was considerably less pleasant when she spoke to the major domo.

"Put Major Lowell's things in the room next to the child's, and the next time, don't be such a stupid ass. This American is the child's father."

She doesn't, Lowell realized, understand that I speak German. That could be interesting, or amusing.

The child didn't come. They had to go find him. Then he hid behind the woman's skirts.

"He's not used to you," she said.

Peter-Paul Lowell had been born in 1947. That made him seven, his father decided, a little old to be hiding behind a woman's skirts. Or is it that I am so formidable a figure?

"What do you say, Squirt?" he said.

The child didn't reply.

"I think, if I may say so," the woman said, "that it would be best to leave him alone. He has the von Greiffenberg hardhead."

"There's some Lowell in him, too," Lowell said. "Well, to hell with him. If he doesn't want the guns, I'll just give them to somebody else."

"What guns?" the boy said.

"It can talk, you see?" Lowell said. "The guns in the brown

bag. The man took it upstairs to my room."

The boy fled the room.

"Major," the woman said. "Forgive me. What can I offer you to drink?"

"Scotch, please," he said.

"I think there's a little left," she said. "Peter-Paul has been waiting for you to come so that he can get you to buy liquor from the army."

"I didn't think to bring any," Lowell said. "And you forgot to tell me who you are?"

"Oh, just another of the displaced relatives Peter-Paul has taken in," she said. "This one from Pomerania. I'm Elizabeth von Heuffinger-Lodz. The countess and my mother were sisters."

I'll bet, Lowell thought, that there's a title that goes with that.

"As you gather, I'm the child's father," he said. "My name is Craig."

She shook his hand again.

I'd like to screw her, he thought, and then he wondered why that thought had suddenly popped into his mind. That would really be a goddamned dumb thing to do, even if she was interested, and there was no reason to suspect she would be.

Peter-Paul Lowell, P.P., came into the room as she handed Craig Lowell a drink. He had on a cowboy hat, a vest, a pair of chaps, on backward, a gun belt, and two enormous six-shooter cap pistols.

"You have your chaps on backward," Craig said.

"Excuse me?"

The European accent and the European manners of the boy made the father sad. He took a large swallow of the weak drink, and then dropped to his knees to show his son how a cowboy wore his chaps.

When he looked up at the woman, he saw her eyes on him. He had the feeling that she was surprised about him, for some reason. She probably expected me to come in here wearing Bermuda shorts, knee socks, and chewing gum, he thought.

V

(One)
The Pentagon
Washington, D.C.
15 May 1954

Major Rudolph G. MacMillan, wearing his pinks and greens
with all his ribbons and overseas bars and the unit shoulder
insignia of both the Armored Center (where he was presently
assigned) and the 82nd Airborne Division (his most significant
World War II assignment), very carefully opened the door of
the men's room cubicle a crack and peered out. Then he closed
the door carefully and slid the lock in place. A colonel had
come in, one he didn't know, and he wasn't waiting for him.

Major MacMillan was off limits. The men's room in which
he sat, trousers up, was a senior officer's latrine, reserved for
colonels and better. Lieutenant colonels down to second lieutenants had their own latrines and the enlisted men had theirs.

MacMillan hated the Pentagon, and Pentagon types hated
MacMillan types, as company clerks hated squad corporals.
But squad corporals could take company clerks out behind the

97

PX beer hall, or waylay them on their way home from the service club and kick the shit out of them when they misused their typewriters.

Corporal Rudolph G. MacMillan had kicked the shit out of a company clerk at Fort Benning in '41 for making a "clerical error" on his service record that kept him from getting the three stripes of a buck sergeant. And the company clerk had told the first sergeant, and the first sergeant had hauled him before the company commander, and both the company clerk and the first sergeant had been sure that he was going to come out of the company commander's office with bare sleeves, and with a little bit of luck, under arrest pending court-martial. But he had had his facts straight then, and he'd come out of the company commander's office as Sergeant MacMillan.

The company commander had made his decision, as Corporal MacMillan had bet his life he would, not so much on fairness, but on what was best for the company. What was right counted, but what *really* counted was what was best for the company.

What Major MacMillan was betting his life on now was the accuracy of his perception that the Pentagon was nothing more than an oversized orderly room. The majors and lieutenant colonels were company clerks who used their typewriters with far greater subtlety when they wanted to screw one of the field troops, and you couldn't grab one of the bastards by his shirt collar and bloody his nose. But a good soldier could still lay the facts out before the company commander, and if he had his facts straight, and what he proposed was good for the army, the Old Man, even if he wore the stars of a general officer instead of a captain's railroad tracks, would do what was best for the outfit.

The hydraulic door-closer whooshed again, and MacMillan cracked open the door of his cubicle again. A lieutenant general walked into the latrine and headed for the urinals, his hand dropping to part his tunic, to get at his zipper.

Major MacMillan pushed open the door of his cubicle and walked to the adjacent urinal. The general glanced at him casually, looked away, and then looked back.

"I'll be damned," the Deputy Chief of Staff for Operations of the United States Army said, shaking himself, tucking himself in, zipping himself up. "Mac MacMillan. How the hell are you, Mac?"

"A little nervous, General," MacMillan said.

"How so?"

They were shaking hands.

"I just punched a company clerk in the mouth, General," MacMillan said.

The general laughed.

"That was a long time ago, Mac. God, that was a long time ago."

"This was another company clerk, General," MacMillan said. "This one is a colonel."

"You're in trouble, Mac?" the general asked, seriously now.

"That'll be up to you, General."

"You didn't really punch...?" the general asked. With MacMillan, the question had to be asked, and not only because when the general had first met Corporal MacMillan, Mac had been about to try out for the post boxing team.

"Figuratively speaking, of course, General," MacMillan said. "The way a major punches a colonel is to wait in a latrine for the general after the colonel has made it quite plain that the colonel has made up his mind and doesn't want to hear any more discussion of an issue. After the colonel has made it an order that I am not to bother the general."

"All you have to do, Mac, to talk to me, anytime, is to call me at the house."

"I'm not here as your friend, sir. I'm here as an officer."

The general's face suddenly turned stern. "If we weren't friends, Mac, I would ask you what the hell you're doing in the senior officer's crapper."

"General, the major requests fifteen minutes of the general's time."

"I heard you were being assigned," the general said. "Hell, I arranged it, Mac. You don't like your assignment, is that it? You don't want..."

"I'm a soldier, General. I go where I'm sent and do the best I can when I get there."

"Then what is it? I thought you'd be glad not to have to work here."

"Sir, the general, in my opinion, has made a mistake in

setting that whole aviation development operation up the way he has," Major MacMillan said.

"Major," the general said, "I am now going back to my office. I will inform my secretary that I have given you an appointment—" he stopped and looked at his watch—"for fifteen minutes at 11:30. I will hear your arguments. Inasmuch as I made the decisions I have made on the advice of Colonel Gregory, I will ask Colonel Gregory to join us."

"Yes, sir. Thank you, sir."

"Or, after pointing out to you that Colonel Gregory will be your efficiency report rating officer, I will completely forget we ever had this little chat."

"Sir, I will be there at half past eleven."

At 11:28, Major MacMillan walked into the outer office of the Office of the Deputy Chief of Staff for Operations and told the receptionist that he had an appointment with the DCSOPS at 11:30.

It is said that the DCSOPS is the man who actually runs the army. Legally, he is coequal with the other deputies to the Army Chief of Staff—DCSPERS (Personnel), DCSLOG (Logistics), and DCSINT (Intelligence)—but as a practical matter, he is the one who makes the recommendations to the Chief of Staff (rarely overturned) about where and when and how the army will fight. Intelligence will tell him about the enemy; personnel will tell him how many troops he can have, and logistics will tell him about supplies. He adds these things up, and decides, taking into consideration the probable intentions and capabilities of the enemy, where to send the troops and their logistical support.

In peacetime, he decides whether the army needs tanks more than artillery, communications more than tanks, or, recently, whether the army needed an air mobility capability more than the tanks and cannon and rifles that armor, artillery, and infantry were screaming for.

When Major Mac MacMillan was shown into the inner office, both Colonel Arthur Gregory, Chief, Aviation Branch, DCSOPS, and Brigadier General Howard Kellogg, Assistant DCSOPS, were already there, sitting, the width of a cushion between them, on a red leather couch against the wall.

"Sir," Major Mac MacMillan snapped, bringing his stocky, barrel-chested body to rigid attention, "Major R. G. MacMillan reporting as ordered, sir."

The DCSOPS returned the salute with a casual wave of the hand.

"Stand at ease, Major," he said. "You know these gentlemen, I believe. You have fifteen minutes."

"With your permission, General," MacMillan said, and walked to the coffee table before the couch. He had a briefcase in his hand. Such had been his parade ground behavior and posture that none of the three officers noticed it until he set it on the floor and began to neatly lay papers from it in stacks on the table.

"Sir," he said, and both the Assistant DCSOPS and the Chief, Aviation Branch, DCSOPS, noticed his use of the singular "Sir" instead of "Gentlemen." MacMillan was making his pitch to the DCSOPS, not to them. That violated the rules. But the DCSOPS was going along with him. It was going to be the Assistant DCSOPS and the Chief, Aviation Branch, DCSOPS, *vs.* Major MacMillan, with the DCSOPS himself hearing the case without a jury. God *damn* MacMillan! Medal or no goddamned medal, that was going too far.

"Sir," MacMillan said, "I am under orders to report to the president of the Airborne Board, Fort Benning, Georgia, for duty as liaison between the Aviation Section of the Airborne Board and DCSOPS."

"We know that, MacMillan," the Assistant DCSOPS said. MacMillan acted as if he hadn't heard him.

"In a very short time," he went on, "the Aviation Section of the Airborne Board will become the Aviation Board, shortly after the reactivation of Fort Rucker, Alabama. Aviation testing and development will then report directly to you, sir, rather than through the Airborne and Artillery Boards."

"We know all that," the Assistant DCSOPS said. "What I don't understand is why we're discussing this with you."

"And that's *Camp* Rucker, MacMillan," the Chief, Aviation Branch, said. "And I was under the impression that whole business was classified. What was your right to know?"

"Let him talk," the DCSOPS said.

"I will then become the liaison officer between the Army Aviation Board and the DCSOPS," MacMillan said. "In other words between army aviation and the army."

"Army aviation is a concept, not a branch of service, Major," the Assistant DCSOPS said.

"Yes, sir," MacMillan said. "That's my point."

"Your point then," the aviation officer said, sarcastically, "is lost on me."

"Let's hear him out," the DCSOPS said, somewhat icily.

"My efficiency report will be written by the president of the Aviation Board, and endorsed by Colonel Gregory," Mac-Millan said. "Whatever information you get up here will come from the president of the Aviation Board via Colonel Gregory."

"Have you a better suggestion?" Gregory asked, sarcastically.

"What's wrong with that, Mac?" the DCSOPS asked. He wasn't overly impressed with MacMillan's intellectual ability, but he knew that MacMillan knew what he was risking by coming here the way he had. MacMillan had paid his dues, the Medal aside, and he was entitled to a full, fair hearing before he paid the price. It had already become apparent to the DCSOPS that he could no longer be assigned to the Aviation Board; MacMillan had already burned that bridge.

"Both Bill Roberts and Colonel Gregory are members of the Cincinnati Flying Club," MacMillan said.

"You refer, I'm sure, to *Colonel* William Roberts," Colonel Gregory said, fury in his voice.

"The Cincinnati Flying Club?" the DCSOPS asked. "What the hell is that?"

"The old-timers, the *establishment* old-timers. They think army aviation belongs to them."

"Define establishment," the DCSOPS said.

"Regulars who stand a chance to make general," MacMillan said. "The WPPA. People like that."

The Association of Graduates and Former Cadets of the United States Military Academy at West Point was widely referred to throughout the army, by officers who had not been privileged to attend that school, as the West Point Protective Association, or WPPA. This appellation was disliked by members of the WPPA.

"I resent that, Major," Colonel Gregory said. "I deeply resent that."

"Make your point, Mac," the DCSOPS said. He now deeply regretted stopping in for a quick leak in the colonel's can. He had a private pisser in his office and he should have used it. He wondered for the first time how long MacMillan had stalked him in there. All morning, certainly. Maybe all week.

"The only information you're going to get, General," MacMillan said, "will be what the Cincinnati Flying Club wants you to hear."

"That's slanderous and insulting!" Colonel Gregory flared.

"Shall I stop, sir?" MacMillan asked.

"No, go on, Mac," the DCSOPS said. "You've already dug your grave. You might as well jump right in."

"Sir, you would be making a mistake to turn army aviation over to the Cincinnati Flying Club."

"MacMillan, I've heard about all I intend to take about the so-called Cincinnati Flying Club," Colonel Gregory said. MacMillan ignored him again.

"You need a separate outfit down there, General," MacMillan said. "Separate from the Aviation Board, separate from the Flying Club. Otherwise, the Flying Club will see that their guys get the command assignments, their projects get the money, and their ideas about how to use aircraft to support the ground troops get to be doctrine and get printed as field manuals."

There was silence for a long moment in the room. The DCSOPS knew that neither Gregory or his own Assistant DCSOPS would be able to let that accusation pass without rebuttal. He wondered what form it would take.

"A special unit, commanded, no doubt, by you?" the Assistant DCSOPS asked, sarcastically.

Ignore it, it'll go away. Ridicule it, it'll be ignored. Not bad, the DCSOPS thought, but it won't wash.

"By Bob Bellmon," MacMillan responded. "Or somebody like him. Somebody who's not artillery. Who's not in the Flying Club. But somebody who's also in the WPPA."

"Bob Bellmon's not even an aviator," the Assistant DCSOPS said, disgust in his voice. "And I resent, Major, your constant and insulting references to a West Point Protective Association."

"I could teach him, or anyone else, how to fly in a month," MacMillan said. "Flying's not as mysterious as some people would have you believe."

"Mac," the DCSOPS said, "you're going off half cocked. You haven't thought this through."

"Yes, sir, I have," MacMillan said. "What we need down there is a Class II Activity of DCSOPS, maybe called 'Combat Developments.' Here it is."

A Class II Activity is an army unit stationed on a military post, which is not subordinate to the post commander, but instead to another—usually higher—headquarters. Hospitals, for example, "belong" to the Surgeon General, not to the commanding general of the post where they are located.

MacMillan handed the DCSOPS a thick sheaf of papers held together with a metal fastener. "Here's my proposed table of organization and equipment. Briefly, it consists of a commanding officer, an executive officer, some logistic and engineering officers, *and* a liaison officer. Plus the necessary enlisted technicians."

The DCSOPS took the material from MacMillan and started to read it. It was immediately apparent to him that somebody besides MacMillan had had a hand in it. It was a finished piece of staff work, and while MacMillan might be the warrior's warrior, he was anything but a staff officer. Whoever had done this for him knew what he was doing.

The DCSOPS thought it over for a moment, then grew angry.

"Mac, who put you up to this?"

"Sir?"

"Goddamnit, somebody did. You didn't write this." The DCSOPS had already made up his mind to hang the sonofabitch who, afraid to state his position publicly, had connived to get poor simple Mac to stand up for him.

"Those are my ideas, sir," MacMillan said. "I had a friend of mine help me put them down on paper."

"Who's your friend?" the DCSOPS asked.

"I can't tell you, General," MacMillan said.

"Why not?"

"Because he said I was committing suicide coming in here

with this, and he wouldn't help me do that."

"What's his name, Mac?" the DCSOPS asked, weighing MacMillan's apparently honest reply in his mind.

"I gave him my word as an officer and a gentleman that I wouldn't say who he was, sir," MacMillan said.

MacMillan was incapable of making that up, the DCSOPS decided. He was so simple, such a virgin in this whorehouse of the Pentagon, that he actually believed in such Guidebook for Officers platitudes as the word of honor of an officer and a gentleman.

"I'm not asking you, Mac," the DCSOPS said. "I'm telling you."

"I'm sorry, sir, I can't do that," MacMillan said. He came to attention.

The DCSOPS looked at him a moment. Then he stood up and tossed the staff study in the lap of the Assistant Deputy Chief of Staff for Operations.

"You take a quick read of that," he said, and then pointed at MacMillan. "And you come with me."

He led MacMillan into his small conference room.

"Mac, I have to know who put you up to this," he said.

"Nobody put me up to it, General," MacMillan said.

"All right, then, who 'helped you with it.' I give you my word as an officer and a gentleman that I won't do anything to him, now or later. But I have to know."

"Why do you have to know?"

"Because what you've done is suggest that there is someone in the service, someone besides yourself—someone rather senior, I would judge, from that staff study—who feels that Colonel Gregory and the Assistant DCSOPS have made a serious error in judgment. Or less kindly, are trying to put something over on me."

"Hell, he's not senior," MacMillan said, chuckling.

"Who is he, Mac?" DCSOPS said. When there was no reply, feeling foolish, he repeated: "I give you my word, Mac, as an officer and a gentleman, that I won't do anything to him."

"His name is Lowell," MacMillan said.

"Rank? First name?"

"He's a major. Craig W. He just finished flight school."

"Lowell? That's the young buck who was screwing the movie star in Korea?"

"Yes, sir."

"And then got involved in Phil Sheridan Parker's boy's court-martial?"

"Yes, sir."

"No wonder he didn't want his name involved. He's got his ass in a deep enough crack the way it is."

The DCSOPS was relieved to find out what he had. And rather surprised that the Lowell kid—he recalled that he was only twenty-six or so—was capable of such good staff work. Pity he'd fucked up his career the way he had. The army had good staff officers and they had good combat commanders, but there had been a severe shortage of men who were both since Valley Forge. The Lowell kid had already made his mark as a combat commander. If he was also capable of staff work like this, he could have gone far and fast.

"It won't go any further, Mac," the DCSOPS said. "You have my word."

"Yes, sir," MacMillan said. "Thank you, General."

They went back into the large office. The DCSOPS looked at his assistant and raised his eyebrows in question. He was not surprised that the two of them were ready with a reply to shoot down MacMillan.

"Sir, we don't need an empire down there," the Assistant DCSOPS said. "Gregory's shop can handle anything that comes out of Rucker. The whole idea in sending Major MacMillan down there is to smooth things out, not make waves. A lot of people would be furious if we tried to shove something like this down their throats. *Armor* doesn't have a special operation for combat developments. *Infantry* doesn't have one. Why should aviation?"

"How do you respond to that, Major?" DCSOPS asked.

"The colonels and the majors at Knox and Benning who are planning for the next war commanded companies and battalions and regiments in the last one," MacMillan said. "There's nobody, *nobody*, in aviation with combat command experience."

Christ, the DCSOPS thought, he's right about that.

"It would be a slap in the face to those officers, myself

included," Colonel Gregory said, "who have worked so long and so hard to get army aviation this far. The suggestion, frankly, infuriates me."

"I respectfully suggest that Colonel Gregory has made my point," MacMillan said. "The Flying Club will be furious if they don't get to spend all the money the army is about to pour into army aviation any way they want to. They mean well, General. But they just don't know about ground combat."

"Is that all you have, Major?" the DCSOPS asked. He saw that Colonel Gregory's face was livid with scarcely concealed fury.

"Yes, sir," MacMillan said, and came to attention.

"I'll look this over, Major," the DCSOPS said. "And have these gentlemen look it over and offer their comments."

"Thank you very much, sir," MacMillan said. "May the major consider himself dismissed, General?"

"You can go, Mac," the general said. MacMillan saluted, did a crisp about-face, and marched out of the office, dipping his knees just low enough to pick up his briefcase as he walked past the coffee table.

There was silence in the room for a moment. Then the Assistant DCSOPS chuckled as he leafed through the proposed table of organization and equipment.

"Well, he's got brass, I'll say that for him," he said. "This thing calls for a colonel, a light colonel, two majors, four captains, and a dozen lieutenants. *And* eleven aircraft."

"*Eleven* aircraft?" the aviation officer asked, a bitter tone in his laugh. "Only eleven?"

"A twin-engine Beech, two Beavers, three Cessna L-19s, two H-19s, an H-34, and two H-13s," the assistant DCSOPS said, reading from the proposed table of organization and equipment. "That's eleven."

"Mac's a nice fellow," Colonel Gregory said (*reverting,* the DCSOPS thought, *to the ridicule it and it'll go away tactic*). "Not too smart, but nice. Let's also give him a B-29, a squadron of P-51s, and maybe a C-54." He and the Assistant DCSOPS enjoyed their laugh.

"I was about to say have a couple of photocopies of that staff study made," the DCSOPS said. "But if there is only one copy, if it leaks, we'll know where it leaked. You take it first, Colonel Gregory, and list your objections to it, and then send it to me through General Kellogg."

"Does the general really intend to put this through the review procedure?" Colonel Gregory asked, in disbelief.

"The general does," the general said. "You and General Kellogg are it, Greg. Review it and get it back to me in a week, will you, please?"

"Yes, sir," the aviation officer said. "Will there be anything else, sir?"

"Yeah. No matter what I decide, MacMillan was right about the efficiency report. Fix it so you rate him, Greg, and I'll endorse it. I may not give him his empire, but I'm sending him down there to work for me, not the Aviation Board. Or what was it he said, 'the Cincinnati Flying Club'?"

(Two)
Marburg an der Lahn
West Germany
23 December 1954

There was a side to Lt. Col. Edgar R. Withers's late-blooming rebirth in the Lord Jesus Christ which worked to Major Craig W. Lowell's advantage. Colonel Withers called Lowell into his office for a little private chat and told him, man to man, that he believed that Ilse's tragic death was the means the Lord had taken to test Lowell, to see if Lowell could measure up to his dual responsibility as a Christian to be both father and mother to the "poor lad."

Withers said he was going to arrange Lowell's duty schedule so that Lowell could make frequent trips to Marburg. He did that, and he even "understood" when Lowell got the spectacular speeding ticket.

Lowell had arranged through Craig, Powell, Kenyon and Dawes's London office to buy a Jaguar convertible "out of routine merchanting," in other words, without having to wait his turn on the waiting list. The Jaguar arrived in Germany two weeks after he ordered it, by coastal ship to Bremen, and he rode up to Bremen to pick it up on a troop train carrying military personnel to the army's maritime facility in Bremerhaven.

He had no sooner got on the Frankfurt-Munich autobahn when a Mercedes whipped past him doing at least ninety. He remembered having heard that there was no speed limit on the autobahn and shoved his foot to the floor.

He was arrested by military police near Hersfeld. The no speed limit did not apply to American officers. It applied only to the Germans. He shortly found himself replying by indorsement to the commanding general of Seventh Army, explaining why he had violated the command's 60-mile-per-hour speed limit by driving his personal vehicle in excess of 110 miles per hour on the autobahn near Hersfeld.

Withers was required to punish him. He could have fined him a third of a month's pay, and written a really nasty letter for his personnel file. He chose instead to "orally reprimand" him, the least of the punishments prescribed, and the oral reprimand consisted in bringing Lowell's attention to the fact that if he should kill himself on the highways, "the lad" would be an orphan.

While technically that was true, Peter-Paul Lowell would not have been left all alone in the world should his father wipe himself out on the autobahn.

Schloss Greiffenberg, now that the Graf von Greiffenberg had returned "from the East"—the innocuous euphemism for Siberian imprisonment—was crowded with displaced Prussian and Thuringian and Pomeranian and Mecklenburgian kinfolk. All of them seemed to have had the foresight to either ship the family treasure out of East Germany before the Russians came, or even sooner to have opened numbered bank accounts in Zurich.

While they bemoaned the loss of their estates to the Bolsheviks, they were living as they had lived for centuries, in castles, tended to by servants, and with little to occupy their time but the investment of their capital—and the care of a little boy.

Elizabeth, the Pomeranian Baroness von Heuffinger-Lodz, Lowell soon learned, was the first among equals of his German in-laws. Shortly after he returned "from the East," not long after Ilse had been killed, Lowell's father-in-law was offered a commission in the Bundeswehr, Germany's new army. There were not all that many ex-colonels around whose opposition to Hitler was certifiable and thus were safe to lead a new German army.

There was no question about accepting the commission. It was his duty to *das Vaterland* to accept an officer's commission, as his ancestors had for seven hundred years. Lowell's father-in-law was now Generalmajor Graf von Greiffenberg, Deputy Chief of Intelligence.

It had seemed entirely logical to the Graf, with his daughter dead, and his American son-in-law at war in Korea, to turn the rearing of his grandson over to a widowed relative. That, too, had been going on in the family for hundreds of years. And when Craig Lowell thought it through, it seemed logical to him, too. The boy was obviously better off here than he would be "at home" in the United States, with a grandmother in a funny farm and the only other "logical" choice for his rearing Craig's cousin Porter Dawes and his wife. There would be time, Lowell had decided, to make the boy aware of his American heritage later. At the moment, his father was busy, trying as best he could to save his military career.

Herr Generalmajor (he was either so addressed, or as "Herr Graf"; it was as if he had no Christian name) seemed confused about Craig's status as an army aviator. There had been two-seater Feisler Storche airplanes in the Wehrmacht, too, flown by people one didn't pay much attention to. It was hardly the sort of thing an officer and a gentleman did.

Lowell did not tell his father-in-law of his difficulty with the army. It wasn't that he was ashamed of what he had *done*—he had had a moral obligation to stand up and be counted when the army had tried to screw Phil Parker, and Ilse had been long dead before he had become involved with Georgia Paige—but rather that his father-in-law, for whom he had a great deal of respect, had simply presumed that Lowell, like himself, was an officer and an aristocrat, and Lowell really liked that.

It would have been awkward to acknowledge that he was on the shit list, or even that he was in trouble at all. As a result, Lowell found himself arguing the case for army aviation with a good deal more conviction than he really felt.

Herr Generalmajor didn't seem to be overly impressed with

Craig's arguments, and often made references to Craig's "next command." There would be no "next command" in tanks, Lowell knew; and he doubted, in his dark moments, if there would ever be an aviation command more important than an aerial motorpool. Even if the dreamers had their way and eventually got their aviation battalions, he doubted that he would be given such a command.

Craig was determined, however, to be close to his son, which meant seeing him often, even if Ilse's relatives seemed to treat him sometimes as the vestige of an unfortunate alliance that would best be forgotten. Only his father-in-law and Elizabeth von Heuffinger-Lodz seemed to really accept him as a member of the family.

To solve Craig's time-in-transit problem, the Graf turned over to his son-in-law an enormous Mercedes sedan, equipped with the special license plates issued to general officers of the Bundeswehr. That kept the German police at a respectful distance, and the U.S. Army Military Police no longer had authority to control speeding German vehicles on the autobahn. Lowell rented a garage in Augsburg, leaving the Mercedes in it when he was on duty and the Jaguar there when he drove to Marburg.

His personal life in the military society at Augsburg was unsatisfactory, but he had expected that, and it didn't particularly bother him. He had decided against taking an apartment "on the economy," although the Generalmajor offered to help him find one. He didn't intend to stay in Augsburg when he had time off anyway, and he didn't want to call attention to himself.

He lived in the BOQ. Despite the notion that "initial utilization tour" aviators were assigned without regard to rank and branch of service, and that he was nothing more than a commissioned jeep driver, he was, de facto and de jure, a major, a field-grade officer.

Nonaviators disliked aviators, as a general rule. Not only were they regarded, once again, as nothing more than jeep drivers with commissions, but salt was rubbed into that wound by flight pay. Aviator lieutenants made as much money as nonflying captains.

The old-time aviators, the ones who ran the Seventh Army

Flight Detachment and told Major Lowell when and where he was to fly, were required to pay to him the military courtesy captains and lieutenants are obliged to show to majors. They lived in company-grade, single-room BOQs, while "young Major Lowell" (how the *hell* did he get to be a *major?*) was assigned a field-grade officer's two-room suite. They might be flight examiners and his instructors in the finer points of helicopter flight, but they were the ones who pulled officer of the day and conducted inventories of the unit supply room. Majors are not expected to do that sort of thing.

Lowell made some friends among them, of course. They weren't all either commissioned cretins or fools. He understood a good deal of the resentment the old-timers felt toward the newcomers. As it became increasingly evident that army aviation was going to grow, it had become just as evident to the old-timers that after having taken all the crap they had all those years, the newcomers were about to take all the gravy.

A letter from MacMillan, eight lines long, and with six misspelled words, reported that a Combat Developments Office had been set up under the DCSOPS at Camp Rucker. Lowell felt more than a little uneasy about that, for Bill Roberts had written shortly afterward, bitterly reporting the same thing and saying it was the first step in the establishment's attempt to take over army aviation. It would be very embarrassing if Bill Roberts found out that Lowell had put MacMillan's thoughts into a presentable form. He had done it for MacMillan primarily because Mac was just back from the escapade in Indo-China, and somehow felt he was paying him back for taking care of Sandy.

Mac would have really looked like the dumb ass he was if he had submitted his proposals to the brass in the form they had been in when he had showed them to Lowell. But Mac had been right: the Army simply couldn't afford to turn a vastly expanded army aviation program over to the Cincinnati Flying Club. Not because the members of the Club weren't competent, for they were about the only people around aviation who were, but because there was not enough of them to go around. When they ran out of Cincinnati Flying Club members for responsible jobs, they would have to get people outside of aviation alto-

gether, for the vast bulk of the other army aviators simply were
unqualified.

The subject of the low quality of aviation officers as a
personnel problem for the future had been the subject of several
of Lowell's long letters to Bill Roberts. Roberts was now a
full colonel at Camp Rucker and president of the Army Aviation
Board. Lowell had suggested solutions, including the periodic
reassignment of officers to their basic branch, so officers would
know something besides flying. Roberts argued that what the
army needed was a separate branch for aviation, Army Air
Corps II. Lowell had concluded that Roberts was wrong and
MacMillan right.

Lowell—after some time—finally acquired adequate skill
as a pilot by the simple expedient of flying whenever he had
the chance, and, where necessary, by using his rank to get the
more interesting flights (ferrying brass around during maneuvers, for example). There was no longer any question in his
mind that he was a competent pilot, but that was not the same
thing as saying that he was a good one. He had to work at it.
He could not swoop and soar like real aviators, who flew as
if they had been born to fly.

It was during a brass-ferrying flight near Bad Tolz that he
had his own rebirth of faith, not in Lt. Col. Edgar R. Withers's
Lord and Savior, but in army aviation.

The brass hat he was chauffeuring was a brigadier general,
the European Command's deputy quartermaster general. Like
most technical service soldiers, the general took his role in the
scheme of things very seriously. He was up at the crack of
dawn, loaded down with steel helmet and field equipment, and
had kept Lowell busy flying between one supply point and
another.

Many of the supply points where the general stopped to jack
up the troops were Class IV, POL, Petrol, Oil and Lubricants.
One of them, inevitably, was engaged in refueling a tank battalion.

As Lowell made the approach to a field beside the road, he
was at first—and automatically—critical. The M48s were too
close to one another. If they were attacked by enemy tanks or
aircraft, or if there was a fueling fire, one exploding tank would

blow up others. The company commanders didn't know what
they were doing, and neither did the battalion commander, or
he would have straightened things out.

But the battalion commander *had* a battalion, Lowell reminded himself. Although Major Craig W. Lowell had commanded a battalion-sized task force and he had fought so well
with it that it was now in the textbooks, he would never be
given command of one again.

He had another thought, as he prepared to land the H-13:

Christ! he thought. *If I had a couple of 3.5 rocket launchers
mounted on the skids of this thing, I could take out two of those
tanks and be gone before they knew what hit them!*

As quickly as the thought came to him, he shot it down.
There was no way to mount rocket launchers on a helicopter's
landing skids, and even if there was, there would be no way
to aim them.

And just as quickly came the solutions. Rocket launchers
had *no recoil*. They kicked up a lot of dust on the ground, but
that wasn't recoil. A rocket's propelling charge recoiled against
the atmosphere. They *could* be fired from choppers. And they
could be aimed by aiming the whole airframe. A helicopter is
capable of movement through all axes.

While the assistant quartermaster general was off shaking
up his troops, Lowell made a sight for rocket fire. He took off
his aviator's metal-framed sunglasses and snapped their lenses
out. Then he bent them into a U at the nosepiece. Then he
found his personal roll of toilet paper, invariably carried when
playing soldier on maneuvers where one crapped where one
found the opportunity. He unrolled it all, and took the paper
tube on which it had been wrapped and shoved it through the
bent frame. Finally, he taped it to the top of the control panel,
and tried to line it up parallel to the center line of the H-13.

When the assistant quartermaster general got back into the
H-13 and ordered himself transported to the next outpost of
his logistic empire, Lowell made a mock rocket firing run over
the parked tanks.

Sighting through the toilet paper tube would work!

"Major," the assistant quartermaster general asked, "what
the hell was that strange maneuver you just made? You some
sort of a hot-rodder?"

Lowell could think of nothing to reply that wouldn't make him look even more foolish in the general's eyes. He said nothing.

"Don't do anything like that again," the general said.

"Yes, sir," Lowell said.

"And take whatever that is you've got taped to the dashboard off," the general ordered. "It's unmilitary."

Unmilitary or not, Lowell thought, as he pulled off his ruined sunglasses and the toilet paper tube and threw them out the door, that's going to affect tank warfare even more than the 3.5 rocket itself did. It gets the rocket to the tank. And the army could swap one $75,000 helicopter for one enemy $500,000 tank. That would be a real bargain, even *if* the enemy got the chopper. By the time the tankers could get the turret-mounted .50 caliber machine gun in action, they wouldn't have time to engage it. Not until the chopper had fired its rockets. He said it in his mind again: the army could afford to trade choppers for tanks all day long.

That night he began to put it all down on paper. A thousand questions arose that would have to be answered. He started looking for the answers. He decided that before he even told Bill Roberts about it, he would have answers for those thousand questions, and maybe, if he could arrange it, he would be able to actually try firing rockets from a helicopter's skids.

Lowell wrote about it right away to Captain Phil Parker, telling Parker to keep his mouth shut. Lowell began to see rocket-firing helicopters as his way out of purgatory. He didn't want some sonofabitch from the Cincinnati Flying Club latching on to his idea and claiming it as his own.

When Phil replied, he said nothing whatever about Lowell's idea. He wrote that he had been granted a Special Instrument Ticket, which meant that he was his own clearance authority. If he figured it was safe to fly, he could take off. Lowell had grown used to being replaced by an old-timer the moment the clouds looked threatening.

Lowell told himself that Phil was flying fixed wing. There was no such thing as instrument flight in helicopters, so it meant nothing. But then he realized that it did mean something: if they were given an instrument flight capability, rotary wing aircraft would be even better rocket launching platforms. He would have to check that out, too.

While Major Craig W. Lowell spent as much time at the controls as he could, as well as long hours working on his rocket-armed helicopter idea, and as much time as possible with his son, he did not enter into a life of dedicated monasticism. He was twenty-six, in perfect physical condition. The juices of life flowed.

There were a number of single American women around Augsburg, service club hostesses, civilian secretaries, and specialists of one kind or another at Seventh Army Headquarters, and he worked his way through them, bedding some of them, being refused by others, never letting it get serious.

He had no desire to remarry. He really hadn't met another woman with whom the idea of sharing his life had any appeal. But it was not true, as the O Club gossip had it, that he worked his way through *each* and *every* female at Seventh Army. There wasn't time for that many women in his life, even if being in his life meant squiring them to the Seventh Army officer's club and little more. After a while, too, the word got around among the women that all the aviator major wanted was somebody in his sack, and that marriage was the last thing on his mind. Dating Major Lowell painted them before other eligibles (even if the other eligibles weren't generally field grade and possessors of a red Jaguar automobile) as girls who had been tried and found either willing or undesirable.

His fluent, unaccented German, acquired from one of a long line of governesses who had acted *in loco parentis* for his "ill" mother, and perfected when Ilse had been alive, came back quickly, and that opened two other sources of females: the girls who hung around the military (these were not, despite their reputation, all semipro hookers looking for a meal ticket, but in many cases young women who simply found Americans more attractive than their German contemporaries) and the Germans in the Augsburg and Munich upper crust, to whom he was known as the widowered son-in-law of Generalmajor Graf von Greiffenberg.

While he didn't score nearly as frequently as the stories went, he scored enough so that his reputation preceded him. If he appeared with a redhead on his arm for the Tuesday

Standing Rib Special at the officer's mess, you could bet that there would be a blond or a brunette the following week.

God only knows where he goes every weekend he can get off, went the talk. It was the general consensus that he used his weekends to diddle the married women whom discretion demanded he diddle at least one hundred miles from the flagpole. It became known that the sonofabitch had a Mercedes 280, with kraut plates, stashed in town.

This suspicious behavior came to the attention of the Counterintelligence Corps. A somewhat disappointed CIC agent, who had really felt that he was onto some sonofabitch on Moscow's, or at least Karlshorst's, payroll, reported that the automobile in question was the property of Generalmajor Graf von Greiffenberg of the Bundeswehr, and that a check of the subject's records indicated that Generalmajor Graf von Greiffenberg was the subject's father-in-law, and had been named guardian of the subject's minor child in the event of his death.

Only the CIC knew that Lowell was spending his weekends and his three-day VOCOs with his son and the Baroness Elizabeth von Heuffinger-Lodz, who was P.P.'s adoptive mother in everything but law. Otherwise, everyone but Lt. Col. Edgar R. Withers preferred to think his weekends were spent in carnal abandon with one straying wife, or oversexed secretary, or another. And the CIC is in the business of investigating people, not issuing character references. Lowell quickly earned a reputation as a swordsman, first class.

The thought of something happening between Lowell and Elizabeth had occurred to both of them and had been weighed and found, in the balance, absurd. They became friends instead.

Although he had passed the Bad Nauheim arrows on the autobahn every time he drove to and from Marburg, Lowell had never turned off for a look at the town where he had met Ilse, where he'd lived with her, where he had made her pregnant. He didn't, he admitted to himself, have the balls.

Elizabeth von Heuffinger-Lodz was responsible for him finally going back. When he arrived at Schloss Greiffenberg to spend Christmas, Elizabeth said she had heard that the army theater in Bad Nauheim was going to have a special Christmas program of cartoons and Walt Disney's *Fantasia* for dependent children, and could he arrange to take them? They could also visit the PX and get Peter-Paul things unavailable at any price on the German economy.

There was no way to refuse. He told himself that he was being foolish, anyway. That was all a long time ago. Sometimes, especially around Elizabeth, whose soft white skin and long, slim legs had their effect on him, he had difficulty even remembering what Ilse looked like.

When Elizabeth asked for the car, the chauffeur misunderstood, and was waiting in the courtyard, all dressed up in his livery, holding open the back door of the 280 for *Frau Baroness, Herr Major, and den süssen kleinen Peter-Paul*. It was easier to let him drive than to make a scene.

The chauffeur elected to take them into Bad Nauheim past the Bayrischen Hof.

It was a bright, crisp winter day, and as the Mercedes drove past the park where Ilse had spent that first night, a jeep came the other way, and a young girl jumped out, legs flashing under her skirt, and ran into the hotel.

Lowell's heart leapt, and he just had time to be amused at that, when a mental image of Ilse lying naked under him, when he took her virginity, filled his mind. She had trusted him, given him her body, given him P.P., when she didn't have a pot to piss in. And here he was, with P.P., in a goddamned chauffeur-driven Mercedes, and she was rotting in her grave. It was so goddamned unfair!

Tears came without warning, his heart went leaden, and it was all he could do to keep from sobbing out loud. He looked away. His eyes fell on P.P., standing up on the back floor, looking out the window. He got control of himself, and let his breath out very slowly.

"She was here with you, wasn't she?" Elizabeth asked.

"Right in there," he said, and met her eyes, not caring that she could see his tears.

"And you loved her very much, didn't you?" Elizabeth asked.

"Yes," Lowell said, surprised at the depth of his emotion. "Very much."

"And you loved who, Papa?" P.P. asked.

"Your mother, P.P.," Lowell said.

P.P. was not interested in his mother, whom he only very faintly remembered.

"And now you love Tante Elizabeth?" P.P. asked.

"Right on the button, Squirt," Lowell said.

"Right on the button?" P.P. asked, confused.

Elizabeth took Lowell's hand in her gloved one, and held it tightly.

After they had taken P.P. to see the Christmas program, and then through the PX to buy him what Lowell later thought of as one each of everything in the toy department, they had dinner in the officer's open mess. Elizabeth was willing to acknowledge that only the Americans really knew how to make a steak, even if there were few other American accomplishments worth mentioning.

On the way home to Marburg, Lowell, convinced that he was now in charge of his emotions, directed the chauffeur to the farmer's house where he had lived with Ilse.

"What are we doing *here?*" P.P. demanded to know, looking at the small farmhouse.

"This is where you come from, Squirt," Lowell said.

"Oh, no, I don't either!"

"This is where your mother and I decided to have you," Lowell said.

"That must have been a *long* time ago," P.P. said. "Can we go in?"

"I don't think so," Lowell said. "Somebody else lives there now." He gestured for the chauffeur to start up.

P.P. fell asleep on the secondary highway to Marburg, lulled to sleep by the swaying of the softly suspended large car. Elizabeth pulled him over her and propped him up in the corner, and then slid over beside Lowell. She took his hand.

"I used to feel sorry for Ilse," she said. "Now I'm a little jealous."

"How do you figure that?"

"You loved her," she said. "That's more than Kurt and I had."

Without really knowing that he was doing it, Lowell put his arm around her shoulder and pulled her closely, affectionately, to him. And then, without thinking about that, either, he kissed her. First a gentle kiss, between friends. Then it became less than innocent, gentle. It was, for some reason, highly exciting.

"This is dangerous," he said.

"What harm can one night do?" she whispered.

He kissed her again, and was not at all surprised when her tongue darted at first teasingly, and then hungrily, into his mouth, or when she violently twisted her body around so that she could press her breasts against him, or when her hand dropped to his crotch.

But that night was the only time it happened. She didn't come to his room again over the holidays, and the next time he got to Marburg, three weeks later, she made it plain within the first couple of minutes that what had happened between them was a freak happenstance, and that it would never happen again.

But they remained friends. The other relatives said they were like brother and sister and privately talked among themselves how fortunate it was that Ilse's American seemed to understand how far better it was for Peter-Paul to remain with Elizabeth, and wasn't it a shame that they hadn't, you know, felt *that* way about each other?

Lowell was personally disappointed when his initial utilization tour was over and he remained assigned to the Seventh Army Aviation Detachment. He had hoped for assignment to one of the divisions, where his rank would demand he be given a staff position. That was obviously the reason he remained assigned to the detachment as an aviator; they didn't want to give him a responsible assignment.

He used his rank to insist that he be checked out in the new, fourteen-passenger Sikorsky H-34 helicopter, and he was the first of the new breed in Seventh Army to be allowed to fly it as pilot in command. That special privilege was generally recognized to be because the Seventh Army aviation officer had heard good things about Major Lowell from Colonel Bill Roberts, while he was in TDY in the States.

He also used his rank to have himself sent to Sonthofen for a ten-week cross-training course in fixed wing flight. He was now what they called dual rated, and sent a copy of his orders to Phil Parker in Alaska. Being dual rated made things more even between them, catching up with Phil now that Phil had the coveted Special Instrument Ticket. Parker responded with a Xerox of his flight log. He had gotten himself checked out, incredibly, by the air force in C-119 Flying Boxcars and C-47s on skis. Parker sent him a photograph in which he was kissing a stuffed polar bear. Lowell sent him a photograph, his head on Rommel's body, of himself as a field marshal, and then had Elizabeth pick out something really nice to send Captain and Mrs. Parker for their first baby, a girl.

VI

(One)
Clayhatchee Springs, Alabama
17 January 1955

Darlene Heatter cleaned up the kitchen as soon as John went
to work, washing the dishes, wiping the table clean, even
mopping the floor. Then she made the bed and dusted the living
room, and then she dressed the kids. Finally, she got dressed,
a nice dress, not a Sunday dress, but nice all the same. She
didn't like to go to the church, even when there weren't any
services, unless she looked nice.

Darlene was an attractive woman, a few pounds shy of being
plump. She had brown hair and brown eyes, and every once
in a while she fantasized about having her hair bleached. She
had been blond as a child, but then, when she was just starting
high school, it had started to turn dark.

She'd put peroxide on her hair to keep it blond, but her
mother caught her doing it and told her that only tramps and
women who hung around beer joints bleached their hair. "If
you want to look loose," she'd said, "you'll have to wait until

you get married and leave home. As long as you live under my roof. you won't bleach your hair, or do anything else to make yourself cheap."

She'd thought about that encounter years later, when she actually did get married, and thought about being free to bleach her hair. but she hadn't done it. She told herself that she was now a young Christian married woman and no more free to look like a tramp than she had been in her freshman year of high school.

Darlene collected the kids and put them in the old pickup. The old pickup was a '47 Ford, red. with the back window gone and a crack in the front one, and pretty well rusted out in the bed from the fertilizer, which just about ate metal. The new pickup was a Ford. It wasn't really new, but it had belonged to the Hessia Peanut Mill supervisor, who hadn't really used it as a farm pickup, so it was the next best thing to a new one. Not worn out or eaten up by rust or anything.

She'd talked John into buying it, without turning the old pickup in as a down payment. They weren't going to give him anything for it, she told him (and that was true, they wouldn't have given him what it was worth, considering all the time he'd put in on it fixing it up and rebuilding it) and he really should have something to use as a spare. You never could tell what would happen, she said.

John was back out at Camp Rucker, thank sweet Jesus for. that, and not only as a fireman, GS-2, but as a fire equipment vehicle operator, GS-3. It wasn't really a promotion, just that he was qualified for the higher job because of his experience and seniority. What it was, officially, was that he had applied for a new job instead of just getting his old one back.

It was sort of funny, he told her, because now that he was a fire equipment vehicle operator, GS-3, there weren't any fire equipment vehicles. Not real ones. They'd auctioned off the old fire engines (some man from Chicago had made the high bid and come all the way down to take them away) when the post was supposed to be closing down for good. The new equipment hadn't come yet, although the army had issued the purchase order for them, and they were supposedly being built. All the fire department at the post had to fight fires with until the new equipment was delivered were some regular trucks with water pumps on the back, and some regular water trucks, regular army trucks. John and some of the others had gone to Georgia, to Fort Benning, to get them. It was the first time John had ever ridden in an airplane.

When she arrived at the Clayhatchee Springs Church of God, a white frame building set on brick piers, nobody was there. She hadn't expected anybody to be there, and would have been disappointed and maybe even a little embarrassed if there had been. She got the door unlocked and turned her kids loose in the nursery and asked them *please* not to tear anything up. Then she went into the church office.

When she got to the door, it occurred to her for the first time that maybe they locked the office. She had keys to the church and even the food cupboards in the kitchen (because she was on the Hospitality Committee and the Ladies Altar Guild), but if they locked the office door, she would have been out of luck. She had no reason to have keys to the office.

The office door was open. And there was the typewriter, right on top of the pastor's desk, with an oilcloth cover over it.

A month before, right after John had gone back to work, Darlene had been in the post office to send some wrong-sized corduroy overalls for Johnnie back to Sears and Roebuck, and she saw the civil service announcements on the bulletin board next to the FBI's Ten Most Wanted Criminals posters.

Fort Rucker was hiring typists, clerk-typists, and typist-stenographers on a competitive examination, and you could write for application blanks or call a number somebody had written in the notice with a Magic Marker. There were vacancies from GS-1 through GS-5 for something they called secretary (stenotyping).

So she called, and the lady in the personnel office said that all you had to do to get taken on as a typist, GS-1 or GS-2, was be able to type. If you typed twenty-five words a minute, you could get hired as a GS-1. If you typed thirty-five words a minute, you could get yourself hired as a GS-2. They would teach you whatever else you had to know once you were on the payroll.

Darlene had given it a lot of thought. John had been a GS-2 before they closed the post, and they'd had all the money they needed. If she could get a job as a GS-1, now that he was a GS-3, that was probably the same thing as two GS-2 paychecks. That was all the money in the world.

The only trouble was that John probably wouldn't want her to work. He would tell her that she should be home with the kids. And she couldn't type; there was that little problem, too.

Darlene Heatter sat down at the pastor's desk and pulled the oilcloth cover off his typewriter. Then, from her purse she took a package of typing paper, wrapped in cellophane, for which she had paid twenty-nine cents in the Piggly Wiggly Superette, and a battered book, bound at the top, which she had borrowed from the Choctawhatchee regional library bookmobile: *Typing the E-Z Way.*

She put a piece of paper in the typewriter and lined it up. She'd already read the first part of the book, and understood what she was to do.

Darlene Heatter put her fingers on the keyboard, and very slowly but with firm strokes, she began to type: aaa lll aaa lll aaa lll alal alal alal lala lala la.

(Two)
The U.S. Army Ground General School
Fort Riley, Kansas
23 February 1955

ROUTINE
HQ DEPT OF THE ARMY WASH DC
0905 21 FEB 55

TO: CG USA GGS AND FT RILEY KANS

1. THE DEPUTY CHIEF OF STAFF, USA, WILL PAY AN INFORMAL VISIT TO THE USA GROUND GEN SCH & FT RILEY KANS 24-25 FEB 1955.

2. GENERAL E. Z. BLACK, USA, AND HIS PARTY, CONSISTING OF ONE VIP CIV, TWO OFF, AND TWO EM, WILL ARRIVE VIA PRIVATE CIV AIRCRAFT AT APPROX 1100 HOURS FT RILEY TIME 24 FEB 55 AND

WILL DEPART FT RILEY BY PRIVATE CIV AIRCRAFT
AT APPROX 0900 HOURS FT RILEY TIME 25 FEB 55.

3. GENERAL BLACK DESIRES TO EMPHASIZE THAT
HIS VISIT IS INFORMAL. THE V/CS USA DOES NOT,
REPEAT NOT, DESIRE HONORS. HE DESIRES THAT ALL
ACTIVITIES AT FT RILEY CONTINUE WITHOUT IN-
TERRUPTION. HOWEVER, THE V/CS USA WILL,
SHOULD THIS BE THE DESIRE OF THE CG USA GCS &
FT RILEY, AND PROVIDING IT DOES NOT INTERFERE
WITH PRESENT PLANS, PARTICIPATE IN GRADUA-
TION CEREMONIES FOR WOCRW FLT TNG CLASS 54-
4 ON 24 FEB 55.

4. THE V/CS USA DESIRES THAT HE AND HIS PARTY
BE PROVIDED TRANSIENT QUARTERS OVERNIGHT.
FIELD GRADE TRANSIENT QUARTERS AND GROUND
TRANSPORTATION ARE DESIRED FOR THE THREE (3)
MAN CIV AIRCREW OF THE CIV ACFT.

5. PROVISIONS OF PARA 3.(B)1 THROUGH PARA
3.(b)16 STANDING OPERATING PROCEDURE NO. 1.3
WILL BE COMPLIED WITH.

> BY COMMAND OF THE CHIEF OF STAFF:
> EDWIN W. BITTER, MAJOR GENERAL, USA
> SECRETARY, GEN STAFF, USA

The TWX posed several questions to Major General Evan
D. Virgil, USA, Commanding General of the U.S. Army Ground
General School and Fort Riley, Kansas, first and foremost of
which was, "Why the fuck is Black coming out here?"

The Chief of Staff, U.S. Army, devotes most of his time
to the Joint Chiefs of Staff, of which he is a member, and to
the President of the United States, the President's cabinet, and
to the Congress. The Vice Chief of Staff, who is also a four-
star general, devotes his time to the U.S. Army.

And he has a role in the scheme of things should the balloon
go up. If the balloon went up, it was entirely likely that there
would be casualties not only in the executive branch of government, but in the Congress and in the Department of Defense
as well. The line of succession to the man who has the authority

to push the button descends through the Vice President to the Speaker of the House of Representatives, various other high elected officials, and only far down the line comes to the military.

As a practical matter, it was tacitly recognized that if the seat of government should go up in a nuclear mushroom, the order to push the button, when received from a four-star general or admiral, would be enough to convince the bright young men in the classified ordnance dumps that they could forego Standing Operating Procedure for Issue of Classified Weaponry and pass out the Nuclears and the Chemical, Biological, and Radiologicals.

It was agreed that the orders would come from the senior surviving four-star general or admiral. It was recognized that the order would be given by the first surviving four-star to be able to get through to the red phones connecting the brass to the men in the classified ordnance dumps.

The first thing the commanding general did on receipt of the TWX was call in his signal officer and instruct him to have radio telephone links with scrambling devices instantly installed in two separate locations, the VIP guest house and a secret concrete bunker, and to insure that each separate link was capable of communication with each of the seven places on the list he was provided.

Then he called in his aides and his sergeant major and put them to work. The junior aide was to see to transportation and quarters for the crew of a civilian airplane. The sergeant major was to make sure that the VIP guest house was made ready for the Vice Chief of Staff of the United States Army. The senior aide was placed in charge of having new programs printed for the graduation exercises of Warrant Officer Candidate Rotary Wing Flight Training Class 54-6, listing General E. Z. Black, Vice Chief of Staff of the United States Army as guest speaker. The Commanding General, USA Ground General School and Fort Riley, Kansas, would introduce the Vice Chief of Staff.

"And I want the band there, all of them, not the ragged collection of clowns I saw the last time," the post commander ordered. "And make sure we have a four-star flag for the platform. I don't care where you get one, get one. Uniform for all

hands will be Class "A" with medals. No ribbons. Medals. The
general staff will attend, and tell them I expect to see their
wives. I don't know what flight training has laid on, but there
will be a reception afterward. A cake. I want it done *right*,
Scott."

"Yes, sir. I take the general's meaning."

"And get with Whatsername, the officer's wives' club ad-
visor..."

"Mrs. Talley, sir."

"Tell Mrs. Talley what's going on and get her to make sure
the WOC wives look like officers' ladies. No slacks. Hats and
gloves, if that's possible."

"Yes, sir."

"Get your show on the road, we don't have much time."

At 1030 hours, the commanding general, the deputy commanding general, and their wives arrived at the Fort Riley
airfield, driving past long lines of Cessna L-19s—used for
training of fixed wing aviators—and long lines of Bell H-13
helicopters—used for training of rotary wing aviators. The
commanding general's junior aide-de-camp and the sergeant
major were already on hand, shepherding a line of olive-drab
Chevrolet staff cars. The junior aide-de-camp had also arranged
for a jeep with a radio tuned to the tower frequency to be on
hand.

At 1050 hours, the radio in the jeep came to life.

"Ah, Fort Riley, this is Martin Three Zero Seven. I am five
minutes out. I have General Black and party aboard. Request
approach and landing."

"What the hell is a Martin?" the commanding general asked
his deputy. The deputy shrugged his shoulders.

"Martin Three Zero Seven, Fort Riley," the tower replied.
"You are cleared as Number One to land on Runway Four Five.
The winds are negligible. The altimeter is two niner niner.
Report on final."

"Understand Number One on Four Five," the aircraft replied.

A glistening black Cadillac came up beside the line of staff
cars. A tall, erect black man in a gray suit got out of the car.

"See who the hell that is," General Virgil ordered.

"Sir, I believe that's Colonel Parker, retired," his aide told him.

"Oh, yeah. I wonder what the hell he wants?"

The tall, erect black man leaned on the fender of the gleaming black Cadillac and, shading his eyes, looked up into the sky.

An airplane appeared, far off, fairly low, and approached the field at a surprisingly high speed. It passed a mile to the left, banked steeply, and started its descent.

"Riley, Zero Seven on final," the radio said.

"Jesus, that's a B-26," the deputy commanding general said.

The airplane, a Martin B-26, a two-engine World War II bomber, was now making its approach. The flaps and landing gear were down. There was a screech as the tires touched, and almost immediately a deafening roar as the props were reversed and the throttles opened. The B-26 slowed very abruptly and started to turn around.

"Riley, Zero Seven on the ground at one minute to the hour. Taxi instructions, please."

"Zero Seven, a FOLLOW ME is en route to meet you."

A jeep with a huge FOLLOW ME sign mounted on its back seat raced out to the B-26, turned around in front of it, and then led the glistening ex-bomber to the line of staff cars. They could see what was painted on the vertical stabilizer now. There was a representation of an oil rig and the words: THE NEWBURGH CORPORATION.

The pilot taxied the airplane nose in to them and shut down the engines. General Virgil led the small procession over to the door, which unfolded from the side of the fuselage. He had a moment's glance at the paneled interior before the door was filled with the body of a huge black master sergeant. He came down the stairs with surprising grace for his bulk, casually saluted the two general officers, said, "Good morning, gentlemen," and then opened a cargo door to the rear of the passenger door and started to take out luggage. His tunic was pulled up as he stretched, and General Virgil saw that he had a .45 automatic in the small of his back.

And then General E. Z. Black got off the plane. He wore an overseas cap, rather than the leather-brimmed headgear normally worn by senior officers, and he wore it cocked to the left, in the armor tradition.

General Virgil saluted crisply. Black returned it idly.

"Good to see you, Virgil," he said. "But you didn't have to come out to meet me." He smiled and nodded at the wives. "Ladies," he said.

A full colonel and lieutenant colonel followed him off the airplane, then a tall, gray-mustached civilian, and finally a younger master sergeant, carrying a briefcase. The unmistakable bulk of a .45 in a shoulder holster was visible under his tunic.

"General, do you know General Young?" General Virgil asked.

"Yes, of course," Black said. "How are you, Young?" Then something caught his eye, and he walked quickly toward the tall, erect, black man.

"Look at this, Carson," he called over his shoulder. "We've been met by the local undertaker."

Colonel Philip Sheridan Parker III, retired, offered his hand to the Vice Chief of Staff of the U.S. Army. He got, instead, a bear hug.

"Slats, God, it's good to see you!" General Black said. The mustached civilian walked up and shook hands with Parker.

"I'm awed by your airplane, Carson," Colonel Parker said. "The last time I saw one of those, it dropped bombs on me. They said it was a mistake."

"I was right there with you, Phil," Carson Newburgh said. "Outside Bizerte. Don't be impressed with the plane. It belongs to the company."

General Virgil filed away for future reference the fact that the retired, outside-the-gate black colonel had friends in very high places.

The colonel, who wore the insignia (lapel pins with four stars and a golden rope through his epaulets) of an aide-de-camp to a full general, walked up to General Virgil.

"The general desires to attend the graduation ceremonies for WOCRW Class 54-6," he said. "But he desires to arrive just as they begin."

"I've, uh, taken the liberty, Colonel, of arranging for the

general to address the graduating class," General Virgil said.

"I don't believe the general had that in mind," the aide-de-camp said. He walked over to General Black.

"You're scheduled, sir, to address the graduating class."

Black frowned, and then shrugged.

"Oh, what the hell," he said. "You want to hear me give a speech, Slats?"

"The general's speeches are usually something to hear."

"Virgil, I don't want to arrive until just before the graduation starts," General Black said. "We have—" he looked at his watch—"fifty-odd minutes. Where can I hide? Better than that, where can we all get a quick drink?"

"My quarters, sir. I'd be honored," the post commander offered.

"Let's open the club," General Black said. "I'll ride with Colonel Parker in his limousine, and the rest of you can meet me there."

They were distracted by the sight of the enormous master sergeant heading their way, more precisely, marching their way. He marched up to Colonel Parker, raised his hand in a salute far more rigid than the one he rendered to the post commander, and barked: "Colonel Parker, sir! Does the colonel remember the sergeant, sir?"

The tall, erect black man saluted, as if he knew he should not salute in civilian clothing, and then put out his hand.

"Of course, I do, Tiny," he said. "I'm just surprised they haven't put you out to pasture."

"Oh, they're trying to, Colonel," he said. "But I got the Vice Chief of Staff on my side, and I'll stay in for a little while longer."

"Come along with us, Wes," General Black said. "You can have a little eye-opener with us."

"No, sir," Master Sergeant Wesley said. "I'll have one with you and the colonel later. I'm going to go see Greer."

"He's not supposed to know we're here," General Black said.

"Hell, General, you know better than that. If it's going on here, Greer knows about it, and has already figured out how to make money on it."

"Indulge me, Sergeant," General Black said. "Do what I tell you."

Master Sergeant Wesley got behind the wheel of the Cadillac.

"You get in the back," he said to Colonel Parker. "It'll be like old times, me driving you someplace."

The master sergeant with the briefcase and the .45 in the shoulder holster got in beside Master Sergeant Wesley. General Black, Colonel Parker, and the mustached civilian, Carson Newburgh, got in the back. The Cadillac drove off.

"Call the club," General Virgil said. "Make damned sure it's open when he gets there."

"I already have, sir," his aide-de-camp replied.

General Virgil impatiently waited for his wife to get in the staff car, and then he took off in pursuit of the Vice Chief of Staff of the United States Army.

At ten minutes after nine the next morning, five minutes after he had watched the B-26 race down the runway, he put in a telephone call to a classmate at the United States Military Academy, presently assigned as Deputy to the Assistant Chief of Staff for Personnel.

"Howard, I just had the most interesting visitor out here."

"I heard he was going out there. What the hell was it all about?"

"Well, you ever hear of a Colonel Philip Sheridan Parker III, retired?"

"Sure. You mean you don't know him?"

"I know he's retired out here."

"His great-great-grandfather retired out there, when Riley was an Indian-fighting cavalry post. There have been Parkers around the army for a long, long time."

"He certainly seems pretty close to General Black."

"They go back a long way together. Parker had a tank destroyer battalion with Porky Waterford's Hell's Circus in Europe. Black had one of the combat commands. That's all it was, war stories week?"

"No. Black hinted strongly that he wanted to address WOCRW 56-4."

"What the hell is that?"

"The sergeants we taught how to fly and made warrant officers out of."

"Is that so? Any particular reason?"

"He showed a particular interest in one of them, a kid named Greer. Had him to dinner at the club, and then they partied all night in the VIP guest house with Black's enlisted men, that great big orderly and the guy with the gun and the briefcase. Very intimate affair."

"Very interesting," the Assistant DCSPERS said. "I'll find out who he is."

"I thought you might be interested."

"Yeah, thanks, Evan."

"Scratch my back sometime."

The Assistant DCSPERS called for the service record of Warrant Officer Junior Grade Edward C. Greer. He found it interesting. He was only twenty years old. They had to waive the age requirement for him to go to flight school. He had been a technical sergeant when he applied for the Warrant Officer Candidate Program. There were not very many nineteen-year-old technical sergeants, either, which was also interesting. Nor were there very many technical sergeants of any age to whom the French government wished to award the Croix de guerre. The State Department had declined to give permission for him to accept it, but the request was in his record jacket.

The Assistant DCSPERS saw that WOJG Greer had been assigned to a Transportation Corps helicopter company for an initial utilization tour.

He called Colonel William Roberts at Camp Rucker, Alabama, and asked him if he could use a rather unusual warrant officer right from helicopter school. Roberts said that he could not. But he suggested that the Aviation Combat Developments Agency might be able to use him.

That name struck a familiar chord in the mind of the Assistant DCSPERS. He had that file pulled. He saw why it had stuck in his memory. They had sent Lieutenant Colonel (Colonel-designate) Robert F. Bellmon down there, with a delay-en-route assignment to the Bell helicopter plant, for a special senior officer's course in helicopter flight.

That was very unusual. But so was Bob Bellmon. He was

Porky Waterford's son-in-law. He'd been a POW in Germany.
The connection was complete. The Assistant DCSPERS told
his secretary to cancel WOJG Greer's orders, and to have new
orders cut assigning him to the Aviation Combat Developments
Office, a Class II activity of DCSOPS, at Camp Rucker, Alabama.

He was pleased; he was able to send General Black, the
Vice Chief of Staff, a personal note saying that he thought
General Black would be pleased to learn of WOJG Greer's
new assignment.

General Black was pleased; one of those chair-warming
assholes in personnel had finally done something right, had
recognized the boy's potential, probably because of the denied
Croix de guerre, and had gotten him a decent assignment as a
consolation prize.

WOJG Greer was pleased; anything was better than an assignment to a Transportation Corps helicopter company.

And Colonel William Roberts was pleased; if there was one
thing Colonel (designate) Bob Bellmon, two weeks out of helicopter school himself, didn't need, it was a chopper pilot not
old enough to vote who had gone to flight school even more
recently.

There were, Colonel Roberts thought, a number of interesting things he could do for Bob Bellmon in the future. Sending an incompetent newcomer to work for an incompetent
newcomer was only scratching the surface of possibilities.

(Three)

The first thing Barbara Bellmon said, in the lounge of the
Hotel Dothan, when her husband met her there after she had
surveyed the post and the available housing was, "I now know
how Grandmother Sage must have felt when she arrived at Fort
Dodge."

"Was it that bad?" Bellmon asked.

"Everything but hostile Indians," Barbara told her husband.
Grandmother Sage had been her great-grandmother, a tall, wiry,
leathery lady who had lived to ninety-seven. She had regaled
her grandchildren with tales of what it had been like as a young

officer's wife living on cavalry posts during the Indian Wars. Some of what she had told them had been true.

"Well, what are we going to do?" he asked. He meant, *What have you decided that we're going to do?* for the division of responsibilities between them gave her housing. She would arrange for it, and he would not complain.

"I thought about trailers," she said.

"Oh, Christ!" he said, earning the disapproving glare of the waitress who had approached the table for his order. "Is it that bad?" Then he turned to the waitress. "You ready for another?" he asked his wife, and when she shook her head, "no," he told the waitress, "Bring me a gin and tonic with a double shot of bitters, please."

"With what?" she asked.

"A double squirt of bitters," he explained. "I like them bitter."

"I'll ask," the waitress said. "But I don't think we have anything like that."

"Ask," he said. "And if you don't, it's OK."

"Welcome to the Wiregrass, you-all," Barbara said, softly, when the waitress was out of earshot.

"You aren't really serious about a trailer, are you?" he asked.

"I don't know what I'm serious about," she said. "I'm really discouraged. There's just no housing, period."

"But a *trailer?*"

"Trailers," she corrected him. "Plural. We'd need two."

"You're serious, aren't you?" he asked. "You're suggesting we rent two trailers."

"We'd do better buying," she said. "They cost about $10,000, for a nice one, and we'd need two, so that would be $20,000."

"Why do we need two?"

"We have children," she said. "Or have you forgotten? And unless you would like one or more of them sharing our bed, we'll need two trailers."

"I thought they made big ones."

"I'm talking about big ones. The little ones are for new-lyweds."

"No houses?"

"The name of the game is screw the soldiers," she said.

"The houses that are available are either tiny, or outrageously priced, or both."

"We need what?"

"Four bedrooms," she said.

"Dick and Billy could double up."

"Three bedrooms. if you are willing to have your children hate you."

"I'm willing," he said. "Can you find a place?"

"How about six bedrooms?" she asked. "I found an antebellum mansion we can have for $650 a month. Six bedrooms. No air conditioning. I guess in the olden days they had colored people waving fans at Massa and Mistress."

"Six hundred fifty bucks a month?" he asked. "That's a hell of a lot of money."

"That's what I thought," she said, sarcastically, "but I thought I'd better check with you."

"Where is it?"

"On Broad Street," she said, "in Ozark."

"Let me finish my bitterless gin and bitters, and we'll go look at it."

"It will be very conspicuous, Bob," Barbara said. "It looks like Tara in *Gone With the Wind*. And it's sort of a stock joke among the officers' ladies."

"How do you mean?"

"'If I thought I could get somebody to buy the children, I'm desperate enough to rent the $650 mansion,'" she quoted.

"Oh," he said, and thought that over for a minute. "Oh, what the hell, honey, I'm a colonel, or will be next week, and there'd probably be as much talk if we rented, or bought, two trailers."

"God, I'm glad to hear you say that," she said.

"Why?"

"Because now I can tell you I gave the man . . . and the man is the mayor of Ozark, *and* a lawyer, *and* a real estate guy . . . a deposit for it."

The reluctance of the Bellmons, separately, to take the antebellum mansion at $650 per month was not because of the rent, although $650 was nearly three times Colonel Bellmon's housing allowance. The Bellmons thought of themselves as "comfortable." Most of their peers, if they had known the extent of their holdings in real estate and investments, would have considered them wealthy. This could be an awkward situation in the army, where most officers lived from payday to payday, and they took great pains not to rub their affluence in anyone's sensitive nostrils.

On the way to Ozark in Barbara's Buick (Lt. Col. Bellmon drove a Volkswagen to work), he told her about WOJG Greer.

"I was assigned a new rotary wing pilot today," he said.

"Oh?"

"By an interesting coincidence, he's the sergeant, the ex-sergeant, who went into Dien Bien Phu with Mac and Sandy Felter."

"How did you arrange that?" she said.

"I didn't arrange it. Bill Roberts arranged it."

"That was nice of him," Barbara said.

"This is no favor," Bellmon said. "He stuck it in me."

"Explain," she said.

"I asked for an experienced warrant helicopter pilot, somebody who had experience in Korea, at the very least. I need experts, honey, not kids who just graduated from flight school."

"Oh," she said, understanding.

"This is the first shot at Fort Sumter," he said. "Open warfare will shortly follow."

"Why?"

"Because Roberts knows what a threat I pose to the aviation establishment," Bellmon said. "And he's a good enough soldier to know that the best defense is a good offense."

"I thought you were sort of friends," she said.

"We were, when I was a tanker, and he was trying to sell aviation to armor as a tool armor needed. But the minute I put on wings, I became a threat, a contender for control of aviation, and that he can't tolerate."

"I don't understand the rivalry."

"He's been studying revolutions," Bellmon said. "He understands that the first thing that usually happens after a successful revolution is that the leaders of the revolutionaries are stood against a wall and shot."

"That's a little strong, isn't it?" she asked.

"What any officer wants is command," he said. "What Roberts fears is that after all the work he's done to convince the brass that aviation is necessary, the commands are going to go to newcomers. Like me."

"Is he right?"

"Right now, the Aviation Board is hot stuff. They've got a bunch of money, and a bunch of people, and they're about to get a bunch of new aircraft, and everything that goes with them. They're going to get their pictures in the paper. But, and Bill Roberts is smart enough to know it, I have the clout. I'm going to be deciding what aviation is going to do with the equipment, and the capability. He knows, in other words, that he's already been shunted over to a support role."

"How come you're so important?" she asked, gently sarcastic.

"I've had a battalion," he said. "The brass trust people who have had commands. And they don't trust aviators. They don't take them seriously."

"Is that fair?"

"What's fair? It's the way things are. The only chance the Cincinnati Flying Club has to keep control of aviation, to keep as much as they can, is to discredit me, people like me. They'll try to make the brass believe that you can't turn over the decision-making to brand-new aviators, because we don't know what we're doing."

"Who's right?"

"That's the bitch, Barbara," he said. "We both are. I don't think the birdmen know, because they haven't been there, what the combat arms need, and what it takes to make a battalion work. And the birdmen don't think that we know, because we haven't been here, what aircraft are, and what they can do."

"So what happens?"

"Darwin. Survival of the fittest. After a good deal of internecine warfare."

"Then you'll win," she said, confidently.

"I'm not entirely sure about that," he said. "And I'm not entirely sure I should."

"Look at Mac," she said. "Trust Mac's instincts."

"What do you mean by that?"

"Mac is the legionnaire in the phalanx," she said. "Nature's natural warrior. No philosophical questions in his mind. He just wants to follow an officer who'll keep him alive and win the battles he's sent to fight. And he enlisted in your army."

"Maybe," he said.

"I remember, I was old enough, when Daddy and I. D. White and Creighton Abrams went to armor from cavalry," she said. "Everybody said they were throwing their careers away. That's what you're doing. They couldn't fight the last war on horses, and they probably won't be able to fight the next one with tanks, or with troops jumping in with parachutes. Army aviation is the answer, and you know it, and you know you're the guy best qualified to figure out how it should be done. Otherwise, you wouldn't have been given the job."

"Have you ever considered a career in the WACs?" he asked.

"I prefer to stand on the sidelines, wearing a big floppy hat, and with a rose in my teeth," she said.

She showed him where to park, before Howard Dutton's office on Courthouse Square in Ozark, directly across the street from the Confederate monument. And they went into Dutton's office, where they met his daughter Melody, and had a cup of coffee. Then they walked down Broad Street where Howard Dutton showed Colonel Bellmon the old Fordham place, which had sat empty for five years, and which he was now going to rent to Bellmon for $650 a month.

VII

(One)
Frankfurt am Main, Germany
17 April 1955

As regulations prescribed, Major Craig W. Lowell was given an efficiency report at the conclusion of his year-long initial ultilization tour as an aviator. It wasn't much of an efficiency report; it wouldn't do him much good.

It said that he had performed the duties required of him in an exemplary manner and had materially increased his skills and knowledge as an aviator. Aviators on initial utilization tours were expected to materially increase their skills and knowledge as aviators. Most of them worked hard at it.

The efficiency report also said: "Inasmuch as subject officer has been on an initial utilization tour during the reporting period, he has not been required to perform any functions of command. Consequently, the rating officer has been unable to evaluate his performance as a commander, or to form any opinion concerning subject officer's potential performance as a combat commander in his present or in a higher rank."

141

In effect, what the efficiency report said was that he managed to put in another year's service without either killing himself in a helicopter or getting into trouble.

What he had become, Major Craig Lowell thought, was a taxi driver to the brass. He was nowhere nearer to doing anything important than he ever had been. There was no reason that a second lieutenant, six months out of flight school, couldn't do what he was doing.

The brass preferred not be flown by second lieutenants. The more senior the brass, the more they could make this known. They felt more comfortable being flown by senior captains and majors and even lieutenant colonels than they did by second lieutenants.

It was Lowell's belief that the younger the pilot, the better. He had prepared a staff study (for Bill Robert's signature; his own signature would make the document meaningless) proposing that fifty enlisted men no older than eighteen years of age, who met the basic requirements for OCS in terms of physical and mental ability, be sent to flight school for training as warrant officer rotary wing aviators. Current practice was to send to flight school deserving noncoms of long and faithful service, technical and master sergeants only, which generally made them twenty-eight or thirty. The performance of the fifty boy pilots over a couple of years would either confirm Lowell's theory, or disprove it.

Roberts had reported that the staff study had caused fits all up and down the Pentagon, particularly with the Transportation Corps, whose senior officer, the Chief of Transporation, had only recently won a major skirmish to have L-20 Beaver and H-34 Choctaw companies designated Transportation Airplane and Helicopter Companies, on the lines of Transportation Truck Companies, and bluntly announced he didn't want a flock of teen-aged warrant officers running loose with his aircraft. The staff study had not been rejected, however. It was "being studied." Rumor had it being studied by the Secretary of Defense himself.

"When you inevitably get us shot down in flames, Lowell," Bill Roberts had written, "we will make a spectacular crash."

Today, leading a flight of eight Bell H-13s, Lowell had

flown up the autobahn from Heidelberg to Rhine-Main Airfield outside Frankfurt, where they had topped off the fuel tanks. After they'd taken off, they'd cut directly across Frankfurt over the Bahnhof and then up Erschenheimer-Landstrasse to the grassy expanse in front of the enormous curved facade of the former I. G. Farben Building, now Headquarters, U.S. Forces, European Theater (USFET).

The seven other Bell H-13s flew in trail behind him in a V, each chopper flying two hundred feet behind and one hundred feet above the bird in front of him. They would make an intentional display of themselves when they all suddenly, and virtually simultaneously, swooped out of the sky to pick up a visiting one-star and his collection of colonels and lower hangers-on and ferry them to Heidelberg, to Headquarters, U.S. Army, Europe.

"All right," Major Lowell said to his microphone, "now let's do it right."

He put the H-13 into a steep turn to the left, his eyes on the white painted *H* of the helipad. He straightened the bird out, dropped like a stone, flared, and touched down. He looked out the plexiglass bubble. Six of the seven choppers were on the ground. The seventh was coming in very slowly, like a bather about to test the temperature in a swimming pool. There's always one sonofabitch who's a minute late and a dollar short, Lowell thought, and then started to shut the helicopter down.

A tall, quite handsome officer, with a glistening star pinned to his overseas hat (you didn't see many of them anymore; the generals had taken to wearing the new olive-green uniform, whose hat was generously provided with scrambled eggs on the brim—far more general-like than an overseas cap) came rapidly striding toward Lowell's H-13.

Lowell hadn't expected them for a good five minutes. But he unsnapped his harness, jumped out of the helicopter, ran under the still rotating blades, and held open the passenger door for the buck general with one hand while he saluted with the other.

The general looked him up and down and got into the helicopter. By the time Lowell got back in, the general had already found the headset and put it on.

"I'm Major Lowell, sir," he said. "Were we by any chance late?"

"No, you were thirty seconds early," the buck general said. "That was pretty spectacular, that swooping pigeons bit. Do you do that all the time, or just to impress visitors?"

"We practice all the time, sir," Lowell said. "So that we can impress visitors."

"One of your pigeons was late," the general said. "Did you notice?"

The other pilots reported in, one at a time, giving just their number, to signify their readiness to take off: Five. Two. Seven. Four. Three. Six.

The needles were in the green. Lowell picked up on the cyclic, swooping back in the air. He saw in the mirror that the rest of the flight had taken off when he did. Perfect. The general hadn't seen that, of course. Just the bastard who was late.

"You're smiling," the general said. "I suppose the rest of your flock got off the ground by the numbers."

"Yes, sir."

"Including Tailgate Charley?"

"Yes, sir."

"Now that we're in the air, don't you think it would be a good idea to ask me where we're going?" the general asked.

"I was informed the general's destination was Heidelberg, sir."

"There has been a change in plans. I want to go to Bad Godesberg. Can you do that, or are you going to have to fuel up someplace?"

"We have enough fuel for Bad Godesberg and a thirty-minute reserve, sir," Lowell replied. He pressed his microphone button and called Rhine-Main area control and told him of the change in flight plans.

"That swooping pigeon bit was very impressive," the general said, when he had finished. "Does it have some sort of bona fide military application, or is it like chrome-plating mess kits?"

"If the general can imagine each of these machines as capable of carrying eight fully armed infantrymen, the general can probably imagine that we can discharge a platoon and its basic load of ammunition in just about the time it took us to pick up the general's party, sir."

"And each of those machines could be flown by a teen-aged boy, right?"

That surprised Lowell to the point where he looked at the general.

"Yes, sir, I think they could."

"You *are* one of Bill Robert's acolytes, then?" the general said.

"I don't think of myself so much as an acolyte, General, as a monsignor to his bishop."

The general laughed. "You've heard about the teen-age pilots, then?"

"I was able to help the bishop draft the appeal to the heavens, sir."

"That suggests you wrote it," the general snapped. Lowell didn't reply. "Either you did, or you didn't," the general snapped. "Which is it?"

"I wrote it, General."

"Then you must be another of the recent recruits to peace on earth through air mobility," the general said. "Another bright young officer throwing his career away in a quest for the Holy Grail."

Lowell didn't trust himself to reply.

"Had second thoughts already, have you?" the general asked.

"No, sir," Lowell said, and then he thought, fuck it, this guy hates army aviation anyway. "I'm in army aviation because I don't have a career to throw away. And, with all respect, sir, I think a lot of people are going to eat their words about Colonel Roberts. He's right, and most of his critics are wrong."

The general said, dryly: "Your loyalty is commendable."

Lowell now knew that whatever he said would be wrong. He said nothing.

The general said, "That was a colorful phrase, didn't you think? 'Another bright young officer throwing his career away in a quest for the Holy Grail.'"

The reply came before Lowell could stop it.

"I don't frankly think much of it, General."

"But you will admit it's colorful? I mean, it has a good deal more class than, for example, 'you dumb fuck, you!' Wouldn't you say?"

Lowell had to chuckle. "Yes, sir, it does."

"General Simmons has always had a flair for the spoken word," the general said. "He just used that Holy Grail line on me, when I told him that I had turned down chief of staff of the 2nd Armored Division to assume command of the Army Aviation Center."

The general was smiling when Lowell looked at him in surprise.

"If you're a monsignor, Major, and Bill Roberts is a bishop, I guess that makes me the Pope." The general made the sign of the cross. "Bless you, my Son," he said. "Go and sin no more." He seemed highly pleased with himself.

After a moment, he asked: "I have two more questions, Major."

"Yes, sir."

"There was a Task Force Lowell in the breakout from the Pusan perimeter. That was you, correct?"

"Yes, sir."

"OK, those blanks are filled in. I've heard about you. Next question. As one old tank commander to another, are these things hard to drive?"

"General, they're a bitch," Lowell said.

"I was afraid you were going to say that," the general said. "Then your thesis is the younger the man, the easier he will be to train?"

"Easier to train, in better physical condition with quicker reflexes, and he can be retained on flying duty for a longer period of time, with consequent reduction of training costs."

"Final question," the general said. "When you can find time, I want you to write down this instantaneous discharge of ground troops from helicopters for me. Send it to me at Rucker, it's in Alabama someplace, I never heard of it. Mark the envelope 'personal.'"

"Yes, sir," Lowell said.

"My name is Laird," the buck general said. "My friends call me 'Scotty.'" He paused. "You can call me 'General.'"

Lowell smiled dutifully at General Laird, who was obviously

delighted with his wit. Lowell had heard that 'you can call me General' line before. And then he remembered where. The first time he had ever seen a general up close, on the polo field at Bad Nauheim. That long ago. Before he had been an officer; before, even, he had met Ilse.

The general had been Major General Peterson K. "Porky" Waterford, then commanding the U.S. Costabulary, the Army of Occupation police force. He had used the same line on his newly formed polo team, which had consisted of the general, two full bull colonels, and PFC Craig W. Lowell, soon to elevate from draftee to second lieutenant, because "Call Me General" Waterford wanted to beat the French. The French played only fellow officers and gentlemen, and PFC Lowell happened to be a three-goal polo player.

Lowell spent long hours in the three weeks after he dropped Brigadier General Laird and his staff off at Bad Godesberg, writing and rewriting a draft field manual, *Helicopter Placement of the Infantry Platoon*.

It wasn't something he had just thought up; the idea had occurred to him a long time ago (and not, he readily admitted, to him alone). The difference was that he had done more than think about it. Encouraged by Bill Roberts's responses to other ideas of his, he had considered the problem as something real and immediate, as if it were going to happen tomorrow. The only imaginary thing in his proposal was the helicopter itself. The army had already begun to take delivery of Sikorsky H-34 helicopters which could, under ideal conditions, indeed lift eight fully armed troops and their combat load.

The yet-to-be-designed, much less built, helicopter described in *Helicopter Placement of the Infantry Platoon* was capable of carrying twelve fully armed troops under all reasonable conditions, plus five hundred pounds of supplies, and the machine was designed so that troops would be off-loaded through doors on both sides.

Lowell played the devil's advocate, trying as hard as he could to find fault with his own idea and its execution. But finally it was done, and he typed it up himself, with five carbon copies, as neatly, he thought, as any clerk-typist of questionable sexual persuasion could type it, each copy having a cardboard cover and bound together with a paper clip.

Typing the address gave him the biggest thrill.

> Brig. Gen. Angus C. Laird
> Commanding General
> The U.S. Army Aviation Center
> Camp Rucker, Alabama 36362
> PERSONAL

Brigadier General "Scotty" Laird had *asked* for it.

Lowell sent a copy to Phil Parker in Alaska. A Xerox copy; he had forgotten about Phil until he was halfway through typing it up. Six weeks later, he got a Xerox of *Emplacement of the Infantry (Ski) Platoon in Arctic Conditions by Ski-Equipped U1A "Otter" Aircraft*.

Phil had adopted his idea to arctic conditions and had used as his imaginary aircraft a sort of super Beaver, a fourteen-passenger DeHavilland single-engine Bush aircraft not yet in the army inventory.

It was the only response Lowell ever got to his proposal. Colonel Bill Roberts acknowledged receiving it, but made no comment. General Laird never even acknowledged receiving it. After several months, Lowell concluded that Laird had just been playing with him, laying some charm on a young officer, getting him to write up an idea that he never intended to seriously consider. He was bitterly disappointed.

And he wasn't doing a goddamned thing of importance now. He was still with the Seventh Army Flight Detachment. He had picked up a bullshit title, "Deputy to the Chief, Special Rotary Wing Missions Branch," but he was painfully aware that he was still playing commissioned jeep driver, ferrying people from one place to another in a flying jeep.

(Two)
Dothan, Alabama
10 July 1955

Rhonda Wilson Hyde examined herself with pleasure in the mirror of the dressing cubicle in Martinette's Finer Ladies Wear in Dothan. She was wearing a matching set, bra, panties, and half-slip, all black. The half-slip was lace from the hem nearly halfway to the waist. The panties were nearly all lace, except where a strip of solid material was necessary here and there to hold them together, absolutely as fragile and delicate and transparent as it was possible to make them. The bra, while it looked as fragile as the panties, was really quite strong. It had to be to hold her breasts up the way it was, and yet it was surprisingly comfortable. It was also surprisingly expensive, even for Martinette's Finer Ladies Wear.

When she had taken the undies out of the sealed cellophane package—which meant that she would have to buy them—she would have bet the thin straps would cut painfully into her shoulders. And she thought the plastic, or whatever it was, that pushed up the half-cups (the tops were open; anyone looking down her dress could see her nipples) was going to dig into the bottom of her breasts and probably jab painfully into the flesh below. But that didn't happen. The bra was as comfortable as any she had ever worn. And sexy!

But God, if Tommy didn't show up, how was she going to pay for it? Doc would blow his cork if he got a bill from Martinette's for $79.95 plus tax. Dentistry wasn't a printing press for money, he would say. Again.

She turned around, looking over her shoulder into the mirror. There was something sexy about the black strap against her white back.

There was a knock at the cubicle door, and someone pushed on it. But it was latched.

"Telephone, Mrs. Hyde," the saleswoman said. "Your husband, I think."

Good God, it better *not* be Doc. She was supposed to be with her mother, and her mother was supposed to be having trouble with her back. She unhooked the latch and an arm holding a telephone appeared in the crack of the door.

"Hello?" Rhonda Wilson Hyde said, when she had the phone to her ear, her free hand pushing the door closed.

"Can you talk?" Tommy Z. Waters asked.

"Hello, darling," she said. "I'm nearly through. I should be home in about an hour."

"I'm up the street," Tommy Z. Waters said.

"How interesting!" Rhonda said. "I'll hurry."

Tommy Z. Waters hung up without saying anything else.

"Good-bye, darling," Rhonda Wilson Hyde said to the dead telephone. Then she opened the door wide enough to put her hand, and the telephone, through.

When the saleswoman took it from her hand, Rhonda latched the door so she couldn't "accidentally" come in. Rhonda wanted to wear the black underwear, and she didn't want the saleswoman to know. She put her own bra and panties in her purse, and paid for her purchase in cash.

The Downtowner Motel up the street was owned by the Downtowner Corporation, whose stock was split among three doctors, a lawyer (Howard Dutton), and a businessman, Tommy Z. Waters.

Five minutes from the moment he had hung up on Rhonda Wilson Hyde, she came through the door of the motel room and pushed it quickly closed behind her.

"I'm always afraid that someone will see me come in here," she said, leaning against the door.

He didn't reply. Cutting through the Downtowner Motel parking lot was a shortcut to the municipal parking lot on the street behind it. If someone you didn't want to see happened to be in the motel parking lot, or walking through it, you just kept walking to the municipal parking lot (where you had parked your car) or onto South Main Street, where the shops were.

Rhonda pushed herself away from the door and went to the refrigerator, where she opened the freezer compartment and took out a small, ice-crusted glass. She put two ice cubes in it, and then walked to where five bottles of liquor stood on a chest of drawers. She filled the glass with gin, added an olive from a jar, and stirred it with her finger.

"Oh, I need this," she said. "You don't want one?"

He shook his head, "No."

"Oh, Tommy, darling, do you have any money with you? I went out without bringing any."

That hadn't stopped her from shopping, he thought. She had three bags.

He took a folded wad of bills from his pocket, spread them out, and extended them to her. There was three, maybe four hundred dollars in the fan he extended to her. Fifties and twenties and tens. Resisting the temptation to take it all, Rhonda pulled two fifties from the fan.

The bra and the panties and the half-slip had cost *almost* that much. It was only fair that Tommy pay for them. She was wearing them for him. Doc would never see her in them. Well, maybe the half-slip, but never the bra and the panties. They would give Doc a fit. She was a respectible married woman, and respectable married women didn't wear open-cupped brassieres and transparent panties with everything showing.

She said thank you, and then tucked the two fifties in her purse, and then she said, "I've got to tinkle."

When she came out of the toilet, she was wearing just the brassiere and the panties. Tommy was already in the bed, naked, with his hands laced behind his head.

"Like it?" she said. "I just bought it."

"Jesus!" he said. "Jesus Christ!"

She was pleased at what he said, and what happened. His cock got stiff. God, he had a marvelous cock! She went and sat on the bed and lowered herself over him, so that he could get his tongue on her nipple.

Afterward, as always, she went to the john first, but this time when she came out, she was dressed.

"What's the hurry?" Tommy asked. That's what he was asking out loud, Rhonda thought. What he was really asking was, "Only once?"

Until recently, Rhonda was in no greater hurry to leave than Tommy was, unless she was late or something. Tommy, in fact, often disappointed her when he just jumped out of bed, Wham, Bam, Thank you, Ma'am. Just like Doc.

"I'm going out to the post," Rhonda said, examining her lipstick one last time in the mirror. "To see about a job."

"What kind of job?"

"I took nutrition at the university," she said. "There's an opening."

"What's Doc think about that?" Tommy Z. Waters asked.

"I haven't told him yet," she said.

She sat on the bed and kissed Tommy, just her tongue, so

she wouldn't muss her lipstick, and she gave his thing a little pump, just for the fun of it, and then she walked out of the motel room, looking around to see if anybody had seen her, and then got in her car.

If she got a job at the post, she decided, that would be the end of the motel room. She was tired of it anyway. Doing it with Tommy was getting to be just about as boring as doing it with Doc.

When Rhonda got the telephone call from the civilian personnel office out at the post, asking if she could come out there for an interview that afternoon, she thought that she was actually going to get the job.

She'd heard about the job at the New Year's Eve party at the officer's club. The military medical and dental people had gone out of their way to be nice to their civilian counterparts. Inviting people who lived in a dry county to a New Year's Eve where Kentucky sour mash bourbon sold for forty-five cents a drink was about as nice as they could be. One of the officers at their table had been a Medical Service Corps officer who had had a hard time keeping his eyes off her boobies. She'd taken a couple of drinks in the afternoon, and that had given her the courage to wear her other open-cupped bra.

Either Doc was so dumb he didn't notice, or he just didn't care, because, despite the way she'd worried about it, he hadn't said a word about it to her. Anyway, the major from the Medical Service Corps had told her, sometime during the evening, that the hospital was looking for dieticians, Grade GS-5. Rhonda had picked right up on that. She had her degree in home economics from the University of Alabama, and she'd had a lot of courses in diet and nutrition, and things like that.

The major said it wasn't up to him to decide—if it was, the job was hers—but that the civilian personnel office made the decision. They went over applications from people and saw whether or not they met the requirements. So Rhonda had filled out the application (my God, the thing was six pages long, and even wanted to know if you had ever been arrested, or been a member of any political organization advocating the violent, or revolutionary, overthrow of the United States government) and mailed it off. And five weeks later, she got the call.

The civilian personnel officer turned out to be a woman, a skinny woman, a 30-AAA cup, training-bra type woman, not an officer, which had sort of disappointed Rhonda. Women aren't interested in well-dressed women; they just get jealous. What the civilian personnel officer, Mrs. Cawthorn, told her was that the dietician, GS-5, job was already filled and that she wasn't qualified anyway. Rhonda was just about to tell her she could have told her that on the telephone and saved her a trip all the way out here, when Mrs. Cawthorn said there was something else.

Something called the Aviation Combat Development Agency had an opening for an administrative officer, Grade GS-7. Rhonda wasn't qualified for that, either, but since she had a college degree, *that* made her eligible for what they called the intern program, which was how the government trained people straight from college with no experience. She could start as a GS-5, and if after a year's probation she learned to do the job, they would make her a GS-7. Mrs. Cawthorn said she wasn't offering her the job. All she could do was set up an interview for her with the executive officer, a Major MacMillan, and see if he was willing to take a chance on her.

Mrs. Cawthorn got on the telephone right then and called Major MacMillan. The major said he could see her if she would get to his office within fifteen minutes.

She had a little trouble finding the place, a converted barracks, and when she went inside, there was a secretary, a Mrs. Heatter, who treated her as if she was collecting money for Russian Relief or something.

"Do you have an appointment?" Mrs. Heatter asked.

"He expects me," Rhonda said. "Civilian personnel sent me over about the administrative officer's job."

Rhonda would have had to be blind not to see that Mrs. Heatter was something less than thrilled to hear that.

"Why don't you tell him I'm here?" Rhonda said, flashing a big smile at her.

Mrs. Heatter picked up her telephone (a funny looking telephone; Rhonda had never seen one like that before) and dialed just one number.

"Major, there is a Mrs. Hyde here, who says you expect

her." Mrs. Heatter then rose and showed Rhonda into another office. "Mrs. Hyde, Major MacMillan."

After all that formal business, Rhonda expected an officer in full dress uniform, at least. The man who said, "Come in, please, Mrs. Hyde," was wearing what looked like a junior league baseball jacket. It was a violent shade of orange and had a snake embroidered on the front with the word MOCCASIN sewn above it.

He shook Rhonda's hand, took her application from her, and offered her a seat. Rhonda regretted all the emphasis she'd given on the application to her nutritional and food preparation experience. It made her sound like a short order cook.

"What the application doesn't show, Major," Rhonda said, flashing him a big smile, and leaning over so that if he wanted to, he could look down her dress, "is that I've been running my husband's office since we were married. All the administration, so to speak."

"Do you type, by the way?"

"No," she said, "not very well." She figured she could get away with that; he had looked down her dress. He was all man, she could tell that.

"That must make things tough in your husband's office," he said, and there was a sarcastic tone in his voice, but he left it there and went on: "Here's a copy of the job description. Why don't you take a look at it and see if you think you'd be able to do it?"

Rhonda sat back and read the job description with what she hoped looked like intelligent interest. When she felt Major MacMillan's eyes on her boobies again, she sat up and leaned over, her eyes still on the job description, to give him a better look. It was either the boobies or nothing; she didn't understand a word of the job description. She told herself that an office was an office, and once she got the job she could figure out what she was supposed to do. She really wanted the job. Major MacMillan was very interesting, indeed, and there would probably be other interesting men, as well.

"I'm sure that once I got my feet on the ground, I could handle this," she said, and flashed him a dazzling smile. "But I have to tell you that I've never had the chance to be around senior army officers before."

"Do you know what a Multilith is?" Major MacMillan asked.

"Yes, sir," she said. "We have one at the church."

All she knew about a Multilith machine was that it was a dirty machine that sat in the preacher's office.

"And you can run it?" he asked. "Or supervise the people that do?"

"Oh, yes, sir."

"I have to tell you, Mrs. Hyde, that this isn't an eight-to-five job," Major MacMillan said. "We would expect you to be available to come into work sometimes very early in the morning, and to work at night, and over weekends. If you're looking for an eight-to-five job, this isn't it."

"My time is my own," Rhonda said.

"What about your husband? And your children?"

"My mother takes care of the children when the housekeeper isn't there," Rhonda said.

"Now, don't tell me that now, and then come in two months and tell me you can't handle the hours."

"I wouldn't do that, Major MacMillan."

"Can you come to work tomorrow morning?"

"Yes, sir."

"About seven o'clock," he said. "We start early sometimes." He wasn't that hard to figure out. He just wanted to see if she meant what she said about being willing to come in early.

"Yes, sir," Rhonda said. That was going to cause trouble. Doc would be furious if she wasn't there to make his breakfast. Too bad. She had a job, and the prospects looked simply fascinating. Doc would just have to get used to making his own breakfast. Hell, they could hire a cook at what she was going to make out here.

(Three)
Camp Rucker, Alabama
16 August 1955

Warrant Officer Junior Grade Edward C. Greer's gray U.S. Air Force issue flight suit was sweat-soaked and showed white lines where the salt tablets, ingested as protection against the heat, had passed out of his body. He carried a white plastic crash helmet loosely under his left arm as he knocked at the sill of the open door of the director, Aviation Combat Developments Agency.

"Come on in, Greer," Colonel Robert F. Bellmon said. The kid looked exhausted. Bellmon really hated to do what he had to do, eat the kid's ass out.

Greer saluted, not especially crisply, but, Bellmon thought, with a flair that represented what a salute was really supposed to be all about, a greeting between practitioners of the profession of arms, not, as most people believed, a symbolic gesture of servitude by the junior to the senior.

"You wanted to see me, Colonel?" Greer asked, but it was more of a statement than a question.

"Little warm outside, is it?" Colonel Bellmon asked.

"I mounted a thermometer on the instrument panel," Greer said. "It went to 125 degrees." Bellmon noticed that that, too, was a statement of fact and not a complaint.

Good lad, he thought. Then, fuck it. I'll eat his ass out later.

"I thought you would be interested in this," Colonel Bellmon said, and handed him the stapled together stack of correspondence:

HEADQUARTERS

U.S. ARMY AVIATION COMBAT DEVELOPMENTS AGENCY

CAMP RUCKER, ALABAMA

20 July 1955

SUBJECT: Request for Flight Training in, and 250 hours of, YH-40 aircraft flight.

TO   : President
        U.S. Army Aviation Board
        Camp Rucker, Alabama

   1. Inasmuch as the USAACDA is charged with determining the future role, if any, of YH-40 aircraft presently undergoing flight testing by the USAAB in the field forces, it is considered absolutely essential that the

USAACDA have access to YH-40 aircraft at the earliest possible time.

2. Request is made herewith that the following personnel of the USAACDA be given, as soon as possible, flight training in YH-40 aircraft assigned to the USAAB. While training by USAAB personnel of all USAACDA personnel listed would be most desirable, should this pose an unusual burden upon the mission of the USAAB, the USAACDA requests the training of Major R. G. MacMillan to a level qualifying him as an instructor pilot, in order that he might accomplish training of the other USAACDA personnel who will be involved with the YH-40, WOJG Edward C. Greer and the undersigned.

3. The USAACDA will arrange to schedule training to meet any USAAB requirements.

Robert F. Bellmon
Colonel, Armor
Director, USAACDA

1st Ind

Hq USAAB, Cp Rucker Ala 23 July 1955
To: Director, USAACDA Cp Rucker, Ala

1. The USAAB board has been assigned three (3) YH40 helicopter aircraft. No additional YH-40 aircraft will be made available in the forseeable future.

2. In order to insure that available aircraft will meet the testing requirements placed upon the USAAB by DCSOPS, it is the policy of the USAAB that only helicopter pilots of great experience will be assigned to fly YH-40 aircraft. Criteria established include seven (7) years experience as a rated aviator; 2,500 hours total flight time; 1,000 hours rotary wing flight time.

3. Further, the flight testing mission placed upon the USAAB by the DCSOPS is such that available flight time for the available aircraft is fully scheduled through 31 Dec 1955.

4. Consequently, the request of the basic communication must be denied.

5. Should the USAACDA wish to furnish the USAAB with any specific flight tests it wishes to have accomplished, the USAAB will make every reasonable effort to have such tests conducted by USAAB personnel already qualified in YH-40 aircraft. The USAAB feels this would be the most economical use of available assets in any case.

William R. Roberts
Colonel, Artillery
President

2nd Ind

Hq USAACDA Cp Rucker Ala 24 July 1955

To: Deputy Chief of Staff for Operations, Hq Dept of the Army Wash 25 DC

VIA: Chief Avn Br DCSOPS Hq DA Wash 25 DC

1. Attention is invited to basic communication and 1st indorsement thereto.

2. Unless USAACDA personnel are trained in YH-40 aircraft and YH-40 aircraft are made available for a minimum of 250 flight hours, the USAACDA will not be able to generate performance and other data on which to base its recommendations for the utilization of the YH-40 in the field force.

3. Request guidance.

Robert F. Bellmon
Colonel, Armor
Director

3rd Ind

Avn Branch DCSOPS Hq DA Wash DC 5 Aug 1955

TO: DCSOPS Hq DA Wash 25 DC

1. The situation described in 1st and 2nd Ind hereto has been investigated by the undersigned, and the following determined:

a. The three YH-40 aircraft assigned to USAAB for USAAB testing are barely adequate for that purpose, and production of additional aircraft in the foreseeable future will be assigned to the USAF for airframe stress and other testing, and to the Transportation Corps for the determination of maintenance and spare parts requirements.

b. The USAAB testing program would be severely hampered by the loss of any YH-40 flight hours, either by the loss of YH-40 aircraft to another agency, or in the event of an aircraft accident.

c. Prudence requires that the available YH-40 aircraft, which, because of their size and power, and because their flight characteristics are not now known, should be flown only by experienced aviators in order to reduce the possibility of their loss due to pilot error or inexperience to an absolute minimum.

d. With the exception of Major MacMillan, the USAACDA aviators for whom flight instruction in the YH-40 has been requested are recent graduates of flight school. Specifically, the provisions of AR 1-670 requiring a one (1) year initialization tour had to be waived in the case of both Col. Bellmon and WOJG Greer in order to permit their present assignment.

e. A review of USAACDA test programs (proposed) by the undersigned indicates that the great majority of such testing could be integrated into present USAAB test programs.

2. It is therefore recommended that the USAACDA be directed to effect such liaison with the USAAB as necessary in order to incorporate those test programs they feel are necessary into present USAAB test programs. This would insure a more efficient use of available assets, and simultaneously reduce, through the use of aviators of long experience, the risk permitting USAACDA aviators to pilot the experimental aircraft would entail.

> Arthur D. Gregory
> Colonel, Artillery
> Chief, Aviation Branch

4th Ind

Office of the Deputy Chief of Staff for Operations,
Headquarters, Department of the Army, Washington
25, DC, 11 August 1955

To: Commanding General, USA Aviation School &
Camp Rucker, Ala.
Chief, Aviation Branch, DCSOPS, Hq DA Wash
25 DC
President, US Army Aviation Board, Camp Rucker,
Ala.
Director, US Army Aviation Combat Developments
Agency, Camp Rucker, Ala.

1. The Deputy Chief of Staff for Operations wishes
to remind all concerned that the USAACDA was established at Camp Rucker for several reasons:

a. In order to provide the DCSOPS with an independent agency capable of basing its recommendations
concerning the future of army aviation in the field forces
on its own independent judgment.

b. In order that it would be in a physical position
to receive what logistic and training support it required
from both the US Army Aviation Board and the US Army
Aviation School and Center.

2. The Deputy Chief of Staff for Operations believes
that very little meaningful data concerning operation of
YH-40 aircraft by personnel with little flight experience,
as would be encountered in a mobilization situation, can
be obtained from test programs in which all of the aviators have seven (7) years flight experience, including
2,500 hours total flight time, and 1,000 hours helicopter
experience.

3. The Deputy Chief of Staff for Operations has received permission from the Vice Chief of Staff to have
twenty (20) graduates from the next two (2) Warrant
Officer Candidate Rotary Wing Flight Classes assigned
for a period of six months to the USAAB for utilization
as pilots of YH-40 aircraft undergoing test. Aviators of
great experience presently assigned to the USAAB will

be assigned to monitor such flight testing, but will *not* participate in flight testing under normal circumstances. It is believed that the pool of aviators possessing seven (7) years and many thousands of hours of flight experience will not be large enough to man the field force envisioned for the future, and that therefore large numbers of inexperienced aviators must be trained.

4. The President of the USAAB is directed to train the officers listed in the basic communication as YH-40 pilots as soon as possible, and to make available to the USAACDA YH-40 aircraft for a minimum flight test program of 250 hours.

5. The Deputy Chief of Staff wishes to state that while he has found this correspondence interesting, he is sure that he will not again be required to devote his time to solving problems that should not have arisen.

BY ORDER OF THE DCSOPS:
Howard G. Kellogg
Brigadier General, USA
Asst DCSOPS

"Jesus H. Christ!" WOJG Greer said. "You sure as hell won that one, Colonel."

"Colonel Roberts went a little too far," Bellmon said. "It was both too obviously chickenshit, and too obviously a grab for power. He lost that fight, but he's smart and he won't make the same mistakes the next time we get into it. Even this, if you think it through, Greer, is not all peaches and cream. I'm really on the Flying Club's—" he caught himself just in time, deleted "shit," and concluded—"list, now."

"Fuck 'em," WOJG Greer said, cheerfully.

"Close your sewer of a mouth, Mr. Greer," Colonel Bellmon said, very sharply, and when Greer looked at him in surprise, added: "And stand at attention, too, please."

Greer came to attention, a look of bafflement vanishing as he froze his facial features.

Colonel Bellmon pushed a lever on his intercom.

"Major MacMillan!"

"Yes, sir."

"Please report to me immediately," Colonel Bellmon said.

"On my way," MacMillan replied cheerfully.

MacMillan came into the office a moment later, walking like Groucho Marx, grinning broadly, and tipping off his fiber tropical helmet.

"Look what I found in the clothing store," he cried, happily.

It was too much for Colonel Bellmon. In the Frank Buck hat, and khaki short pants, MacMillan looked like a burlesque comedian.

"I asked you to report to me, Major," Bellmon said, icily.

MacMillan looked at him in surprise, and then saw he was serious. He sailed the Frank Buck tropical helmet out the door, came to attention, and saluted.

"Major MacMillan reporting as ordered, sir," he said.

MacMillan, Bellmon thought, didn't look much older than he had ten years before, when, as Technical Sergeant MacMillan, he had been with Bellmon in the stalag.

"The reason I have asked you gentlemen in to see me," Bellmon said, "is that it has come to my attention that you are guilty of conduct unbecoming to officers and gentlemen."

MacMillan and Greer stole quick, confused looks at one another.

"And the reason I have you standing here at attention is to convince you that I consider this whole matter quite serious."

"May I inquire what the colonel makes reference to, sir?" MacMillan asked, still at rigid attention.

"Your filthy mouth, Mac," Bellmon said. "And yours, Mr. Greer."

They both looked confused. Bellmon let them sweat a minute, and then went on.

"Mrs. Heatter was in here," Bellmon said. "In tears. Crying. She said she had to have a transfer."

"I'm not sure I follow you, sir," MacMillan said. "What was she crying about?"

"She said she liked her job, but that she was a Christian woman, and she could not continue to work under such conditions."

"What conditions, Colonel?" Greer asked. Bellmon thought

he looked about sixteen years old.

"Your filthy goddamned mouth is what I'm talking about, Mr. Greer," Colonel Bellmon said. "Your constant blasphemy and obscenity."

"Yes, sir," Greer said.

"Just Greer's filthy goddamned mouth, Colonel?" Mac-Millan asked, too innocently. "Or my goddamned filthy mouth, too?"

Bellmon stared at MacMillan in disbelief. Was MacMillan actually daring to mock him?

And then he recalled his own words.

"Shit!" he said. They all laughed.

He got control of himself in a moment.

"Oh, stand at ease," he said. "But listen to me, you two. I'm serious about this. Mrs. Heatter was really in here. She was really crying, and she was really upset. I've got enough trouble without her filing a complaint with civilian personnel about you two."

"I don't know what the hell she's talking about," Greer said, seriously. "I know what she's like. She carries Bible study lessons in her purse and reads them when she eats lunch. You don't think I was making a pass at her, or anything like that, do you?"

That thought hadn't even occurred to Bellmon.

"She's the kind who thinks that 'hell' is a dirty word, Greer," Bellmon said. "So don't use it."

"I thought I was watching it," Greer said. "But yes, sir, I'll watch it even more closely."

"We're all guilty, I'm sure," Bellmon said. "But she especially complained about you, Greer."

"Not about me?" MacMillan said.

"She said you don't seem to care what kind of filthy language he uses," Bellmon said. "So you watch Greer, and I'll be watching you. Understood?"

"Yes, sir."

"Take a look at this, Mac," Bellmon said, and handed him the YH40 correspondence.

"Jesus Christ," MacMillan said. "When Gregory and Roberts saw this, the shit must have really hit the fan."

Colonel Bellmon did not correct him, Greer noticed. Because it would have been necessary to eat his ass out if he had? Or because he had agreed with MacMillan's assessment and really didn't notice the language?

"So we're going to get a YH-40 to play with, are we?" MacMillan said.

It was another of MacMillan's classic examples of saying the right thing the wrong way. They weren't going to "play" with the YH-40. MacMillan knew as well as he did what they were going to do with it.

The YH-40 was a nine-passenger helicopter, powered by an 1,100 horsepower turbine engine. It was intended to replace the Sikorsky H-19 and H-34, which had a reciprocating gasoline engine—neither efficient nor entirely safe in helicopter operations. It was faster, smaller, and carried as many passengers (nine, without equipment) as the H-34. It was obviously going to be the helicopter with which the army would be equipped in the 1960s.

The "Y" in the designation stood for prototype, an acknowledgement that the production helicopters (the H-40s) would be different from the prototype YH-40s in detail. They would be changed to reflect what would be learned about them when they were tested.

It was Bellmon's job as director of the Aviation Combat Developments Agency to test the machine to see what it was capable of and to adapt this capability to what had become known as the "Flying Army." He would then request that changes be made to the machine so that it could better accomplish its duty.

Both looking after the changes and testing to see if the modified aircraft did what it was supposed to do was the function of the Aviation Board. They had tried and failed—by painting themselves as the only experts—to usurp Bellmon's responsibility and authority. The fight had gone as high as DCSOPS, and DCSOPS had cut the Cincinnati Flying Club off at the knees.

But getting a YH-40 for 250 hours was only the beginning of the fight. Bellmon could count on the Cincinnati Flying Club finding fault with any conclusion he reached which did not entirely agree with one of their own. He would have to be able to prove every point he made about the YH-40.

That was not, as MacMillan put it, getting a "YH-40 to play around with."

But Bellmon didn't correct him. He knew he hadn't heard the end of the battle with Colonel Bill Roberts. He felt very much alone, alone in a way neither MacMillan or Greer could understand. Right now, they were the only two people he could really count on. It would have made no sense to hurt Mac's feelings by correcting him.

VIII

VIII

(One)
The Officer's Open Mess
Camp Rucker, Alabama
22 August 1955

"Mrs. Hyde? I'm Barbara Bellmon," the woman said, walking briskly over to Rhonda with a smile on her face, and her hand extended. "I'm so glad you could come."

"It was very nice of you to ask me," Rhonda Wilson Hyde, Administrative Officer (Probationary) of the USA Aviation Combat Developments Agency said to the wife of the Director of the USAACDA.

"I thought we should get to know one another," Barbara Bellmon said. She led Rhonda into the barroom of the officer's open mess and waved her into a chair at a table. A GI waiter was immediately at their side.

"What can I get you, Miz Bellmon?" he asked.

"Oh, I think I'll have one of your wave-the-vermouth-cork-over-the-neck-of-the-gin-bottle martinis," Mrs. Bellmon said.

"Yes, Ma'am," the waiter said. He looked at Rhonda.

"The same for me, please," Rhonda said.

She liked this. Respectable married women in Dale and Houston counties did not go by themselves to a bar and order martini cocktails at lunchtime.

"I always like a martini before lunch," Barbara Bellmon said. "But I feel wicked if I do it at home."

"I know what you mean, Mrs. Bellmon," Rhonda said.

"Oh, call me 'Barbara,' please," Mrs. Bellmon said.

"And you call me 'Rhonda,'" Rhonda said, pleased with that too.

"We should have had lunch sooner," Barbara Bellmon said. "But I was out of town."

"Oh?"

"A wedding," Barbara Bellmon said. "Scotty Laird's sister's boy married my cousin Ted's daughter. That's pretty involved, I guess, isn't it? If you're an army brat, as I am, you simply presume that everybody knows who you mean."

"'Scotty' Laird? Is that the general who's coming here?"

"Yes," Barbara Bellmon said. "We grew up together, as the kids did. Army brats seem to wind up married to each other."

"That sounds very nice," Rhonda said. She found it interesting that Mrs. Bellmon was a friend of the incoming post commander. She had certainly started off in the right circles.

The waiter delivered the martinis.

"Here's to you and your new job," Barbara Bellmon said, raising her glass.

"Why, thank you," Rhonda said, and took a sip of the really icy, *really* dry martini.

"Do you like your job?" Barbara Bellmon asked.

"I'm just learning it," Rhonda confessed. "But I'm fascinated. I've been on the long distance telephone more in the last two weeks than I've ever been in my life."

"I'm sure it's quite a change from what you're used to," Barbara Bellmon said. There was something in her tone that Rhonda didn't like, but she couldn't put her finger on it.

"Yes, it is," she said smiling.

"You'll quickly learn that the army is a small world of its

own," Barbara Bellmon said. "Everybody knows everybody else."

"Your husband," Rhonda said, and then corrected herself, "Colonel Bellmon and Major MacMillan are old friends, I know that."

"They met in a POW camp," Barbara Bellmon said. "During World War II."

"That must have been tough on you," Rhonda said, sympathetically.

"We have a friend," Barbara Bellmon said. "Major Craig Lowell. I think you'd like him. Well, as proof of my small army world theory: the commandant of the stalag, which is what they call a POW camp, was a Colonel von Greiffenberg. He and my father had been classmates at the French cavalry school at Samur together."

"Was your father a soldier?" Rhonda asked.

"My maiden name was Waterford," Barbara Bellmon said.

It took Rhonda a second or two to pick up on that.

"General Waterford? The one with the tanks?"

"That's right," Mrs. Bellmon said.

"Well, my God, I'm impressed," Rhonda said.

"You shouldn't be," Barbara Bellmon said. "His friends called him 'Porky.'"

"You know, you just can't imagine anybody calling a *general* 'Porky.'"

"Only other generals called him that," Barbara Bellmon said. Rhonda wondered why she was getting this whole business, why Barbara Bellmon was trying to impress her with her army connections. Then she realized that if she had been the daughter of a famous tank general, a friend of Eisenhower and Patton and people like that, she'd want people to know, too.

"I'm really impressed," Rhonda said, truthfully.

"Well, I'm telling you what a small world it is," Barbara Bellmon went on. "After the war, my father met a young soldier who really impressed him, and he arranged for him to be commissioned."

That was the truth, Barbara Bellmon realized as she spoke, but it was not the whole truth and nothing but the truth. What had impressed her father about Private Craig W. Lowell was that he was a three-goal polo player.

"Can generals do that? I mean, make officers out of soldiers?"

Barbara Bellmon signaled the waiter for a second martini.

"Generals can do practically anything they want to do," Barbara Bellmon said. "That's why everybody wants to be a general." They laughed together.

"I was telling you about Craig Lowell," Barbara said. "Well, he married a German girl—"now that I admit I am stretching the truth, she thought, the distortions come so easily!—"and that's something that young officers just don't do. Like making a pass at their commanding officer's daughter. Or wife."

"I understand," Rhonda said.

"And who do you think the girl turned out to be?"

"I really can't guess," Rhonda replied.

"The daughter of Colonel, now Generalmajor, von Greiffenberg," Barbara Bellmon said. "They named their son after the general, who was then in a Russian POW camp. He wasn't released until 1950."

"But then everybody lived happily ever after? What a charming story!"

"Not really," Barbara Bellmon said. "When Craig was in Korea, the girl was killed in an automobile accident."

"Oh, how terrible!"

"Yes, it was. And what made it worse was that the man who killed her was also an army officer. A quartermaster major. He was cashiered, of course, but that didn't bring Craig's wife back."

"What happened to the baby?"

"He's being raised by his mother's family," Barbara Bellmon said.

"You really are just one big family then, aren't you?"

"Yes," Barbara Bellmon said, and then to the waiter: "Oh, that was quick!" The waiter set fresh martinis before them.

"I'm go glad you told me all of this," Rhonda said. "It helps me to understand so much!"

"There's one other thing you should understand," Barbara Bellmon said.

"What's that?"

"Army wives don't like to share their husbands," Barbara Bellmon said.

For a moment, Rhonda wasn't sure that she had heard right.

"I'm sure," she said, "that I don't know what you mean." She tried to sound as indignant as she could. While it was true that she thought that Colonel Bellmon was quite a man, and to be absolutely truthful about it, she had wondered what it would be like with him, that had been fantasy. She was not about to get involved with her boss. Especially since he had shown absolutely no interest in her.

"You know exactly what I mean," Barbara Bellmon said.

"I don't know . . ."

"You're not Bob's type," Barbara Bellmon said. "But on the other hand, if any man has it waved in his face often enough, he's going to take a sniff."

"I just don't know . . ." Rhonda protested.

"Mac MacMillan," Barbara Bellmon said, "is something else. He's not quite as bad as Craig Lowell, but he has been known to stray. When that happens, Roxy MacMillan is very unhappy. And when Roxy MacMillan, who is one of my very best friends, is unhappy, I'm unhappy. And if I'm unhappy, I can make things very unpleasant for you, Rhonda."

"You have no right to say these things to me!" Rhonda said.

"I have the right," Barbara Bellmon said. "I'm what they call the colonel's lady. And it's not all pouring tea, Rhonda. You'd better understand that, too."

Rhonda was now speechless.

"All I'm saying to you is stay away from the married men, officer and enlisted," Barbara Bellmon said. "If you're not getting what you need at home, and you can't find it off the post, stay away from our married men."

"I don't have to sit here and be insulted this way!" Rhonda said.

"If you want to satisfactorily complete your probationary period, you do," Barbara Bellmon said. "I'm holding all the aces. When my father taught me to play poker, he told me to go for the jugular."

She met Rhonda's eyes and held them for a moment.

"Have a go at young Mr. Greer," she said. "I'd rather have him involved with someone like you than have him get caught by one of the local belles."

Without thinking what she was saying, Rhonda said: "Greer is just a kid!"

"He's big enough," Barbara Bellmon said. "And they're supposed to be better when they're young. Just keep in mind, though, that Greer's part of the family. Sort of a little brother."

"I don't quite understand you."

"Get Mac to tell you about him sometime. They had quite an escapade in Indo-China together."

The waiter appeared.

"Your table is ready, Miz Bellmon," he said, handing her the check. Barbara Bellmon signed it.

"You know, of course, Rhonda," she said, "that when you complete your probationary period, you'll be eligible to join the officer's club." She met her eyes again. "Shall we have our lunch?" she asked.

"I'm famished," Rhonda said.

"Probably the martinis," Barbara Bellmon said and led Rhonda into the dining room.

(Two)
Augsburg, West Germany
26 September 1955

Major Craig W. Lowell spent most of the morning (from 0950 until 1215 hours) of 26 September 1955 in the PX cafeteria at the Hersfeld Kaserne of the 24th Armored Cavalry Regiment, drinking nickle coffee from a china mug and reading *The Stars and Stripes* and *Cavalier* and *True* magazines.

Major Lowell had flown to Hersfeld a full colonel of the Ordnance Section of Headquarters, Seventh Army, who was uneasy being flown about by junior officers and who had requested Major Lowell as pilot. Once in Hersfeld, however, reasoning that since Lowell was not an ordnance officer and therefore had nothing to contribute to his business with the 24th's commanding and ordnance officers and was in fact nothing more than a pilot, the ordnance colonel had told Major

Lowell to "go catch a cup of coffee somewhere, and I'll get word to you when I need you."

At 1215 hours, Major Lowell was summoned from the PX cafeteria to the officer's open mess by the ordnance colonel, who at that time had reasoned he had an obligation to see that his pilot was fed. Even if he was an airplane driver, he was a major, a field-grade officer; common military courtesy required that he be invited to eat with them.

Luncheon at the 24th Armored Cavalry officer's open mess was a little awkward for Major Lowell. The colonel commanding the 24th Armored Cavalry was there, as was his executive officer, his S-3 plans and training officer, his S-4 supply officer, and the commanding officers of Troops "A," "C," and "D." All of these officers were naturally armor officers, and most of them looked curiously at Major Lowell when the ordnance colonel introduced him as "my pilot."

Major Lowell was wearing the cavalry sabers superimposed upon a tank insignia of armor, an Expert Combat Infantry Badge (second award), and his aviator's wings. In contravention of regulations, he was not wearing any of the ribbons representing any of his many medals.

Lowell typically ran into two classes of armor officers, those who knew about Task Force Lowell and those who didn't. Of those who did know about it and knew that he had been its commander, eighty to ninety percent felt that both its reputation and the promotion and decoration of its commander were so much bullshit. These rather rejoiced to see that the army had finally caught up with him and thrown him out of armor on his ass. Those other armored officers (including a rare one here and there who had been in Task Force Lowell), who felt that it was one of the better operations in that fucked-up war in Frozen Chosen and that its commander fully deserved his Distinguished Service Cross and the gold leaf, were even more awkward when encountered. They were embarrassed to see the man who had led forty-four M46 tanks faster and further than anyone else reduced to flying a whirlybird.

Those two groups together consisted of perhaps ten percent of all armor officers. The other ninety percent had never heard of Task Force Lowell or of Major Craig Lowell. They were cavalrymen, stationed in a fort on the enemy's border, ready at a moment's notice to heed the sound of the trumpet and charge off to do battle, and they thought as much of an armor major who arrived driving a helicopter as they would have thought, a hundred years before, of a cavalry major who arrived at Fort Riley driving a mess wagon. Any cavalryman who would do something so degrading wasn't very much of a cavalryman.

There were no officers present at luncheon who had served under Major Lowell at the time he led Task Force Lowell, but there were, he was sure, at least two officers who connected him with Task Force Lowell and would thus have something to talk about when he was gone. The commanding officer of the 24th Armored Cavalry was one of them.

"Didn't you at one time work for General Paul Jiggs, Major?"

Brigadier General, then Lieutenant Colonel, Paul Jiggs had been the commanding officer of the 73rd Heavy Tank Battalion, from which Task Force Lowell had been formed.

"Yes, sir."

"I thought so," the colonel said. He did not pursue the subject. He had pegged Lowell for who he was, and whether he had pegged him as a brilliant armor commander or a spectacular fuck-up didn't matter; Lowell either deserved better than being a fucking chopper jockey or he was a real fuck-up. In either case, his presence was an embarrassment.

After luncheon, Major Lowell returned to the PX cafeteria and sat there among the off-duty enlisted men and the dependent wives until 1515 hours, when a sergeant came and fetched him. The ordnance colonel now desired to be flown back to Augsburg.

Lowell told himself that this was just not his lucky day. It would not have been pleasant if the ordnance bird had wanted to RON (Remain Over Night), for that would have meant spending the night in the O Club of the 24th Armored Cavalry. On the other hand, since the ordnance colonel had decided that he did not wish to spend the night on the East German border, this meant Lowell would be back in Augsburg in time for the monthly formal dinner dance, which he would be expected to attend.

Lowell dreaded unit parties. Because they bored him out of his mind, he generally managed to have himself sent away on a RON flight when they were scheduled. This time, he thought as he parked the Bell H-13 and supervised its refueling, he would not be successful in ducking the formal dinner dance.

Dress, mess, or Class "A" uniform with black tie was the required uniform for formal dinner-dance affairs. Dress or mess uniform were recommended but not prescribed. Dress and mess uniforms cost a small fortune, and commanders were reluctant to make the junior officers spend the money.

It had occurred to someone at Seventh Army, however, that aviators were paid more money every month than their non-flying peers, and what better way for them to spend that money than on mess and/or dress uniforms? Once they got the flyboys into mess and dress, maybe the others would be shamed into buying the uniforms.

Major Lowell knew that he was expected to show up in at least a dress uniform. He was a bachelor. Bachelor majors could afford uniforms. He elected to go in mess dress, which was the most elegant and most expensive of the options. He wasn't sure if he was trying to be a conscientious member of the staff, or whether he was doing it for himself. Perhaps it was just to remind himself—after the scornful looks of the armor officers at Hersfeld—that he had once been a pretty good tank commander himself, despite what he was now doing.

There are cavalry yellow stripes down the seams of armor officer's mess dress trousers, and the lapels are cavalry yellow. Each sleeve has golden cord, sewn in an eleborately curved pattern. Second lieutenants get one cord, colonels six. As a major, Lowell got to wear four golden cords. And a golden cummerbund.

He pinned his three rows of minuature medals to the right lapel. Around his neck, on a three-inch-wide purple ribbon, he hung the saucer-sized medal which signified that he had been named to the Order of St. George and St. Andrew by the King of Greece.

He looked, he thought, like something from a Sigmund Romberg operetta.

He dined with the chaplains; a Baptist who was visibly

uncomfortable in a place where the booze flowed like rivers, and the Roman Catholic, whom Lowell suspected of being a pansy. As soon as he decently could, he left them and went to the bar.

Though Lt. Colonel Withers had become a teetotal when he had been born again, he still believed in unit parties because they were family affairs. Withers came to him at the bar and, in the belief that he was skillfully killing two birds with one stone, suggested to Major Lowell that he dance with the officers' ladies.

The first three dances were uneventful. The fourth lady, the wife of a newly assigned captain, pressed her breasts and ungirdled belly against him. When this produced an involuntary reaction in his external reproductive anatomy, he made a valiant effort to withdraw from further close physical contact. This proved impossible to accomplish. The lady's midsection stayed riveted to his, and her fingers played with his ear. When the dance was over, she led him back to her table, hand in hand, her breast pressed against his arm. And then as he thanked her for the dance and politely nodded to her husband and the other captains and their wives, she loosened her hand from his and groped him.

He was profoundly grateful to Lt. Col. Withers for catching him at the bar after the dance. He was still in possession of ninety-eight percent of his common sense and recognized a dangerous situation when he saw one. He spent the rest of the party drinking plain soda water and listening to Lt. Col. Withers extoll the merits of membership in the Augsburg Military Post Christian Men's Club.

For the next week, he took his meals either in the unit messes, where dependents were not authorized, or on the economy, thus avoiding the club and the chance of seeing the captain's wife.

He learned that her husband, Captain Suites, was assigned to Special Rotary Wing Missions Branch. Captain Suites was an archtypical army aviator, who saw as his sole *raison d'être* the piloting of aircraft. He was personally an amiable moron, with a high-pitched giggle. Lowell dismissed him from thought after he'd given him a check ride and reported to the senior flight instructor (another amiable moron, a lieutenant colonel who affected highly polished half-Wellington boots and was seldom seen without his aviator sunglasses) that Captain Suites (pronounced "Soots") was safe to fly people from hither to yon in his H-13.

Lowell flew Monday, Tuesday, and Wednesday of that week: two missions, and four three-hour check rides. The next day, Thursday, he would have to spend at his desk. Lt. Col. Withers had learned of his paper-pushing skill and turned over to Lowell as much of it as he could. Since he would not be flying the next day, he could have a couple of drinks.

(Aviators were officially forbidden to drink more than one beer the night before flying. Lowell never even took the permitted one. The army's official opinion of his flying ability was a good deal higher than his own. He had no intention of taking off with alcohol dulling his senses or impairing his coordination, and drank only when he was not scheduled to fly.)

But he resisted the temptation to take a drink at the club. The lady who had groped him might be there. He went instead to the movies, and the movie turned out to be incredibly bad. He tried but failed to suffer through it and got up after an hour and walked out. Fate, he decided, had pointed him toward the booze. To avoid going to the club, he went downtown in the Jaguar and went to the Café Klug, an establishment catering to the wealthier Germans, where the patronage of Americans was discouraged both by the prices and a thoroughly nasty maître d'hôtel who took great pleasure in making it clear that they would be far more welcome elsewhere.

He made an exception for Major Lowell, however. The unusual *Amerikaner* not only never showed up in uniform, but was reliably reported to be closely connected with some very important people indeed, a rumor supported by the fact that the major spoke impeccable high-class German.

Lowell was given an on-the-spot, maître d'hôtel's promotion to *Herr Oberst* and bowed into the premises. He went to the bar and ordered a triple Johnny Walker black. (A triple in the

Cafe Klug, costing the equivalent in deutsche marks of $4.50, contained roughly as much whiskey as a thirty-five-cent single did in the officer's club.)

He sat there, half listening to the orchestra, dimly aware of inviting smiles from several women alone at the bar and thinking what he thought of as quasiphilosophical profundities:

There was a military version of *The War Is Over; Soldiers and Dogs Keep Off the Grass!* He stated it in his mind, and restated it, until he was satisfied; *When the War Is Over, Warriors Interfere with the Smooth Running of the Peacetime Army.*

He thought of others:

An Ambitious Officer Is Like a Brazen Prostitute; He Makes Ordinary People Uncomfortable.

If Men Ride Motorcycles Because It Is Symbolic Power Between the Legs, Then the Helicopter Is the Ultimate Motorcycle: Any Moron Can Get It Up.

Simple Problems May Be Corrected in the Army Provided the Solution Is Complex; Simple Solutions to Complex Problems Are Not Tolerated.

He had just ordered his fifth drink and told himself that it was the last when the maitre d'hôtel coughed behind him, and, his tone making it clear he hoped it wasn't really true, announced that the "lady" at the door said that she was joining the *Herr Oberst*.

"I thought," Mrs. Suites said in a somewhat hurt tone of voice, "that you would call."

He didn't reply, just put a question on his face.

"You did send Ken on that Remain Over Night, didn't you?" she asked.

She swiveled on her barstool, gave him a conspiratorial laugh over her shoulder, and swiveled back again. This time her knee pressed his groin.

"Aren't you going to buy me a drink?" she asked.

Without really thinking what he was doing, he signaled the barman to give her a drink.

(Three)

"I have looked the other way, Lowell," Lt. Col. Edgar R.

Withers said, "when your other escapades have been brought to my attention, but this time you've gone too far."

There is no way I can explain to this man—because he is incapable of understanding—that Phyllis Suites pursued me like a shark, Lowell thought. But it wouldn't matter if Lt. Col. Withers did understand what really had happened. If he saw Phyllis for what she was, a horny slut, I have still broken Army Commandments XI and XII; THOU SHALT NEVER DIDDLE A BROTHER OFFICER'S WIFE and THOU SHALT NEVER, NEVER, NEVER STICK YOUR DICK TO THE WIFE OF A SUBORDINATE.

Phyllis was both: the wife of a brother officer and the wife of a subordinate. He said what he was feeling.

"I am deeply ashamed of myself, Colonel," he said.

"And well you should be, Lowell. What in God's name were you thinking about?"

There was no response to that. He couldn't think of a thing to say. He certainly couldn't tell the colonel, who was president of the Augsburg Military Post Christian Men's Club, that Phyllis Suites had overcome his nearly valiant efforts to avoid her and had run him to ground in the Cafe Klug. Or that he was half in the bag when she found him, and consequently paying less than usual attention to his ethical obligations as an officer and a gentleman. Or that he was suffering from the symptoms of close to six weeks' self-imposed celibacy and thus easy prey to the sinful lusts of the flesh. He had not thought of Phyllis Suites as a wife and mother when she grabbed his wang; he had thought that if she was so interested in the object, then it could be reasonably presumed that she would make a marvelous cocksucker. And so she had turned out to be.

"I was deeply ashamed of myself," the Colonel said, "when Captain Suites came in here and asked for my help."

Oh, Jesus Christ!

"I'm sorry, very sorry, that you have become involved, Colonel," Lowell said.

"I will interpret that to mean that you are sorry I am involved, and not that you're sorry only because you've been caught."

"Yes, sir."

"I'll tell you frankly, Lowell, that my first reaction was to bring you up on charges. If I have ever seen a case of conduct unbecoming an officer and a gentleman, this is it. You have betrayed your oath of office, and the entire officer corps."

Rather than being offended by having my ass chewed by this self-righteous, self-important little bastard, Lowell thought, I seem to be reveling in it. I deserve it. I really *am* a shit. I knew what an amiable jackass Suites is, the archtypical husband of the woman who plays around. For that reason I should have stayed completely away from his wife, even if that meant jumping out the goddamned window of the Cafe Klug when she came in there.

"Out of consideration for Captain and Mrs. Suites and their children, however—and it is their interests with which I am concerned, not yours—I have decided to keep the resolution of the mess you have generated unofficial."

"Yes, sir," Lowell said.

"I know that you don't think much of us who believe in the Lord Jesus Christ as our Savior, Lowell," the colonel went on. "But it's come to your defense. 'Judge not,' it says in the Bible, 'lest ye be judged.' I am aware that you have lost your wife and that your loss probably has made you bitter. What I have tried to do, therefore, is find a Christian solution to this problem."

There followed a sixty-second silence during which the colonel looked at Lowell with mixed loathing and compassion.

"A requirement has been laid upon us to provide a rotary wing aviator to the military attaché at the United States Consulate General in Algiers. The requirement is for company grade, but I have obtained permission to send you. You will be gone six months. You will leave in two days. That doesn't give you much time, I realize, but you'll have to make do with what you have. You will not, repeat *not*, make any attempt to communicate with Mrs. Suites in any way before you leave, and I think it would be a good idea if you took your meals in one of the unit messes."

"Yes, sir," Lowell said. "I'd like to thank you, Colonel."

"After you read your efficiency report, Major, you won't want to thank me for anything. Just be grateful that you weren't court-martialed. There is simply no excuse for your conduct."

(Four)
Ozark, Alabama
22 December 1955

Melody Dutton came by her father's office during her lunch period to pick up the 1953 Ford so that she could run up the highway to Brundidge to get something for her mother's birthday. "Daddy, if I had my own car," she said, "I wouldn't have to take yours and leave you walking."

"Honey," Howard Dutton replied, "you're still a little girl, and still in school."

"Oh, Daddy!" she said, in exasperation, but she smiled at him.

She was not a little girl. She was a freshman at the university. She was eighteen, soon to be nineteen. She was wearing a tight skirt and a loose sweater, the current fashion, and you could see, *anybody* could see, that she had a young woman's body. The young men were already sniffing around her.

He didn't know how he was going to handle that, when she got a young man, when she fell in love with a young man, when she left him for a young man. Howard Dutton had loved his Melody from the time she was in her crib, all pink and smelling good. Not that he didn't love Howard, Jr. (who was sixteen) or Marcia (who was fourteen). They were wonderful children, too, but not like Melody. He had to try very hard to be fair and decent and not to let it show how much more he loved her than the other two.

Melody was tall, lithe, blond-haired and blue-eyed, and gentle, shy, and loving. There was nothing that made him happier than to sit in the living room and hear her play something good, like Chopin, on the piano. Prissy had told him he was out of his mind when he bought her the Steinway. Melody wasn't a musical genius or a prodigy, or whatever, she was just a thirteen-year-old girl who'd had three years of piano lessons, and she didn't need a piano like that.

About the only thing he could do for Melody now, aside from what he was going to do today, was see her through college and set her up for marriage. The trouble with that was every time he really started to think about that, he was reminded that he was going to lose her.

It was God's way, Howard reasoned. God made teen-aged girls beautiful so they would attract the men and have babies and start the whole cycle all over again. Howard had once thought he would give away half of everything he owned, or would ever own, if he could have just one more year of things the way they were, without them changing. That was when Melody was thirteen, and they'd gotten the braces off her teeth, and she was just turning into a young woman, though young enough still to sit on his lap and snuggle up and let him kiss her on the top of her head.

That was five years ago. Five years from now, Melody would possibly be holding her own baby on her lap. He would be a grandfather and she would be a mother, and it made a nice picture, but he didn't like to think about it.

"I don't think he's busy, Tommy," he heard Prissy say. "Why don't you stick your head in and see?"

The way she should have done that was to push the button on the intercom and *ask him* if he was free. And she should have said, "Mr. Waters is here," and not called Tommy "Tommy." But she wasn't really his secretary, she was his wife, and she did things the way she wanted to do them, and not the way a secretary was supposed to.

"Come on in, Tom," Howard Dutton called. Tom Z. Waters was wearing an open-collared plaid sport shirt, a zipper windbreaker, white Levis, and oil-tanned, brass-eyeleted boots, not hunting boots, but the kind engineers and surveyors wear. He looked like an apprentice surveyor, Howard thought. The only way you stopped thinking about Tom Z. Waters as a nice young man—the kind you want to give a boost up the ladder—was after you had a look at his balance sheet, his 1040, and the contents of the safe in the office upstairs over Zoghby's Emporium.

"You about ready, Howard?" Tommy asked.

Howard nodded, and walked around his desk to the door.

"Tommy and I are going out to Woody Dells," Howard said to his wife.

"You're going to be out there all the rest of the afternoon?" Prissy asked.

"We've got a lot to look at," Howard replied. Goddamn,

when he got his own private secretary, after they moved into the new bank, *she* damned well had better not ask him questions like that. All his private, personal secretary had better say was, "Yes, sir, Mr. Dutton," not ask him if he was going to be out all afternoon.

Parked at right angles to the curb was Tommy's GM carryall. They weren't going to be at Woody Dells all that long, and they wouldn't be going off the pavement, so they didn't really need the carryall. Another man would have come and picked him up in a car. But if he had come in a car, Prissy might have asked questions.

They drove out North Broad Street, out of town, crossed the highway, and drove two miles farther. They turned left and started down a steep hill. There was a sign, a regular-sized billboard. "WOODY DELLS," it said. "A Fine Place to Live. Homes from $19,550. FHA, VA, and Conventional Mortgages. Miller County Construction Company, Inc."

It had been a tree farm, loblolly pine planted in what the Rural Reclamation Administration had determined to be submarginal farmland—worked-out cotton fields.

There were two finished sample houses near the entrance (brick pillars, with split pine fencing running fifty yards the other side of the entrance). Each had a sign on the lawn saying, "FURNISHED SAMPLE. Sales Representatives on Duty." Another nearby had just the framing up. That would be another sample when it was finished.

Beyond the sample houses was a three-lane macadam road with concrete curbs and street signs reading Broad Vista Avenue. Two-lane macadam streets branched off it. There were signs of construction, bulldozers pulling out pine stumps and leveling lots, more bulldozers cutting more streets, pulpwood trucks hauling the pine off for the paper mills in Mobile, teams of men pouring concrete slabs, teams of rough carpenters putting up the frames.

"Is there anything out here you want to show me?" Tommy asked.

"No," Howard said, "I just needed a place I could say I was going."

"Thought so," Tommy said. He came to the end of the

pavement, slowed almost to a stop, then drove over the edge. Engine groaning in low gear, he continued over a graded dirt road, ready for macadam, and then off that onto raw land, following the guttered tracks of pulpwood trucks.

"Where the hell are you taking me?" Howard asked.

"I used to shoot quail out here," Tommy said. "You'd be surprised how close we are to the highway."

He had no sooner said it that Howard saw the highway. He would have sworn it was at least a mile further on, and he'd walked these hills all his life. Tommy drove roughly parallel to the highway for a quarter mile, until he found a place where he could ease the carryall up the steep shoulder and onto the pavement.

Thirty minutes later, Tommy drove the carryall right into the garage of Dothan Ford and Mercury, and parked it in a service stall. Then they walked into the showroom.

There it was, right in front, where people driving by could see it. Flaming fire-engine red with highly polished chrome. The roof was down, and that canvas thing—whatever they called it—was snapped in place over the folded-down top. White sidewall tires and white vinyl seats. The entire works.

"Well, Mayor Dutton, what do you think of it?" the owner of Dothan Ford and Mercury said, shaking his hand. "You need a car like this, Tommy," he added to Tommy Z. Waters.

"Wish I could afford a car like that," Tommy Z. Waters said.

"If you'll give me the papers," Howard Dutton said, "I'll give you the check. Tommy's going to drive it home for me."

Potted plants and chrome-and-plastic couches were moved out of the way, and the double glass doors in the front opened. Tommy very carefully maneuvered the convertible out of the showroom. The tires squealed on the polished linoleum whenever he turned the wheel, and the exhaust sounded like a motorboat.

"Mayor," Tommy said. Tommy always called him "Mayor" when they were in situations like this, sort of a token of respect. "If it's all right with you, I'll just go along now."

"Be careful with it," Howard Dutton said.

"I'll be there with it at seven thirty sharp," Tommy said.

"You better be," Howard said.

He didn't give a damn, he *really* didn't give a damn what Prissy was going to say, and when Tommy showed up at seven thirty sharp, she was going to have plenty to say. What really mattered was that so long as she lived, Melody would remember that when she was eighteen, her daddy had given her a flaming red Ford convertible with white seats and every option that Ford made, including air conditioning and power seats. That's what she would remember, being daddy's girl, getting a fantastic Christmas present from her daddy.

To hell with Prissy.

IX

(One)
Camp Rucker, Alabama
22 December 1955

Major General Angus Laird walked out of his office and through the front door of post headquarters where a Bell H-13D two-passenger helicopter sat parked. It was a special H-13D. Although it was mechanically identical to every other H-13D in the Aviation Center fleet, it was painted white. The others were painted olive-drab. The seats were upholstered in white leather, and there was an eight-by-ten-inch red plaque mounted on either side of the cockpit with the two silver stars of a major general (Scotty Laird's second star had come in the month before).

The helicopter was the aviation evolution of Patton's jeep, General Laird had often thought. There was no mistaking whose H-13 it was. It was as flashy as they could make it. General Laird believed along with General Patton that generals should stand out visually from the troops in the ranks.

General Laird walked around the H-13 and made the pre-

flight visual inspection. Then he got in the pilot's seat and
fastened his lap and shoulder harness and put the earphones on
over his cap with the two silver stars pinned to it. He threw
the master switch and heard the gyros for the artificial horizon
start to whirl. He adjusted the mixture and tuned in Ozark
Army Army Airfield local control on the radio. He reached down and
pulled up on the Engine Start switch. The starter whirred, and
the engine coughed blue smoke and then started.

It was a lot more complicated to start than a jeep, he thought,
but once you were in the air, it more than made up for it. It
would have taken him thirty minutes to drive a jeep to Hanchey
Field, where they were just starting to turn 3,500 acres of pine-
covered clay and sand into the world's largest airport designed
solely for rotary wing aircraft. He would be there in no more
than ten minutes in the chopper.

The engine and transmission oil temperature gauges moved
their needles to points on the circular dial where a strip of green
tape indicated the proper operating temperatures.

The rotor was making its fluckata-fluckata-fluckata noise
over his head. He pulled on the mike switch.

"Ozark local, this is Center Six."

"Go ahead, Center Six."

"Center Six on the ground at post headquarters. Request
clearance for a low level flight to Hanchey Field," General
Laird said.

"Ozark Army local control clears Center Six for a low level
flight to Hanchey Field. Be aware of traffic in the area. Have
a nice flight, General."

"Thank you," General Laird said. "Center Six light on the
skids."

He picked it up, moved into transitional lift, and then out
of ground effect. He lowered the nose and began to accelerate
quickly across the parade ground. It was a wonderful feeling.
God*damn*, it was like being a bird! He picked it up and flashed
a hundred feet over a line of barracks in a climbing turn to the
left.

The soaring was the best part. It was almost dreamlike. You
just pulled up on the cyclic, and you had your own personal
elevator.

He liked the feeling. He held the cyclic where it was and kept his eyes on the rotor rpm and the engine rmp needle indicators, which were both on the same gauge. The needles had to be superimposed. If you pulled too much cyclic, tried to take more power from the engine than it had to offer, you were in trouble. He wasn't running the risk of doing that. He wasn't a fool. He was well within what they called "the safe flight envelope."

He was over the pine forest now. He would be over the pine forest until he reached Hanchey Field.

His eyes flicked to the altimeter. The altitude it indicated was a couple of seconds behind where he really was. It worked on a diaphragm, and the dampening necessary made the indicator a couple of seconds slow. It was 1,000 feet, so he figured he was probably at 1,200 feet, maybe 1,300. High enough.

He just started to ease off on the cyclic when the engine above and behind him coughed. Coughed again. And died. The rotor and engine rpm needles split. The engine rpm needle swooped counterclockwise to zero. The rotor rpm indicator slowed less rapidly, but frighteningly.

What the hell?

He clamped the stick between his knees and pulled on the Engine Start switch. He heard it whine, thought he heard the engine cough.

In the last few seconds before the white H-13D struck the pine trees, Major General Laird knew what happened: *Carburetor ice! Carburetor ice! If you want to climb that fast, you are supposed to turn on the carburetor heat! Otherwise the carburetor intake, which is a venturi tube, loses temperature so rapidly that it freezes the moisture in the air passing through it and stops the fuel flow.*

He was going in. He reached forward and killed the Master switch.

Major General Laird and the white-painted H-13D hit the ground at a thirty-three degree angle at ninety knots. The helicopter sheared off the first two trees it hit and then struck a larger tree squarely in the middle. The trunk came through the plexiglass bubble and the instrument panel and crushed him against the seat. A fraction of a second later, the engine, torn loose from its mounts, smashed into the rear of the seat. He was probably dead before the gasoline rushed from the ruptured tanks through the remains of the bubble and soaked his flight suit.

WOJG Edward C. Greer was two miles away at the controls of an H-19. He had been in Montgomery, Alabama, at the Air War College, simultaneously running an errand for Colonel Bellmon and practicing low level flying. According to the standing operating procedure of the U.S. Army Aviation Center, aircraft commanders who wish to leave the area, or practice low level flight, were required to seek permission of the Ozark Army Airfield operations officer.

In the case of aircraft leaving the area, there was generally some officer trying to catch a ride, either to Montgomery or Atlanta, because of the lousy commercial service available from Dothan. In the case of aircraft wishing to practice low level flight, the operations officer generally directed the aircraft to areas on the post which were virtually flat.

Warrant officers junior grade were in no position to deny rides to senior officers or to protest that the whole purpose of practicing low level flight was to learn how to go between hills and mountains and over electric power lines.

The USAACDA policy, unofficial of course, was simply to ignore the U.S. Army Aviation Center standing operating procedure and to use one of their own. Greer had radioed the USAACDA operator when he was taking off from Ozark Army Airfield, and he telephoned him immediately upon landing at Maxwell Air Force to let him know he had safely arrived.

He had telephoned Mrs. Heatter just before he took off from Maxwell, and had been just about to reach for the FM radio to call in and say he was back on the Rucker Reservation when he saw the H-13D drop out of the sky.

He tuned the radio instead to 121.5 megacycles and called "MAYDAY! MAYDAY!" even as he put the Sikorksy into a steep, diving turn toward the crash site.

"Aircraft calling MAYDAY, go ahead."

"H-13 down halfway between Hanchey and the post," Greer reported. "No sign of fire. I'm landing."

"Down or crashed?"

"He went in from six seven hundred feet, anyway," Greer said. "Crashed."

Greer raised the nose of the H-19, to lose speed, and then put it quickly on the ground, as close as he could to the wrecked H-13. He unfastened his harness and climbed out of the cockpit window. His foot missed the spring-loaded cover of the step in the fuselage wall. He pushed himself away from the helicopter and fell to the ground. He fell on his back, hard, and it knocked the wind out of him. It took him a moment to get it back.

Then he ran through the pines to the wrecked helicopter. Only when he was close enough to smell the avgas did he recognize the H-13D as the white-painted bird of the post commander. He saw the twisted frame, and the twisted body inside.

And he smelled the gas again.

Sonofabitch was very likely to blow.

If it blew, there wouldn't be enough left of the body to fill a fire bucket.

He ran to the machine, shuddered, and then threw up when he saw what the crash had done to the body. In moments, though, he steeled himself, reached in, and tried to tug the body loose. The release for the seat and shoulder harnesses was jammed. He reached into the ankle pocket of his flight suit and took out his knife.

The knife had begun life as a bayonet for a .30 caliber U.S. carbine. Sergeant Ed Greer had ground it down to half the original length even before he'd left the 223rd Infantry to go to XIX Corps (Group). It was as sharp as he could make it, and the only time he had ever had a chance to use it (running around in the goddamned Indo-Chinese jungle with MacMillan and Felter), it had proved to be as good a people killer as he hoped it would be. A lot better than that thin English Fairbairn commando knife a lot of people had thought was hot enough shit to pay forty-five bucks for.

He sliced through the shoulder and lap belts and pulled the body from the wreck. He grabbed it as well as he could under the armpits, and he was twenty yards from the wreck when it exploded.

And then the body burst into flame. Greer looked down in horror and saw that the front of his flight suit was on fire. So were his sleeves and his legs and even his leather flying gloves.

He pulled the gloves off frantically and started to work the long zipper that ran down the front of the USAF flight suit. His fingers fumbled, and terror swept through him. He calmed himself, put both hands to the opening of the flight suit, and ripped it open with brute force.

When he had it off, he started throwing sand on the flaming body.

When the ambulance helicopter arrived a couple of minutes later, they found him wearing nothing but jump boots, and charred skivvies. He was sitting on the ground near the body retching from an empty stomach.

(Two)
Camp Rucker, Alabama
23 December 1955

HEADQUARTERS

CAMP RUCKER & THE ARMY AVIATION CENTER

CAMP RUCKER, ALABAMA

23 December 1955

SUBJECT: Christmas activities

TO: All subordinate units of USAAC

INFO: US Army Aviation Board
US Army Aviation Combat Developments Agency
US Army Signal Aviation Test & Support Activity

1. Mrs. Angus Laird has informed the undersigned that she and the other members of the family of the late Major General Angus Laird, while they appreciate the expression of sympathy implied, desire that General Laird's death in no way interfere with Christmas and New Year's activities previously scheduled at Camp Rucker.

2. No cancellation of activities scheduled to mark the Christmas and New Year's holidays is encouraged or desired.

3. A memorial ceremony honoring Major General Angus Laird will be conducted at Parade Field #2 at 0815 hours 26 December 1955. Participation of all USAAC subordinate units is expected. Participation by USAAB, USAACDA, and USASATSA is invited.

4. Major General Angus Laird will be interred at the cemetery of the United States Military Academy at West Point at 1600 hours 26 December 1955.

> William F. Adair
> Colonel, Corps of Engineers
> (Acting) Commanding Officer

The army does not know how to cope with civilian dignitaries in matters of protocol. The tendency is to attempt to equate civilians of surrounding communities with their military counterparts.

Prissy (Mrs. Howard) Dutton barely knew Jeannie (Mrs. Angus) Laird, but when she and her daughter Melody showed up at Quarters # 1 to pay their respects to the widow, they were immediately ushered into the room (which had been Scotty Laird's study) where the widow was surrounded by the senior ladies of the post. Prissy Dutton was the mayor's wife and thus Jeannie Laird's peer.

Jeannie Laird was glad to see her, not for the ritual expression of sympathy, but for the ritual offer to help in any way she could, which she was sure would follow.

"There is something," she said, "now that you mention it."

"Anything," Prissy said. "Anything at all."

"Do you have your car with you?" Jeannie Laird asked.

"We came in my daughter's car," Prissy said.

"I want to go over to the hospital," Jeannie Laird said. "And I want to do so as quietly as possible. Could I borrow your car? And perhaps Melody to drive me?"

"Certainly," Prissy said. "Would you like me to go with you?"

"No, what I want Melody to do, if you would, dear, is bring your car up to the kitchen door. And then I'll just run out and jump in, and no one will see me. We won't be gone long. But there is something I have to do."

In the Ford convertible on the way to the hospital, Jeannie Laird told Melody that the pilot of another helicopter had seen her husband crash, had immediately landed to see if he could help somehow, and in pulling General Laird's body from the wreckage, had been badly burned.

"I think they're going to decorate him," Jeannie Laird said. "But I wanted to thank him myself."

When they got to the hospital, Jeannie Laird sent Melody inside alone to ask what room WOJG Edward C. Greer had been assigned. When Melody found out, Jeannie Laird told her where to drive in the maze of hospital buildings.

"You sure know your way around here," Melody said.

"I've worked here three afternoons a week," Jeannie Laird said. "Two afternoons pushing the library cart around and one afternoon in the maternity ward teaching young mothers how to wash their babies." She paused. "I'm going to miss it," she said.

She showed Melody where to park the car, next to one of the interconnected single-story frame buildings, and then she led her inside through a door above which was written, "FIRE EXIT ONLY—NO ADMITTANCE."

Melody followed her down a polished linoleum corridor to a ward marked BURNS.

Melody didn't know what to do. She didn't want to see somebody all burned up, but she couldn't back out.

Jeannie Laird knocked at a wooden door, and without waiting she walked in.

There was a young man in the bed, both hands wrapped in white gauze. There was more gauze wrapped around his otherwise bare chest, and still more around his right leg.

The only clothing he was wearing was a pair of pajamas. The right leg of those was cut off above the knee. Melody could see the hair around his thing peeking out of the fly. She flushed and looked away. He didn't have any eyebrows. Where they were supposed to be, he was coated with a pink grease.

She realized his eyebrows had been burned off. He didn't look old enough to have done what Mrs. Laird said he had done.

"Ladies, I am sorry to say I think you're in the wrong place," Greer said.

"I don't think so. I'm Jean Laird."

"Jesus!" Greer said, then: "Sorry."

"And this is Melody Dutton," Jeannie Greer said. "She was kind enough to drive me over here."

"Hi!" Melody said. Greer looked at Melody and nodded his head, just once.

"I wanted to thank you, Mr. Greer," Jeannie Laird said, "for what you tried to do for Scotty."

"Nothing to thank me for," Greer said.

"Everyone has been telling me he went quickly, without pain," Jeannie Laird said. Greer nodded. "If that happens to be true, I'd like to hear that from you. You saw it. No one else did."

"He went quick," Greer said.

"He was dead when you got there?" Jeannie Laird asked.

"Oh, yeah," Greer said. "He died when it hit."

"Then why did you . . . risk what you did, to do what you did?"

Greer looked at her a moment. Then he shrugged.

"Then you did what you did more for me, than for my husband?" Jeannie Laird asked. After a moment, Melody realized that what Mrs. Laird was asking was why Greer had risked his life to pull a corpse from a wreck. And then she understood why: because otherwise the body would have burned.

"I did it because I would want somebody to do the same thing for me," Greer said.

"If it makes you feel any better, Mr. Greer, Scotty would have done the same thing for you had the circumstances been reversed," Jeannie Laird said, and then, for just a moment, her voice broke and there was the suggestion of a sob. Then she got control of herself.

"I've brought you something, Mr. Greer," she said. She reached in her purse and came out with a battered silver flask. She handed it to him.

"I don't want that," Greer said, uncomfortably.

"If it wasn't for you, Mr. Greer," Jeannie Laird said, "it would have melted."

"Jesus Christ!" Greer said.

"I'm sure giving it to you would be what Scotty would want me to do with it," she said. She laid it on the bed. He picked it up awkwardly in his bandaged hands. Melody saw there were tears in his eyes.

"There's something in it," Greer said.

"Then I think we should drink it," Jeannie Laird said. "Don't you?"

"Why not?" Greer said. His voice broke.

Jeannie picked the flask up, opened it, and tilted it up.

"Good brandy," she said. "That was his medicine for everything."

She started to hand him the flask, and then saw how encumbered he was with the bandages. She held it to his mouth. He took a healthy swallow. Then Jeannie handed the flask to Melody. Melody didn't want to drink straight liquor, and she especially didn't want to do it from a dead man's flask. But she realized there was nothing she could do. She took a swallow. It burned her throat. It made her cough.

"I don't think your friend is used to booze," Greer said.

The door opened. Bob and Barbara Bellmon started to come into the room, but stopped when they saw Greer had visitors. They continued when they saw who it was.

"You all right, Jeannie?" Colonel Bellmon asked.

"We've just been having a little drink," Jeannie said. "Recognize this, Bob?"

"How well," he said.

"Scotty carried that for twenty years," she said. "Longer."

"I think you'd better hang on to it, Mrs. Laird," Greer said. "Thank you just the same."

"I've told Mr. Greer that Scotty would want him to have it. Do you think he would?"

"Absolutely," Barbara Bellmon said. "Absolutely."

Colonel Bellmon took the flask, shook it, and opened it.

"Here's to you, Scotty," he said, and took a large swallow, and then handed it to his wife. Barbara Bellmon took a large swallow, but said nothing.

They passed the flask between them, Melody included, until it was empty. Jeannie Laird and Barbara Bellmon took turns holding it to Greer's mouth.

"Now that it's all gone," Jeannie Laird said, "that probably wasn't the best thing we could do for Mr. Greer."

"I just checked with the flight surgeon," Colonel Bellmon said. "He'll be out of those bandages tomorrow except for his hands. He looks worse than he is."

"Hell, I was hoping for a thirty-day convalescent leave," Greer said.

"You've got it," Colonel Bellmon said.

"I was only kidding, Colonel," Greer said.

"I'm not," Colonel Bellmon said. "By the power vested in me by God and other senior headquarters, the hospital commander and the flight surgeon concurring, you are, as of midnight, on thirty-days' convalescent leave."

"Thank you," Greer said.

"Can I help you get home?" Jeannie Laird asked. She turned to Bellmon. "We can have him flown home, can't we, Bob?"

"He can be flown anyplace he wants to go," Bellmon said.

There was something about the reply that wasn't right, and Melody Dutton picked up on it.

"I'm going to have to get back to my quarters," Jeannie Laird said. She walked to the bed and shook Greer's wrist above the bandages. "Thank you again, Mr. Greer."

"I'm really sorry, Mrs. Laird," Greer said.

"If there's room for me," Barbara Bellmon said, "I'll catch a ride with you. Bob can pick me up over there."

In Melody's Ford, Mrs. Laird said, "A fine young man. He's just a kid. You expect warrant officers to be bald-headed and middle-aged."

"He's not old enough to vote," Barbara Bellmon said. "Or drink. You heard about him and MacMillan in Indo-China, didn't you?"

Jeannie Laird had not heard. Barbara Bellmon told her. And Melody Dutton was fascinated, awed. And then, because it gave them something else to talk about, besides Scotty Laird, Barbara Bellmon told Jeannie what else she knew about Warrant Officer Junior Grade Edward C. Greer.

"Bob got the CIC/FBI Complete Background Investigation report on him when he had to have a Top Secret security clearance," she said. "It reads like a cheap novel. He was raised in a carnival. His father ran a freak show. His mother, who never bothered to marry his father, ran off when he was four months old. He was raised by whatever women his father happened to be playing house with at the moment."

"That's terrible," Jeannie Laird said.

"And then by a court reporter in Indiana," Barbara Bellmon said. "The court reporter felt sorry for him and took him in when his father went to jail. She taught him to use one of those little machines . . ."

"Stenotype?"

"Right. And then he ran off and joined the army. He wound up working for E. Z. Black, and Black sent him to flight school."

"Then he doesn't have a family?" Jeannie Laird asked.

"Just his father, and he's still in prison," Barbara Bellmon said.

"Then where's he going on his leave?" Jeannie Laird asked.

"The BOQ, probably. Oh, we asked him for Christmas. And so did Roxy MacMillan. Mac is alive because of Greer, and Roxy can be very determined when she wants to be. I guess he feels uncomfortable with families."

Melody Dutton repeated the story that night at supper, leaving out the details she knew would drive her father and mother up the wall. In her version of the story, WOJG Greer was an orphan who had no place to go for Christmas.

As Melody thought she would be, her mother was touched by the story of an orphan with no place to go for Christmas dinner. She telephoned WOJG Greer at his BOQ the next day. WOJG Greer politely thanked her but told her that he had a previous engagement.

Melody next saw him at the memorial services for General Laird on Parade Ground No. 2. Mrs. Laird had seen to it that a seat had been reserved for him on the VIP stand, in the section reserved for "friends of the family."

Melody saw that someone must have dressed him in his dress uniform, for his hands were still swathed in bandages. She saw that the Vice Chief of Staff of the U.S. Army, General E. Z. Black, who had been visibly bored when he was introduced to her father, wrapped his arms around Greer's shoulders when he saw him.

And she heard what he said, not able to entirely hide his emotions:

"Goddamnit, Greer, I'm glad to see you."

"Aw, shit, boss," Greer said, and then Greer and the Vice Chief of Staff of the U.S. Army laughed together.

And her mother went up to him, and said: "Mr. Greer, we're having a few people in for a buffet afterward. We'd like you to come. We'll take you back and forth, of course."

While her mother was talking to him, Greer was looking at Melody. That gave her a very strange feeling in the pit of her stomach, and when she saw him nodding his head, she felt her heart beat a little faster.

When the memorial ceremony was over, they transferred General Laird's flag-covered casket from the M48 tank on which it had come to the parade ground to the H-34 which would fly it to Ozark Army Airfield. There an air force transport waited to fly it to West Point along with all the generals who had come here for the ceremony. Afterward, Melody's mother went and led Greer by the arm to their Mercury.

He rode up in front with her father and didn't say a word all the way into Ozark. Melody saw that he had a scar on his neck. She wondered if he had gotten the scar as a boy, jumping over a fence or something, or whether he had gotten it as a soldier.

In the Dutton house, he made himself as inconspicuous as possible. Melody found him in her father's office, trying without much success to turn the pages of a magazine with his bandaged hands.

She got him a plate from the buffet and fed him. When their eyes met, she had a weak feeling in the pit of her stomach again.

"You're uncomfortable here, aren't you?" she asked.

He just looked at her and said nothing.

"Come on," Melody said. "I'll take you out to the post."

"Thank you," he said.

On the way to the post, she asked: "Where are you going to spend New Year's Eve?"

"At the club, probably. Not the main club. The annex."

"Who's going to hold your drink for you?" she asked.

"What do you want from me?" he asked.

"I was hoping for an invitation," she said.

"Why would you want to do that? Don't tell me you don't already have a date."

"You want to take me or not?"

"You're not my kind of people," he said.

"We won't know that until we know each other better, will we?" Melody replied.

"You wouldn't want to go to the annex," he said.

"I want to go to the main club with you," Melody said. "I'll pick you up and take you home. You can't drive, anyway."

"I drove to the parade ground," he said. "I can drive."

She interpreted that as an acceptance. After she dropped him by his car at the parade ground, she went home and called the boy she had had a date with at the Ozark Country Club. She told him she was sorry, but she wouldn't be in town.

She tried to call Greer three times between then and New Year's Eve, but he never answered the telephone. On New Year's Eve, she got dressed about half past six in an off-the-shoulder evening dress. She tried to call him again. This time his phone gave her a busy signal. When she kept trying, and still got the busy signal, she decided the phone was off the hook, whether by accident or intentionally.

When he didn't show up by seven thirty, she wondered if she had the courage to go out there. She worried that she was frightening him off. When it was time for her parents to go out to the post, and he still hadn't showed up, she lied to them. She told them he had called and was delayed, and that they should go out. She would be along later.

When he didn't come by half past eight, she went out and got in the Ford convertible, and crying, told herself that she was going to go out to his BOQ and really tell him off. If he didn't want to take her out, he should have been enough of a gentleman to tell her so, not let her get all dressed up and then not show up.

When she got to the post, she realized she didn't know where he lived. She turned around and went back to the MP house at the gate, where an obliging MP, who made it plain he thought she was something special as a woman, looked up

GREER, Edw C WOJG (USAACDA) in the post telephone book. He lived in BOQ T-108, he told her, which was down behind the field house.

Melody found T-108, one of three identical two-story buildings in a row, without any trouble. And Greer's car was in the parking lot, the only one there.

His name was on a small cardboard sign stapled to a door on the second floor.

She knocked on the door.

"Go the fuck away!" he called out.

Melody flushed and started to turn to leave. But then she realized that he didn't know, couldn't know, that it was her.

She went to the door, and raised her hand to knock again. Then she changed her mind and pushed it open.

He was sitting in an upholstered chair, a magazine in his lap, a bottle of whiskey and a glass on a table beside him. A television set was playing.

When he saw her, he looked away. Then he got up and looked out the window. She saw that he was wearing a purple bathrobe and white pajama bottoms. A pair of white hospital slippers was in front of the chair. He had stolen them, she realized. Then she thought, if I knew he didn't have a bathrobe or pajamas, I would have bought them for him for Christmas.

"What the hell's the matter with you?" he asked, his back to her. "Coming to a BOQ?"

"I thought we had a date," she said.

"You thought that," he accused. "I didn't say anything."

"I broke my date to go with you," she said.

"Jesus H. Christ!" he said.

She started to cry.

"Oh, for Christ's sake!" Greer said. "What the hell is the matter with you anyway?"

"Why didn't you call me?" she asked. "You could have at least called me."

"I thought you'd get the message," he said. "Jesus, what do you want from me, anyway?"

"This is how you're going to spend New Year's Eve? All alone? Getting drunk by yourself? What's wrong with you, anyhow?"

"Look, Melody, or whatever your name is..."

"You know damned well what my name is!"

"Look, honey," he said, "you don't want to get involved with somebody like me."

"Why not?"

"Because I'm a fucking soldier, that's why," he said. "There's more," he added darkly.

"Your father's in jail, is that what you mean?"

"Who the hell told you that?" he asked, genuinely surprised that she knew. "Yeah, that's what I mean. Among other things."

"I'm not afraid of you," Melody said. "And I don't care about your father."

"Yeah, but just wait until His Honor the Mayor hears about it."

"Is that all that's bothering you?" Melody asked.

"That's just for openers," Greer said.

"Where's your uniform?" Melody asked. "I told my father and mother we'd meet them at the club, and we're going to meet them."

"What happens to me when he finds out?" Greer said. "About my father, I mean? And you can't tell me he's pleased with the notion of you going out with a soldier in the first place."

"Where's your uniform?" Melody asked, and when he didn't answer her (at least he hadn't told her to get out), she went looking for it. She found the BOQ consisted of two rooms, the room she was in, sort of a living room, and a bedroom. In the bedroom there was a doorless closet, which was covered with a cotton curtain. She pushed the curtain aside and saw that it was jammed full of uniforms.

"Which one of these?" she asked. She looked over her shoulder. He was standing in the doorway.

"What do you plan to do, dress me?" he asked.

She met his eyes. "Yes," she said. "You can't dress yourself."

"The blue one," he said. She turned and took a blue tunic and trousers from the closet.

"Jesus!" he said. "Just put it on the bed."

She laid the tunic on the bed.

"And get me a white shirt from the dresser drawers," he said. When she was sliding drawers open, he said: "Christ, you're even going to have to put my socks on."

"Sit down and I'll put them on," Melody said.

He sat down on the bed. She found socks in the chest of drawers and then remembered underwear. She found jockey shorts and a T-shirt in another drawer, and then thought about a necktie. She didn't know how to tie a man's necktie. What was she going to do about that?

She went to where he was sitting on the bed. He avoided looking at her. She squatted and forced a laugh, and said, "I don't have much experience doing this."

She tugged his sock on. She looked up at him, pleasure in her eyes.

"There!" she said. "One down and one to go!"

"Shit!" he said, and it was a cry of anguish. He twisted on the bed to get around her, to get up. When he did, she saw his thing, hard, erect, poking out of the fly of his pajamas.

He got that because he was looking down my dress at my breasts, she thought.

"Goddamnit, why don't you just get out of here?" he said, when he had gained his feet.

"Obviously," Melody heard herself say, "because I don't want to."

"Don't tease me," he said. "Goddamnit, don't you tease me."

"I'm not going to tease you," she said.

"You know what's going to happen to your little schoolgirl's ass if you don't get it out that door, don't you?" he said.

Melody Dutton, as if she was in a dream, stood up, contorted her body, and reached behind for the zipper on her evening gown. The gown had a built-in bra, and when she stepped out of the gown, she was naked except for a brief pair of panties. Meeting his eyes, she slid them down off her hips. She went to him and untied the cord of his pajama pants. Then she lay on the bed.

"You dumb little shit," Ed Greer said to her no more than two minutes later. "What did you do that for?"

"I wanted to," she said.

"I never copped a cherry before," Greer said.

"How did it feel?" she asked, nastily, aware that she was close to tears.

"Oh, Jesus Christ!" he said, and hugged her to him, and it was all right.

"Did you hurt your hands?" Melody asked and sat up and held them gently in her own.

"Who cares?" he asked. She smiled down at him.

"It didn't hurt as much as I thought it would," she said. "In case you're wondering."

"But it did hurt?" he said.

"Not after a while," she said.

"You're sure?" he asked. "I mean, I didn't break anything, did I?"

Melody leaned over and kissed him.

"Happy New Year," she said.

"Jesus, your parents," he said. "They're at the club."

Howard Dutton *knew* the moment he saw Melody and the soldier with the burned hands walking across the floor to their table. There was a look in Melody's eyes (not guilt) that had never been there before. And there was proof later, the way they looked at each other, the way that Melody blushed a little.

Prissy didn't suspect a thing. That was to be expected. Prissy didn't have the brains she was born with. All Prissy saw in this boy was the orphan needing a family.

But Howard Dutton knew. While the boy went to the men's room, he'd told Melody he thought Greer was an unusual young man, and when Melody had said, "I'm going to marry him, Daddy," he wasn't all surprised.

Howard Dutton said—calmly—because he knew there was nothing else he could say, "We'll talk about it, honey."

And he decided that first off, they would have to get the boy out of the army. He didn't want Melody running off to the four corners of the world like a camp follower. He wanted her right here in Ozark. There was plenty of room for the boy. If not in the bank, then in one of the companies.

X

(One)
The Consulate General of the United States
Alger, Département d'Algéier, République Française
22 June 1956

Major Craig W. Lowell, with Sergeant William H. Franklin beside him, flew the Hiller H-23 over the desert due north from the foothills of the Atlas Mountains until he reached the Mediterannean. Then he turned right, several hundred yards out to sea, and flew along the beach and the coastal highway very low until he reached Algiers. He picked it up to a thousand feet then and flew directly across the city itself to the airport.

The crew chief came out while they were still shutting the bird down to deliver the message that the military attaché, a starchy infantry full bull colonel wanted to see Major Lowell right away. Then he said, in awe: "Holy Christ! Did you see that?" He pointed to the tail structure of the Hiller, where half a dozen bullet holes stitched the covering.

"Yeah," Sergeant Franklin said, dryly sarcastic. He was a tall, pleasant-faced, twenty-one-year-old black man. "I happened to be there when it happened."

"You better get a picture of that, too, Bill," Major Lowell said. "First a shot of the holes, and then rip the covering away and see what damage it did inside."

"Jesus Christ, Major," Sergeant Franklin said, examining the damage closely. In his dusty khaki shirt and shorts, he looked very much like the Norman Rockwell painting of an Eagle scout. "They came a hell of a lot closer than I thought they did."

"These things are a lot tougher than anybody believes," Lowell said. "And can take much more of a beating. As your properly focused, perfectly exposed movies are going to prove."

"Can I wait till I stop shitting my pants?" Sergeant Franklin said. He opened the side of a Paillard Bolex 16 mm motion picture camera, removed the exposed film it contained and reloaded it. Lowell had bought the expensive Swiss-made camera when the issue Eyemo camera had given Sergeant Franklin trouble. "Otherwise, the flick will shake a lot."

Lowell patted him on the shoulder.

"I am sure that you will do your usual splendid work," he said.

Franklin responded to the sarcasm in kind. "Yah, suh, boss. I does mah best foah you, boss."

Lowell affectionately punched his arm and got out of the helicopter and walked to his Jaguar. He started for the consulate, debating en route whether to report as he was—that is, in a short-sleeved, somewhat sweaty, open-necked tropical shirt and trousers—or to stop by his suite in the Hotel d'Angleterre on the Avenue Foch and change into something more in keeping with the formal atmosphere of the Consulate General. He elected to change uniforms. The military attaché was a starchy old bastard, and all he needed from him was a lousy efficiency report to go with the lousy efficiency report he'd received from Lt. Col. Withers.

He parked the Jag behind the elegant baroque villa that served as the Consulate building and had himself let in the back door by one of the Marine guards. When he saw that the military attaché had chosen that day to wear a white uniform, he was happy that he had changed into fresh tropical worsted tunic and trousers. He went through the prescribed ritual, "Sir,

Major Lowell reporting to the military attaché as ordered," and standing at attention until given at ease. It seemed a little absurd in the baroque splendor of the villa, but he sensed the colonel expected it.

"Rest, Lowell," the colonel said. "Would you like a little something to cut the dust?"

"I would be profoundly grateful for a vodka tonic, sir."

"But you'll take a little neat scotch, right?"

"Yes, sir, with equal gratitude."

"How did it go?" the attaché asked, taking a bottle of scotch and what looked like Kraft cheese glasses from a drawer of the enormous mahogany desk.

"They put in a company and a half—a company, plus half the heavy weapons platoon and a signal section—in about five minutes. Against automatic weapons fire I would rate at medium to heavy," Lowell said.

"What kind?"

"German and U.S. light .30s, I think. A couple of Browning .50s."

"And they didn't get their whirlybirds shot down?"

"They all got in all right," Lowell said. "Several of them are going to have to be either repaired on site or destroyed. They won't fly."

"And you have all this in your movies, right?"

"Yes, sir."

"That really surprises me," the colonel admitted. "I would have given good odds that a good PFC with a BAR could knock those things out of the sky like a skeet shooter."

"I'm really impressed with how tough the H-21s are. For that matter, all of them: I took half a dozen hits in the H-23 and didn't know it until we landed."

"Sergeant Franklin all right?"

"Yes, sir. Have we got anything on hazardous duty pay for him?"

"Yeah, they turned it down. And they turned down flight pay, too. It's not authorized. What I'm going to do is up his housing allowance. The State Department pays for that, and they're willing to go along. In money terms, he'll do better than he would with flight and hazardous duty pay. It's not right; he should get credit for sticking his ass in the line of fire, but it's the best I can do."

"Thank you, sir," Lowell said. "I appreciate your efforts."

"You're not leaning on him, are you, Lowell? I mean, he really is a volunteer?"

"Yes, sir."

"I don't like to lean on troops," the colonel said, and then in the next breath: "What do you intend to do about your efficiency report?"

"Sir?"

"I've been waiting for your 'Exception to Rating and Indorsement,'" the colonel said.

"Colonel," Lowell said, "I'm guilty as charged."

"Bullshit," the colonel said. "You're guilty of getting your wick dipped, not of 'conduct suggesting a lack of the high moral standards required of an officer.' You'll never get rid of the gold oak leaf if you let that stay in your record."

"Sir, I don't know what I can do," Lowell said.

The colonel took a sheaf of paper and carbons from his desk drawer and threw it on the table.

OFFICE OF THE MILITARY ATTACHE

THE CONSULATE GENERAL OF THE UNITED STATES

ALGIERS, ALGERIA

APO 303, C/O POSTMASTER, NEW YORK, N.Y.

> 201-LOWELL, Craig W. Maj 0439067
> 21 June 1956

SUBJECT: Exception to the Efficiency Report of 30 November 1955 and the Indorsement Thereto.

TO: Secretary of the Army
            Department of the Army
            Washington 25, D.C.

In the absence of any specific allegations concerning the moral conduct of the undersigned, the undersigned

protests the entire tone of subject efficiency report and
the indorsement thereto and requests that it be expunged
from his record.

Craig W. Lowell
Major, Armor
Assistant Military Attache

1st Ind

Office of the Military Attache
United States Consulate General   23 June 1956

Algiers, Algeria, France
TO: The Chief of Staff
    United States Army
    Washington, D.C.

1. Recommend approval.

2. In the period subject officer has been assigned to the
Office of the Military Attache, U.S. Consulate General, Algiers, Algeria, he has been under the close and personal su-
pervision and observation of the undersigned. Not only has he
demonstrated the highest personal standards to be expected of
an officer, but has virtually daily risked his life in observing
the operations of the French Army against the Algerian insurgents.

3. That his conduct has reflected credit upon the United
States, as well as the United States Army, is made evident by
the letter of commendation from the Consulate General (attached as Enclosure I) and by the citation accompanying the
award to subject officer of the Legion of Honor, Class of
Chevalier, by the Governor General of Algeria in the name of
the French Republic. (Translation of citation attached as Enclosure II. The medal and the citation is currently being for-
warded, through State Department channels, to the Office of
Congressional Liaison, U.S. Department of State, requesting
Congressional approval of the Award of a Foreign Decoration
to a Serving Officer in Peacetime.)

4. It is clear to the undersigned, based on his twenty-nine
(29) years of commissioned service that this officer has been
grievously wronged in a personal vendetta, in all probability

based on personal jealousy. Not only has this officer been promoted to his present grade long before his contemporaries, but is obviously destined, in the absence of petty chicanery against him, for much higher grade and responsibility.

5. The undersigned has been authorized to state that the Consul General concurs in this indorsement.

Ralph G. Lemes
Colonel, Infantry
Military Attache

The indorsement was already signed.

"I don't know what to say," Lowell said.

"Just don't believe any of that heroic diplomat bullshit," the colonel said. "And for Christ's sake, keep your pecker in your pocket from now on."

"You didn't have to do this," Lowell pursued.

"No," the colonel said. "I didn't."

It took four months to come back.

HEADQUARTERS

DEPARTMENT OF THE ARMY

WASHINGTON, D.C.

26 October 1956

Major Craig W. Lowell
Office of the Military Attache
The United States Consulate General
Algiers, Algeria, France
(Via Diplomatic Pouch)

Dear Major Lowell:

Reference is made to your letter of 21 June 1956, in reference to your efficiency report and the Indorsement thereof, covering your service while assigned to the Flight Detachment, Headquarters, Seventh United States Army.

The efficiency report and the Indorsement thereto has been expunged from your service record and the following substituted:

"While assigned to the Flight Detachment, Headquarters, Seventh United States Army, Major Lowell performed in a wholly satisfactory manner all the duties to which he was assigned.

"The exigencies of the service having made the rendering of an efficiency report covering this service impossible, it is directed that any personnel actions being based on Major Lowell's record consider his service while assigned to the Office of the Military Attache, U.S. Consulate General, Algiers, Algeria, as also applying to his service in Seventh Army."

The Secretary of the Army believes this to be an equitable resolution of the problem and has asked me to tell you that he extends every good wish for a successful career in the future.

Sincerely,
Ellwood P. Doudt
Major General
Special Assistant to the Secretary of the Army

Of the two acts, betraying a subordinate officer by screwing his wife, or making the chief of Rotary Wing Special Missions back down from the lethal efficiency report rather than make it public knowledge that Phyllis had dallied in his bed, the latter made Lowell feel more ashamed of himself. That was really conduct unbecoming an officer and a gentleman.

It made him more than a little ashamed of himself, for he was guilty as charged, and he was afraid that he hadn't seen the last of the chief of Rotary Wing Special Missions. If he was ever assigned under him (or even near him), he would get an efficiency report he couldn't protest.

His orders came a month after the letter from the Special Assistant to the Secretary of the Army.

HQ DEPT OF THE ARMY 16 DEC 1956
MILITARY ATTACHE
US CONSULATE GENERAL
ALGIERS, ALGERIA

MAJOR CRAIG W. LOWELL 0439067 ARMOR RELVD OFC MIL AT-
TACHE US CONSULATE GEN ALGIERS ALGERIA TRF AND WP VIA
MIL OR COMMERCIAL AIR TRAN FT LEAVENWORTH KANS RUAT
CG US ARMY COMMAND AND GENERAL STAFF COLLEGE NOT LATER
THAN 2400 HRS 6 JAN 1957 PURP ATTENDING USACGSC COURSE NO.
57-1. OFF WILL REPT OFC OF MIL LIAISON, THE PENT WASH DC EN
ROUTE NLT 1200 HRS 29 DEC 1956. PCS. OFFICER AUTH TRANS PER-
SONAL AUTO AND HOUSEHOLD GOODS. NO REPEAT NO DELAY EN
ROUTE LEAVE AUTHORIZED BECAUSE OF TIME LIMITATIONS.

FOR THE ADJUTANT GENERAL:
STANLEY G. MILLER
COLONEL, AGC

It was more than he had dared hope for. The year-long
"Long" Course at the Command and General Staff College. If
he ever was to get promoted before being "passed over" twice
by a promotion board and thrown out of the army, or if he was
ever to be given any kind of command or even a responsible
job on a staff, he had to have C&GSC. Now that he had been
given C&GSC, he realized that he had refused to think about
his chances of a meaningful career. He had been living day to
day.

He wondered why C&GSC had come through now. He
suspected that it had something to do with his protesting the
efficiency report. Maybe they had asked questions about him,
unofficially, a telephone call here and there. He decided that
that was probably it, and that he had been lucky, that the
telephone calls had been directed to people, Paul Jiggs, for
example, who would go to bat for him.

He had no idea what the OFC OF MIL LIAISON he was supposed
to report to was. He had never heard of it.

Colonel Lemes asked what he intended to do with the Jaguar.
Impulsively, Lowell offered to sell it to him and quoted a price

he later found out was far below the market value. Colonel Lemes snapped it up. Lowell later wondered whether the colonel was just taking advantage of a bargain or whether he considered it a favor, tit for tat, a Jaguar at a bargain basement price in return for a salvaged career.

(Two)
Washington, D.C.
29 Dec 1956

Lowell flew home via Paris on his first transcontinental jet. He spent the night at Broadlawns in Glen Cove and took the first flight he could catch to Washington the next morning. Just to stick the needle in, he telephoned his cousin Porter Craig and told him that he was going to decide, after discussing his future assignment in Washington, whether or not to stay in the army. Then he thought about that, and afraid that Porter would make another telephone call to the senator, called him back and took him off the hook.

The OFC OF MIL LIAISON turned out to be a small, three-room suite in the next-to-the-inner of the five rings of Pentagon offices. They were waiting for him and had a shiny staff car ready to take him back across the Potomac into Washington. The car went into the basement garage of a huge, monolithic building, where a squeaky clean young man in civilian clothes ritually offered his hand, identified himself as Captain Somebody, and took him in an elevator into a conference room on the fifth floor for what he said would be a "routine debriefing."

The squeaky clean young captain had a looseleaf notebook stuffed with paper. When they were joined by a secretary using a court reporter's stenotype machine, he opened the notebook and began to ask questions. Lowell was astonished at the amount of information the questions represented. They knew not only the names of most of the French officers with whom he had had contact, but a good deal about them as well.

Once the questions had been asked and answered, the lights were dimmed and a slide projector introduced. The slides had been made from the miles of film Sergeant Bill Franklin had made of French Army (in particular, the Foreign Legion's and the parachutists') actions against the Algerian insurgents. Each slide represented a question the film had left unanswered.

During the slide show, someone else came into the room, sat against the door, and watched without speaking. When the lights were finally turned back on, Lowell turned and saw the newcomer was Sandy Felter. He was in civilian clothing.

"Are you through with him, Captain?" Felter asked.

"Yes, sir," the captain said. There was something in the captain's demeanor, something in his tone of voice, that told Lowell he was paying Sandy Felter far more than the ritual courtesy paid by a captain to a major.

"Then I guess I'll take him home with me and feed him," Sandy said, walking over and putting out his hand.

"I didn't know you knew the major, sir," the captain said.

"Oh, yes," Felter said. "Major Lowell and I are old friends."

In Sandy's Volkswagen, on the way to the far reaches of Alexandria, Sandy said: "My neighbors don't know I'm in the army. In case it comes up."

"Super Spook, huh?"

"Nothing like that," Sandy said. And then changed the subject to ask about P.P.

Sharon laid out a full dinner; that meant she had known he was coming. *That* meant that Sandy had known he was coming. What the hell was he doing?

"Where did you get my film?" he asked. "I sent it to Bill Roberts."

"We asked Roberts for it and copied it," Sandy replied. That asked more questions than it answered.

There were two kids now, and Sharon was as big as a house with her third. She told him, after hearing about Elizabeth, that he had done the right thing to leave P.P. in Germany with her.

He spent the night on the Felter's couch, which unfolded into a bed. In the morning, Sandy drove him by his hotel where he changed into a fresh uniform and then over to the huge building again. Sandy parked the Volkswagen in a reserved spot near the elevator.

That meant he was important around here, Lowell realized, and then laughed at himself. He was becoming a spook himself, noticing details and reaching conclusions.

He wasn't in the building long. Overnight, what the stenotypist had taken down had been transcribed. He was asked to go over it, and make sure that the transcription and his answers were correct. Afterward, Felter appeared again and apologized for not being able to take him to the airport. He told him that when he got his feet on the ground at Leavenworth, he should plan to come to Washington and spend some time with them.

And then, almost idly, Felter asked if Lowell had had any thoughts about his replacement in Algiers.

Lowell was surprised at the question. What was Felter doing involved in officer assignments?

"I thought they had a school for attaché types," Lowell said.

"I don't want an attaché type," Felter said. "I want someone like you over there, who won't regard the assignment as a two-year cocktail party tour. I want somebody who'll really report on how the French are fighting that war. I suspect we're going to have one of our own to worry about pretty soon."

"You've answered your own question, Mouse," Lowell said. "You need a chopper jockey who's not afraid to get shot at. One who speaks French. Most important, one that nobody else wants."

Felter smiled at him.

"What business is that of yours, anyway?" Lowell asked.

"What business do you have, asking me what business I have?" Felter responded with a smile.

"Screw you, Mouse," Lowell said, affectionately. Then he hugged Felter and got into a plain (but obviously government-owned) Chevrolet and was driven to Washington National Airport.

Sandy Felter returned to his office.

The reason Lowell had done so well with the French was that he was a gutsy combat type who spoke French fluently. Felter knew another gutsy combat type who also flew choppers and spoke French. Who was an honorary member of the *3ième Régiment Parachutiste de la Légion Étranger*.

He didn't know if the soldier could get a Top Secret clearance, and he was only a warrant officer, which wouldn't do. But a commission would be easy enough to arrange.

He called the office of Military Liaison in the Pentagon and told them he wanted the service record of WOJG Edward C. Greer on his desk within the hour.

(Three)
Kansas City, Missouri
15 January 1957

The sales manager of Twin-City Aviation, serving Kansas City, Missouri, and its twin across the river, Kansas City, Kansas, was three-quarters convinced that he was wasting his time with his present "up," a walk-in customer who was making inquiries about either renting or buying an airplane.

He had walked in the door at half past eight in the morning, half an hour before Twin-City Aviation officially opened. He was, well, a little flashily dressed (there were not many people who had the balls to wear a silk foulard in an open-collared dress shirt around KC) and had announced that since he would be in the area for the next ten months or so, he had been thinking about either renting or buying an airplane to "get around."

The sales manager told him that he had certainly come to the right place, and just what sort of airplane did he have in mind?

The guy with the foulard and the tweed jacket with leather patches on the sleeves said he wasn't sure, that the whole idea had just occurred to him.

"You are a pilot, of course?"

"Yes," he said.

The sales manager looked out the window to see what kind of a car he was driving. A four-door Chevy. A new one. Did that mean anything?

It meant that he was a possible customer for a Cessna 172, a very nice little single-engine four-seater, with a complete set of Narco navigation equipment. Cruised out at 120 knots, burned about six gallons an hour.

"Be happy to take you up for a little spin," the sales manager said. "Now, I'm not trying to talk you into anything you don't want to do, but if you're going to be flying regular, renting is going to eat you up. We have to charge, you understand, for time you'd be sitting on the ground somewhere, in addition to the flight hours, which on a long term, regular basis, would run you $17.50 an hour.

"I've never flown a 172," the man said.

"Easiest airplane in the world to fly," the sales manager said. "You make a mistake, it gives you ten minutes to think it over."

"All right, let's try it," the man said.

They flew for fifteen minutes up the river to Leavenworth, and that was when the sales manager learned that the guy was in the army, at the school the army ran at Leavenworth for people they thought might be full colonels and generals.

"There's a fleet of H-13s and L-19s there," the guy said, "for proficiency flying. But I'm the junior aviator, which means I would have to get my proficiency time in from three to six on Sunday mornings."

"Oh, you're in the army, are you?"

"I'm a major. One of two in my class. Everybody else is a light bird."

Well, there goes the sale of this sonofabitch, the sales manager decided. There was no way a soldier could come up with the down payment on a 172, much less the payments, and *no way* he could afford the insurance and the maintenance. Not on army pay.

Well, what the hell, he'd probably spring for maybe ten hours of rental before he decided he'd better do his flying free, even if that meant—what was it he had said—"from three to six on Sunday mornings."

"Had about enough?" the sales manager asked, already making a 180 degree turn back toward KC.

"Yeah, this isn't going to do it."

"Look," the sales manager said. "There's a couple of Pipers around I could let you have, if you agreed to take, say, fifty hours over six months, for about $12.50 an hour. Nice little airplanes."

"That wouldn't do it either, I'm afraid," the major said.

They got back on the ground and parked the Cessna 172. The started walking back to the office.

"What's that?" the man said, turning to peer in the plexiglass window of an aircraft.

"That's an Aero Commander," the sales manager said. "Just got it in."

"Beautiful," Major Craig W. Lowell said. He had never seen one before. It was a sleek-looking, high-winged, twin-engined aircraft that looked, and probably was, fast. The one he was looking at was painted a high gloss white, with red trim.

"Gorgeous," the sales manager said. "That's a classy airplane."

"You say it's yours?"

"Until I can sell it, it belongs to me and the First National Bank of KC," the sales manager said.

"How about taking me up in this?" Lowell asked.

Jesus, the nerve of some people!

"If I had it as a rental ship, out for rent, which I don't, I'd have to charge a hundred an hour. You're looking at a hundred and twenty-five thousand dollars' worth of airplane, Major."

The major reached into his pocket, pulled out a folded wad of bills, and peeled off a hundred dollar bill.

"If you don't have anything else to do," he said. "I'd really like to take a ride in that."

What the hell, the sales manager thought. Why not? That way the morning won't be a complete loss.

"I'll get the key," he said, and pocketed the hundred dollar bill.

"It feels as if you're dragging your ass on the ground, doesn't it?" the major said, when they were taking off.

He didn't ask to fly the airplane, and the sales manager didn't offer to let him fly until the hour (well, forty-five minutes, who was looking at a clock?) was just about over.

He let the major land the airplane. He had a little trouble getting it on the ground. The Aero Commander's fuselage was eighteen inches off the ground, and that took some getting used to. For the first couple of landings, it was like you were going to fly right through the runway.

When they had it back in line and the engines were shut down, the sales manager could see the major was really reluctant to get out. He turned around in the copilot's seat and looked at the passenger compartment, with its elegant paneling, and ran his hand almost lovingly over the closest of the four glove-leather upholstered seats.

"This is a very fine airplane," he said.

"It sure is," the sales manager said.

"And frankly, I like the panel," the major said, turning to point at the instrument panel, which had a full array of the latest Aircraft Radio Corporation communication and navigation equipment.

That's very gracious of you, Mac, the sales manager thought, as he heaved himself out of the pilot's seat and then walked down the aisle to the door.

The major stayed another two minutes, which seemed a lot longer, before he got out of the copilot's seat and reluctantly got out of the airplane.

"What did you say it's worth?"

"It lists out, with all the equipment, at $129,480," the sales manager said.

"But you would take $125,000 cash, right?" the major asked, jokingly.

"Right," the sales manager replied, with a smile.

"How about $120,000, even?" the major said.

"As a special favor to you, I'd take $120,000 cash," the sales manager said. He was feeling pretty good. The bottom line was that he'd gotten nearly an hour in the Commander, which was a jewel to fly, and this guy had paid for it.

When they got back in the office, and the sales manager was getting paper and pencil out to rough out some figures for a fifty-hour use of a Piper, the major asked if he could use his telephone for a collect call.

"Sure," the sales manager said.

The major called a New York City number, collect to Porter Craig from Major Craig W. Lowell.

"Porter," he said, when his party came on the line, "I'm in Kansas City. Who do we do business with out here?"

Then he covered the mouthpiece with his hand and spoke to the sales manager: "You did say the First National Bank of Kansas City was your bank, didn't you?"

"Yeah," the sales manager said. "That's what I said."

"I'm about to write a rather substantial check, Porter," the major said. "Specifically, one for $120,000. And I don't want to wait until it clears. Would you call the First National Bank here and do whatever has to be done?"

The sales manager looked at him in confusion and disbelief.

"I'm buying an airplane, Porter, is what I'm doing," the major said. "Have the bank call a Mr. Sewell at Twin City Aviation and tell him my check is good, will you?"

Then he asked the sales manager for a blank check and filled it out. It was for $120,000. Where the name of the bank was supposed to be, he had written Craig, Powell, Kenyon and Dawes, N.Y.C.

"What's this here, instead of the bank's name?" the sales manager asked.

"That's a bank. Or rather a firm of investment bankers," Major Lowell explained.

"Never heard of it," the sales manager said.

"Few people have," Major Lowell said. "Listen, I think it will take maybe thirty minutes to arrange for that check. I'm on my way to New Orleans. I'll need charts, and I'd like to read the Dash-One on that for a few minutes. Would it be all right if I took the keys and went out to it?"

The major was wrong about it taking thirty minutes to arrange for his check to be cleared. Five minutes later, the executive vice president of the First National Bank of Kansas City telephoned the sales manager of Twin City Aviation and told him the bank had received a telephone call from the chairman of the board of Craig, Powell, Kenyon and Dawes, the New York investment bankers, and that he could accept any check drawn against them by Major Craig W. Lowell, up to a quarter of a million dollars.

(Four)
Fort Benning, Georgia
15 January 1957

Lieutenant Colonel J. Peter Hawkins, Deputy Chief of the Platoon Tactics Branch, Tactics Division, of the U.S. Army Infantry School, had six months previously submitted (under the provisions of AR 615-301, and Department of Army Personnel Pamphlet 615–15) an application for consideration for assignment as a military attaché.

Shortly afterward, he became aware that he was the subject of a new complete background investigation, conducted among the military by personnel of the U.S. Army Counterintelligence Corps and in civilian areas by agents of the Federal Bureau of Investigation. Lt. Colonel Hawkins already had undergone a complete background investigation and held a Top Secret security clearance. That wasn't enough, apparently.

Two months before, he had been placed on orders to the 2nd Infantry Division in Korea. Although he presumed that to mean he had not been selected for duty as a military attaché, he had not been so officially notified. He had prepared to move to Korea, which meant that he had had to find off-post housing for his wife and children. Dependents were not authorized in Korea, and government quarters were authorized only for personnel assigned to a post.

He had purchased a four-bedroom, two-bath ranch house in the Riverview subdivision of Columbus, Georgia, taking over the mortgage from an ordnance major who had been reassigned to the Redstone, Alabama, Ordnance Depot.

And then his orders to the 2nd Infantry Division were cancelled. He received a telephone call from the Office of the Assistant Chief of Staff, Personnel, in the Pentagon, saying that he might expect other orders in the near future. The caller could give Lt. Colonel Hawkins no indication of what those orders might be.

Four days previously, there had been a TWX:

HQ DEPT OF THE ARMY
CG FT BENNING & THE INF CENTER, GA

IT IS ANTICIPATED THAT LT COL J. PETER HAWKINS 0386567 INF THE INF SCHOOL WILL BE ORDERED TO AN OVERSEAS POST WITH FOURTEEN (14) DAYS. DEPENDENTS WILL REPEAT WILL BE AUTH TO ACCOMP OFF. TVL BY MIL AND/OR CIV AIR IS ANTICIPATED. OFF WILL INSURE DEPENDENTS POSSESS PROPER PASSPORTS AND HAVE COMPLETED IMMUNIZATION SERIES. THIS IS ALL THE IN-

FORMATION PRESENTLY AVAILABLE AND INQUIRIES ARE NOT DE-
SIRED AND WILL NOT BE ENTERTAINED.

FOR THE ASST C/S PERSONNEL:

STEPHEN MASON

LT COL, AGC

And last night there had been a telephone call from the aide-
de-camp to the post commander. He was to be at the army
airfield at Fort Benning at 1000 hours. He was to be in a Class
"A" uniform. He was to take with him enough linen and extra
uniforms to spend three days away from Fort Benning. Transportation from Benning to where he was going would be by
military air. The aide-de-camp had no further information.

When Lt. Colonel Hawkins went to Base Operations at 0915
the next morning and identified himself, they had no information to give him. They knew nothing.

At 0955 hours, Lt. Colonel Hawkins watched as a very
unusual airplane taxied up to Base Operations. It was an Aero
Commander. Colonel Hawkins had not known that the army
had acquired any Aero Commanders, which were high-priced
civilian business aircraft, the kind used by corporate big shots
too impatient to take airliners. From the markings there was
no question, however, that this was an army aircraft, for it was
painted in army colors. But Colonel Hawkins had never seen
any other army aircraft painted like this one. The paint was
glossy, not flat, and most of it was gleaming white, not olive-
drab. While it had the standard star-and-bars identification on
the fuselage, the insignia looked much smaller than normal.
The only place it said US ARMY was on the vertical stabilizer,
high up, in letters no more than four inches tall.

A VIP aircraft, obviously. But there was no general officer's
starred plaque mounted anywhere on the fuselage.

The door in the fuselage behind the high wing opened and
an officer got out. He was wearing a Class "A" uniform, not
a flight suit. There were wings on the tunic, so it was logical
to presume he was the pilot, or copilot. In an airplane like that,
obviously, flight suits were not necessary.

The pilot, a young captain, wearing the Military District of
Washington shoulder insignia and a West Point ring came into

Base Operations. He took one look at Lt. Colonel Hawkins
and walked right to him. He saluted.

"Colonel Hawkins?"

Ask not, Lt. Col. Hawkins thought, *for whom the bell tolls.
It tolls for thee.*

"Yes, I am," he said.

"Good morning, sir. Are you ready to go? Can I help you
with your luggage?"

"Where are we going?" Lt. Colonel Hawkins asked.

"Let me have that bag, Colonel," the captain said, and then
held the door out to the flight line open for him.

The captain stowed Colonel Hawkins's bag in the rear of
the cabin and then walked forward.

"Good morning, Colonel," a little Jew in civilian clothing
said. "I'm Sanford Felter."

"How do you do?" Lt. Colonel Hawkins asked, wondering
just who the hell he was. There were two other passengers on
the airplane.

"May I present General de Brigade des Fernauds?" the little
Jew said, and then switched to French. *"Mon Général, je
présente le Colonel Hawkins."*

Hawkins had kept up his French. Four years of it at the
Point, further practiced when he'd been in Germany.

"I am honored, my General," Hawkins said in French.

"I am very happy to meet you, Colonel," the French brigadier said, in English.

"General des Fernauds is the military attaché," the little Jew
said.

The Aero Commander was already moving.

"Everybody ready back there?" the pilot called. Lt. Colonel
Hawkins slipped into a seat. He just had time to fasten the belt
when the plane turned, the engines roared, and it began to race
down the runway.

Lt. Colonel Hawkins realized he still had no idea where
they were going.

Thirty minutes later, they landed at Camp Rucker, Alabama.

Out the window, Lt. Colonel Hawkins saw workmen erect-
ing a sign on the Base Operations building: LAIRD ARMY AIR-
FIELD. He remembered hearing somewhere that the field had

been renamed in honor of Scotty Laird.

The captain who had fetched him at Benning came down the aisle again, but before he reached the door it was opened from the outside and a warrant officer stuck his head in.

"I didn't know they let lousy civilians on military airplanes," he said.

"Bonjour, mon petit," the Jew said, smiling broadly, looking almost playful.

The warrant officer climbed inside and was followed by a major. Hawkins saw, with the surprise that comes even to old soldiers when they actually see one, the blue-starred ribbon of the Medal of Honor among the major's many other decorations.

"I swore I'd never get on another plane with you," the major said to the little Jew. "The last time, you nearly got my balls blown off."

"It's nice to see you, too, Major MacMillan," the little Jew said, with a wide smile.

"What the hell is all this, anyway? Bellmon's going to blow his cork when he comes back and finds both of us run off with you."

"Get on, sit down, and shut up," the Jew said to him. "Try to remember that you're supposed to be an officer and a gentleman."

When the warrant officer came into the cabin, he saw the French general.

"Pardonez-moi, mon Général," he said.

"Hello, Greer," the French general said. "It's good to see you again, my friend."

The warrant officer slipped into a seat across from Lt. Colonel Hawkins.

"Good morning, sir," he said, formally.

"Good morning," Lt. Colonel Hawkins said. The Aero Commander was already turning away from the Base Operations building.

Not two hours later, the Aero Commander turned off a taxiway at New Orleans Lake Front Airport and parked beside a civilian Aero Commander. A tall man, blond and mustached, was leaning against its nose.

Felter was the first one out of the airplane. Lt. Colonel

Hawkins followed him out the door.

Felter walked up to the civilian and they shook hands.

"I thought you were coming in commercial," Felter said to him. "What brings you here?"

"I just landed," the man said. "I heard your pilot give his ten-minutes-out report, and I had a hunch it was you."

"What did you do, rent a plane?" Felter asked, a hint of tolerant disgust in his voice.

"Actually, I just bought it," the man said. "Just this morning. What do you think?"

"I think that's more ostentatious than Patton's polo ponies," Felter said.

The tall man shook hands with the man with the Medal.

"What do you say, Mac?" he said.

"Did I hear you say you bought that?" MacMillan asked.

"Yeah, you like it?"

"Who are you going to get to fly it for you?" MacMillan asked, innocently.

"You must be Greer," Lowell said, putting out his hand. "Bob Bellmon tells me you're the final solution for Mac-Millan."

"And what's that supposed to mean?" MacMillan asked.

"A twenty-four-hour-a-day keeper to read road signs and menus for you, that sort of thing," Lowell said.

They were smiling, but Hawkins sensed that there was a degree of genuine hostility between them. Or maybe contempt.

"What's this all about, Mouse?" Lowell asked. "I appreciate getting an excuse for teacher to get out of school and an excuse to fly my new little bird down here, but I *am* a little curious."

"This is Lieutenant Colonel Hawkins," Felter said. "He's going to take your place in Algiers."

"Oh," he said. He put out his hand to Hawkins. "I'm Major Lowell, sir."

"How do you do?" Hawkins asked. He decided that he had not heard correctly or else that Major Lowell was joking about just having bought the civilian Aero Commander. Majors simply do not have that kind of money.

"*Mon Général*," Felter said, "may I present Major Lowell?"

"*Mon Général*," Lowell said, almost coming to attention

before the general put out his hand to him.

"I'm happy to finally meet you, Major," the general said. "Especially under such circumstances."

"May the major inquire into the nature of those circumstances, *mon Général?*" Lowell asked.

"You have been a hero, again, Craig," Felter said. "And they are going to give you a medal, again."

Hawkins wondered just who the hell the little Jew could be. Probably someone from the State Department. He realized that he had just heard that not only had his application for attaché duty come through, but that he had been told where he was going. To Algiers.

They rode into downtown New Orleans in a Cadillac limousine with a Corps Diplomatique tag mounted above the license plate. They were taken to a turn-of-the-century mansion on Saint Charles Avenue. A brass plate mounted to the brick fence pillar identified it as *Le Consulat Générale de la République Française*.

They were ushered into the office of the consul general. Hawkins saw through French doors leading to another room that there was a buffet laid out, with half a dozen bottles of champagne in coolers.

"May I suggest, *Monsieur le Consul*," the French general said, "that we have our little ceremony? And then we can have, perhaps, something to drink."

"Until just now," Lowell said to Felter, "I thought you were kidding."

The consul took a blue-bound folder from his desk.

Felter pushed the warrant officer and Major Lowell into line before the consul.

"Dans le nom de la République française!" the consul announced, dramatically. The French general came to attention.

He read a citation. For valor in action in leading survivors of a shot-down aircraft through enemy lines in the vicinity of Dien Bien Phu, French Indo-China, Major Rudolph G. MacMillan, U.S. Army, was invested with the Legion of Honor, in the grade of Chevalier. General des Fernauds pinned the medal of the Legion of Honor on MacMillan's tunic and then kissed his cheeks.

"Dans le nom de la République française!" the consul announced dramatically again. For his gallantry in action in flying a helicopter through intense enemy small arms fire to bring succor to French soldiers wounded in counterinsurgency operations in Algiers on at least twenty occasions, Major Craig W. Lowell was invested with the Legion of Honor in the grade of Chevalier.

"Dans le nom de la République Française!" the consul general announced, a third and final time. Majors MacMillan and Felter and Warrant Officer Greer were invested with the Croix de guerre for their heroic rescue of a French Foreign legionnaire from the Viet Minh.

The champagne was served, and General des Fernauds raised his glass.

"To those we left behind," he said. Everyone raised his glass, and drank. Then the general dropped his glass to the carpet and ground it with his heel. Lowell and MacMillan, Felter and Greer, one a time, did the same thing. Lt. Colonel Hawkins was about to drop his glass—when in Rome, do as the Romans—when the consul stayed his hand.

"Only those who were there," he said, softly.

Hawkins was touched by the ceremony but wondered again why he had been brought all the way down here to witness it. And then he had the insight: somebody wanted him to know what was expected of him when he got to Algiers, and what was expected of him in Algiers was not taught at the Infantry School or at the Command and General Staff College. And then he had a second insight: the one who wanted him to know, the one who had arranged for him to come down here, was the little Jew.

XI

Rhonda Wilson Hyde had "requested" Darlene Heatter to come in on Saturday to answer the telephones until noon, and there wasn't anything that Darlene could do about it.

It wasn't that she minded working; she got paid time and a half for overtime. It was just that she didn't like the way Rhonda Wilson Hyde was always ordering her around. But there wasn't anything she could do about it except act as if she didn't mind. Rhonda was the administrative officer and her immediate boss. The only person she could complain to was Colonel Bellmon. Though Darlene knew that she generally could get what she wanted from Colonel Bellmon, there was such a thing as wearing out your welcome.

Darlene was sure that things were going to catch up with Rhonda, anyway. It said in the Bible, "Judge not, lest ye be judged," and Darlene tried not to judge anyone, but there was no getting away from the fact that Rhonda Wilson Hyde was carrying on like a you-know-what.

About the only good thing you could say about her was that she wasn't fooling around with the married officers, just the bachelors, or else the married officers who were visiting USAACDA for a week or ten days without, of course, their wives.

At first, Darlene had thought that Rhonda was nothing more than a flirt, but she couldn't keep thinking that in the face of all the evidence. Rhonda *was* going to bed with them, and there was no denying a fact when it stared you in the face.

Darlene couldn't understand how a married woman could do that, go to bed with a man who wasn't her husband. Just going to bed for lust. The sinful lusts of the flesh. She had come across that phrase in a book of prayer from the Episcopal Church in the pastor's office when she had been learning how to type.

It was the work of the Devil, too. Sort of contagious, like a disease. Charlene had caught herself wondering what it would be like to do it with somebody other than John. Before she realized what she was doing, caught herself, and stopped, she had wondered what it would be like with Mac MacMillan, of all people.

She knew what had set that off: MacMillan and one of the other officers had been going into and out of the men's room at the same time. One going in while the other was coming out. MacMillan had put his hand right through one of the panels on the door, and they'd had to cut him out of it, to keep him from cutting his wrist any more than he had already cut it.

And Mr. Greer had laughed when he heard about it, and said, "What do you expect? Mac's built like a fucking tank."

The way they swore so much, the words were even usually used incorrectly. He didn't mean that a tank actually you know what. But that had started her thinking. Mac MacMillan *was* built like a tank. Large and powerful. Not that John wasn't all man or anything like that. But one of MacMillan's arms was about as big as one of John's legs, and his neck was about twice the size of John's and it was a perfectly natural thing for her to wonder if he was twice as big as John, all over. And what it would be like.

She was ashamed of herself when she realized what she was

thinking, and she stopped herself right then. And every other time she had thoughts like that. She was a Christian wife and mother, and what she was thinking was sinful and indecent.

The temptation of Satan was awful. She had even thought of that when she was doing it with John. When she thought about it, sort of pretended that it was Mac on top of her, it made doing it with John better. It made her, you know, *convulse*. Or whatever it was called.

Maybe, she thought, it was the uniform. Uniforms were supposed to be appealing to women, and maybe that was it. They really had looked nice, the whole unit, when they'd been at USAACDA this morning.

They were giving Mr. Greer a commission as an officer, a promotion from the lowest grade of warrant officer to first lieutenant. Darlene thought it had something to do with the medals he and Mac had won in Indo-China.

When Colonel Bellmon had been up at Fort Benning, and Major MacMillan was acting as commanding officer, there had been a telephone call from the DCSOPS in the Pentagon in Washington, D.C., which was the boss of USAACDA, telling Major MacMillan that a plane would land at Laird Field, and take them someplace for a day or two.

When Colonel Bellmon came back from Fort Benning and found the both of them gone, he got sore and called the DCSOPS to find out what was going on. Because she just happened not to hang up after she'd placed the call for him, she heard a general tell him that it was combined politics and intelligence. The French were going to give them medals and a certain "unnamed Jewish major friend of yours" was involved. They would be gone no more than forty-eight hours.

Whatever it was, there had been a big party at the Pontchartrain Hotel that night, and they hadn't come back until late the next afternoon. And then in a private airplane. She'd overheard that conversation, too, when the control tower called and asked Colonel Bellmon if he expected a civilian Aero Commander to land. He'd said, no, he didn't, and then a couple of minutes later, the tower had called back and said that the pilot of the airplane was a Major Lowell and that he had Major MacMillan and Warrant Officer Greer aboard, so Colonel Bell-

mon had said it was all right for them to land and told the tower
to pass the word to Major MacMillan that he wanted him to
come directly from the field to his office.

Both Major MacMillan and Mr. Greer were a little drunk,
or at least a little sick from being drunk. They said that Lowell
had dropped them off at Rucker on his way back to Leavenworth and that Felter had taken some colonel she had never
heard of back to Washington with him after the party in the
hotel.

"Where did Lowell get the Aero Commander?" Bellmon
asked.

"He bought it," MacMillan replied, laughing. "Where else?"

"And he's flying it, as drunk as you two are?"

"No, he stopped at midnight," MacMillan said. "He's not
that kind of a fool."

The TWX about Mr. Greer getting promoted came in that
night.

HQ DEPT OF THE ARMY WASH DC 0950 22 JAN 56
DIRECTOR, USAACDA CP RUCKER ALA

THIS TWX CONSTITUTES AUTH TO HON DISCH FR THE MIL SERVICE
WOJG GREER, EDWARD C W727110 FOR THE PURP OF ACCEPTING
A DIRECT COMMISSION AS 1ST LIEUTENANT ARMOR AUS AND CON-
CURRENT CALL TO ACTIVE DUTY. OFF WILL REMAIN ASGD
USAACDA. OFF IS ALERTED FOR OVERSEAS SHIPMENT 26 JAN 1957.
DA GENERAL ORDER 20 1956 IN PREPARATION WILL BE FURNISHED
WHEN AVAILABLE.

BY ORDER OF THE DCS PERSONNEL:
EDMUND T. DALEBY
COLONEL, AGC

Normally, USAACDA didn't march in the regular Saturday
morning parade on Parade Ground No. 2, but Colonel Bellmon
had made them march this time. They would swear in Mr.
Greer as an officer during the parade, and the colonel thought
the unit should participate. Afterward, there was going to be
a company party at Lake Tholocco, to say good-bye to *Lieutenant* Greer.

Everybody in the unit, civilians included, was invited, but
Darlene didn't think that she would go, even when duty hours
were over at noon, and she would be free too. There would
be a lot of drinking, she knew. There was a whole jeep trailer
filled to the top with iced beer, and that meant that there would
be a lot of drunken people. Since she believed that the body
was the temple of the Holy Spirit and that drinking was soiling
that temple, Darlene didn't think she ought to go.

But Colonel Bellmon and Major MacMillan and a couple
of the other officers came in after the parade. Colonel Bellmon
seemed surprised that Rhonda Wilson Hyde had made Darlene
come to work.

"We should have just had the switchboard refer calls to the
staff duty officer," he said, and Darlene was glad that Rhonda
Wilson had been caught doing what she had done.

"If you want to leave your car here, Darlene," Colonel
Bellmon said, "you can ride out to the lake with us."

Since he expected her to go, there was nothing she could
do about it, Darlene decided, and she sort of liked the idea of
Rhonda Wilson Hyde seeing her show up out there with the
colonel. She didn't have to drink any alcohol, she decided.
There would surely be Coke and things like that out there.
Maybe even some punch.

When she got there, she saw that it wasn't (except for the
jeep trailer full of beer) very much different from a church
picnic. A little more elaborate, maybe. Church picnics were
generally covered dish. USAACDA was serving individual
steaks cooked on charcoal with baked potatoes and baked beans.
Mrs. Bellmon and the other officers' ladies had "arranged for"
the food and drinks (in other words, paid for it), and the enlisted
wives would help prepare and serve it.

Darlene helped the enlisted wives serve the food on the
serving line, and then, because it was like a church picnic, she
walked over to where the enlisted men, the privates and the
technicians, had gone off by themselves, feeling a little out of
place with the wives and children.

She knew how to make people feel comfortable, how to
join in the fellowship with the others.

They had one of those enormous stainless steel kitchen pots, and it was full of fruit punch. She was glad to see that not everybody was drinking. The enlisted men smiled at her when she asked if she could have some of the fruit punch. When she sipped at it, she realized for the first time how thirsty she was and how good the punch was. She drank everything in the paper cup and held it out to be refilled.

"I'm absolutely dry!" she said.

(Two)

Melody Dutton was absolutely furious with Ed Greer. She and her mother were trying to involve him as much as they could in the preparations for the wedding, and he just didn't seem to give a damn.

She had told him that the caterer from Dothan would be at the house from nine thirty Saturday morning and that she wanted him to help with the selection of the menu.

She knew that the whole idea of a big wedding made him uncomfortable, but they had talked that through. It was going to be more than just her reception, it was going to be a chance for people from all over the state to meet him, and that was going to be very important to him when he got out of the army and went to work as vice president of Dale County Builders, Inc.

He didn't know half the people he would have to know once he started to work, and the reception was as important to his future as anything Melody could think of.

Not only didn't he show up after that stupid parade as he had promised, but he didn't even call up and say he was tied up or something. There was no question in Melody's mind where he was. He was sitting drinking beer, in that stupid little bar, Annex 1 next to the BOQ, that's where he was.

When he finally showed up, she was really going to give him a piece of her mind.

The caterer waited as long as she could, and then she left. By then it was half past two in the afternoon. Just wait till he showed up!

Melody went to her room, took off her dress, and put on shorts and a T-shirt. Her mother had made her change into the dress before Mrs. Angie Gell, the caterer, had come. Mrs. Gell, who was from a fine old family, had her standards, and Melody should, in deference to them, put on a dress and look like a young woman about to be married, not like a tomboy.

Melody called the post number. When the operator came on the line, she asked for Annex 1.

"May I speak with Mr. Greer, please?" she asked, when one of his drunken cronies answered the phone.

"Not here, honey," the drunk said. "Would you settle for a lonely first lieutenant?"

Melody slammed the phone down in its cradle.

She wasn't going to have this out with him when he finally, in his own sweet damned time, elected to show up; she was going to have it out with him now.

She made the tires squeal as she backed the convertible out of the driveway (one of their wedding presents was going to be a new car; she had heard her father talking about that on the telephone). They were getting a house in Sunny Dale Acres and all the furniture, as well. She reminded herself angrily that Ed hadn't been very enthusiastic about that, either. She had had to pick out all the furniture herself. Ed said that he didn't know or care much about furniture. As long as it had four legs and a soft cushion, that was all he cared about.

She drove well above the speed limit (no Dale County deputy sheriff in his right mind would ticket Howard Dutton's daughter for speeding) until she reached the post. There she had to slow to thirty-five, because the MPs would give out speeding tickets, and they were a lot of trouble when you got one; you had to go to the federal courthouse in Dothan and pay it to a U.S. magistrate.

She jumped out of the car when she got to Annex 1 and went inside. The place was jammed with young officers and a bunch of girls she would just as soon not have had to say "hello" to, but Ed Greer wasn't there.

"Hey, Schatzie," one of them called to her as she was leaving. She hated to be called "Schatzie." Ed had told her that was what the soldiers called their German girl friends. Their frauleins. Ed had also told her that they called the frauleins "fur-lines," which Melody thought was really gross.

She turned to glower at whoever had called her name.

"I just remembered," a young warrant officer said, "that USAACDA is having a beer bust out at the lake. That's probably where he is."

"Thank you," Melody said.

That was just like him. He had told her about the beer busts. Once a month, the officers chipped in most of the money and provided the enlisted men with steaks and all the beer they could drink. That's where he was, out with the enlisted men swilling beer when he should have been arranging for the reception, which was just as important to him as it was to her. He preferred drinking himself silly on beer with the enlisted men to meeting his obligations and responsibilities to her.

Sometimes she just hated him!

It took her twenty-five minutes to find the USAACDA beer bust. There were three other beer busts, and she had to stop at each one long enough to find out it was the wrong one.

By the time she finally found the USAACDA beer bust, Ed was drunk. She could tell that from the bemused look on his face when he saw her. He was sitting on the hood of a jeep. The jeep was towing a trailer, and the trailer was full of huge chunks of ice and beer. The pine straw on the ground was just about covered with empty beer cans.

One of the enlisted men, a young sergeant, walked up to him just before Melody got to him and pointed to a group of GIs around a woman. Ed Greer laughed, and then grew serious.

"If the colonel finds out, he'll have your balls for breakfast," Melody heard him say.

"Hi," Melody said. Now that she was actually facing him, she really couldn't be angry.

"Hi," he said.

"If the colonel finds out what?" Melody asked.

"The troops have been feeding punch to our born-again Christian wife, mother, and Get-Thee-Behind-Me-Demon-Rum secretary," he said, and laughed.

"What's funny about that?"

"There's three half-gallons of vodka in that pot," he said. "Darlene is bombed out of her mind."

Melody looked over and saw Darlene Heatter, her face flushed, her hair mussed, with the group of GIs. Two of them had their arms around her shoulders. They were singing and laughing idiotically.

"And you think that's funny?" Melody snapped.

"It will do until something funnier comes along," Greer said.

"Why didn't you come and meet with the caterer?" Melody asked.

"A very good question," he said. He was really drunk, she saw. She had never seen him this drunk before.

"Or at least call and say you weren't coming?"

"You are looking at Old Mr. Ball-less himself," Ed said.

"What's that supposed to mean?"

"I didn't have the balls to call," he said. "As a matter of fact, before you showed up here—uninvited, I must point out—I was just about to decide that I would write you a letter."

"A *letter?* What kind of a letter?"

"A Dear John letter," Greer said, looking at her through somewhat fuzzy eyes. "In your case, a 'Dear Melody' letter."

"Saying what?" Melody asked. She had a sick feeling in the pit of her stomach.

"Saying, 'Dear Melody, dear sweet Melody, we have made one hell of a mistake.'"

"You're drunk," she said.

"Getting there," he agreed. "Getting there."

"If you have a point, I don't know what it is," she said.

"The army's sending me to Algeria," he said.

"The army's doing *what?*"

"Algeria," he said. "They're sending me to Algeria. To-morrow."

"They can't do that!" Melody protested. "Your resignation was approved."

"I have withdrawn my resignation," he said.

"I don't believe any of this. Is this some kind of sick joke?"

"Believe it," he said. She knew then he wasn't lying.

"But why?" she asked.

"Because when I thought about it," he said, "I realized that

I would much rather be a first lieutenant in the army than a vice president of Dale County Builders, Inc., despite the very nice fringe benefits."

"They offered to make you a lieutenant, if you'd stay?" she asked.

He put his hand to his collar point and exhibited it to her. There was the silver bar of a first lieutenant.

"Why didn't you talk this over with me?" Melody asked.

"Because you probably could have talked me out of it," he said. "And this opportunity wasn't going to knock again."

"What opportunity?"

"Algeria," he said. "Doing something important."

"I'm not important? Is that what you're saying?"

He didn't reply.

"We're supposed to be in love," Melody said.

"I thought about that, too," Greer said. "What we are is in lust. We've been fooling each other."

"How do you mean that?"

"You know what I mean," he said, mysteriously.

"We're supposed to be married on the tenth of February," she said. "What about that?"

He just looked at her and shrugged his shoulders.

"I'll be a laughing stock," she said.

"Sorry about that," he said.

"You never intended to marry me!" she accused, and now she was shrieking hysterically. "You bastard, you never intended to marry me! All you wanted was a piece of ass!"

"No. That's not true," Greer said. "I just finally stopped thinking about fucking and started thinking about the way things really are. We couldn't hack it, Melody. You're daddy's girl, and I'm a soldier."

"I hate you!" Melody shrieked. She didn't care that people were watching her. "You *bastard!*" she screamed.

She slapped his face and stormed toward her car. Halfway there, she turned around. Tears streaming down her face, she shook her fist at him. Then the fist turned into the finger. Then she screamed, "Fuck you!"

Then she got in the car and somehow got it started and put

it in gear. With the wheels spinning on the pine straw, she started off.

Greer sat on the hood a moment longer and then tossed his beer can away. He walked over to the officer's table where there was whiskey. He made himself a scotch and soda in a paper cup.

MacMillan walked over to him, stood silently for a moment, then said:

"Does that mean the engagement is off?" he asked, innocently.

"Yeah, I suppose it does," Greer said, chuckling.

"You're not going to do anything foolish like get yourself shit-faced, are you?" Mac asked. "Sandy Felter frowns on drunks. What time are you due in Washington?"

"I'm on the 8:20 flight out of Dothan in the morning. I'll be in Washington National about 1500."

"You want me to get a plane and take you up there?"

"No, thanks anyway, Mac."

"Why don't you come over to the house tonight?" MacMillan asked.

"I've got to finish packing," Greer said. "Thanks anyway."

"Well," MacMillan said, "say hello to Felter. And don't do nothing heroic over there."

They shook hands. Greer walked to where he had parked his car. He was going to leave the car parked behind his BOQ. MacMillan would advertise it in the *Daily Bulletin* and sell it for him. Major Lowell (now *there* was a character—his own personal Aero Commander!) had talked to him at some length about what to expect in Algeria and had told him the smart thing to do for wheels in Algiers was buy a new Renault 4CV. With a diplomatic passport, he could get one tax free.

He was almost to the car when he saw Darlene Heatter. She was walking unsteadily toward the rest rooms. She would pass by the officers and their wives. He didn't give a damn about Darlene; so far as he was concerned, she could fall flat on her ass in front of Bellmon. But Bellmon would find out that the troops had been feeding her vodka-spiked punch. Bellmon would not think that was funny.

He caught up with her.

"Mrs. Heatter," he said, "I'm going back to the post. Can I offer you a ride?"

She looked at him uncomprehendingly for a moment, then smiled broadly.

"Why not?" she said, and took his arm.

He had a little trouble getting her into the car, she was that bombed.

"I feel so silly!" she announced, when they were on their way from the lake to the post.

"There was a lot of vodka in that punch you were drinking," he said. "In case you didn't know."

"I know," she said. "I figured that out myself."

"You did?"

"Yeah," she said. "When I started feeling so good, I figured that out myself."

"I see."

"I figured, since everybody else was doing it, why not?"

"And you like it?"

"It's different," she said. "But how am I going to go home?" She giggled.

Christ, now he was stuck with her. If she went home that way, her husband, another tee totaler, would cause all kinds of trouble. He decided he would take her to the snack bar and get her a cup of coffee and then dismissed that idea. She would be obviously drunk in the snack bar.

"If you'd like," Greer said, "I could make you a cup of coffee. In my BOQ."

She thought that over a moment.

"That's all you have in mind?" she asked.

He laughed.

"Word of honor. A couple of cups of coffee and you'll feel a lot better."

"Thank you," she said. "Thank you very much. If my husband ever found out about this, he'd kill me."

"Well, we'll just make sure he never finds out," Greer said.

She was unsteady on her feet going up the stairs to his room, and he was grateful that there was nobody in the BOQ corridors.

He installed her in one of the armchairs and got the electric coffeepot going. There were still two bottles of beer in the refrigerator, and he took one.

"I never tasted alcohol until today," Darlene said, when she saw him.

"Is that so?"

"And I've never tasted beer," she said.

"Don't you think you've had enough?"

"I want a taste of the beer," she said. He handed her the bottle. She took several swallows, licked her lips, and said it was good.

"If you drink the rest of that, the coffee won't do you any good," Greer said.

"So what?"

"What about your husband?"

"I was lying about him," she said. "He won't be home. He'll be at the fire station. Did you know that my husband is a fireman?"

"Yes, I did," Greer said.

"Well, he won't be home until nine tomorrow morning," Darlene said. "And the kids are at my mother's, so if I want to drink a beer, nobody has to know a thing about it."

"Help yourself," Greer said.

"Thank you, I will," she said, archly.

He took the last bottle of beer from the refrigerator and opened it. When he turned around again, Darlene was reading *Playboy*.

"I can't understand why girls pose for pictures like that," she said. "I mean, people they know would know."

"I guess they pay them," he said.

"I'm not a prude," Darlene said. "I know men like to look at naked women." She laughed. "And I guess women like to look at naked men, too. Somebody should start a magazine for women with naked men inside. I'd buy it."

Greer was suddenly alarmed. *Fuck the coffee*, he thought. *Just get her out of here!*

"You about ready to go, Darlene?" he asked.

"You trying to get rid of me, or what?"

"Don't you think you'd better start thinking about getting home?"

"I bet if I took my clothes off, you'd want me to stay," Darlene said. "I'll bet you would."

Greer didn't say anything.

Darlene stood up, and started to unfasten her blouse.

"What do you think you're doing?" Greer asked.

She had been looking down at her buttons. Now she looked up at him.

"I just thought," she said. "You're going away tomorrow. For good."

"Yeah," he said. "I am."

"So nobody would ever know," she said. She lowered her head and looked at her fingers on the buttons, but she stopped moving the fingers. "You want to, or not?" she asked.

Fuck it, Greer thought. *It's probably just what I need.*

"Yes," he said.

(Three)
The Pentagon
Washington, D.C.
1 June 1957

The Vice Chief of Staff of the U.S. Army caught the Chief of Staff of the U.S. Army as he was preparing to enter his black Cadillac limousine.

"I'm on my way to see the President, E. Z.," the Chief of Staff said.

"Fuck him, let him wait," E. Z. Black said. "This is important."

Shaking his head, smiling, the Chief of Staff took the sheet of paper extended to him. It contained just three names. There was a neat check mark by one of them.

"You think that's it, huh?" the Chief of Staff said.

"Yes, sir. That is my recommendation."

"There's going to be howls of rage," the Chief of Staff said. "Cries of favoritism, cronyism. They're going to read into this more than I think you intend."

"With a little bit of luck," General E. Z. Black said, "I'll be able to blame it on the outrageous interference of the Deputy Secretary of Defense on Internal Army Affairs."

The Vice Chief of Staff leaned over the roof of his limousine and scribbled his initials on the sheet of typewriter paper.

"Thank you, sir," General Black said.

"I'll be burned in effigy," the Chief of Staff said.

"They'll probably take your bust out of the Airborne Hall of Fame," General Black said. "Or use it for a dart board."

"Tell me. Because he's the best man? Or because you think aviation is the flying cavalry?"

"A little of both," Black said. "I've always been a little afraid of the airborne's idea of 'acceptable losses in the assault.' A tanker has been trained since he's a second lieutenant to conserve his assets."

"Yeah," the Chief of Staff said. "That's just what I decided. Right now, I mean. Trying to read your mind."

The Chief of Staff started to get into the limousine.

"Give my most respectful regards to our Commander in Chief," E. Z. Black said.

"I just might do that, E. Z.," the Chief of Staff said.

Because it had been far more political, the selection of a general officer to replace the late Major General Angus Laird as commanding general of the U.S. Army Aviation Center had been somewhat more difficult than the selection of a replacement commander for another of the combat arms or technical services schools would have been.

For one thing, there was no legally established aviation branch, and thus the slot was not reserved for an infantry general, as would have been the case had the commanding general of Fort Benning, the Infantry Center, suddenly died. Or for an artillery general, if the commander of the Artillery Center at Fort Sill had died. Or an armor general, had the commanding general's slot at Fort Knox suddenly come open.

As a matter of fact, it had been originally and rather universally believed that the new Rucker commander would not be an armor General. Scotty Laird had been armor, and logically—fairly—the new commander should not be. Now that armor had had its turn, it was now infantry's, or airborne's, or maybe even artillery's or, remotely, transportation's.

There are normally seven four-star generals on active duty. The Chief of Staff; the Vice Chief of Staff; the Commanders in Chief Europe and Asia; the Commanding General of Continental Army Command; and the Commanding Generals, U.S. Army Forces, Europe, and U.S. Army Forces, Far East.

Next down the line come the twenty-five to thirty lieutenant (three-star) generals, who command the eight armies, the larger corps, and serve as deputies to the four-stars. The Assistant Chiefs of Staff for Operations, Personnel, Logistics, and other general and special staff functions are normally lieutenant generals.

There are nearly two hundred major (two-star) generals and over three hundred brigadier (one-star) generals. It was from this latter group of more than five hundred one- and two-star generals, almost all by definition thoroughly qualified officers, that the selection would have to be made.

But numbers were deceiving. Not all of the five hundred brigadier and major generals were available for consideration. The technical service general officers were immediately eliminated from consideration. The Surgeon General and his subordinates were obviously out of the running, and so were the general officers who had spent their careers in the Finance Corps, the Signal Corps, the Ordnance Corps and the Quartermaster Corps. The Corps of Engineers made a halfhearted attempt to let it be known that it would not stagger the imagination to have an engineer general command Rucker, especially in view of the massive construction projects underway in Alabama.

The Transportation Corps made a serious attempt to gain the slot, coming up with a skillfully written staff study attempting to prove that aviation was really nothing more than an assemblage of flying trucks and jeeps. If the army of the 1960s, it argued, was indeed to be air mobile, then the bulk of the "aerial vehicles" would be flying trucks, as the vehicles of the present army were predominantly wheeled ones.

As vehicles of transportation, the Transportation Corps argued, it was simply logical to place the training of their crews and maintenance personnel under the Transportation Corps, which already had responsibility for wheeled vehicles and their serving personnel. They had an in-place. tested system, the Transportation Corps argued. that with obviously simple modifications could and should be adapted for army aviation. Finally, they argued, there was no place in the army better able to accept the thousands of warrant officer pilots than TC. When, for one reason or another, the warrant officer pilots could no longer fly, work would have to be found for them. Those who could not be absorbed in aviation-type functions could be employed in other TC rail, road and water operations.

The arguments advanced were logical, but the proposed TC equation lacked one essential ingredient. The Transportation Corps was a technical service, not a combat arm. While the odd TC officer, here and there, might have had to send out a truck convoy somewhere or other where it might come under fire, no TC officer had ever had to look his lieutenants in the eye and announce to them they were expected to lead their men over the next hill; or set the fuses to zero and fire point-blank; or push disabled tracks to the side of the road and keep moving.

There are three official combat arms—infantry, artillery, and armor—and a fourth, unofficial, but equally powerful politically, made up of officers of the three combat arms trained in the technique and philosophy of vertical envelopment, the airborne.

Airborne had always wanted aviation, and felt that it was logical for it to absorb it. Aviation was really nothing more than the evolutionary development of vertical envelopment. The helicopter, so to speak, was nothing more than an improved and vastly more efficient means for delivering the guy with the rifle safely behind enemy lines.

Infantry, although there were very few infantry generals who had not gone through the three-week jump school at Benning and who in consequence did not wear parachutist's wings, had by and large reached the consensus that airborne was so much elitist bullshit.

Their argument ran that it made very little sense to spend a great deal of time and money training people as parachutists only to lose somewhere in the neighborhood of twenty-five percent of them in parachute accidents before they fired a shot in combat. These accidents ranged from broken ankles, legs, and backs to electrocution and incineration on high tension power lines. This sin was multiplied when airborne tried to

246 W. E. B. Griffin

insist that airborne privates have Army General Classification Test scores of 100, only ten points below the AGCT required to send a man to OCS.

The function of an army, those disenchanted with airborne said, was not to die yourself but to kill the enemy.

Artillery's claim on the empty commanding general's office at Camp Rucker was by right of lineage. Army aviation had entered the army as Piper Clubs flying during War II as artillery spotters. It was theirs, they argued, and there was a corps of company and field-grade officers coming up who had spent their careers in aviation.

It was pointed out by the Signal Corps, however, that aviation, period, had entered the army, period, via the Signal Corps. The first aviator's "wings" had been a representation of the Bald Eagle clutching signal flags in his claws. There was no reason the Signal Corps should not send one of its generals to command Rucker. No one really took their bid seriously.

Armor maintained that aviation should be an armor function. For those who *really* understood military history and the lessons it taught, it was clear that the three combat arms were infantry (the man with the pike, or the bow and arrow, or the rifle, whatever the individual hand-held weapon); artillery, (the people who fired the catapults, the cannons, and the rockets); and cavalry (those who moved rapidly around the infantry and the artillery in battle, once on horses, presently in tanks, and quite obviously in the future on mechanical horses called helicopters). They were willing to grant that George S. Patton had made one mistake. He had gone along with the misguided when they wanted to change cavalry's name to armor. They pointed out that General I. D. White, who had gotten the 2nd Armored Division to the Elbe when General Porky Waterford was still hung up around Kassel, had thrown a famous I. D. White fit in the office of the Chief of the Staff after the war, the result of which was that cavalry sabers were superimposed on the tank in armor's insignia.

The arguments reduced the number of candidates to fill Scotty Laird's vacancy from nearly five hundred to about fifty. The selection process moved into the inner offices of the Pentagon. Further recommendations were not desired, nor would they be entertained.

The list was distilled down to three general officers, a straight-leg infantry major general, presently commanding the 1st Infantry—"the Big Red One"—Division in Germany; a jumping general, presently deputy commander, XVIII Airborne Corps, at Bragg; and a brigadier general, whom both the Chief of Staff and the Vice Chief of Staff (but few others) knew had just been selected for promotion to major general. The brigadier general was presently serving as Special Assistant to the Deputy Secretary of Defense for Research and Development.

At eight o'clock that same night, General E. Z. Black, Vice Chief of Staff of the U.S. Army, walked up to the charcoal grill erected in the garden behind Quarters No. 3 at Fort Meyer, Virginia.

A white-jacketed orderly was broiling steaks. A slight, erect man in civilian clothing watched him.

"Staying close to the fire, Paul?" E. Z. Black said.

"A cavalryman always knows enough to stay close to the food, General," Brigadier General Paul Jiggs said.

"And how are things in Research and Development?"

"I'm thinking about resigning and running for public office," General Jiggs said. "Obviously, politicians live much better than we do. They eat inside with linen on the table and everything."

Black laughed.

"I've got something for you, Paul," E. Z. Black said. He put something in Jiggs's hand. "Keep it under your hat until it's official."

Jiggs looked at the small silver pin in his hand. It was rank insignia: two stars joined together.

"Thank you, sir," he said.

"There's a catch, Paul. There's no free lunch."

Jiggs looked at him.

"Rucker and the Army Aviation Center," General Black said.

"I didn't think I was even being considered," Jiggs said. Black sensed that Jiggs's surprise was genuine.

XII

(One)
Camp Rucker, Alabama
12 June 1956

HEADQUARTERS

THE U.S. ARMY AVIATION CENTER

CAMP RUCKER, ALABAMA

12 June 1956

The undersigned herewith assumes command of the United States Army Aviation Center and Camp Rucker, Alabama.

Paul T. Jiggs
Major General, USA
Commanding

(Two)
On his third day as commanding general of the Aviation Center and Camp Rucker, Major General Paul T. Jiggs walked

out the back door of the headquarters building and across the
street and into the officer's open mess. He was trailed by his
two aides-de-camp (one of whom he had brought from Washington, the other appointed that day; the latter had been functioning as unofficial aide to the colonel who had been in
temporary command since General Laird's death) and a lieutenant colonel from the Department of Flight Training who had
been named as the general's instructor pilot.

General Jiggs got in the cafeteria line, going to the end of
it like everybody else instead of going into the dining room,
where there was waiter service and a table reserved for the
commanding general.

He put a bowl of gelatin with pineapple chunks embedded
in it on his tray, then pork chops, no gravy, and held his hand
up to refuse mashed potatoes. He took a roll, no butter, and a
glass of water and a mug of coffee. He initialed the bill he was
given by the cashier and found a table in the crowded cafeteria,
uncomfortably aware that people were staring at him. They
tried not to, but they did.

Apparently, Scotty Laird had not carried his own tray to eat
with the peasants and had otherwise accepted the benefits of
the myth that rank hath its privileges. Jiggs had already seen
that the colonel who had been holding the fort had wallowed
in the prerogatives of the base commander.

"Good afternoon," General Jiggs said to the adjacent table
of second and first lieutenants, who responded—until he stopped
them with a wave of his hand—by jumping to their feet.

The general's party joined him. They unloaded their trays
and the junior aide collected all of them and put them on a tray
table before sitting down himself.

The general's party became aware that something in the
cafeteria dining room had caught the general's attention. He
kept looking at something. They narrowed it down. The general's attention was drawn to two officers sitting at a table.
One was a very large, very black captain, wearing stiffly starched
fatigues and the Aviation Center insignia. The other was a
young-looking major in a Class "A" tropical worsted uniform.
One of General Jiggs's first official acts as commanding general
was a change in the center uniform regulations. Wearing of

tropical worsted uniforms during normal duty hours was discouraged. It was a good change, doing away with both chickenshit and high dry-cleaning bills. It was a lot cheaper to have khakis or fatigues washed and starched than it was to have TWs dry-cleaned. It was difficult in the Alabama heat to make a uniform last a full day before it became sweat-soaked.

The general spoke: "Across the room," he said, "are two officers. A major in TWs and a captain in fatigues. Do you see them?"

"Yes, sir," the general's party replied, almost in unison.

"I want you to carry a message to the major," the general said to the aide he had acquired since coming to Rucker.

"Yes, sir."

"You will tell the major that if he cannot afford to offer to buy the commanding general a cup of coffee, the general is willing to loan him the money to do so."

"Yes, sir," the aide said, confused, uneasy, getting to his feet.

"Wait a minute, I'm not through," General Jiggs said. "You will say to the captain that if he is indeed sweet little Phil Parker, the general will buy him a cup of coffee, too."

"Yes, sir," the aide said, and walked across the room. He returned almost immediately, with the major and the captain trailing him.

"Good afternoon, sir," they said.

"Long time, no see, Lowell," General Jiggs said.

"Yes, sir, it has been some time, hasn't it?"

"And you, Captain, were once known as sweet little Philip S. Parker, IV, am I correct?" he asked the six-foot four-inch, 235-pound officer.

"Yes, sir."

"I'm an old friend of your father's," General Jiggs said.

"Yes, sir, I know."

"I was under the impression you were at C&GSC, Lowell."

"Yes, sir, I am."

"You're a long way from Leavenworth."

"I came to see Captain Parker, sir."

"Birds of a feather?"

"Yes, sir."

"What do I have you doing here, Parker?" General Jiggs asked.

"I'm an IP in Rotary Wing Advanced, sir," Captain Parker said.

"That's fascinating," General Jiggs said. "Are you any good at it?"

"I believe I'm competent, sir."

"As I was walking over here, it occurred to me that having a lieutenant colonel—no offense, colonel—detailed full time to teach me how to fly when I am not otherwise occupied was not a very efficient utilization of resources. Is there any reason, Colonel, why Captain Parker could not be detailed to teach me how to fly, permitting you to return to duties more appropriate to a senior officer?"

"Sir, I'd have to review Captain Parker's records," the lieutenant colonel said.

"He's either a competent instructor pilot or he isn't," General Jiggs said, his voice suddenly very cold. "Which?"

"I'm sure that Captain Parker is competent, sir," the lieutenant colonel said, uncomfortably. "But we like to take a little extra care with general officers, sir."

"Bullshit," General Jiggs said. "Captain Parker's father was my instructor in equestrianism at Riley when I was second john. I always told myself I'd get back at him someday. You arrange for it, Colonel."

"Yes, sir."

"How long do you plan to be AWOL from Leavenworth, Lowell?"

"I'd planned to turn myself in in the morning, sir."

"In that case, you'll be free to come to supper," General Jiggs said. "We eat at seven. At half past six, we serve drinks."

"Yes, sir."

"Are you married, Parker?"

"Yes, sir."

"Would it be convenient for Mrs. Parker?"

"I'll have to check, sir," Captain Parker said, a little uncomfortably.

"It's Dr. Parker, sir," Lowell said. "She's a contract surgeon at the hospital."

"If it would be convenient for *Dr.* Parker, I would be honored to make her acquaintance," General Jiggs said. "Now go finish your lunch."

General Jiggs ate two mouthfuls of pork chop.

"That was Captain Philip Sheridan Parker IV," he said. "A direct descendant of some of the first Negro soldiers in the army. His great, great, whatever it is, grandfather rode with Sheridan, and named his first-born after him. In the last great war to end all wars, that boy's father, Colonel Parker III, led an armored column into East Germany and snatched Bob Bellmon and two hundred other American officer prisoners from the Russians."

There was no reply.

"The other one is Lowell," General Jiggs said. "Anybody ever heard of Task Force Lowell?"

The aide he had inherited, who wished to remain assigned as an aide, had done his homework. In Korea, as a lieutenant colonel and later as a colonel, General Jiggs had commanded the 73rd Heavy Tank Battalion (Reinforced). A task force, Task Force Lowell, from the 73rd had made the breakout from the Pusan perimeter and linked up with General Ned Almond's X Corps after the landing at Inchon. It was described in the book the lieutenant had read as "a near classic utilization of an armored column in both the breakthrough, and in disrupting the enemy's rear." After he had read it, the lieutenant remembered reconstructing the operations of Task Force Lowell at the Point. They'd done it twice, once on the maps and the sand tables and again as an exercise in logistics: how to supply a fast-moving armored column with the almost incredible amount of fuel, ammunition, and other supplies it consumes, by whatever means are available.

"Yes, sir," he said.

"Tell them," General Jiggs said.

The word spread, beginning that afternoon, that all the rumors were true. Armor was taking over. The first party the general had thrown was pure armor. Some jigaboo captain, whose father had taught the general how to ride, no shit, a horse, back when there still was cavalry; Colonel Bellmon, armor, director of the Aviation Combat Developments Agency;

Major MacMillan, the guy with the Medal; his exec, also armor. And some hotshot major from C&GSC who's the guy who flew into Laird Field in that red-and-white civilian Aero Commander. Also armor. Shit. The Armor Association would probably turn out to be worse for army aviation than the Cincinnati Flying Club and the West Point Protective Association.

(Three)
19 June 1957
Oran, Algeria

The tourists, mostly members of Local 133, International Brotherhood of Master Machinists, Tool Makers and Die Cutters, United Automobile Workers of America, but including (to fill up the forty-four passenger buses used by African Tours, Ltd.) a trio of middle-aged schoolteachers; two rather willowy gentlemen from New Hope, Pennsylvania, who thought that Native Art was going to be important in their interior decorating business; and three others arranged for by the Oran office of American Express, gathered at 7:15 in the morning in the lobby of the Hotel de Normandie in Oran.

There was some confusion, of course, and someone, naturally, had overslept, and it was a few minutes after eight (not 7:30 *sharp!*) before the bus pulled away from the hotel. In thirty minutes the bus was out of Oran, which looked to most of the Americans not too different from European cities, except for the Ay-rabs in their dirty robes.

The bus—Dutch, diesel, enormous, with lots of glass and surprisingly comfortable and roomy seats—swayed not unpleasantly down the highway as the green of Oran and its environs turned into the brown of the desert.

Sidi-bel-Abbès, legendary home of the French Foreign Legion, was their first stop. It was something of a disappointment. The museum was interesting, but you can only take so many museums, and Local 133 had been on tour for sixteen days so far, and they had enough museums to last them awhile.

The legionnaires, except for their funny hats, looked disappointingly like Americans. Their uniforms were American khaki and U.S. Army work clothes, and they drove jeeps and Dodge three-quarter-ton trucks and GMC six-by-sixes, some of which, the machinists and tool and die makers agreed among themselves, *they* had made back in Detroit. The legionnaires were armed with good old U.S. M1 Garand rifles and Thompson .45 submachine guns and Colt .45 automatics.

And then something happened that made everybody really hate the goddamned French Foreign Legion. No sooner did they get out of Sidi-bel-Abbès, than they got stuck behind a French Foreign Legion convoy that moved down the road like a goddamned snail.

"Pass the sonsofbitches!" the machinists yelled at the bus driver, but the bus driver simply shrugged his shoulders.

It was not that there was any good reason to go faster, and they really couldn't have gone a hell of a lot faster on the narrow, winding roads. It was simply that they were part of their culture, and a vehicle in front of them going five miles an hour less than they were capable of going was almost insulting.

Not that it was uncomfortable in the air-conditioned bus. There was a refrigerator with soft drinks (Coke and some local orange soda that the Americans didn't like and some Algerian beer, which was nearly as bad). And the scenery was spectacular, if you liked rocks. Everybody oohed and aahed at first, and then they got bored with the mountains.

They went through Tiemcen to Geryville. They stopped in Geryville for lunch, and everybody was pleased with that. It gave them a chance to stretch their legs, take pictures of camels and great big Arabs on little tiny donkeys, and have a little lunch. And the French Foreign Legion convoy had disappeared. They wouldn't have to swallow their dust from here on in to wherever the hell they were going next. But when they left Geryville, the Legion convoy was on the road ahead of them again. Bastards!

They were going next to Colomb Béchar, via Ain Sefra. Fourteen miles out of Ain Sefra as the crow flies, and thirty-six miles out as the road wound its way up and around the mountains, four 105 mm artillery shells furnished by the United

States of America as military aid to the Republic of France and captured by the *Armée Nationale pour la Libération d'Algérie* were detonated under the road.

The plan was to blow the shells when the bus was directly over them. The ANLA *sous-chef* who pressed the plunger had been well trained when he had been in the French Army, but he was a little nervous, and he pressed the plunger a half-second early.

The charge exploded under the bus's engine. The force was sufficient to send what was left of the engine sailing fifty feet into the air, and to neatly sever the bus's frame immediately behind the engine compartment. The driver and Mr. and Mrs. Rudolf Czernik, of Hamtramck, Michigan, who were riding in the forwardmost passenger seats, died instantly.

The back of the bus pushed what was left of the severed front of the bus approximately ten meters farther down the road before it dug into the macadam surface and stopped.

Six more tourists, including one of the interior decorators from New Hope, Pennsylvania, died in the initial explosion. Four others, riding near the front of the bus, suffered injuries that were to be fatal. Many others were injured, some seriously, some slightly.

But the ANLA plan to kill all on board was a failure: those to the rear of the bus were either unharmed, slightly injured, or simply badly shaken up.

Within moments of the explosion, legionnaires from a jeep which had been following the bus managed to get the rear door of the bus open. They began to unload first the unharmed passengers and then the injured passengers. The dead were left where they were.

The surviving passengers were herded into a ditch by the side of the road and told by a legionnaire with a heavy German accent to stay down and not move.

There was weapons fire now, the sharp crack of .30 caliber rifles and light machine guns, the heavier, booming crack of .50 caliber machine guns, the crumping boom of mortars. The noise was deafening. One of the members of Local 133, ignoring his screaming wife, crawled out of the ditch and reclaimed an M1 Garand and two bandoliers of ammunition from a legionnaire who lay in the road with half of his head blown off. He crawled back into the ditch, opened the action halfway to see if the rifle was loaded, and then crawled to the lip of the ditch.

He couldn't see anything, but he emptied the clip into the granite mountain above them, and then he loaded a fresh clip into the Garand. He turned to his wife: "Francine, for the love of God, shut the fuck up!"

The firing lasted about five minutes. The smell of gunpowder was in the air.

Then there was silence.

There came the sound of helicopters. The lithe, blond woman recognized that sound. Help was on the way. Help had come. She put her hand on her ankle. The pain made her want to scream. She had thought she had sprained it. She now realized, dully, that it was broken. It was already swelling and turning blue.

The sound of the helicopters came closer and closer, and then two flashed overhead. Over the sound of their engines and the fluckata-fluckata-fluckata of their rotors she could hear the sharp cracking roar of machine guns. She waited for the sound of helicopters landing. She had seen helicopter ambulances on television. If they had helicopters with machine guns, they were certain to have helicopter ambulances.

But there were no helicopter ambulances, and in about ten minutes the sound of the helicopters with the machine guns died out. The helicopters were now flying high, back and forth along the road.

Legionnaires had now formed a defensive line around the surviving tourists in the ditch. A legionnaire with a medical kit came over to her and looked a moment at the ankle and took a hypodermic needle from his bag. He smiled at her.

"I don't want that," she said. She hurt, she hurt as badly as she had ever hurt in her life, but she wanted to be conscious. She didn't want to be unconscious, not knowing what was going on, here in the middle of nowhere, where she didn't really know what had happened, only that she had almost been killed.

"No, *non*," she said, then, *"nein,"* remembering that some of the legionnaires seemed to be German.

He pinned her hand painfully to the ground with his knee, grabbed her arm roughly with one hand, and injected her through her blouse sleeve with the other.

"Damn," she said, and then it was as if the lights and the sounds and everything else went off.

She became aware, first, of an old-fashioned ceiling fan turning and creaking above her. She focused her eyes on it. Then she smelled the smell of a hospital. It was disinfectant, what she thought of as chloroform, even though she knew that wasn't what it was.

Her mouth was absolutely dry. When she tried to lick her lips, her tongue was dry. She pushed herself up on her elbows. She had the worst headache she had ever had. Even her eyeballs hurt, as if something was pushing them from inside her skull.

There was a pitcher of something, probably water, and a plastic glass on a small table beside her. She rolled on her side to reach for it. Then she became aware of her leg. There was no pain, but it felt very heavy. She threw the sheet off her and looked.

She was in a rough white hospital gown. No buttons. It tied in half a dozen places. Whoever had tied her into it hadn't done a very good job. Her body was exposed from the waist down. She pulled the gown closed over her midsection and upper legs.

She wondered where her clothing was; there was no closet in the room. Her foot and ankle were in a dirty white plaster of Paris cast. She moved it from side to side. There was a dull pain, nothing that really bothered her.

She wondered where she was, and looked around for a button to call for a nurse, or a doctor, or somebody. She found it, but someone had tied it in a loop, for some reason just out of her reach.

She pushed herself upward on the bed and decided that she would sort of crawl up the headboard and reach the damned cord.

Then there was a knock at the door.

She slid quickly back into the bed, pulling the sheet over

her, and tried to pull the hospital gown, which had ridden up, back down again. The sheets were thin, translucent, and she didn't want whoever it was at the door to see her hair down there.

There was a second knock.

"Come in," she called, and then she remembered something from her high school French. "*Entrez,*" she added.

He was an officer in a French Foreign Legion uniform, a parachutist's camouflage uniform. He was as deeply tanned as she had ever seen a man tanned. His muscular arms, exposed to the biceps by the neatly rolled up sleeves, were almost chocolate brown. His hair was bleached nearly white. His eyes were hidden behind gold-framed aviator's glasses. He was, she realized, the most handsome, sexiest, most masculine man she had ever seen.

He sort of backed into the room, as if finishing a conversation with someone in the corridor.

"Good afternoon," he began, artificially cordial, reassuring. "I'm Lieutenant Edward C. Greer, of the United..." He stopped in midsentence. "Holy shit!" he said.

She didn't say anything. Just waited for him to go on.

"United States Army," he picked up. "I'm temporarily stationed with the French Foreign Legion in Colomb Béchar. You're in a French Foreign Legion hospital. The doctors assure me that you are in no danger. Arrangements are being made to fly all the Americans from the tour out of here. It will take a few more hours to make the arrangements. In the meantime, if you will give me a name and address of someone you would like notified, the American consul general in Algiers will telephone them and assure them that you're all right."

She nodded.

"Except, of course," Lieutenant Greer said, "I don't need your address."

"I thought maybe you'd lost it," Melody said.

"If we can get you into a wheelchair," he said, "I can get you through on the radio. That would be better for your parents, if they heard from you, yourself, rather than one of those State Department assholes."

"I'm fine, Ed," Melody said. "How are you?"

"What the fuck are you doing here, anyway? Are you out of your mind?"

"I'm not here," Melody said. "Today I'm in either Strasbourg or Cologne, I forget which, looking at a cathedral."

"You almost got your ass blown off, you know that?" he said, angrily.

"You look pretty good yourself," Melody said. "That's a really nice tan."

"You're not telling me you came here just to see me?" he challenged.

"I'm queer for desert and rocks," Melody said.

"Hey, that was a long time ago," he said.

"Six months. I thought maybe six months would change things."

"There have been bandits in this area since before the time of Christ," he said. "While the French make every effort they can to police the area, obviously they aren't always successful."

"Those weren't bandits," Melody said. "Whoever it was, was trying to kill us."

"And the French Foreign Legion isn't exactly a police force, either."

"What was that, a speech someone told you to give?"

"His Esteemed Excellency, the Deputy Consul for Public Affairs himself," Greer said. "I told him he'd better come give it himself, but he said he was going to be needed in Algiers to handle the public relations end of this 'incident.'"

"What are you doing here?"

"Learning," he said.

"Learning what?"

"That escorting a civilian bus with a platoon of troops doesn't always guarantee the safety of the bus, for one thing," he said.

"Don't you care that I love you?" Melody asked.

"If that fucking charge had gone off a second later," Greer said, "we'd be sending what was left of you home in a rubber bag."

"Were you out there?" Melody asked.

"I was in one of the gunships," he said.

"Why didn't you land and help us?" Melody demanded.

"That was their game plan," he said. "They set that charge

conveniently close to an area big enough to take a couple of H-21s."

"That's the one with a rotor at each end?" she asked.

"Yeah, the Piasecki. Flying Banana. We gave the French fifty, sixty of them. What we were supposed to do was lose our cool when we heard about the bus, and then rush in with H-21s and medical people. When we did that, they would knock out the H-21s."

"But we were civilians," Melody said.

"You were either French or American, which is nearly as good. You blow away one Frog *or* two Americans and you get a guaranteed ticket to heaven."

"Would that have bothered you?" she asked.

"Would what have bothered me?"

"If the bomb had blown me up?"

"What they're doing now," he said, "is sending patrols through the mountains over the airfield. As soon as they've been cleared, the air force is sending in a couple of transports from Morocco. They'll fly you to Algiers."

Melody started pulling open the bows fastening her gown.

"What the hell are you doing?" Greer asked.

"Looking," she said.

"You're all right. You must have slammed your ankle into a seat or something. You weren't hit."

"I may not have been hit," Melody said. "But I'm not all right."

"What's the matter with you?" he asked, and she heard the concern in his voice. Her nipples were standing up. She was glad for that. She knew he liked it when her nipples were erect.

"You tell me," she said. "You're the one who runs away from me."

"Hey, I thought that was all settled. Different folks. You're your kind of people, and I'm my kind of people. You want to close your goddamned robe? Before somebody comes in here, for Christ's sake!"

"Have you had a lot of girls since you came here?" Melody asked.

"What do you think?"

"Tell me."

"Lots of girls."

"You used to tell me I had the prettiest teats in the world," she said. "You find anybody with prettier teats, Ed?"

"Jesus Christ! You're really a fruitcake, you know that?"

"I went to bed with six different guys," she said.

"Shut up!"

"I fucked six different guys, some of them two and three times, and it was never like it was with you," she said.

"Goddamn you, will you shut up!"

"So I figured it was worth the trip over here," she said. "It took a little doing to get the money from my father. After what I got into with you, he decided I needed a keeper. I had a hard time ditching her. The cops in Coblenz are probably dragging the river for my body."

She looked up at him and forced a smile on her face, and then she saw his cold eyes and rigid jawline and that was too much. The whole trip, even nearly blown up, had been for nothing.

She let out a little howl, and threw herself on her side. "Get the hell out of here!" she said. "Leave me alone!"

She heard footsteps and figured that it was him, leaving the room. But then the bed sagged, and she knew he was sitting on it. She held her breath for a moment, and then rolled over to him, her arms out, reaching for him.

"Oh, baby," he said. "Jesus Christ, I've missed you."

"That's why you sent me all the letters, right? Not even a lousy postcard!"

"I just didn't want you to get into something you shouldn't," he said.

She moved her face to his, found his mouth. She put her tongue in his mouth, felt him shiver, as he always did. Then she thrashed around in his arms.

"Let go of me!" she said. He let go of her, surprised.

"What are you doing?" he asked.

"What does it look like I'm doing?" she asked, as she shrugged out of the hospital gown.

"Jesus, Melody, what about your ankle?"

"Fuck my ankle," she said. "Take your damned clothes off!"

(Four)
Extract from the Southern Star
Volume 87, No. 42
Ozark, Alabama
30 September 1957

OZARK, Sept 30—Mayor and Mrs. Howard Percy Dutton announce the wedding of their daughter Melody Louise, to First Lieutenant Edward C. Greer, United States Army, in Algiers, Algeria, September 28.

The previously scheduled nuptials, delayed because of Lieutenant Greer's reassignment from Camp Rucker, were conducted in the English Church in Algiers (Episcopal) by the Rev. Ronald I. Spiers, chaplain to the British Consulate General in Algiers.

Lieutenant Greer is an assistant military attaché at the United States Consulate General, Algiers, where the couple will reside.

XIII

(One)
Washington, D.C.
1 September 1957

At the conclusion of his first day on the job as Deputy Chief, Plans and Requirements Section (Fiscal), Aviation Maintenance Section, Office of the Deputy Chief of Staff for Logistics (DCSLOG), Major Craig W. Lowell caught a cab at the Pentagon and had himself driven to the Park-Sheraton Hotel.

He had arrived the night before from Frankfurt, and there were a number of things he had to do, starting with unpacking, thinking about getting a place to live, and getting an automobile.

But the first thing he did when he got to the Park-Sheraton was walk in the bar and order a very dry martini. He had reached the conclusion within an hour of reporting for duty that he was not going to like his new assignment at all. He was going to be a glorified clerk, despite his awesome title, and he was surrounded with horse's asses from his immediate superior, a Lieutenant Colonel Dillard, upward.

He quickly downed the first martini and was halfway through the second when the inevitable thought occurred to him: if he was going to have to spend his time moving paper around on a desk, he had might as well do that at Craig, Powell, Kenyon and Dawes, where he at least owned half the store.

He realized then that both the thought—and martinis—were dangerous at the moment. He set the martini down, scribbled his name on the bar check, and walked out of the bar and to the desk, where he asked for his key.

The desk clerk handed him a telephone message along with the key: "Please call Col. Newburgh." There was a number.

He didn't know a Colonel Newburgh, and he wondered how Colonel Newburgh, whoever the hell he was, had found him at the Park-Sheraton. The temptation was to crumple the message up and forget about it, but he knew he could not afford to offend any of his new superiors. He went to his room (there had been no suites available, something else that annoyed him) and took off his tunic, pulled down his tie, and dialed the number.

"Burning Tree," an operator announced, and for a moment, Lowell thought that he had dialed the wrong number. Burning Tree liked to refer to itself as the President's golf course. There were few colonels among its members.

"Colonel Newburgh, please," he said, however, just to make sure.

"May I ask who's calling?" the operator said.

"Major Lowell," he said.

"Colonel Newburgh is expecting your call, sir," the operator said. "He's in the steam room. Will you hold, please?"

In a moment, a deep, somewhat raspy voice said, "Newburgh, here."

"Major Lowell, sir," Lowell said. "Returning your call."

"Glad I caught you, Lowell," Newburgh said. "What I had in mind was a couple of drinks and dinner. I hope you haven't made other plans."

"Sir, do I know you?"

"We've met," Newburgh said. "And we have a number of mutual friends."

"May I ask who, sir?"

"Bob Bellmon, for one," Newburgh said. "Paul Jiggs for another. He is, that is, *Bob* is going to eat with us."

"That's very kind of you, Colonel," Lowell said. "What time?"

"I don't suppose you've had time to get a car. So if I sent mine for you, that'd give you half an hour to get ready..."

"I'll just jump in a cab," Lowell said.

"You know where it is?"

"I'm sure the cabbie will be able to find it," Lowell said.

"I'll leave your name at the door," Newburgh said. "Give them mine, and they'll pass you right in."

"Thank you," Lowell said, and hung up.

He took a shower and changed into civilian clothing, a tweed jacket, gray flannel slacks, a dress white shirt with a foulard in the open collar, and loafers. Then he took a taxi to Burning Tree Country Club.

"Major Lowell, as the guest of Colonel Newburgh," he said to the porter at the door.

The porter looked confused, checked his file, and announced: "I don't seem to have any record of that, sir. But I believe the colonel may be here, and if you'll be good enough to have a seat, I'll see about straightening this out."

"How about this?" Lowell said, handing the porter a card. It was the personal calling card of the executive vice president of the Riggs National Bank, who was also chairman of the Burning Tree House Committee. On it was written "Mr. C. W. Lowell. All privileges, pending action of membership committee."

"Oh, yes, sir," the porter said. "We've been told to expect you, sir. Go right in. I'm sure our manager would like to explain our facilities."

"Just point out the bar, please," Lowell said, with a smile.

"Yes, sir. Up the stairs, through the double glass door."

"Thank you," Lowell said, and found the bar.

There was a stand-up bar and a number of leather upholstered chairs before small tables. Lowell sat down at one of the tables. A waiter in a white jacket appeared immediately.

"Scotch, not much ice, and water," Lowell said.

"You're Mr. Lowell, sir?" the waiter asked.

"That's right."

"Your first night with us, sir, you're a guest of the club. And our manager just called to say he's tied up at the moment, but he looks forward to meeting you personally in just a few minutes."

"That's very nice," Lowell said. "Thank you very much."

When the waiter delivered his drink, a good stiff shot in one glass, a glass with ice, a bowl of ice, a small pitcher of water, and a plate of salted almonds, Lowell asked the waiter if he knew Colonel Newburgh.

"Yes, sir," the waiter said. "That's the colonel at the end of the bar, sir."

"Would you give the colonel another of what he's drinking, with my compliments?" Lowell asked.

"Yes, sir, Mr. Lowell, be nappy to."

A minute later, Colonel Carson Newburgh, a tall, ruddy-faced man in his late fifties, in a splendidly tailored glen plaid suit, walked to Lowell's table. Lowell stood up.

"You one-upped me, Lowell," he said, offering his hand. "I guess I asked for it."

"What was the little game at the door?" Lowell asked. Newburgh sat down, and motioned for Lowell to sit.

"My intention was to teach by example," he said. "The point I was trying to make was that it is very hard for most people to gain access to these exalted premises. How'd you get in?"

"I had lunch with the chairman of the house committee in New York a month ago, and when he heard I was coming to Washington . . ."

"You're up for membership?"

"Yeah. He said the committee meets only once every three months."

"And decides which of the applicants, who applied two, three years ago, is the most worthy," Newburgh said.

"Some pigs," Lowell said, "as Mr. Orwell pointed out, are more equal than other pigs."

"It's nice to be rich, isn't it, Lowell?"

"It's way ahead of whatever is in second place," Lowell said. "I gather you are 'comfortable' too, Colonel?"

"I think you could say that," Newburgh said, and smiled at him.

"I'm really curious to know what this is all about," Lowell said. "Until you played games with me at the door, I thought my cousin was somehow involved, that he wanted me to meet the respectable people."

"No, the only contact I've had with Porter was to find out where you were staying," Newburgh said. "I don't really know him. But we have some mutual friends."

"So do we, you said," Lowell said.

"Bob Bellmon's coming over," Newburgh said. "He should be here right about now. I think the plane gets in at 5:55."

"Don't forget to leave your name at the desk," Lowell said.

"I won't have to," Newburgh said. "Bellmon's a member. His grandfather was a member."

"I shall have to remember to be nice to him," Lowell said. "Until after his chance to drop a blackball has passed."

"Barbara wouldn't let him do that," Newburgh said. "Barbara likes you."

"Just who the hell are you, Colonel?" Lowell asked. "And what the hell is going on?"

"My name is Carson Newburgh," he said. "As in the Newburgh Corporation."

"Then you *are* 'comfortable,'" Lowell chuckled.

"It's also been Lieutenant Newburgh," he said. "And since I did such a superb job as E. Z. Black's housekeeper in Korea, Colonel Newburgh."

"Now I know who you are," Lowell said. "Sure."

"And I know who you are, of course," Newburgh said, and chuckled. "You have been described to me as the consummate fuck-up."

"I've heard that," Lowell said.

"And also as a brilliant combat commander with a real genius for logistic planning."

"That would have to be Barbara Bellmon."

"Actually, it was Paul Jiggs."

"I'd love to be able to quote that to him, and use it as a lever to get me the hell out of the Pentagon."

"We now get to the point," Newburgh said. "You can, if

you're willing to, make a greater contribution to the army sitting on your ass in the Pentagon than you made leading Task Force Lowell," Newburgh said.

Lowell's eyebrows raised in mocking disbelief.

"In case you're wondering," Newburgh said, smiling broadly, "why I called this little meeting."

Lowell chuckled, and held up his empty drink for a refill. "What do I have to do?"

"One thing that will probably amuse you, and give you some satisfaction, and a number of other things that you will probably dislike intensely. Both are equally important."

"Tell me what will amuse me," Lowell said.

"There is an H-19 at Fort Lewis, Washington," Newburgh said, "that has been wrecked. Nearly totaled. You're going to have to find enough money in your appropriated-for-other-purposes funds to have it rebuilt, and do so without anyone knowing about it."

"And what happens to the H-19 when I do this? Some general has a flying command post?"

"Mac MacMillan gets a test bed for rocket-armed helicopters," Newburgh said. When he saw the look on Lowell's face, he added: "I told you that it would give you some pleasure."

"Is that why I got that paper shuffler's job?"

"That's part of the reason."

"Drop the other shoe, Colonel," Lowell said.

"From what I've heard about you from the Bellmons," Newburgh said, "and from my personal observations, you'd make a lousy politician. That's a shame."

"Why do you say that?"

"Because what the army needs from you is political influence."

"Porter refers to our distinguished solon as *our* distinguished solon," Lowell said.

"And I have one, actually three, too," Newburgh said. "But we need more than that."

"For what purpose?"

"To keep army aviation alive," Newburgh said. "The air force is going for the jugular."

"I'm not good at that sort of thing," Lowell said.

"No. But you're going to have to try. We'll help."

"I don't really know what the hell you're talking about," Lowell said.

"This town functions over Swedish meatballs and scotch on the rocks," Newburgh said. "More power is wielded at parties than in the Capitol buildings. It's pretty revolting, but that's the way it is."

"And where do I fit in?"

"The way you walked in here," Newburgh said. "I made my point with a demonstration, it seems, even if it wasn't the point I had in mind."

"I don't think I follow you."

"You plan to play some golf while you're in Washington, do you, Major Lowell?"

"Probably."

"Here?"

"Unless I can find someplace more convenient."

"Out there, Major, in Chevy Chase and Silver Spring, in the District itself, are several hundred congressmen, and God only knows how many thousand members of their staffs—and understand, Lowell, right away, that staffers are often more powerful than the men they work for—who can't get past the porter at the door to this place. And places like it. They would be deeply grateful to be asked to play golf with you, Lowell, and they would not risk losing your friendship by voting with the air force. Get the picture?"

"I get it, and I don't like it. I don't think it will work."

"It'll work."

"I wouldn't know our senator if he walked in the door."

"But he knows you, and you're going to be invited out by him. And you will go, and you will have a good time, and you will entertain him in return. And he will find himself sitting next to a very charming colonel, who will make our pitch in his ear."

"Jesus!"

"I don't want to wag the flag in your face," Newburgh said. "But this sort of thing is important, Lowell. And because you are—what did you say?—'comfortable'? Because you are comfortable, you can afford to do it."

Lowell looked at him for a long moment and then shrugged his shoulders.

"How do I start?"

"Call your friend at the Riggs Bank and tell him you want a nice little town house in Georgetown. Get one with a big kitchen and a big dining room. Nothing ostentatious, but efficient. Two or three in staff. Getting the picture?"

"A well-outfitted brothel," Lowell said. "I have the picture."

"And knock out the flip remarks. Act as if you like it."

Lowell put up his hands in surrender.

"That probably means drinking soda water with a squirt of bitters to give it a little color. Your guests can, and it is to be hoped, will, get drunk. You will not."

"Will I get an R&R?"

"Sure. Just take somebody valuable with you. Congressmen from Mobile, Alabama, love to go riding in Aero Commanders."

Newburgh raised his own glass over his head for a refill, and then he glanced at the door, and said, "Oh, there they are."

Lowell looked over his shoulder and saw Bob Bellmon, in uniform, walking into the bar beside a tall, muscular man in civilian clothing. He had never seen the muscular gray-haired man out of uniform before, and it was a moment before he recognized him to be General E. Z. Black, Vice Chief of Staff of the U.S. Army.

Lowell first thought that it was really very clever. Black's very presence lent credibility and authority to his new role as a lobbyist. (He had almost immediately had the irreverent thought that he was about to become the male Perle Mesta.) And Black's hands would be clean. The discussion was over. *Black* hadn't told him to wine and dine the provincial congressmen, or to take funds appropriated for one purpose and use them for another, probably illegal purpose. And rebuilding a wrecked H-19 with funds intended for something else, and then arming it, in violation of the Key West Agreement of 1948, which forbade the army to arm its aircraft, was certainly illegal.

But that wasn't why General Black had come to have a little chat with an obscure major.

An hour later, General Black lifted his eyes from the cracker on which he was spreading Camembert.

"I want you to stay away from Sanford Felter, Lowell," he said.

"Sir?"

"You heard what I said."

"May I ask why, sir?"

"Felter is our man in the White House," Black said.

"I don't know what that means, sir," Lowell said.

"I was about to say that it doesn't matter if you know or not—I gave you an order, and I expect it to be executed—but I suppose you are entitled to an explanation. Felter is the President's liaison man with the intelligence community. It's supposed to be a big secret, but he carries the rank of Counselor to the President. I don't want that role of his compromised in any way. Not by somebody making the connection between this lobbying activity of yours, or this armed chopper business. Clear?"

"Yes, sir," Lowell said. "But how do I explain this to Felter?"

"You're a bright fellow, Lowell," E. Z. Black said. "You'll think of something."

(Two)
Georgetown
The District of Columbia
4 July 1958

It was nearly midnight when Lowell's Eldorado turned onto his street, and he pushed the switch on the dash that triggered the automatic door-opening device on his town house garage. He'd had a little party for a small (30) group of people aboard a rented 55-foot Hatteras. They'd cruised the Potomac starting at half past five. Cocktails, a seafood buffet, and then champagne as they watched the fireworks.

He'd worked in the Pentagon most of the day, and the party had been a real pain in the ass. What he wanted now, desperately, was a drink. He got out of the Eldorado, pushed the button that closed the garage door, and entered the town house through the kitchen. The servants were gone, but there was a stack of bills awaiting his attention on the kitchen table.

He went out of the kitchen through the dining room, and then through the living room to the bar, where he found a bottle of scotch. He carried it back into the kitchen, mixed a strong drink with very little ice, and sat down at the table and wrote checks. While he wrote the checks, he had two more stiff drinks.

It was hot and muggy, and when he checked the thermostat, he saw that one of the servants, who didn't like air conditioning, had the temperature set at eighty. It came on with a thud, but when he climbed the stairs to his bedroom, it seemed as if every stair he took raised the temperature another two degrees.

It was too goddamned hot to even try to sleep. On an impulse, he took a pair of swim trunks from his dresser and carried them back downstairs with him. He undressed in the living room, throwing his clothes on a couch, went into the kitchen, and looked out the breakfast nook windows at the pool.

"What the hell," he said. "Why not?"

He turned on the floodlights and the underwater lights in the pool and walked into the backyard. The backyard was walled with a ten-foot brick fence. He walked down the terrazzo to the deep end of the pool, set his drink down on one of the umbrella-topped tables, and took a running dive into the pool.

Goddamned water must be ninety degrees, he thought. It was like jumping into a hot bath.

He climbed out of the pool halfway down and walked back to pick up his drink.

"Howdy, neighbor!" she called.

Shit, that's all I need. Constance.

Constance was his neighbor. Constance was the wife of a very important senator. The senator was sixty-eight, and said he was fifty-eight. Constance was thirty-odd and pretended she was twenty-two. Constance had short black hair which she wore pressed close to her skull.

He picked up his drink, put a smile on his face, and turned around.

"Howdy, neighbor!" he parroted. "I hope the lights didn't wake you up."

"Couldn't sleep," she said. Then she said, "Don't go away!"

What the fuck is *that* supposed to mean? he wondered.

He walked back to the house, stopping to look for a towel

in the pool house. There was none. He went into the kitchen and toweled himself with dish towels. He hoped that Constance was not going to come over. He waited for the sound of the chimes, and when they didn't come in a reasonable time for her to have come over, he went and looked out the window. The street was deserted.

He could go to bed. The temperature would be lower, if not cool. He had to go to work in the morning and he needed his sleep.

"Hi!"

Constance, wearing a two-piece bathing suit that would have been appropriate for a late-blooming thirteen year old, came in from the kitchen.

"How did you get over the wall?" he asked, in surprise.

"Love always finds a way," she said.

He smiled at her and went to look. He was mystified.

"At the end by the house," she explained, coming to stand close to him. "They made sort of steps in the wall."

"I never noticed," he said.

"There's a lot you never notice," she said.

He smiled.

"Do you want to be wet outside or inside?" he asked, thinking he was being clever, offering her a choice between a dip in the pool or a drink. Constance chose to misunderstand.

"That's getting right down to the nitty-gritty right away, isn't it?" she asked. "Can I have a drink first, or should I just jump in bed?"

"Certainly, you jest!" he said, making that as much a joke as he could.

"I didn't mind you ignoring me when I thought you were queer," she said.

"You thought I was queer?"

"You're so beautiful, I thought you had to be," she said.

"I'm crushed," he said.

"And then I saw you paddling around with that newspaper reporter," she said. "And I just happened to notice that she left her car on the street all night."

"Engine trouble," he said.

"Certainly," she said.

"Would you like a drink?"

"I don't need one," she said. "But if it makes you feel any better."

He went to the kitchen to make her a drink. She followed him, and ran her fingers over a faint, fifteen-inch-long scar on his back.

"Where'd you get that?" she asked.

"A long time ago in Greece," he said.

"It's just enough to accent the rest of the perfection," she said. Her hand ran down his back and rested on his buttock. Either her fingers or her breasts coming out of the negligible top of her suit or the damp suit itself was enough to give him an erection. He was now afraid to turn around.

"Your britches are wet," she said. "If you don't get out of them, you'll catch your death."

"This conversation is getting dangerous," he said.

"Isn't it interesting?" she said.

"Neither one of us could afford anything like that," he said.

"What you couldn't afford, darling, is me going to my aging, impotent, but nevertheless insanely jealous husband and telling him you made improper and unwanted advances."

She moved her hand around to the front of his trunks, grabbed him, and chuckled deep in her throat.

"Take off your britches, darling," she said. "Like a nice boy."

(Three)
Alexandria, Virginia
7 November 1958

The Cadillac Eldorado, which bore a District of Columbia license plate, a bumper-mounted decal authorizing the vehicle to be parked in Lot C-5-11 of the Pentagon parking area, drove slowly down Kildar Street while the driver swore aloud.

"These fucking rabbit hutches look all alike," he said.

And then he spotted a battered Volkswagen parked beside a Buick estate wagon. He turned off Kildar Street and pulled into the driveway and stopped behind the huge Buick and had a nasty thought: *Little Men Like Big Cars.* He had no idea why that thought had popped into his mind, and was immediately ashamed of himself.

The Deputy Chief, Plans and Requirements Section (Fiscal), Aviation Maintenance Sections, Office of the Deputy Chief of Staff for Logistics, was in uniform, the new olive-green shade 51 uniform. On his shoulder was the insignia of the Military District of Washington. There was a major's gold oak leaf on each epaulet. He wore the lapel insignia, a silver star on which was superimposed the national eagle, of the General Staff Corps, and on his tunic pocket was the insignia awarded to officers who have served a year on the Army General Staff. He wore no ribbons or qualification badges. Pinned to his tunic, above the left pocket was a name tag with white letters on a black background. It read LOWELL.

He got out of the Eldorado, let the heavy door swing closed of its own weight, and walked up to the door of 2301 Kildar Street.

The chimes played "Be it ever so humble" when he pushed the door bell, and as always, he winced.

Sharon Felter, a slight, feminine, black-haired woman wearing a full apron, opened the inner door. She squealed with pleasure when she saw him, and pushed open the screen door. She pulled him to her and kissed him, not quite on the mouth.

"Things never change," he said.

"What things?"

"The first time you ever kissed me, you smelled of freshly baked bread," Lowell said.

"Don't knock it, I could open a business."

"I would speak at that man you're married to," he said.

"He's not home yet, Craig," Sharon Felter said.

"I saw the pile of rust," Lowell said. "I thought he was here."

"Somebody from the office picked him up," Sharon said. "I think he had to go into Washington."

"But he is coming home?"

"He should be here any minute," she said. "Can I get you a drink?"

"Will you have one with me?"

She thought that over a moment, and then nodded her head. "To celebrate," she said.

"I suppose I'm expected to ask what you're celebrating."

"The visit of an old and dear friend, who, although he lives in Washington, might as well live in Anchorage, Alaska, or someplace, how often he comes to see us."

"I stand before you suitably shamed," he said. "But you know what would happen, if I did this very often? I would ply you with booze and carry you off into a life of sin."

"Would there be room for me?" Sharon replied. "You're not as young as you used to be, you know."

"Touché, Madame," Lowell said.

"What will you have to drink?" Sharon asked.

"Scotch, straight up," Lowell said. He was surprised when Sharon made herself a scotch on the rocks, a stiff one, not measuring the liquor.

"Has that man you live with been teaching you evil ways?" he asked, nodding at her drink.

"Doctor's orders," Sharon said. When she saw his eyebrows raise, she added: "Cross my heart."

"Is there something wrong with you?" Major Lowell asked, and the concern in his voice was intense and evident.

"Nothing, according to the doctor, that a little scotch and water won't cure."

"I'm not very good at games," he said. "And neither are you. What's wrong?"

"Tension. High blood pressure. Nerves. Lady's complaints," Sharon said.

"Because of what he's doing?" Lowell asked, almost angrily.

"All he does is work very hard," she said.

"Has he been up to his disappearing-act spy games again? Is that it? And don't tell Uncle Craig you're not supposed to talk about it."

"Just hard work," she said.

"Why he doesn't get the hell out of that business, I'll never know," Lowell said.

There was the sound of a car door slamming, and then of the front door opening.

"Hello, Craig," Sandy Felter said, coming into the kitchen. He was in a baggy, gray business suit. He did not seem either surprised or especially pleased to see Lowell.

"Let me guess," Lowell said. "This week, you're disguised as a bureaucrat."

"What brings you over here?"

"I heard you were out of town and thought it would be a splendid time to seduce your wife."

"Well, this was your chance," Felter said. "The kids are in Newark. You could have had her all to yourself if you'd come over earlier."

"I don't think either of you are funny!" Sharon said.

"From what I hear," Lowell said, "wife swapping is all the rage among up and coming D.C. bureaucrats."

"If anybody could check that out, you're the man," Felter said. "From what I hear, there have been so many women going into and out of a certain Georgetown town house the cops thought somebody had opened a store."

"Sandy!" Sharon said.

"He's just jealous, Sharon, that's all," Lowell said. "Some of us have animal magnetism, and some of us don't."

"And some of us are too smart to get involved with senator's wives," Felter said. He took off his jacket and opened the hall closet. The butt of a Colt .45 pistol was visible in the small of his back.

"That cannon makes your wife nervous, you know," Lowell said, as Felter took the pistol from its skeleton holster and laid it on the closet shelf. "From the time you leave until the time you walk back in, she has visions of you being ambushed by the NKVD in front of the Falls Church A&P. It's driving her to drink."

"I don't think that's particularly funny," Sanford Felter said.

"I wasn't trying to be funny. Before you sneaked through the door just now, in your inimitable imitation of Humphrey Bogart, I was saying to your wife that it was high time you stopped playing spy and went back to being a soldier."

"Just for the record, Craig," Felter said, coldly, "I am a soldier."

"In that bureacrat suit, you sure could fool me," Lowell said.

"To what do we owe the honor of your visit?" Felter asked, coldly.

"Enough!" Sharon said. "I don't know what it is with you two. You're closer than brothers, and you act like . . . I don't know what."

"How about brothers?" Lowell asked, innocently. There was a moment's pause and then Felter laughed.

"How about giving my little brother a belt?" Lowell asked. "He looks as if he can use one."

"Sandy?" Sharon asked.

"Why not?" he said. Sharon jumped up and walked quickly into the kitchen to make her husband a drink.

"Mud in your eye," Felter said, taking a sip of his drink.

"Mazeltov!" Lowell replied. Felter looked at him and shook his head.

"You're amazing," he said. "Amazing. That came out anti-Semitic."

"Well, screw you," Lowell said. "I was simply trying to be charming."

"If you're trying to be charming, you want something," Felter said.

"Right," Lowell said.

"That figures, that figures," Felter said. "What?"

"I was dealing with one of your pals today," Lowell said.

"Oh?"

"Yeah. He came into my office, looked under the desk and in the wastebaskets to see if any Russians were lurking about, and flashed his badge on me."

"What kind of a badge?" Felter asked.

"CIC."

"Craig, I have nothing to do with the CIC. You know that."

"Creepy little bastard, drunk with authority," Lowell said. "He was asking questions about a friend of mine."

"What friend?" Felter asked.

"I want to know why he was asking the questions," Lowell said. He reached in his pocket and handed over a slip of memo paper. "That's the name."

"And what am I supposed to do with this?"

"Find out what kind of trouble my friend is in, and what I can do to help," Lowell said.

"You know I can't do anything like that!"

"Yes, you can. You may not want to, but you know you can."

"You can't believe I would even think about doing something like that," Felter said.

"Get on the goddamned phone and call somebody up," Lowell said.

"I'll tell you what I'm going to do," Felter said. "I'm going to go upstairs and take a shower. And I'm going to even forget that you asked me what you did."

"Kiss my ass, Sandy," Craig Lowell said. He stood up, and put his drink down.

"You're not leaving!" Sharon Felter said. There was an awkward silence. Sandy saw that Sharon was close to tears.

"No, of course not," Lowell said, after a moment.

"I'll make us another drink," Sharon said. Lowell saw that Sharon's glass was empty.

Sanford Felter walked up the stairs to his bedroom. The sonofabitch had no right to ask him things like that; he had no right to upset Sharon. God only knows what the human stud had been saying to her before he got home. Felter had noticed how quickly his wife had drained her glass.

God*damn* him!

Felter walked to the chest of drawers and unloaded his pockets. There were a couple of bills crumpled into a ball; a dollar or so in coins; a sweat-stained wallet; a leather folder containing a badge and a plastic identification card identifying him as a Deputy United States Marshal (which served, in case some zealous cop got curious, to justify the .45) and a plastic card, riveted to an alligator clip, containing his photograph, his name, and three diagonal red stripes. This granted him access at any time to any area of the Pentagon, the Defense Intelligence Agency, the State Department, and the CIA, as well as access to any information he might ask for.

In the classified files of DCSINTEL, where his service records were kept, was a copy of the Department of Army general order which had placed Major Sanford T. Felter, Infantry (Detail: Military Intelligence) of the Defense Intelligence Agency, on temporary duty with the White House. In the Eyes Only safes of the Secretary of Defense, the Secretary of State, the Director of the FBI, and the Director of the CIA, was a short note on White House notepaper:

THE WHITE HOUSE

WASHINGTON

Effective immediately, and until further notice, Major Sanford T. Felter, USA, is relieved of all other duties, and will serve as my personal liaison officer with the intelligence community with the rank of Counselor to the President. This appointment will not be made known publicly. Major Felter will be presumed to have the Need To Know when this question arises.

                                              DDE

There was a photograph on the dresser. It had been taken in Greece, near the Albanian border. It showed two very young officers. They were wearing American khaki shirts. The rest of their uniforms were British. The smaller of them, First Lieutenant Sanford T. Felter, twenty-two years old, cradled a Thompson .45 caliber submachine gun in his arms, like some bootleg era gangster. The taller of them, Second Lieutenant Craig W. Lowell, aged nineteen, had an M1 Garand slung over his shoulder like a hunter. There were two 8-round cartridge clips pinned to the Garand's leather strap.

Felter remembered, very clearly, other photographs that had been on that roll of 35 mm film. In an act of incredible stupidity, he had sent it home to Sharon to have it developed and printed. And when it came back from the Rexall drugstore on the corner of Aldine Street and Lyons Avenue, one block down from the Felters' bakery, Sharon, his wife of eight months, had seen what his room in Greece looked like and what the dog they had acquired somewhere looked like, and what his new friend Craig Lowell looked like. Two of the photographs had told Sharon much more about what he was doing in Greece than he wanted her to know. The two photographs showed Craig Lowell in the traditional pose of the successful big game hunter, smiling broadly, cradling his rifle proudly in his arms, kneeling on the fruits of the hunt. What he was kneeling on was a pile of three bodies. One of the bodies was looking at the camera with a look of surprise on his mustached face. There was a neat little .30 caliber hole in the middle of his forehead. The back of his head had been blown away.

Sharon had kept the print and the negatives until he came home, and then wordlessly given them to him. He had wordlessly burned them. Felter looked at the photograph of them together, way back then, and then he forced his eyes away and went into the bathroom and took a shower.

There was such a thing as pushing a friendship too far, he told himself. Craig expected too much.

As he soaped his balding head with Sharon's woman's shampoo (if he used soap, or regular shampoo, his skin flaked), he remembered how Craig W. Lowell had solved the problem of what he was going to tell Sharon and his mother and father and her mother and father about what he was doing in the hospital in Hawaii. While they were airlifting him from the hospital ship in Pusan Harbor to Hawaii, Craig, Porter, Kenyon and Dawes, investment bankers, had sent a nice young man around to Felter's Warsaw Bakery. The nice young man had a limousine, and the nice young man had traveled with them to Hawaii, just in case someone in the airlines hadn't gotten the word that the Felters and the Lavinskys were personal friends of the man who owned half of the firm that had just loaned the airline however many millions of dollars it took to make a down payment on a fleet of intercontinental transport aircraft.

And when they carried him into his room on the stretcher, they had all been there, and Sharon was hugging him and crying, and nobody could talk, except his mother.

"So, Sanford," his mother said, "you wouldn't believe our hotel. Would you believe we got two whole apartments? On the beach. You can look out from the porch and see these Hawaiian *schwartzes* riding on those boards. The Royal Hawaiian, yet."

And he remembered what Sharon had told him, after he'd come back from Dien Bien Phu. That Craig W. Lowell had sat in the chair where he was now sitting, swilling down booze and crying like a baby.

"In a way, Sandy, it was funny," Sharon said later. "Here

we were, the widow and the orphans, and what we were doing was trying to make Uncle Craig stop crying."

"Shit!" Sanford Felter said. He stepped out of the shower, wrapped a towel around his waist, and went to his bed and sat on it. He opened the door of the bedside table and took out a black telephone with several buttons on it.

He dialed a number.

"Liberty 7–1936," a male voice said.

"Scramble Four Victor Twenty-Three," Felter said.

"Confirm Four Victor Two Three," the voice said, after a moment. "Go ahead."

Felter pushed the appropriate buttons on the special telephone.

"This is Felter," he said. "Get onto somebody in G-2 or the Defense Intelligence Agency and find out (a) why the CIC is investigating a man named Franklin, William B., and (b) what the investigation has come up with so far."

"Yes, sir," the male voice said. "Will you spell, sir?"

"Franklin, as in Poor Richard's Almanac," Felter said. The name rang a bell, but he couldn't put his finger on it. There were so many names.

"Yes, sir."

"I'm at my home," Felter said. "Get back to me here."

"Yes, sir."

Felter replaced the handset in the receiver without saying anything else. He put the phone back in the space under the bedside table. Then he stood up and walked back into the bathroom and put the towel in the hamper.

What he had done was absolutely a breach of the authority with which he had been entrusted. There was no other way to look at it. On the other hand, it was equally clear that he would get away with it. He reported to the President—and nobody else. Even if the directors of the FBI or CIA somehow heard about this, there would be no questions asked. For a long time now, he had been one of the very few who were given the benefit of any doubt.

He put on a sports shirt and a pair of slacks and went downstairs.

Craig was in the kitchen with Sharon. Sharon was making

a salad. Craig was pressing roughly ground peppercorns into a steak with his thumb.

"So how were things in Germany?" Felter asked. "Is there any more whiskey, or did you two drink it all up?"

"How'd you know I was in Germany?" Lowell asked.

"I spoke to your father-in-law yesterday," Felter said. He found the bottle of scotch and made himself a drink. That killed the bottle. He was sure there had been four inches of whiskey in it when he'd gone upstairs. He saw that both his wife and Lowell had full, dark glasses.

"We took Peter hunting for his first time," Lowell said.

"Craig, you didn't!" Sharon said. "My God, he's only nine years old."

"He's a real kraut," Lowell said. "He loved it."

"He's half-American, Craig," Sharon said.

"He finds that somewhat embarrassing," Lowell said.

"Oh, Craig!" Sharon said.

Felter pushed the curtain on the kitchen door aside to see how the charcoal was coming.

"You haven't started the fire," he accused.

Lowell snapped his fingers. "I knew there was something I had to do besides stick peppercorns in this."

It wasn't that funny, but Sharon and Craig thought it was.

It took forty minutes for the charcoal to achieve what Major Craig W. Lowell thought was the proper grayish hue. Time, Felter saw, for two more drinks. Sharon, he thought, is going to get sick to her stomach. Then, aware that he was being petulant, he enjoyed the notion that it would serve her right.

Lowell insisted on red wine to go with the meal. That was really going to make Sharon sick.

They had just about finished eating when the door chimes played "Be it ever so humble."

Felter drained his wine glass and went to answer it. A stocky, gray-haired man in a business suit, carrying a briefcase, stood before the door. Felter saw a black Chevrolet four-door sedan in the driveway behind Lowell's Eldorado. There was someone behind the wheel. He opened the door.

"Good evening, sir," the gray-haired man said.

"Come in, please, Colonel," Felter said, opening the door.

Felter led him into the dining room.

"You know Mrs. Felter, of course," Felter said.

"Ma'am," the colonel said.

"Colonel," Sharon said.

"This is Major Lowell," Felter said.

"How do you do, sir?" Lowell said. They shook hands, but the colonel did not offer his name, and Felter didn't use it.

"Can I offer you a glass of wine, Colonel? Or a drink?" Felter asked.

"Thank you, sir, no. I have the duty."

"You apparently have some answers for me," Felter said. The colonel looked uncomfortable.

"I rather doubt that either my wife or Major Lowell will rush to the nearest telephone to inform the Russian Embassy of this conversation," Felter said.

"Yes, sir," the colonel said. "Sir, I wasn't given much to go on, so I decided it would be best to bring you what I have myself."

"I'm sorry you had to drive all the way out here," Felter said.

"Sir, there are three Franklins, William, under investigation," the colonel said. He sat down at the table and opened his briefcase. "Two are routine background investigations. I have their summaries with me. The third, Lieutenant Colonel Franklin, who I would guess is the subject of your interest, has been, we believe, sexually compromised—we're not quite sure by whom—in Yokohama."

He laid three folders on the dining room table.

"Colonel Franklin's file, sir, is the thick one," the colonel said.

Felter nodded. He looked through the two thinner files, then pushed them toward Lowell. Their eyes met. Lowell selected one of the two thinner files and flipped through it quickly. Felter read the file concerning Lieutenant Colonel Franklin, who had apparently discovered at age thirty-six an interest in young, relatively hair-free male youths.

"Colonel," Felter said, "when you have finished this, would you be sure that I get a copy and otherwise be kept up to date?"

"Yes, sir," the colonel said. "Of course, sir. Sir, if there are any areas of particular interest to you?"

"Nothing your people are not presently covering very well, Colonel," Felter said. "I'm afraid that my concerns here amount to much ado about nothing."

"It never hurts to make sure, does it, sir?" the colonel said.

"It sometimes inconveniences people," Felter said. "Lowell, have you any questions for the colonel?"

"No, sir," Lowell said, straight-faced. "The colonel's people are obviously on top of the situation."

The colonel's pleasure was evident on his face.

"I feel rather bad about getting you all the way out here, when it turns out that there is no problem," Felter said. "Are you sure you won't have a drink? Or perhaps something to eat?"

"Thank you just the same, sir," the colonel said. "I have the duty."

The colonel stuffed the files back into his briefcase and Felter walked him to the door.

"Thank you again, Colonel," Felter said. "I'm very impressed with your response time."

"Thank *you*, sir," the colonel said.

Felter closed the door, walked into the kitchen, and made two drinks. He walked into the dining room and set one before Lowell. Then he sat down and stared at him. They stared at each other for a long time, and then they began to chuckle, and then to laugh.

There was a touch of hysteria in the laughter.

"Is that a private joke?" Sharon asked, pleased that they were laughing together.

"The things you get me to do, you bastard," Felter said.

"From now on, that poor fruitcake in Yokohama won't be able to take a leak without three creeps from CIC timing him with stopwatches," Lowell said.

"Are you going to tell me or not?" Sharon demanded.

"I don't know why the hell I'm laughing," Felter said. "It really isn't funny."

"There is an element of overkill, isn't there?" Lowell asked, chuckling.

"I'm getting mad, Sandy, I mean it," Sharon said.

"When Don Juan here was in Algiers," Felter explained, "he had a Signal Corps photographer sergeant named Franklin, William. The kid did his time, and got out of the army, and went back to Canton, Ohio, where, after a couple of months, he decided that he really didn't want to spend the rest of his life taking photographs of weddings. So he re-upped and put in for the warrant officer candidate helicopter pilot program. Before they give them their warrants, they give them a complete background investigation. The kid naturally listed Craig here as a reference. The kid figured that a field-grade officer of such an impeccable reputation was a good reference to have."

"So?" Sharon said.

"So MDW sent some sergeant in civilian clothes around to ask Major Lowell if he had, in fact, known Franklin, William B., and to inquire if he would recommend Franklin, William B., for a position of great trust and responsibility."

"Well, he could have been in trouble," Lowell said. "How was I supposed to know?"

"If he was a friend of yours, you could almost count on his being in trouble," Felter said.

"I still don't understand," Sharon said.

"What happened, honey," Felter said, "was that Don Juan did it to me again. I just put what is laughingly known as the intelligence community in high gear. The deputy chief of Army Counterintelligence rushed out here devoutly believing he was involved in a security matter of the highest priority. If he really knew what it was all about . . ."

"Hell, Sandy, you made his whole week. He'll be waiting for his boss at 0700 to tell him Super Spook himself told him personally he was impressed with his reaction time."

"I don't know why I'm laughing," Felter said. "Goddamn you, Craig, you're dangerous."

"Hand me the phone, Sharon, honey, will you?" Lowell asked.

"Don't you dare!" Felter said. "God knows who he wants to call."

"I'm going to call Franklin, that's who I'm going to call."

"No, you're not," Felter said.

"Why not?"

"For one thing, you're drunk," Felter said. "The last thing that kid needs now, two months before he graduates, is a telephone call from a drunken officer."

"*I'm* drunk? You're the one who could barely pronounce 'reaction time,'" Lowell said.

"Don't call him, Craig," Felter said. "You'd just make trouble for him."

"What Craig wants to do is see if he needs anything," Sharon said, somewhat thickly, defending him.

"Right. What's wrong with that?" Lowell demanded of Felter.

"You're just going to call attention to him," Felter said. "That's the last thing he needs right now."

"I'll call Phil Parker," Lowell said. "He's down there."

"Don't call anybody," Felter said. "Quit while you're ahead."

Lowell thumbed his nose at Felter and picked up the telephone.

Felter was pleased when Lowell could not complete his call to Captain Philip Sheridan Parker IV, and was limited to a brief, maudlin conversation with Dr. Antoinette Parker.

Antoinette assured him that she would have Phil check to see what, if anything, Warrant Officer Candidate Franklin needed, and then asked to speak to Sharon.

Lowell moved to an armchair in the living room while the women talked, and fell asleep. That solved another problem, Felter decided. Lowell was obviously too drunk to drive back into Washington. Virginia police were death on drunken driving. The chair was reclining. Felter got Lowell into a nearly horizontal position, loosened his necktie and belt, removed his shoes, and draped a blanket over him.

Sharon was still talking to Antoinette when he finished.

He waved at her, and went upstairs and got in bed.

He heard her come into the room ten minutes later, listened to the sound of her undressing, felt the bed sag as she got in beside him.

"You awake?" Sharon asked.

"I am now," Sandy replied.

"Antoinette wants us to come down there for New Year's Eve," Sharon said.

Felter didn't reply.

"I want to go, Sandy," Sharon said.

"It's a thousand miles down there," Sandy said. "You really want to go a thousand miles to sit around an officer's club full of drunks in dress uniforms?"

"Yes," she said.

"What did you say?"

"I want to go," Sharon repeated. "I want to walk into an officer's club with you, in uniform. I want to wear my West Point ring, and I want you to wear your West Point ring, and I want you to wear your uniform with all your ribbons and all your medals. I'm just a little sick of pretending the man I'm married to is an economic analyst for the goddamned CIA."

She's really drunk, Sanford Felter realized. Sharon rarely swore.

The confirmation of that analysis came when he rolled over and put his arms around her and found that she was naked.

"Surprise, surprise," she said.

"Not that I mind, of course, but what brought this on?" Felter asked.

"I got very horny, Sandy," Sharon said, solemnly, "when Colonel Whatsisname was here."

"Let me have that again?" he asked, amused. Her hand moved to his groin. "Women are turned on by strong and powerful men," Sharon said. She giggled as he started to grow erect. "Wheee!" she said.

He put his hand to her breast. It was firm and the nipple erect.

"You were the strongest man in the room," she said. "Stronger, Sandy, than that colonel. Stronger than Craig."

He was, he realized, deeply flattered. Even if she was drunk. *In vino veritas,* he thought.

"But I never get a chance to show you off," she said. "I want to show you off, Sandy. I never get a chance to be an officer's lady. That's important to a woman. You're a man and you don't understand that."

"If you really want to go to Rucker, we'll go to Rucker," he said. He was a little ashamed of himself. Going to Rucker was a preposterous idea. What he wanted to do was screw. A stiff prick, he told himself, has no conscience.

Sharon was a good solid woman. This was the third time since they had been married that he knew for sure she was drunk. She had gotten drunk after they buried Craig's wife, and she had gotten drunk when her father died. When he thought about that, there was something unnerving about her being drunk now. Was 'her nerves' that serious a problem?

He put that thought from his mind. There was something wicked about her being drunk now and wanting him to screw her. He liked it. In the morning, she would be a little embarrassed about taking too much to drink, about what she was doing now. She would realize then that going to Rucker was really absurd.

She twisted away from him.

"What are you doing?" Sandy asked.

The bedside lamp came on.

"I want to see," Sharon said. "I want to watch!"

"You little vixen, you!" he said, and knelt between her legs. He could feel his excitement in his chest. He thought that it would be four days before the kids came back from Newark. He thought he would bring a bottle home some afternoon.

"Fuck me, Sandy!" Sharon hissed in his ear. "Fuck me good!"

He did.

When Sanford Felter went downstairs in the morning, Sharon was making Craig eat scrambled eggs, despite his protests that all he wanted was a cup of coffee.

She avoided her husband's eyes when he sat down at the table. She scrambled some more eggs and put them before him, with toast and grape jelly and grapefruit juice. Then she sat down at the table, and stirred her coffee.

"Craig," she said, "if Sandy can get off, will you take us to Fort Rucker for New Year's Eve? Antoinette asked us."

Lowell, surprised, hesitated before replying. Sandy knew that Craig didn't want to spend New Year's Eve at the Rucker officer's open mess any more than he did.

"Madame," Lowell said, "Lowell Airlines is at your beck and call."

Sharon looked at Sandy, met his eyes.

"The kids can stay with Mama Felter," Sharon said.

XIV

(One)
Fort Rucker, Alabama
11 November 1958

> QUESTION: *What is a WOC?*
> ANSWER: *Sir, a WOC is*
>   *something one fwows*
>   *at a wabbit.*

It had been rumored among both the staff of Warrant Officer Candidate Battalion, the U.S. Army Aviation School, and among the WOCs themselves that an amnesty would be granted by the commanding general to mark the Thanksgiving holiday. Major General Paul T. Jiggs, the post commander, who had otherwise earned a reputation as a starchy bastard, seemed to take some kind of a perverse pleasure in freeing WOCs from restrictions imposed by the WOC staff on whatever slim excuse he could find. Thanksgiving, to both the restricted and the restrictors, seemed to be just the sort of excuse the general would be pleased to have available.

Of the 254 WOCs in Companies A through D, thirty-two WOCs were under restriction of varying degree. Those WOCs whose academic grades were below acceptable standards, and who were guilty of no other offense against the rules and regulations, were restricted to the WOC area, but permitted to sign themselves out at the orderly room and visit the post exchange and the post theater. This authority specifically excluded visiting the post exchange cafeteria.

WOCs guilty of other violations were under progressively more restrictive restraints, in proportion to their offenses against the regulations. The most severe restriction imposed (beyond which punishment was expulsion from the WOC program) required that the WOCs, between the 0600 and 2200 hours, confine themselves to their rooms. During this period, dressed in a Class "A" uniform, they had the option of standing or sitting at their study desk. They were not permitted to smoke. Aside from a thirty-minute period during which they were permitted to read the daily newspaper, their reading material was limited to official textbooks and army manuals. The operation of radios, televisions, or other electronic amusement devices was proscribed.

The most common violation with which the WOCs on restriction were charged was "conduct unbecoming a warrant officer candidate and a gentleman." The specific charge was most often "use of vulgar and/or obscene and/or blasphemous language."

Ninety percent of the WOC class of which WOC William B. Franklin was a member consisted of regular army noncommissioned officers between the ages of twenty years and six months and twenty-six years and six months, and in the grades of E-5 through E-7, that is to say staff sergeants, sergeants first class, and master sergeants, or their technical counterparts, specialists five, six, and seven. There were tank commanders and cartographers, first sergeants and budget analysts, infantry platoon sergeants and medical corps x-ray technicians. There were aircraft mechanics and avionic technicians, photographers, small arms artificers, and even one farrier, who had come to flight school from Fort Meyers, Virginia, where he had been in charge of the horses used in the military funerals held half a dozen times a day at Arlington National Cemetery.

What they had in common, in addition to generally splendid physical condition, an average of 6.7 years of enlisted service, and Army General Classification Test (AGCT) scores averaging 123.6 (an AGCT score of 110 is required of officer candidates), was the desire to become both helicopter pilots and warrant officers.

They were old soldiers; they had been around. They knew that the pay scale for warrant officers was precisely that of officers in the ranks of second lieutenant through major. They would put up with whatever bullshit the army threw at them for six months, or however long it took, and they'd come out of it with a warrant, and it would be *sayonara* and *auf Wiedersehen* to the bullshit that went with being a goddamned EM. If they liked the life of an officer, they could wangle a commission and go for thirty, and if it turned out to be a pain in the ass, they'd just put in their twenty (drawing flight pay meanwhile) and retire at fifty percent of their base pay.

Getting through the bullshit was going to pose no problem at all. They weren't a bunch of fucking recruits, for Christ's sake. They knew the army game, and they knew how to play it. Cover your ass, keep your shoes shined, your pants pressed, your hair cut, and your mouth shut.

The army, for Christ's sake, was not going to fuck around with a bunch of old soldiers.

The orders which assigned them to the U.S. Army Aviation Center, Fort Rucker, Alabama, specifically forbade travel by private automobile and clearly stated that since the warrant officer candidates would be restricted to the barracks for the first six weeks of their training, "dependents are discouraged from accompanying sponsors."

Well, bullshit! Let the Old Lady drive the car, get a motel or a room someplace, and then it would simply be a matter of going over the fence at night to share the nuptial couch.

The orders which had sent them to Fort Rucker four months before further stated, specifically, that incoming students would report not earlier than 2000 hours and not later than 2200 hours, in Class "A" uniform, and that civilian clothing and other personal equipment would be turned in for storage to the quartermaster before they left their camp, post, or station to report the Fort.

Sergeant Franklin had found a garage in Daleville, outside the gate, where he could leave his car and his civvies. He had taken a cab to the post, and had more or less expected to see what happened: starting at 2005 hours, a line of civilian automobiles owned by married noncoms appeared at the WOC area. Senior enlisted men, carrying for the first time in a long time a standard GI duffel bag, got out of the cars, perfunctorily kissed their wives, and marched up the sidewalk to the orderly room.

There they were greeted by cadre, corporals, and buck sergeants. They knew the routine. There was a roster. Their names were checked off. They signed in. They were given room assignments and informed that they were restricted to the company area.

They, like Franklin, were pleased with what they initially found. For one thing, they had BOQs. Regular goddamned officer's BOQs, a sitting room study with a desk and even a desk lamp. A bedroom with a real bed, not even a GI bed, a real bed, with a real mattress. There was a shower and a crapper, shared with the guy next door. It wasn't quite the accommodations Sergeant Franklin had had in the Hotel d'Angleterre in Algiers, but it was far more spacious and comfortable than he expected.

The guys next door were a surprise. Goddamned buck ass private recruits, fresh from Dix or Bragg or another basic training post, still showing the signs of the thirty-second haircut they'd got on their first day in the army. Bright kids, starry-eyed and bushy-tailed, but goddamned *rookies*. What the fuck they were doing here was something that would have to be figured out.

At 0600 the next morning, a somewhat scratchy phonograph recording of reveille was played over the public address system. This was almost immediately followed by the announcement, repeated twice, that the uniform of the day was Class "A" with ribbons and qualification badges. Breakfast would be served at the WOC mess. WOCs would form at 0625 hours in front of the barracks. They were told to determine among themselves who was the senior noncommissioned officer, and he would form the company. A member of the cadre would serve as guide for the march to the WOC mess.

Five master sergeants ambled outside at 0620. They were wearing immaculate uniforms and all their ribbons. They crisply saluted a five-foot-three-inch second lieutenant who was standing outside, and cheerfully barked, "Good morning, sir!" to him.

He returned their salute, gave them a half-smile, and stood watching with his arms folded.

They compared dates of rank, and it was determined that First Sergeant Kenneth G. Spencer, until three days before top kick of Dog Company, 508th Parachute Infantry, 82nd Airborne Division, was the ranking noncommissioned officer.

"What we'll do is have each of you take a platoon," First Sergeant Spencer said. "And you," he added to the fourth master sergeant, "will be the guide."

While it had been some time since some of the master sergeants had marched anywhere, they knew what the hell they were doing. When the rest of the incoming class came out before the barracks, they quickly formed them into three platoons, each headed by a master sergeant. The second john (who looked as if he had gotten out of the Point last week) gestured to the cadre corporal to present the roster to First Sergeant Spencer.

Roll was called.

First Sergeant Spencer performed an impeccable about-face, snapped his right hand to his right eyebrow in an impeccable demonstration of the hand salute, and barked: "Sir, all present and accounted for."

The shavetail returned the salute.

"Very good. March the men to the mess, Sergeant."

"Yes, sir!" First Sergeant Spencer said. He did another impeccable about-face.

The mess was a pleasant surprise too. Most school mess

halls were pretty goddamned bad. This wasn't. There were four-man tables, each with pitchers of milk, condiments, table clothes, even napkins and flowers. More like an officer's mess than an EM mess hall. And the chow wasn't at all bad. Eggs any way you liked them, biscuits. First class.

Nobody had said anything about marching back to the company area, but First Sergeant Spencer had apparently decided it wouldn't hurt to play it safe and do things by the book, for when Franklin came out of the mess hall, Spencer was already there to form the troops again. When they were all assembled, he marched them back to the company area. Shiny Balls the Second John was waiting there for them. First Sergeant Spencer had guessed right. He had been expected to march the men back from the mess.

He formed the company into platoons, did an about-face, and saluted.

"Sir, the company is formed," he barked.

"Prepare the company for inspection in ranks, Sergeant," Shiny Balls the Second John said.

First Sergeant Spencer saluted, about-faced, stood at rigid attention and barked:

"Open ranks, MARCH!"

The first rank took two large steps forward; the second rank took one large step forward. The third rank did not move.

"Dress right, *dress*. Ready. FRONT!"

First Sergeant Spencer followed Shiny Balls the Second John up and down the ranks. Shiny Balls stopped in front of each man, examined him from tip of cap to tip of shoes. Shiny Balls, thought Staff Sergeant William B. Franklin, really ate that inspecting-officer shit up.

Finally, it was over.

Shiny Balls stood in front of the company.

He reached inside his tunic and took from it something that First Sergeant Spencer had never seen before. It was Shiny Balls's collection of ribbons and qualification badges. Shiny Balls, Sergeant Franklin saw, wasn't quite the fresh-from-the-Point shitass he had appeared to be. Shiny Balls had his own collection of qualification badges. There was a CIB, and below the CIB a set of aviator's wings, and then, below a double line of four-abreast ribbons, a set of jump wings. There was a Silver Star and Purple Heart with a cluster among the ribbons. Franklin was surprised to see the patch of ribbons and insignia on Shiny Balls. The only other officer he'd ever seen with a set like that, which could be put on or taken off with such ease, was Major Craig W. Lowell; and Lowell had class.

"Gentlemen," Shiny Balls said, "my name is Oppenheimer, and I am your tactical officer. Now, ten percent of you, those who have joined us directly from basic training, will probably accept this without question. The other ninety percent of you, the noncommissioned officers, the backbone of the army, are doubtless at this moment entertaining certain questions.

"It is practically an item of faith within the noncommissioned officer corps that second lieutenants have a value on a par with a rubber crutch for a cripple, or lactation glands on a male camel.

"I believed this myself, gentlemen, when, before I was afforded the opportunity of an education at the United States Military Academy at West Point, I served as a platoon sergeant with the 140th Tank Battalion.

"Ninety percent of the commissioned officers with whom you will be associated during your stay with us, as well, of course, as one hundred percent of the warrant officers, have had service as noncommissioned officers.

"I would therefore like to make the friendly suggestion that any thoughts that any of you have regarding beating the system because of your vast and varied experience as soldiers in sundry assignments around the planet Earth should be dismissed as wishful thinking.

"We are going to teach you two things while you are here. We are going to teach you how to fly rotary wing aircraft. Since you are all in excellent physical condition and possess a degree of intelligence at least as high as that of officer candidates, and since flying, frankly, is not all that difficult, that phase of your training should pose no problem.

"We are also going to make a valiant effort to turn you into officers and gentlemen. An officer is someone charged with the responsibility for other men's lives; there is no greater responsibility placed on any human being. A gentleman is someone who has earned the respect of his peers and subordinates by his personal character. His word is his bond. He accepts and executes orders without any mental reservations whatever.

"There is no bed check here, gentlemen. There will be no guards posted to keep you from walking out the gate and spending the night with your wives in the Daleville Motel—or wherever else you have stashed them. When you are ordered to be in your quarters, you are expected to be in your quarters. Your very presence here means that you have given your word to faithfully execute all orders.

"You will not be punished, in other words, for going AWOL. You will be dismissed from the program as being unfit to be an officer and a gentleman because your word cannot be trusted.

"Neither do we function here on the buddy system. You will cover for your friends at your own risk. A gentleman is not a snitch who will run to his superiors to report the misbehavior of his peers. On the other hand, to give you a specific example, should it come to our attention that someone missed a formation, that someone failed to appear at the appointed time, at the appointed place, in the proper uniform, and that whoever was in charge of the formation covered for him, the result would be immediate dismissal for both individuals.

"That's all the explanation of how things operate that you're going to get, with this final exception. You will be marched from here to the quartermaster warehouse, where you will receive a complete issue of uniforms, from T-shirts and shorts to flight suits. Those uniforms will be adorned with the insignia prescribed for the various grades of warrant officer candidates, and with no, repeat no, other insignia of any kind. It will be impossible to tell, for example, a former first sergeant of a parachute infantry company from a former recruit E-1. And that, gentlemen, is the point.

"From the moment you put on those new uniforms until you graduate, or are dismissed, you can forget that you are a noncommissioned officer whom a grateful government has seen fit to equip with authority, and the symbols of that authority, as well as the symbols for whatever unusual contribution you may have made to the profession of arms in the past.

"You are all equal. What you are now, gentlemen, is WOCs. And what a WOC is, is something one fwows at a wabbit."

It was not, Staff Sergeant Franklin had decided, your typical bullshit welcoming speech.

(Two)

By 21 November 1958, when Captain Philip Sheridan Parker IV marched into Dog Company WOC Battalion, Shiny Balls Oppenheimer, having completed eighteen months of satisfactory service, had received an automatic promotion to first lieutenant. His charges had gone through various stages of ground school, and phases I through IV of flight instruction. They would graduate just before Christmas, on completion of phase V (Light and Medium Transport Helicopter Operation Under Field Conditions).

Shiny Balls saw the Chevrolet staff car with the Collins VHF antenna mounted incongruously on its roof pull up before the company and correctly concluded that it was a messenger from On High; specifically, since only the post commander's staff car was equipped with the Collins antenna and the radios to go with it, an officer from the post commander's staff bearing amnesty for the WOC sinners.

He waited in his office for the little ballet to be carried out.

The WOC charge of quarters, at a little desk by the door, bellowed "Atten-hut" when the general's messenger entered the building. A moment or two later, the command was repeated as the general's messenger entered the orderly room.

"Sir," the WOC officer of the day barked crisply, "WOC Stewart, J. B., officer of the day, sir."

"Stand at ease," the general's messenger said. "Would you please offer my compliments to the tactical officer and inform him that I would have a word with him. My name is Parker."

The WOC officer of the day (the position was rotated daily among the WOCs) knocked at Shiny Balls's open door, was told to enter, entered, saluted, and said, "Sir, Captain Parker offers his compliments and requests to speak to the lieutenant, sir."

"Ask the captain to come in," Shiny Balls said, and prepared to stand up behind his desk.

"Sir," the WOC officer of the day said, at rigid attention, "Captain Parker, sir."

"Lieutenant Oppenheimer, K. B., sir," Shiny Balls said, saluting.

"Good afternoon, Lieutenant," Captain Parker said, returning the salute. He looked at the WOC officer of the day. "Be good enough to close the door when you leave," he said. The door was closed.

"It is the general's desire," Captain Parker said, "that your sinners be pardoned for all sins."

"Yes, sir," Oppenheimer said. "I suspected that might be the purpose of the captain's visit."

"I wish the announcement of the general's gracious gesture to be withheld from the troops until I have a word with one of them," Parker said. "One who is, I understand, a genuine, no question whatever about it, wise-ass."

"Who would that be, Captain?"

"Warrant Officer Candidate Franklin, William B.," Parker said.

Shiny Balls looked uncomfortable.

"May I say something, Captain?"

"Certainly."

"Now, I'm not trying to excuse what he did. It was wrong. I know it was wrong, and he knows it was wrong. But..."

"But?"

"He's a good man, Captain. Solid. And it isn't as if he had only 135 hours of flight instruction, if the captain gets my meaning."

"Your loyalty is commendable, Lieutenant," Captain Parker said, dryly. "And duly noted."

"Yes, sir. Shall I send for him, sir?"

"Just tell me where I can find him," Parker said. "I am going to have a word with him here, and then I am going to

take him away from the company area for further counseling.
You may make announcement of the general amnesty after we
leave."

"Yes, sir," Shiny Balls Oppenheimer said. He turned to a
chart on the wall and pointed out to Captain Parker the location
of WOC Franklin's WOCQ. (WOCQ stood for warrant officer
candidate's quarters. It was pronounced WockYou. It was far
more often mispronounced.)

Captain Philip Sheridan Parker IV rapped once with his
knuckle on the doorframe of WOC Franklin's WOCQ.

WOC Franklin, who had been sitting at his study desk,
jumped to his feet.

"Sir, WOC Franklin, W. B., sir!" he barked.

"Stand at case, Mr. Franklin," Captain Parker said. Franklin
assumed the position of "parade rest" rather than the somewhat
less rigid "at ease."

"My name is Parker," Captain Parker said. "In addition to
my other duties, I am the post equal opportunity and antidiscrimination officer."

"Yes, sir," Warrant Officer Franklin said.

"It has come to my attention that you have been charged
with, and are being punished for, a rather serious violation of
flight safety rules."

"Yes, sir."

"The army generally and the commanding general specifically are determined that there be absolutely no discrimination
based on race, creed, religion, or country of origin."

"Yes, sir."

"I am here, Mr. Franklin, to determine whether you are
guilty as charged or whether this is an incident where you are
being discriminated against because of the pigmentation of your
skin."

"Yes, sir."

"Well?"

"Sir, I am guilty as charged. It had nothing to do with me
being colored."

"'Colored'?" Captain Parker asked, in an incredulous tone.
"I was under the impression that the descriptions now in vogue

to describe those of the Negro race were 'black' and 'Afro-American.' I haven't heard the term 'colored' used in some time."

Franklin, visibly uncomfortable, took a moment before replying.

"Sir," he said, "it had nothing to do with my race."

"As I just informed you, Mr. Franklin," Parker said, "I am the post equal opportunity and antidiscrimination officer. It is my function, not yours, to determine whether or not the charges that you 'recklessly endangered an aircraft' are based on fact, or are one more manifestation of racial prejudice against those whom you quaintly chose to refer to as 'colored.'"

"Yes, sir," WOC Franklin said.

"To that end, Mr. Franklin, I am about to subject you to an unscheduled check ride."

"Yes, sir," Franklin said, visibly surprised.

"Get your helmet and your flight suit, Mr. Franklin," Captain Parker said. "I will wait for you in a sedan parked in front of this building." He turned on his heel and walked out of the room.

WOC Franklin jerked open his locker and took out his gray flight coveralls and his helmet. He debated for a moment whether to put the flight suit on now, or wait until they got where they were going. He decided it would be best not to keep this Captain Parker waiting. He folded his flight suit over his arm, put the helmet on his head, and ran down the corridor toward the stairs.

Parker was sitting in the back of a Chevrolet sedan. Franklin saw the Collins antenna on the roof, and thought: Jesus Christ, this is the general's staff car!

He got in the front seat beside the driver.

"You know where we're going," Captain Parker said to the driver. The driver was a sergeant first class. Sergeants first class normally do not drive staff cars, unless they happen to be the general's personal driver.

What the fuck is going on? thought Franklin.

"Yes, sir," the general's driver said.

He drove them to post headquarters.

The general's white-painted H-13H sat on the helipad before post headquarters. The general's staff car pulled into the reserved parking place, and the driver jumped out to open the door for Captain Parker.

"Thank you, Sergeant," Captain Parker said. He beckoned with his finger to WOC Franklin to follow him and walked across the road to the general's H-13H.

Franklin trotted after him.

"The general," Captain Parker said, "as an indication of his deep concern that the colored should not be discriminated against, has graciously made his personal helicopter available for your check ride."

Franklin was now wholly baffled.

"The general," Captain Parker went on, "was taught to ride a horse by a colored soldier when he was a very young officer. That colored, so to speak, the general's thinking about the colored. He finds it difficult to accept the fact that some coloreds, from time to time, really do really stupid things." Parker paused. "I have been led to believe, Mr. Franklin, that you have been instructed in the techniques of preflight inspection of aerial vehicles such as the one before you. If so, please conduct the inspection."

Franklin conducted the preflight. Captain Parker strapped himself in the passenger seat.

"Fire it up, Mr. Franklin," he said, and Franklin started the engine.

Parker depressed the mike button on his stick.

"Laird local control, Chopper One on the pad in front of the CP for a local flight to Hanchey. The Six is not aboard."

"Laird local control clears Chopper One for a local flight to Hanchey."

"Were you aware, Mr. Franklin," Captain Parker politely commented over the intercom, "that Major General Angus Laird took off from this very helipad and, the application of carburetor heat having slipped his mind, flew a machine just like this one into the trees?"

Franklin looked at Parker. Parker put both hands out in front of his body and made a lifting motion, and then pointed in the general direction of Hanchey Field.

Franklin saw that the needles were in the green, and inched back on the cyclic.

"Laird local, Chopper One light on the skids," Parker's voice came over the helmet earphones.

Ten minutes later, his voice came again.

"Now that you've demonstrated you can get it up," he said, "let's see if you remember how to put it down." He pointed to a clearing in the pine forest in the center of which was a whitewashed circle with a fifteen-foot-tall "H" in the center.

Franklin made what he thought was one of his better landings.

Parker made a cutting motion across his throat with his hand. Franklin killed the engine, and the fluckata-fluckata-fluckata sound of the rotor changed pitch as it slowed.

"Tell me true, Franklin," Parker said, "out here where no one can hear us, as one Afro-American warrior to another, just how much bootleg chopper time do you have?"

"About 600 hours, sir."

"My, you really must have worked at it, getting that much time."

Franklin didn't reply.

"The safety-of-flight allegations made against you, which may yet see your black ass thrown out of WOC school, accuse you of flying one of these things hands-off, in order that you might take snapshots."

"Yes, sir," Franklin said.

"'Yes, sir, that's what they say I did,' or 'Yes, sir, that's what I did'?"

"I was taking pictures, sir. I used to be a photographer."

"So I understand," Parker said, dryly. "Purely to satisfy my personal curiosity, will you show me how you performed this aerial feat of legerdemain?"

Franklin looked at him for a moment, as if making up his mind.

"What you have to do, Captain," he said, "is lock the cyclic under your knee. Like this."

He demonstrated how to fold the left leg over the cyclic control, the sticklike control to the left of the pilot's seat which controls both the angle of attack of the rotor blades and the amount of fuel fed to the engine.

"All you really can do is hold your attitude," Franklin explained. "You control the stick with your left foot and your right knee."

"Jesus Christ!" Parker said. "And somebody saw you doing this?"

"Yes, sir."

"The only reason they haven't thrown your ass out is probably because nobody believes it can be done."

"Am I to be thrown out, Captain? Is that what this is all about?"

"No, you're going to graduate. The 'incident' report has been lost."

"Jesus Christ, I'm glad to hear that," Franklin said.

"You really want to fly, huh?"

"Yes, sir, I do."

"You were doubtless inspired by some aviator with whom you had contact?"

"Yes, sir."

"Who taught you how to fly, despite regulations to the contrary?"

"Yes, sir."

"Who probably came up with this 'no-hands' technique of flying?"

"After he taught me how to fly," Franklin said, "we used to practice at 3,500 feet. He'd try to do it, and I grabbed the controls when something went wrong."

"In other words, one hell of a pilot, huh?"

"Yes, sir."

"Handsome devil, who when he is not doing something terribly John Wayneish, spends his time deciding which of the attractive ladies who gather around as moths to a candle he is going to honor with a screw?" Parker said. "A great big honky named Major Craig W. Lowell?"

"Do you know the major, sir?" Franklin asked.

"I wouldn't admit this to just anybody, Mr. Franklin," Captain Parker said, "but not only do I know the bastard, he's my best friend."

They grinned at each other for a moment.

"What happens now, sir?"

"I take you home for supper, what else?" Parker said. He

made a wind-it-up signal with his index finger. Franklin reached out and held down the Engine Start switch.

"The colored guy I told you taught the general to ride?" Parker's voice came over the earphones.

"Yes, sir?"

"My father," Parker said. Then there was a click as he depressed the microphone switch on the stick to the second detent, activating the transmitter. "Laird local, Chopper One in the Hanchey area. Request low level clearance to Pad One."

He looked at Franklin, and made the pick-it-up gesture with his hands.

"Both hands, Bill," he said. "Use both hands."

XV

(One)
Quarters No. 3
Fort Meyers, Virginia
11 December 1958

Every week or so, the Chief of Staff of the U.S. Army "got together" with the Vice Chief of Staff of the U.S. Army. The meetings were social and unofficial. In the hourly logs of their activities carefully maintained by their respective aides-de-camp the time blocks contained the abbreviation "AIQ." Alone In Quarters.

Very rarely were they alone, and only from time to time were they actually in their quarters. They were never, of course, completely alone. There was always a master sergeant or a warrant officer hovering around someplace with a .45 pistol in the small of his back or an M2 carbine in the golf club bag. There were generally, too, a junior aide around to grab the phone and a driver; and more remotely officers with the duty of being instantly available should they be needed (physicians and military policemen; cryptographers and public relations officers; ad infinitum) kept themselves aware of the locations of *the* Five and *the* Six and of the shortest, fastest way to get from where they were to where *they* were.

Alone meant that *the* Five and *the* Six were not officially or semiofficially entertaining anyone, including each other. Alone meant that what was said in the room where they happened to be would stay within that room. Not because the room had been swept to make sure it contained no clever little listening devices (although that of course had been done) but because the people at their little get-togethers were absolutely trustworthy.

At 1840 hours, twenty minutes to seven, the Chief of Staff of the U.S. Army said to his wife and his senior aide, "I'm going to walk over to E. Z. Black's. I'll be back after a while."

As soon as *the* six had gone out the door, the senior aide made a couple of telephone calls to pass the word where *the* Six would be and where he himself would be, and then he went home. Unless he was grossly mistaken, *the* Six would stay in place for the next five or six hours.

At 1843 hours, *the* Six entered Quarters No. 3, General E. Z. Black's quarters, through the kitchen door. There he found Master Sergeant Wesley, who had been with Black since they wore riding breeches (they spent a lot of time on the backs of horses), Senator Fulton J. Oswald of South Carolina and the Military Affairs Committee, Carson W. Newburgh, chairman and chief executive officer of the Newburgh Corporation, and, of course, *the* Five, General Black.

"What can I get you to drink, General?" Master Sergeant Wesley asked. The men nodded at each other, but none spoke or offered a hand to be shaken.

"Has he got any of that good scotch left, Wes?" the Chief of Staff asked.

"Yes, suh, twenty-four years old an' as mellow as it's gonna git," Sergeant Wesley said, turning and taking a bottle from a kitchen cupboard.

"Carson brought the chow," the Vice Chief of Staff said. "You have your choice between steak or pheasant. The pheasant'll take Wes about an hour to fix."

"I'll have the steak, then," the Chief of Staff said.

"Does the general want it cooked like a steak?" Sergeant Wesley inquired. "Or are you gonna eat it raw like Colonel Newburgh and the senator?"

"Steak tartar?" the Chief of Staff asked, chuckling. "Why not?"

"It's guaranteed to put lead in your pencil, General," the senator said.

"It'll take a hell of a lot more than some chopped beef and an egg yolk to put lead in my pencil, Senator," the Chief of Staff said.

Sergeant Wesley handed him a glass, dark with barely diluted scotch.

"If you gentlemen would like to go into the study, I'll start seeing about supper," Master Sergeant Wesley said.

"Give us half an hour, Wes," General Black said. "Time for another drink."

"Anybody else coming?" the Chief of Staff asked as they walked into the study. A table covered with an army blanket had been set up in case they decided to play poker.

"This is it," E. Z. Black said. "I was about to ask you the same thing."

"Tell E. Z. what you told me, Senator," the Chief of Staff said.

"The air force knows about your rocket-armed helicopters," the senator said. "I got that straight from the horse's ass, the distinguished senior senator from Rhode Island."

"Helicopter," General Black said. "Singular. One."

"One is one more than I knew about, E. Z.," the Chief of Staff said.

"Does the air force *think* we have them, or do they *know* we have them?" He corrected himself: "That we have *one* of them?"

"They have still and motion pictures," the senator said.

"Dirty bastards must have planted a spy," General Black said, angrily.

"Maybe that's what I should have done," the Chief of Staff said. "Instead of relying on you to keep me up with the interesting minutiae of the field army."

"I try to spare you the minutiae, General," E. Z. Black said. "To save you for politics."

"If this isn't politics, then what the hell is it?"

"I spent an hour this afternoon, for example," E. Z. Black went on, "trying to decide what to do about an ordnance light colonel in Japan who's also been in the movies. He happens to have the key to the tactical nukes."

"What kind of movies?"

"Stag movies. Queer stag movies. He's the star," E. Z. Black said. "I was going to bring that minutia to the general's attention for a decision."

"Jesus!" the senator said.

"There are several options," E. Z. Black went on. "The CIC and the G-2 want him removed and court-martialed, or at least cashiered. Some other people want the game to go on, to see who's dealing."

"What other people?" the Chief of Staff asked.

"CIA," E. Z. Black said. "And Felter."

"And you want to go with Felter, right?" the Chief of Staff asked.

"That is my recommendation. Yes, sir."

"Let's get back to your armed helicopters," the Chief of Staff said. "We both know that Felter will call the tune in the end anyway. The President thinks he's a goddamned genius."

"Isn't he?" the senator asked.

"He's a goddamned major in the U.S. Army," the Chief of Staff said. "That's all he is."

The senator laughed. "Bull*shit!*" he said. "All he is is a major in the army who gets to whisper in the President's ear once a day."

"I'd be a lot happier if he'd resign and just..." the Chief of Staff began. Black interrupted him.

"Get a hard-on for the army?" he said. "Felter thinks of himself as an army officer, and I think that's just fine."

"The question is, does he? I mean, does he really?"

"Yes, he does," Black said, firmly.

The Chief of Staff looked at the Vice Chief of Staff for a moment. They didn't like each other. The Chief of Staff was

West Point and infantry/airborne. The Vice Chief of Staff was Norwich and armor. The chemistry was bad between them. They had known and casually disliked each other for a quarter of a century. A mutual respect between them had slowly blossomed as their parallel careers had brought them to the top. They now deeply respected each other, but they were not friends.

Master Sergeant Wesley brought in a fresh tray of drinks and some cheddar cheese on toothpicks. The Chief of Staff put a cheddar chunk in his mouth.

"Tell me about your armed helicopters," he said.

"The idea's a natural," Black said. "I've been playing with it since before I went to Korea. When I commanded Fort Polk, Mac MacMillan strapped a 3.5 rocket launcher onto the skid of an old H-23 and showed me what he could do to M3 and M4 hulks on the known distance range."

"So Mac's involved in this?" the Chief of Staff asked. As an 82nd Airborne Division regimental commander, the Chief of Staff had recommended that Technical Sergeant Rudolph G. MacMillan of the Regimental Pathfinder Platoon be directly commissioned as a second lieutenant. Before MacMillan could be sworn in, he had been captured (at the time, it was thought he had been killed) under such circumstances that he had been recommended for the Medal of Honor.

"Mac and Bob Bellmon," E. Z. Black said.

"You realize this is liable to cost Bellmon his star?" the Chief of Staff asked.

"I am sure Colonel Bellmon recognized the inherent risk to his career," Black said.

"Anybody else?" the Chief of Staff asked. "E. Z., I'm getting a little annoyed pulling these details out of you like twelve-year molars."

"The chain of responsibility is me to Bellmon to MacMillan. There are two other officers involved. There's a young lieutenant named Greer, who served with the French Foreign Legion—who, as you know, regularly arm their choppers—in Algeria. He's at Fort Hood with the helicopter, and a couple of mechanics and an Ordnance Corps warrant officer I borrowed from Ted Davis."

"In other words, General Davis is also involved?"

"No, sir. General Davis could honestly testify that he had no inkling whatever of what was going on. I asked him for a competent ground rocket man who knew his way around ordnance depots. He didn't ask any questions, and I didn't volunteer any information."

"OK," the Chief of Staff said.

"And there's one more man, an officer in DCSLOG, here."

"What's his function?"

"This has cost a lot of money," E. Z. Black said. "This guy's good at getting it from other appropriations. He was also in North Africa and knows what's going on."

"Has he got a name?"

"Lowell. Major C. W. Lowell."

"What was that name, E.Z.?" the senator asked.

"Lowell. Major Craig Lowell," Black said.

"Oh, shit," the senator chuckled. "Well, that brings us to Item Two on the agenda," he said.

"I beg your pardon?" General Black asked, genuinely confused.

"E.Z.," the senator said, "I really hate to ask you if you know what else your Major Lowell has been up to."

"I don't understand," E. Z. Black said. He was a little worried that the senator was going to tell him Lowell's parties were getting to be too much the talk of the town.

"He's gotten himself involved with a senator's wife," the Chief of Staff exploded.

"It's probably really not his fault," the senator said. "But it could be awkward."

"What do mean, it's 'probably not his fault'?" the Chief of Staff snapped.

"The senator is old and rich. The senator's wife is young and healthy. The major is young—and a bachelor."

"Actually a widower," Carson Newburgh said.

"You know him, Carson?" the Chief of Staff asked.

"Yes, I know him. Fairly well, as a matter of fact," Newburgh said. "I didn't know about this, however. Who's the lady?"

"Constance," the senator told him.

"And who else knows about it?" Newburgh asked.

"Everybody, probably, but the husband. And I'm not too sure about that."

"Jesus H. Christ!" the Chief of Staff said. "E.Z., you really know how to pick them!"

"I didn't know about this," E. Z. Black said.

"You don't live in Georgetown," Carson Newburgh said. "All sorts of interesting things go on there."

"Lowell lives in Georgetown?" the Chief of Staff asked.

"Right next door to the senator whose wife we're talking about," the senator said.

"How the hell does he afford that?" the Chief of Staff asked.

"He's comfortable, General," Carson Newburgh said. "Very comfortable."

"What the hell does that mean?" the Chief of Staff asked.

"Are you familiar with Craig, Powell, Kenyon and Dawes?"

"Stockbrokers?" the Chief of Staff asked.

"That, too, but primarily investment bankers. There are two major stockholders. Porter Craig, chairman of the board and chief executive officer, who owns half. And his cousin, Major Lowell, who owns the other half."

"What the hell is a rich man like that doing in the army?"

"I wasn't aware that being poor was a soldierly virtue," Carson Newburgh said, icily.

"Georgie Patton was rich," E. Z. Black said. "He was a good soldier. So was Carson. So is Lowell, for that matter. He ran the breakout, Task Force Lowell, from Pusan."

"Oh, yeah," the Chief of Staff said. "I know about him. He's the wise-ass who then got up and testified in a court-martial that he could see nothing wrong with shooting officers who were running in the wrong direction. I knew he had a big mouth, but I didn't know he was rich." He stopped, then went on: "Nothing personal, Carson, goddamnit, you know that."

"You gennlemen just say when you want to eat," Master Sergeant Wesley said, from the door to the study.

"In fifteen minutes, Wes," General Black said.

"George Patton didn't go around fucking senator's wives," the Chief of Staff said. Black saw that he was working himself into a rage and wondered why.

"It can be controlled," the senator said. "I just thought it was worth mentioning."

"You bet your sweet ass it will be controlled," the Chief of Staff said. "We'll send the sonofabitch to Greenland and let him screw a polar bear."

"Hey, come on," the senator said. "The major is not the first soldier to get his ashes hauled outside the nuptial couch. MacArthur had a Eurasian mistress stashed in an apartment when he was Chief of Staff. Even the chastity part of Eisenhower's wartime sainthood had been questioned."

"You don't believe that cheap gossip, do you?" the Chief of Staff snapped. "I'll remind you, you're talking about the President."

"Of course, *I* don't believe it," the senator said, angrily, thickly sarcastic. "And *I was there*. *I* believe he commissioned that big-teated Limey as an American officer *solely* because she did such a splendid job driving his jeep. I also believe in the tooth fairy."

The Chief of Staff glowered at him.

"I just remembered something else about your man Lowell, General," he said to Black.

"What's that, sir?"

"Remember the flap when *Life* ran the story with the pictures of the M48 with 'Blueballs' painted on the turret? And that actress that doesn't wear any underwear with her arms around the crew? Georgia Paige? I remember that some damned fool of a young officer took her up to the front, and subsequently screwed her on every available horizontal surface, and I just remembered his name. That was your man Lowell, wasn't it, General?"

"I believe it was," Black said. "So what?"

"He gets around, doesn't he?" the senator chuckled.

"What do you mean, so what?" the Chief of Staff demanded, angrily.

"You remember, I'm sure," Black said, "what Phil Sheridan said about soldiers that don't fuck."

"He was speaking of soldiers, not officers of the General

Staff Corps," the Chief of Staff said, so furiously that spittle flew.

"I don't give a good goddamn if he screws orangutangs," Black said. "So long as he does his duty and does it as well as this particular, young, unmarried officer does his."

"Hey! Hey!" the senator said. "Tempers, gentlemen!"

The Chief of Staff glowered at him and then at E. Z. Black. In a moment he got control of his voice.

"To sum up," the Chief of Staff said icily, "what we have here is a clear and blatant violation of the Key West Agreement of 1948, which says the army will not, repeat not, under any circumstances arm its aircraft. We have been caught with our ass hanging out. And for the cherry on top of the cake, one of the *officers* and *gentlemen* involved in this breach of good faith is involved with a senator's lady."

"I am the officer primarily involved, General," Black said. "And so far as the senator's lady is concerned, you can make that 'was involved.' I'll see that it's stopped."

"That still leaves us with your goddamned armed helicopters, which I'm sure the air force is sure to bring to the attention of the *Washington Post* just as soon as they can," the Chief of Staff said.

"I've been thinking about this helicopter thing," the senator said. "What I think you should do is go public with it. Call a press conference. Show the goddamned thing off. If it works, the air force would look pretty goddamned silly bitching about it."

"It works," E. Z. Black said. "And the bottom line is that we can afford to swap helicopters for tanks all day long."

The Chief of Staff looked at him for a long moment.

"I don't see where we have any other alternative to this mess in which the Vice Chief of Staff has enmeshed us," he said.

"You're going to have to get off the dime, General," the senator said, "before the air force lowers the boom."

"Wesley!" the Chief of Staff called out.

Master Sergeant Wesley appeared.

"Yes, suh?"

"Get somebody on the horn, please, Wes. See if you can find the Chief of Information. Ask him if he's free to join us for a drink. If you can't find the Chief of Information, get his deputy."

"Yes, sir," Sergeant Wesley said.

(Two)
Ozark, Alabama
12 December 1958

"Mr. Dutton's office," Howard Dutton's private secretary purred into the telephone.

"I have a collect call for anyone from Mrs. Greer in San Antonio," the operator's somewhat twangy voice announced.

"This is Mr. Howard Dutton's office," Howard Dutton's secretary repeated."

"I have a collect call for anyone from Mrs. Greer in San Antonio," the operator repeated.

"Just a minute, Operator," Howard Dutton's secretary said. She laid the phone down and walked to Howard Dutton's office.

"Mistuh Dutton, we got a collect call for anybody from some Mrs. Greer," she said. "What do I tell her?"

"Good Christ!" Howard Dutton said, spinning around in his high-backed leather chair to face the credenza with the telephones on it. There were two telephones, each equipped with buttons that lit when the line was in use. There were four buttons on each telephone. Of the eight buttons, four were lit.

Howard Dutton got the San Antonio operator on the third try.

"Put it through, put it through," he had twice announced to somewhat startled users of the telephone.

"Go 'head, please," the operator finally said.

"Daddy?"

"How's my baby?" Howard Dutton asked. "Nothing wrong, honey, is there?"

"Daddy, could I come home a little early for Christmas?"

"Honey, you can come anytime you want to come home," Howard Dutton said. "What's wrong, honey?"

The baby began to cry.

Goddamn that bastard! What has he done to my Melody?

"He's throwing up again, damn him," Melody said. "All over my dress."

"Now, you just calm down, honey," Howard Dutton said. "Everything's going to be all right."

"Could I come home this afternoon? Or tonight, really? On the eight thirty-two flight from Atlanta?"

"Eight thirty-two," Howard Dutton repeated. He turned to his desk for a pencil, and saw his secretary. "Write this down," he snapped. "Eight thirty-two from Atlanta." He took his hand off the telephone mouthpiece.

"I'll be there, honey," he said. "I'll be waiting for you when you get off the plane."

He remembered that the call had been collect. Did that mean she didn't have any money?

Why doesn't she have any money?

"Now, you just tell me what's wrong," Howard Dutton said, "and your daddy'll take care of it."

"Nothing's wrong, Daddy," Melody said.

"Where's your husband?" he demanded.

" '*My husband*,' " Melody mocked him, "is halfway to Rucker in the Big Bad Bird. He got orders this morning to bring the Big Bad Bird to Rucker ASAP."

"I don't know what that means," Howard Dutton confessed, unhappily.

"He's flying the gunship up there. ASAP: As Soon As Possible. The orders said for a minimum period of thirty days. So I'm on my way, too."

"You sure you got enough money? I could call the bank down there, and see that you had some money right away."

"Eight thirty-two, Daddy," Melody said, and hung up.

Howard Dutton put the telephone back in its cradle and spun the chair around. His secretary was standing there with her pencil poised over her steno book. Stupid damned female! He sometimes almost wished that Prissy was back.

"I'll be at my house," he said to her and walked out of the office.

Prissy was sitting at the kitchen table having a cup of coffee with the maid when he walked in.

"What are you doing home?" she asked.

"Melody and the baby are coming on the eight thirty-two from Atlanta," he said. For some inexplicable reason, making the announcement made him feel like crying.

"Where's Ed? Is he coming?" Prissy asked.

"He's flying up by himself," Howard Dutton said.

"Why aren't they flying together?" Prissy asked.

Stupid damned female.

"I think they have a rule against flying infants in army helicopters," he said, sarcastically.

"You could have explained that he was flying with the army," Prissy said. "Well, we'll just have to get ready for them."

"She said they'll be here for at least thirty days," Howard said.

"Eight thirty-two? That's plenty of time. You didn't have to come home. You could have called from the office."

He went to his office and opened a drawer and took a long pull at the neck of a quart bottle of Jack Daniels.

Between a stupid female at home and a stupid female in the office, it was a miracle he hadn't lost his mind. He sat down at his desk and reached out and adjusted a double photo frame so that he could look at it better.

The left was Melody's graduation picture. The right was of Melody and the baby. She looked like a madonna, Howard Dutton thought. There was no other word to describe the way Melody looked holding her baby.

He took another pull at the bottle of Jack Daniels and then looked at his watch. It was nine forty. Melody would be home in less than twelve hours.

(Three)
U.S. Army Aviation Combat Developments Agency
Fort Rucker, Alabama
12 December 1958

"You understand, Colonel, I'm sure, that I've had only the briefest of briefings. About the only orders I got from the general were to get my show on the road."

The speaker was Colonel Tim F. Brandon, Chief, Special Operations Branch, Media Relations Division, Office of the Chief of Information, Department of the Army.

"What general is that?" Colonel Robert F. Bellmon asked, innocently.

"The Chief of Information," Colonel Brandon said.

"Of course," Colonel Bellmon said. He had just noticed that if one was to judge from the display of ribbons on Colonel Brandon's tunic, he had managed to rise to colonel of infantry without ever once having heard a shot fired in anger.

"Now, this little operation of ours enjoys a very high priority," Colonel Brandon said.

"So I understand," Colonel Bellmon replied. He had received a telephone call at 11:30 the night before from the Vice Chief of the Staff of the U.S. Army, informing him that a couple of PIO assholes would be coming to see him; the decision had been to go public with the rocket-armed gunship.

The Big Bad Bird itself had already been ordered from Hood to Rucker and Hood had been ordered to fly the technicians and their equipment to Rucker as soon as that could be arranged.

"Go along as far as you can with these guys, Bob. Lean over backward. But if you need me, get on the horn."

"Yes, sir," Bellmon had said to the Vice Chief of Staff.

There was a knock on the door. Bellmon looked up and motioned for MacMillan to come in. MacMillan was in a flight suit. He had just returned, successfully, to judge from the OK sign he made, from arranging for a portable hangar to be erected to house the gunship out near Hanchey—and far from prying eyes.

"Colonel Brandon," Colonel Bellmon said, "this is Major MacMillan. Major MacMillan is the man you'll be working with."

"I had hoped that we would be working directly, so to speak, together on this," Colonel Brandon said.

"Major MacMillan knows as much, more, about the Big Bad Bird than I do," Colonel Bellmon said.

"I see," Colonel Brandon said.

"You got an ETA on the Bird, Mac?" Bellmon asked.

"Greer called from Dallas," MacMillan said. "About thirty

minutes ago. Said he'd be on the ground about an hour. Unless he's called since, he's at Love Field."

"That's an unfortunate term," Colonel Brandon said.

"I beg your pardon?"

"'Big Bad Bird,'" Colonel Brandon said. "We need something stronger. Like 'Tiger.'"

"'Tiger' is a German tank," MacMillan said.

"We'll work on that later," Colonel Brandon said. "'Big Bad Bird' is just not going to cut the mustard. Now, what about this guy with the Medal? What's he look like?"

MacMillan looked at Colonel Brandon in disbelief. Colonel Bellmon smiled broadly.

"I was told one of your officers has the Congressional," Colonel Brandon said. "I'm hoping two things: first, that he has been connected with the gunship and second, that he's photogenic and can talk."

"Say something for the colonel, Mac," Bellmon said.

"I beg your pardon, Major," Colonel Brandon said. "Certainly, no offense was intended. What I was saying was that I hoped you would turn out to be someone we can put on camera. Obviously, you're more than I hoped for."

Bellmon pushed his intercom button. "Darlene, would you have someone bring some coffee in here, please? And if Mrs. Hyde is in the building, would you run her down and ask her to come in here, please?"

"Now that we have the problem of the talking head solved," Colonel Brandon said, "we can think about a new name for the gunship. I don't even know what it looks like. There must be a photograph of it around somewhere?"

"They're classified Secret, Sensitive," Colonel Bellmon said. "I haven't been informed that you're so cleared, Colonel."

Rhonda Wilson Hyde knocked at the door and came in without waiting to be invited.

"Colonel," Colonel Bellmon said, "this is Mrs. Hyde, our administrative officer. Rhonda, this is Colonel Brandon, of the Office of the Chief of Information."

Colonel Brandon and Mrs. Hyde smiled at one another. Major MacMillan looked at Colonel Bellmon and mouthed the word "Geronimo."

"Mrs. Hyde will take care of getting you cleared, Colonel," Bellmon said. "And otherwise take care of your needs. And now, if you'll excuse us, I have some other matters to discuss with the Talking Head."

(Four)
McLean, Virginia
15 December 1958

The morning briefing, as it sometimes did, had become the afternoon briefing, and the blinds had been drawn against the afternoon sun in Conference Room III.

Sanford T. Felter stayed behind, as he sometimes did, when the briefing officers and the analysts were dismissed.

"Are you going to be in town over the holidays?" Felter asked, when everyone else had left the room.

"Yes," the Director said. "Special reason for asking?"

"If it can be worked in, I'd like to take a little leave. Say, ten days from the twenty-first?"

"You don't have to ask me, Felter."

"I hoped you'd take over briefing the boss," Felter said.

"Sure," the Director said. "Where you going?"

"To Fort Rucker," Felter said.

"What the hell is going on down there?" the Director asked. Felter looked at him curiously. The Director went on: "I noticed a memo that E. Z. Black is going to be at Rucker over the holidays."

"I'm not going with him," Felter said. "I'm just going to visit some friends."

"Well, at least the communications will be in. We can get the army to pay for them. Just have them get you a couple of secure lines."

Felter's curiosity got the best of him. He walked to one of the telephones on the conference table and dialed a two-digit number.

"Army liaison," a voice said. "Colonel Ford."

"Sanford Felter, Colonel," Felter said. "Why is General Black going to be at Fort Rucker over the holidays?"

"Sir, the army is going to go public about its helicopter

gunship. There's going to be a press junket. The general's going to make the announcement himself."

"Thank you," Felter said and hung up.

The Director looked at him curiously.

"It would seem the air force has caught the army arming its helicopters," Felter said. "And have decided the best defense is a good offense. Black is going to make the announcement himself."

"Christ!" the Director said. "Well, at least we're not involved."

"No," Felter said.

"Who do you think is right, Sandy?" the Director said.

"The army," Felter said. "Was that the response you expected of me?"

"I'm sure it's based on your analysis of the problem," the Director said, "and not because you march in the rear rank of the Long Gray Line."

"We furnished the air force with the material generated in Algeria," Felter said. "They didn't do anything with it. Arming helicopters is an idea whose time has come. The army just filled the vacuum."

"The air force is going to cry 'foul,'" the Director said.

"The air force still believes they won the war in Europe with bombers," Felter said.

The Director chuckled. "Now, *that* was a voice from the Long Gray Line," he said.

Felter looked uncomfortable.

"Just kidding, Sandy," the Director said. "Just kidding."

XVI

(One)
U.S. Army Aviation Combat Development Agency
Fort Rucker, Alabama
16 December 1958

Colonel Bellmon pushed the lever on his intercom.

"Darlene, I can't raise Mac. Is he in the building?"

"No, sir. He's out at Hanchey."

"What about Mrs. Hyde?"

"She's out there, too, with Colonel Brandon and the camera crew."

"Come in here a moment, will you please, Darlene?"

When she came into his office, he told her that he wanted her to take the staff car and driver and go out to Laird Field.

"You've met Major Lowell, haven't you?"

"Yes, sir, I have."

"Major Lowell is about to land at Laird in a civilian airplane. I want you to meet him. Tell him that I sent you to bring him directly here. There may be other people meeting him. But you are to make him understand that he is to come directly here to

325

see me before he does anything else. Can you handle that?"

"Yes, sir, I'm sure I can," Darlene Heatter said.

Darlene was waiting at the Base Operations building at Laird Army Airfield when the glistening, sleek Aero Commander taxied up to the transient parking area and was shown where to park.

When she started to go out the glass door, she almost bumped into a nigger woman. When she looked more closely, she recognized her as that nigger woman *doctor* they had over at the hospital, an object of some curiosity and a good deal of discussion.

"After you," Darlene said, priding herself on this demonstration of lack of prejudice.

"Thank you," the nigger woman doctor said and went through the glass door and started for the Aero Commander. The door in the back of the airplane opened and Major Lowell got out and stretched his arms and legs. Then he leaned back inside the airplane and took out a tunic. He put it on, and then he saw the nigger woman doctor.

"Well, as I live and breathe," he said, "my favorite lady chancre mechanic!"

He kissed her, as if it was the most natural thing in the world.

Well, that wasn't the only thing she'd seen at Rucker that she would never have believed in a thousand years.

"Phil's out stamping out racial prejudice," the nigger lady doctor said. "So here I am."

"Major Lowell," Darlene said, "do you remember me?"

He looked at her.

"I'm afraid not," he said, after a moment.

"I'm Colonel Bellmon's secretary," Darlene said. "He sent me to fetch you."

"I've already been 'fetched,'" he said.

"Colonel Bellmon said I was to bring you back to him before you did anything else," Darlene said. "I got the staff car."

"That sounds like an order," the nigger woman doctor said. "As opposed to a friendly invitation."

"Doesn't it?" Lowell said. "Well, let me see what he wants, and then I'll come over to the hospital."

"I'm on duty until half past four," the nigger woman doctor said. "But the maid knows you're coming; and Phil, I'm sure, will get loose as soon as he can."

"Sorry about the wild goose chase," Lowell said.

"Don't be silly," the nigger woman doctor said and kissed him on the cheek.

Lowell went back inside the Aero Commander and came out with several pieces of luggage, two limp garment bags, two suitcases, and a rigid oblong case that Darlene recognized after a moment as a gun case. The driver saw them and ran over to help with the luggage.

As they rode from Laird Field through Daleville onto the post, Darlene Heatter wondered what it would be like to do it with Major Lowell. Even if he did let himself get kissed by a nigger woman. Maybe it *was* true, what they said, about niggers really being good at it. Maybe nigger women were as good as it as the men were supposed to be.

Lowell knocked at Colonel Robert F. Bellmon's door.

"Come," Bellmon said.

Lowell marched in, saluted, and stood at attention.

"Sir, Major Lowell reporting as ordered, sir."

"Not quite as ordered, I'm afraid," Bellmon said. He walked over and closed his office door, and that was all that Darlene could hear.

"Oh, sit down, Craig," Bob Bellmon said. "You want a cup of coffee, or something?"

"No, thank you. I drank coffee all the way down."

"As I understand your orders, you were to proceed here by the first available commercial air transportation," Bellmon said. "And I further understand that you were taken to Washington National by an officer, to encourage you to carry out your orders."

Lowell said nothing.

"Well?"

"It didn't make a hell of a lot of sense to me to leave my airplane there at National," Lowell said. "What's the difference?"

"That's always been your trouble, Craig," Bellmon said. "You ask yourself what's the difference, and you answer yourself. 'none,' and then you do what suits you. In this case, to be honest, the answer is that it makes no difference whatever."

"If I've somehow embarrassed you, Bob, I'm truly sorry."

"Hell, yes, you've embarrassed me."

"I'm sorry," Lowell said.

"You don't really have any idea the trouble you're in, do you?"

"I have the feeling that I have someone *on high* a bit annoyed," Lowell said. "I'm not exactly sure who."

"I might as well get right to the point, Craig," Bellmon said. "I hope the senator's wife was a good lay."

"Oh. So that's it."

"Because that piece of ass has wiped you out," Bellmon said. "You're finished, Craig. I've got the unpleasant duty of making that clear to you."

"Define finished," Lowell said.

"You are on thirty days' temporary duty here," Bellmon said. "If you do not resign in that period, and it is hoped that you will resign today, you will be reassigned to U.S. Army, Caribbean. It will not be a flying assignment. Until they can think of some clever way of speeding up the process of separating you from the service as unfit, you'll probably be assigned as dependent housing officer, or special assistant to the garbage collection officer."

"Come on, Bob," Lowell said. "I'm not about to be, I'm not about *to let myself be* thrown out of the army over some horny woman."

"The horny woman was the straw that broke the camel's back, I'm afraid," Bellmon said.

"What else am I alleged to have done?"

"The air force knows about the Big Bad Bird."

"I'll bet I knew that before you did," Lowell said.

"We need a sacrifice," Bellmon said. "You're it."

"*That* needs an explanation."

"Here's the new scenario, which I don't think you've heard, because I got it on the telephone less than two hours ago."

"From whom?"

"Do you know Dan Brackmayer?"

"Dog robber to the Chief of Staff?"

"*Colonel* Brackmayer is Special Assistant to the Chief of Staff."

"I know who he is."

"This is the way it goes, Craig," Bellmon said. "We plead guilty."

"What's that mean?"

"The Chief of Staff admits that we have violated the Key West Agreement of 1948 by arming a helicopter. An over-zealous officer, you, is responsible."

"And?"

"Most important, now that we have it, of course, it would be foolish to give it up. But since orders must be obeyed, the officer responsible must be punished. He will resign to spare the army embarrassment and himself the possibility of a court-martial."

"In other words, I take the rap for everybody? The West Point Protective Association forms a circle to fight off the Indians?"

"I offered to take full responsibility," Bellmon said.

"Oddly enough," Lowell said, "I believe that."

"Thank you," Bellmon said. "Oddly enough, it's very important to me that you do believe that."

"Where does E. Z. Black fit into all this?"

"The Vice Chief of Staff has given his word to the Chief of Staff that you'll resign."

"He seems pretty goddamned sure of himself," Lowell said.

"There was a last straw with him, too, Craig," Bellmon said.

"Which was?"

"He told you to stay away from Felter. I heard him, as a matter of fact. He told you to stay away from Felter, and why, and you haven't."

"I had Sharon and the kids over to that whorehouse I set up at Black's request a couple of times, so the kids could use the pool."

"You were ordered to stay away from Felter, and you didn't, period."

"Well, fuck him!"

Bellmon didn't respond to that.

"Everybody seems to think that I'll just take this lying down," Lowell said. "It must have occurred to somebody that I just might open the closet and show all the skeletons to the air force."

"I was asked that question," Bellmon said. "And I said there was absolutely no risk of that at all. I'm not sure the Chief of Staff believed me, but all your friends did."

"Why am I flattered by that?"

"Because you're a soldier," Bellmon said.

"'You're a soldier,' says the vice president of the WPPA, 'now get your ass out of the army.'"

"The Big Bad Bird is what's important, Craig," Bellmon said.

"Oh, shit," Lowell said. "Don't wave the flag at me, Bob."

"I wasn't," Bellmon said. And then he corrected himself. "OK, I was. What's wrong with that?"

"You want to hear about this dame?" Lowell said. He went on without waiting for a reply. "She climbed over the wall into my backyard. Actually climbed over the fucking wall. And groped me. And when I suggested that might be a little risky, she said what was risky was her going to the senator and telling him I had made lewd advances."

"Oddly enough," Bellmon said, "I believe that, too."

"So what the hell do I do with my life, now?" Lowell asked. "The army's all I know."

"Well, you won't wind up on welfare," Bellmon said. "I'm sure that was a factor in the equation."

"I could go to Germany, I suppose," Lowell said. "God knows, I don't want to work for the fucking firm."

"Buy yourself an airline," Bellmon said.

"What am I going to tell my father-in-law?" Lowell said.

"The truth," Bellmon said. "He'll understand."

"In his army, they handed an officer a Luger with one round and let him do the honorable thing," Lowell said. "I've still got my Luger someplace, come to think of it."

"Don't be melodramatic," Bellmon said. "You don't mean that."

"I wouldn't have the courage," Lowell said. "When I was in Greece with Felter, the day we got there, the guy in the next room to us stuck a .45 in his mouth and pulled the trigger. That sort of thing is very messy."

He looked at Bellmon and smiled.

"Don't look so stricken, Colonel," he said. "I'm really not all that fucked up by this involuntary sacrifice I'm making."

"If there's ever anything I can do for—" Bellmon began. Lowell interupted him by holding up his hand.

"Resigning today is out of the question," Lowell said.

Bellmon's eyebrows went up.

"Why?" he asked.

"Well, there are several reasons. For one thing, I'll have to...you'll have to...find someone trustworthy to whom I can turn over the secrets of where I stole the money for the Big Bad Bird. If that doesn't get blown up, you can get money there again."

"And the other reason?"

"It's the holiday season," Lowell said. "Old Home Week. Sandy Felter is bringing Sharon down here. The little bastard has her on the edge of a nervous breakdown with his spy business. She wants to be an officer's lady on New Year's Eve, and I want her to have that."

"You're in no position to announce what you want," Bellmon said.

"Get on the phone, Bob," Lowell said. "Call Brackmayer and tell him I will silently steal away as of 1 January 1959. Not one day before. At least not quietly."

"OK," Bellmon said, after thinking it over. "I'll call Brackmayer. I'll tell him that you understand the situation and will do what is expected of you. I'll tell him that I need you to tie up the loose ends for the Big Bad Bird. I'll reassure him that his concerns about skeletons are groundless."

"Fuck him, tell him the opposite. Let him lose a little sleep."

"Until a decision is made, Major Lowell," Colonel Bellmon said, formally, "You will find yourself a BOQ, and you will stay in that BOQ, or the club, and you will not leave the post."

"I'm staying with Phil and Antoinette Parker," Lowell said.

Bellmon nodded. "All right, Lowell," he said. "So long as you understand me about keeping yourself under wraps."

"I understand," Lowell said. "Is that all, Bob?"

Bellmon nodded.

Lowell stood up, saluted, and walked out of the room.

(Two)
Auxiliary Field Three
Hanchey Army Airfield
Fort Rucker, Alabama
22 December 1958

The hangar was constructed of plasticized cloth in the manner of an inflatable life raft. It had been erected in fifteen minutes. First four stakes were pounded into the ground at precise distances from each other. Then what looked like a pile of camouflaged tenting was spread out. Each corner was attached to one of the stakes.

A five-horsepower gasoline generator was started. The engine drove an electric motor, and the electric motor powered an air compressor. The pile of camouflaged tenting seemed to sit, then to grow and subside, grow and subside, until it rather suddenly assumed its ultimate shape, ninety feet long, forty feet wide, and fifteen feet high at the center. An enormous empty toilet tissue center half buried in the ground.

Whenever the pressure of the air in its hollow walls dropped below 7.5 psi, the generator started up automatically. There were doors of the same construction. There was another generator—larger, diesel, jeep-trailer mounted—which provided electricity, heat, and compressed air for the aircraft mechanic's tools.

The Kit, Hangar, Service, Field, Inflatable, Self-Contained, also included poles and ropes and camouflage netting. When the whole thing was in place, properly inflated, and covered by the netting, it was very hard to see from the air or the ground, even if you knew it was there.

The Big Bad Bird sat in the balloon, as the hangar inevitably came to be called, its fifty-six-foot-diameter rotor blades parallel with the fuselage.

The Big Bad Bird had been one of the very first Sikorsky H-19s the army had purchased. It had seen service in the Korean War, and had later been assigned to a transportation helicopter company at Fort Lewis, Washington. It had suffered three minor and two major accidents. After the second major accident, it had become a hangar queen at Fort Lewis, losing most of its remaining functioning parts as replacements to keep newer, better H-19s flying.

Just over a year before, it had left Fort Lewis on a truck, and had been dropped from Fort Lewis's property books. It had been acquired by Plans and Requirements Division (Fiscal), Aviation Maintenance Section, DCSLOG. It was thereafter logically assumed by those who knew Tail Number 50–3003 that the old wreck would be sold for junk, or maybe used as a target on a tank range, or something. It would never fly again, that was for goddamn sure.

The Army Aviation Base at Anchorage, Alaska, was that year scheduled to receive two new fire engines and three ground power generators. It got one of each. The Army Airfield at Fort Sill, Oklahoma, which was supposed to get two fire trucks got none, and neither did Kitzigen, Germany, or Headquarters, U.S. Army, Panama.

The Walla Walla (Washington) Flying Service, which operated civilian models of the Sikorsky H-19 in timber applications, received a purchase order from the Plans and Requirements Division (Fiscal) of the Aviation Maintenance Section, DCSLOG, to make such repairs as were necessary to restore H-19 50–3003 to minimum standards of flight safety. The funds expended had been intended for fire engines and ground power generators.

Double Ought Three, the Big Bad Bird, was not what someone coming across its listing in the inventory of Aircraft, Non-Serviceable, Awaiting Evaluation, would have envisioned. It had been restored to flyable condition and modified.

It had a new (actually rebuilt) engine, a new power train and rotor head, and new rotors. At Fort Hood, the fuselage had been modified.

The standard H-19 has one cargo compartment door, on the right. The Big Bad Bird had another cut through the left fuselage wall. The interior of the passenger compartment had been strengthened, the seats were removed, and "stores racks" installed.

The landing wheel struts had been reinforced, and on each strut was a circular canister, holding three 3.5 inch rockets with explosive heads. The canister functioned very much like the cylinder of a revolver. As the canister revolved, the rocket was fired, just as a cartridge is fired in a revolver when its cylinder is aligned with the barrel. (There was, of course, no barrel on the Bird's rocket canisters.) A feed chute ran from each canister into the Bird's fuselage. The chute was connected to a bin. The bin and the feed chute were filled with 3.5 inch rockets.

When the rocket launching device was activated (by a switch mounted on the pilot's control stick), an electric motor turned and an electric firing circuit was activated. The canister revolved 120 degrees, moving a 3.5 rocket into firing position, where it was fired. Then the canister revolved 120 degrees again, the empty cylinder picking up a 3.5 from the chute, and the chute picking up a 3.5 from the bin. There were a total of fifty-four 3.5s in the bins, the chutes, and the canisters, twenty-seven on each strut. They could all be fired in fifteen seconds.

There was no tank known to military intelligence with armor strong enough to resist a direct hit from a 3.5 inch rocket during the "most efficient" phase of the rocket's flight. That is to say, when the target was from 50 to 350 yards from the point where the rocket had been launched. It took the rocket about 50 yards to get up to speed, and after 350 yards it began to lose speed. But within the "most efficient" phase of its flight envelope, the rocket would pass through the armor of any known tank like a drop of molten steel through a stick of butter. And then it would explode.

The testing that the Big Bad Bird was going through now had little to do with the practical military application for which it was intended. It was now preparing for what the Big Bad Bird People, as they called themselves, had chosen to call its "screen test."

Colonel Tim F. Brandon was not particularly amused by this attitude, but he had been around long enough to understand that troops in the field seldom (if ever) understood how important public relations was to the army as a whole. And he also understood that it was unlikely that no explanation would ever change the attitude of the troops. It was something he just had to live with, meanwhile doing the best job he was capable of.

And he was correctly convinced that he could do one hell of a good job.

The debut of "the Viper" (which is what Colonel Brandon had decided to call the Big Bad Bird) would take place early in the morning of 27 December 1958. All three television networks were sending camera crews, and there would be the army crew to make film available to other outlets. A special camera platform had been erected. Additionally, three remote-controlled cameras had been set up in sandbag-protected emplacements along the route of the tank, so that the actual strike of the rockets on the tank could be filmed closeup.

Colonel Tim F. Brandon, again correctly, considered the tanks proof positive that he knew just what the hell he was about.

Eleven Russian T34 tanks had come into American possession from various sources. They had been studied in great detail by armor and ordnance tactical and technical experts and then turned over to Fort Riley, Kansas (less one tank which went to the Ordnance Museum at Aberdeen Proving Ground and another which went to the George S. Patton Museum at Fort Knox, Kentucky). Fort Riley had a unit trained in Soviet Army tactics, which was used in maneuvers. The availability of genuine Red Army T34s lent an aura of authenticity to the maneuvers that could be accomplished in no other manner.

They had bellowed in outrage when the TWX came.

HQ DEPT OF THE ARMY WASH DC 17 DEC 59
COMMANDING GENERAL FT RILEY KANSAS

TWX CONFIRMS TELECON CG FT RILEY AND VICE DSCOPS 0900 HRS 17 DEC 59:
CG FT RILEY WILL IMMEDIATELY TAKE STEPS TO MOVE THREE (3) OPERATING T34 TANKS PRESENTLY ASSIGNED USA MANEUVER GROUP FT RILEY TO USA AVIATION COMBAT DEVELOPMENTS AGENCY FT RUCKER ALA. PRIORITY OF FT RUCKER OPERATION REQUIRES TANKS ARRIVE IN OPERATING CONDITION NOT LATER THAN 2400 HOURS 20 DEC 59. CG FT RILEY WILL ASSURE THAT SUFFICIENT REDUNDANT

PERSONNEL, EQUIPMENT, AND TRANSPORT EQUIPMENT ARE
INVOLVED TO ACCOMPLISH THE FOREGOING. DSCOPS DI-
RECTS THAT THE MOST REPEAT MOST SERVICEABLE OF
AVAILABLE T34S BE SENT TO FT RUCKER.

BY COMMAND OF DCSOPS:
WALTER HAGEMEN, BRIG GEN, USA

When the convoy arrived from Riley, the crews of the T34s
were somewhat ambivalent about what Colonel Tim F. Brandon
was going to do with their T34s. On the one hand, they had
nursed them along for several years now, a difficult task in
which they took justifiable pride, and it seemed like a goddamned shame to just blow the bastards away.

On the other hand, the T34s had been a real bitch to drive
and maintain, and if the sonsofbitches were blown away, the
army would have to come up with M46s or M48s for them.
Their jobs would be a hell of a lot easier. If you needed a track
for an M48, you called up Chrysler. You didn't have to make
the sonofabitch yourself.

It looked like it was going to be one hell of a show, too.

More than one of the crew sergeants, after seeing what was
going on, rethought his decision that the WOC program was
so much bullshit.

They were particularly impressed with Warrant Officer Junior Grade William B. Franklin. Mr. Franklin told them he had
just graduated from the WOC program and had been assigned
to Aviation Combat Developments because of his service as
an EM in Algeria.

Flying something like the Bird seemed to be a far more
pleasant occupation than nursing a T34 or for that matter an
M48 through the mud. Lieutenant Greer, the Big Bad Bird
pilot, was also an ex-EM who had gone to WOC school earlier
on. They'd just laid a commission on him.

And in the back of all their minds was the thought that if
the Bird did what it was alleged it could do—blow away
tanks—then it followed that the Russians would figure out how
to do it, sooner or later, and they might one day find themselves

sitting in an M48 with a Russian chopper ready to shoot a 3.5 up their ass.

And one of their number, a guy who had been in Korea in the early days, reported that he had run into his CO.

"I seen that 73rd Heavy Tank patch on his shoulder, and officer or not, I slapped his back, and it was an officer, all right. It was the goddamned post commander. But he remembered me, so it was all right. Even remembered my name, and told me if I wanted to apply for the WOC program, he'd do what he could to help me.

"And I tell you who else I saw here. I'm sure it was him. 'The Duke.' They called him that. Would you believe he was twenty-four years old when he made major? No shit. Twenty fucking four years old. He ran Task Force Lowell, forty-eight M48s and flock of half-tracks with multiple .50s on them, and just forget the flanks, fellas, through the gooks like shit through a goose. You see people like that around and you got to admit that everybody in aviation isn't a candy-ass who can't piss standing up. I'm getting a little sick of running around making like a fucking Russian anyhow. I'm thinking very seriously of giving this aviation a try. What have I got to lose?"

Colonel Tim F. Brandon believed in "practice makes perfect" nearly as devoutly as he believed in Murphy's Law.

In order that absolutely nothing could go wrong with the events scheduled for 27 December 1958, he not only ran dry runs, but dry runs of the dry runs.

He acquired control of two adjacent ranges, built as 105 cannon ranges in the 1940s. One of the ranges would house the actual demonstration for the media. The other was the dry run range.

There was only one "Viper," and the colonel had no intention of running any risk of damaging the Viper that wasn't absolutely necessary. After it did its thing (destroyed a *moving*, absolutely legitimate, Red Army T34 with rocket fire), it would immediately land in Area "A," where it would serve as a backdrop for the announcement by General E. Z. Black of the army's latest accomplishment to guarantee the peace. Major MacMillan would be there, wearing the Medal. Behind them, to show that the army was a youthful outfit which offered black youth an opportunity limited only by their ability, would be that colored warrant officer and Lieutenant Greer. Greer would actually fly the Viper during the demonstration, but it would be implied that MacMillan, the old soldier/hero figure had done so. Greer didn't look old enough to be the chief test pilot. It would look as if the army didn't have the sense to put someone mature in charge of something as important as the Viper.

The Viper had been painted. The Viper now had fangs. Colonel Brandon had gotten the idea from the P40s flown by the American Volunteer Group in China before War II. Colonel Brandon knew what the Big Bad Bird People thought about the Viper and the painted fangs. But he didn't even try to bring them around to his way of thinking. He had more important things to do with his time.

On Demonstration Day there would be no one in the moving, bona fide Russian T34, of course. The controls would be locked in place. The tank would be started across the range by one of the troops from Riley, who would then jump off to be picked up by a waiting jeep. He would then have ninety seconds—plenty of time—to get out of the way before the first rocket could possibly be fired.

In the dry run for the dry run, conducted on Alternate Range B, a regular unarmed H-19B from the post fleet was used. The dry run for the dry run was primarily to come up with times for the scenario. Once they had the rough times, they would move to the Demonstration Range for several levels of dry runs, starting out with the regular H-19B from the post fleet. On 26 December came the dress rehearsal, which would be identical to the actual demonstration, except that there would be no one there but the participants. The Viper would be flown, and the T34 would be moving with its controls locked in place, and the Viper would fly by the camera platform close enough to permit the army cameramen to get a good shot of the fangs and the canisters, and then the Viper would destroy one of the T34s.

The film of that event would be processed overnight in Atlanta (an L-23 with a backup had been laid on for that purpose), and copies would be available to the networks the next

day immediately after the demonstration, in case something
went wrong when they were filming the real thing.

There would be only one practice use of the Viper. Colonel
Tim F. Brandon felt that was a risk he was just going to have
to take.

Col. Brandon was not all surprised when he saw the white-
painted H-13H of the post commander making an approach to
the inflatable hangar. The Chief of Information had told him
on the telephone that morning that he was personally going to
call General Jiggs to make him aware of how important it was
that everything go smoothly on 27 December, and thus insure
General Jiggs's wholehearted cooperation.

When he saw that the general was alone in the H-13H,
Colonel Brandon had another thought: *flying generals!* That
ought to be worth ninety seconds on the six o'clock news.
Maybe he could even get some mileage out of it during the
demonstration. He decided he would put that on the back burner
for a while, give himself some time to think about it. His next-
to-first thought now was that he should save it for a later day.

Colonel Brandon walked out to the H-13H. Some of the
Big Bad Bird People had started to do the same thing, but when
they saw him, they stopped.

General Jiggs put his cap on before he pushed open the
plexiglass door in the H-13H's bubble. That would make a
good shot, Colonel Brandon thought. That would be the first
time the viewer would realize he wasn't looking at some ordinary captain or major. He'd see instead the two stars on the
general's overseas hat.

Colonel Brandon saluted.

"Good afternoon, General," he said. "I'm Colonel Brandon."

"I was just talking about you," General Jiggs said.

"You were, sir?"

"Your boss just called me up," General Jiggs said, "to inquire if you were causing me any trouble. I told him that so
far as I knew, you were behaving yourself and staying out of
the way as much as possible."

Colonel Brandon didn't know how to take that. He said
nothing.

"I understand Major Lowell is out here," General Jiggs said.

"Yes, sir," Colonel Brandon said. "He's working on the Viper ordnance."

"The *what* ordnance?"

"I have tentative approval for 'Viper' as semiofficial, that is to say, popular nomenclature for the gunship, sir."

"Fascinating," General Jiggs said. "Is Lowell in that tent?"

"I'll get him, sir," Colonel Brandon said.

"I'll find him," General Jiggs said. When Colonel Brandon fell in step with him, he added: "I want to see him alone, Colonel."

Major Lowell and Lieutenant Greer and Warrant Officers Franklin and Cramer (fifty-five, gray-haired, and leather-skinned, the old-model warrant officer) were doing something to the rocket launcher feed mechanism.

Mr. Cramer was the first to see the general approaching. He nodded his head, calling attention to him, but did not call attention. The others kept working. Mr. Franklin looked a little nervous, as if he was wondering if it was his function as the junior officer to call attention.

"That's all right, gentlemen," General Jiggs said, dryly sarcastic, "stand at ease."

They stood up from bending over the rocket launcher feed mechanism.

"Hello, Dutch," he said to CWO (W4) Cramer. "Long time, no see."

"Nice to see you again, General," Cramer said.

"If you had come by the office, Dutch," the general said, "my aides have orders to throw rocks only at certain people. You're not on their list." He looked at Franklin, and then put out his hand to him.

"You're the one that went right from WOC to experienced expert, right?"

Franklin looked very uncomfortable.

"You think this thing is going to work, Mr. Franklin?" the general pursued.

"Yes, sir. The problem the French had was aiming. Unless you're lucky, it takes three, four rounds to get on target..."

"You walk the rockets?" the general interrupted.

"Yes, sir," Franklin said, visibly less nervous now that he was talking about something he knew. "And if you only have six in the canister..."

"What have we got here?" the general asked.

"Twenty-seven," Franklin said. "With luck, that gives you up to five good runs."

General Jiggs nodded his comprehension.

"Where's MacMillan?" General Jiggs asked. "Also known as 'the Talking Head.'"

"I thought you knew, sir," Lowell said. The general shook his head. "He and Phil Parker took my plane to get the Felters," Lowell said.

"The way Captain Parker phrased his request was to ask if I minded if he 'picked up a little dual time.' In my innocence, I had pictured him as shooting touch-and-go's at Laird."

"They should be back in a couple of hours, General," Lowell said.

"You got a minute, Lowell?" the general asked.

"Yes, sir, of course."

The general took Lowell's arm and led him across the inflatable hangar, where they were alone.

"There's no good news and bad news," General Jiggs said. "It's all bad. I just made my pitch for you to Black. I got about as far as your name."

"I didn't expect you to do that much, sir," Lowell said. "But thank you."

"A senator's wife! What the hell were you thinking about?" Lowell chuckled.

"I don't think it's funny," Jiggs said. "It's not funny at all, goddamnit."

"There's more to it than that," Lowell said. "And I don't think even Black could get me out of this one if he wanted to, and I have it on good authority that he doesn't."

"There aren't many majors," Jiggs said, "who manage to get the Chief of Staff of the U.S. Army personally pissed at them."

"Can it be kept quiet until after New Year's?" Lowell said. "Or is it getting to be pretty common knowledge?"

"I don't know," Jiggs said. "Bellmon won't talk about it."

"Bellmon's all right," Lowell said. "He'll make a good general."

"What are you going to do?"

"I think I'll go to Germany for a while. For six months or a year, anyway. It'll give me a chance to spend some time with my son."

"I'm sorry, Craig," General Jiggs said. "I really am."

"I appreciate that," Lowell said.

"I don't want you to sneak off this post," Jiggs said, visibly emotional. "You understand what I'm saying?"

Lowell smiled at him.

"You can come out to Laird on New Year's Day," Lowell said. "And wave so long. But between now and then, I don't want anybody, particularly the women, to know. I want the last party to be a good one."

"I'll do what I can," Jiggs said. "But I think that's wishful thinking. Men do the gossiping, not the women."

Lowell nodded and shrugged.

"I'll see you around before you go," General Jiggs said.

"I'll be around," Lowell said.

General Jiggs nodded and suddenly turned and walked out of the inflatable hangar to his H-13H.

Lowell walked back to the feed chute for the rocket launcher.

"Made his pitch to Black about what?" Greer demanded. Lowell looked at him in surprise.

"Interesting characteristic of these curved ceilings," Greer said, "is that when somebody talks close to one side, somebody on the other side can hear everything."

"You just keep your goddamned mouth shut about what you think you heard," Lowell said.

"What I heard," Greer said, "is that you're getting thrown out as of 1 January."

"Where did you get that?"

"My wife got it from her mother," Greer said.

"I don't know your wife or your mother-in-law," Lowell said.

"You don't know any of the lieutenants or the warrants in Annex 1, either," Franklin said, joining the conversation. "But they know all about the major who was run out of Washington on a rail."

"Honest to God, Bill?" Lowell asked.

"I'm afraid so," Franklin said.

"Well, you guys just keep your mouths shut. It's done. It came down from the Chief of Staff himself. I just don't want it to ruin the holidays."

"MacMillan knows," Lieutenant Ed Greer said. "He knows why you asked him to pick up Major Felter. By the time they get to Washington, you can bet Parker will have heard."

"Let's hope they have enough sense to keep their mouths shut," Lowell said.

"Ah, hell, yes," Greer said.

(Three)
Washington National Airport
The District of Columbia
22 December 1958

The first thing Sanford Felter did when MacMillan crawled out of the Aero Commander at Butler Aviation at Washington National Airport was take him aside to confide what he somewhat bitterly described as the "final chapter in the Lowell sexual saga."

"I went to Black," Felter said.

"And?"

"He told me this was the one time I should remember that I was a major in the army," Felter said.

"Shit," MacMillan said.

"Well, we shall all pretend that nobody knows," Felter said. "We can at least do that much."

"Dumb sonofabitch," MacMillan said. "That pecker of his has had him on the edge of something like this as long as I've known him. And I've known him a long goddamned time."

Sharon walked over.

"I guess Sandy told you?" she asked.

"I knew," MacMillan said.

"So that means Roxy knows," Sharon said.

"Roxy's mad at Craig," MacMillan said. "Barbara's mad at Bellmon for not trying hard enough to get him out of it."

"Bellmon couldn't do anything," Felter said. "Nobody could. The Chief of Staff is after Craig's scalp, and Black has apparently made up his mind to let him have it."

"Well, the best thing we can do is pretend we don't know," Sharon said.

"Yeah," MacMillan said.

"I hate that damned woman!" Sharon said, and flushed.

MacMillan leaned over and kissed her.

XVII

(One)
Auxiliary Field Three
Hanchey Army Airfield
Fort Rucker, Alabama
26 December 1958

They had to roll the Big Bad Bird (a/k/a the Viper) out of the hangar twice. When they rolled it out the first time, it occurred to Colonel Tim F. Brandon that a crew consisting entirely of enlisted men pushing it out would make a better shot than what he had, one sergeant, three warrants, and two field-grade officers.

So it was pushed out again with the motion picture cameras rolling, and Colonel Brandon set up another shot: Major MacMillan and Lieutenant Greer first looking at a map, then walking around the helicopter to check the rocket canisters.

"You got about enough of your fucking pictures, Colonel?" MacMillan snapped finally. "Can we get the goddamned Bird in the air now?"

It was clearly disrespectful and insubordinate, but Colonel Brandon swallowed his resentment.

"Give me five minutes to check things on the other field," he said and climbed into his jeep and drove off.

"Pissant," MacMillan said, watching him drive away.

CWO (W4) Dutch Cramer checked the bins and the chute and the canisters a final time, and nodded his approval.

Lieutenant Greer climbed up the side of the fuselage, and through the pilot's window, and strapped himself in the seat.

"Off we go into the wild blue yonder," he crooned and reached for the Engine Start switch.

His eyes fell on Major Lowell, and for a moment their eyes met. Lowell gave him a wink. Greer gave Lowell a mocking, but friendly salute, and lowered his eyes to the instrument panel as the engine began to run.

He told himself the worst part was over. They'd all gotten through Christmas without anybody bringing up what was to happen to Lowell as of 1 Jan 1959. It had been decided among the women that they would spend Christmas eve and Christmas morning with their families (which meant that Lowell was with the Parkers) and then get together for Christmas dinner. At first, Barbara Bellmon insisted on having it at the Bellmon quarters, but she lost out to Dr. Parker, who pointed out that her quarters in the hospital (*hers,* as Contract surgeon, with the assimilated rate of colonel, not Captain Parker's), were much larger and better able to hold everybody.

There had been an enormous turkey, a standing rib of beef, a ham, and lots of booze. All Greer had been able to drink, however, was a glass of champagne when they got there and a glass of wine with dinner. He would be flying the Big Bad Bird today.

Everybody else had gotten pretty well sauced up, and even General Jiggs had appeared uninvited, with his wife.

"Can any old cavalryman come in here?" he had asked, when he walked in. "Or does being able to read and write disqualify me?"

Nobody mentioned what was about to happen to Lowell, but Jiggs came pretty close when he handed Lowell a Christmas-wrapped package.

"What the hell is this?" Lowell asked, embarrassed. It had been decided among them that there would be no exchange of gifts.

"One could reasonably presume it's your Christmas present," General Jiggs said. "Open it up."

Inside the silver foil imprinted with scenes of a White Christmas in Old England was a battalion guidon, a small flag bearing a unit's number. Guidons had come into use on battlefields before the telephone and radio as a unit identifier the troops could "guide on." The only place they were still used for that purpose in the modern army was flying from a tank radio antenna to identify the tank of the unit commander.

The guidon General Jiggs gave Major Lowell was frayed and stained. It was for a tank battalion, the 73rd, and someone had lettered on it, crudely, with a grease pencil: T/F LOWELL.

"I thought you should have that," General Jiggs said.

Major Craig W. Lowell looked very much as if he was going to cry.

"Paul," Mrs. Jiggs said, quickly, "tell them what Wonder Boy said to the colonel from X Corps. That's a marvelous story."

"Yeah," General Jiggs said. "Yeah. Well, I got the story from his operations sergeant. Let me set the stage. Lowell and forty M46s had just gone up the Korean peninsula to link up with X Corps, which had landed eleven days before at Inchon. With his well-known modesty and reticence, he'd modified the guidon he had flying from his tank. That one. I mean, what the hell, if you're going to be in the history books, make sure they spell your name right, right?

"Well, he went a little further and a little faster than the OPSORDER called for. I'd just found them myself, in an old L-4. He was a hundred miles further than he was supposed to be and about thirty-six hours ahead of the time he was supposed to be a hundred miles back, if you follow me. X Corps is nosing around just south of Suwon, when all of a sudden, balls to the leather, around the bend come a half dozen tracks, with multiple .50s and 20 mm Bofors, chased by the first of the M46s.

"The tracks were shooting at anything that moved or looked

like it could move, and that included the people from X Corps. So they waved some flags, and Task Force Lowell stopped shooting at them. Lowell drives through the tracks, and rolls up to the people from X Corps. At the time he was a major with about two hours' time in grade.

"Well, the colonel from X Corps consults his OPSORDER and announces, 'You're not expected here, Major, and you're not expected for another thirty-six hours.' So you know what the Duke says? 'What would you have me do, Colonel? Go back?'"

They had all heard the story before, but they all laughed, and it took some of the tension away. Then Mrs. Jiggs handed Lowell a Christmas-wrapped tube. Lowell unwrapped it, glanced at it, and then started to roll it up again.

"Pass it around, Duke," Mrs. Jiggs said. "Some people haven't seen it."

"Hell," he said, but he handed it to Melody, and Greer read it over Melody's shoulder. It was a photograph of the front page of the *Chicago Tribune*, and it had been sealed in plastic. It was obviously a product of the post photo lab, and Greer suspected that it had just been made.

KOREAN REPORT: The Soldiers
by John E. Moran
United Press War Correspondent

SEOUL, SOUTH KOREA (UP) (Delayed) September 26—The world has already learned that Lt. General Walton Walker's Eighth Army, so long confined to the Pusan perimeter, has linked up with Lt. General Ned Almond's X United States Corps, following the brilliant amphibious invasion at Inchon.

But it wasn't an army that made the link-up, just south of a Korean town called Osan fifty-odd miles south of Seoul, it was soldiers, and this correspondent was there when it happened.

I was with the 31st Infantry Regiment, moving south from Seoul down a two-lane macadam road, when we first heard the peculiar, familiar sound of American 90 mm tank cannon. We were surprised. There were sup-

posed to be no Americans closer than fifty miles south
of our position.

It was possible, our regimental commander believed,
that what we were hearing was the firing of captured
American tank cannon. In the early days of this war we
lost a lot of equipment to the enemy. It was prudent to
assume what the army calls a defensive posture, and we
did.

And then some strange-looking vehicles appeared a
thousand yards down the road. They were trucks, nearly
covered with sandbags. Our men had orders not to fire
without orders. They were good soldiers, and they held
their fire.

The strange-looking trucks came up the road at a
goodly clip, and we realized with horror that they were
firing. They were firing at practically anything and everything.

"They're Americans," our colonel said, and ordered
that an American flag be taken to our front lines and
waved.

Now there were tanks visible behind the trucks—M46
"Patton" tanks. That should have put everyone's mind
at rest, but on our right flank, one excited soldier let fly
at the trucks and tanks coming up the road with a rocket
launcher. He missed. Moments later, there came the
crack of a high-velocity 90 mm tank cannon. He was a
better shot than the man who had fired the rocket launcher.
There was a soldier in front of our lines now, holding
the American flag high above his head, waving it frantically back and forth. Our colonel's radio operator was
frantically repeating the "Hold Fire! Hold Fire!" order
into his microphone.

His message got through, for there was no more fire
from our lines and no more from the column approaching
us.

The first vehicles to pass through our lines were Dodge
three-quarter-ton trucks. These mounted two .50 caliber
machine guns, one where it's supposed to be, on a ped-
estal between the seats, and a second on an improvised

mount in the truck bed. They were, for all practical purposes, rolling machine-gun nests.

Next came three M46 tanks, the lead tank flying a pennant on which was lettered Task Force Lowell. The name "Ilse" had been painted on the side of its turret. There was a dirty young man in "Ilse's" turret. He skidded his tank into a right turn and stopped. He stayed in the turret until the rest of his column had passed through the lines.

It was quite a column. There were more M46s and some M24 light tanks, fuel trucks, self-propelled 105 mm howitzers, and regular army trucks. We could tell that the dirty young man in the turret was an officer because some of the tank commanders and some of the truck drivers saluted him as they rolled past. Most of them didn't salute, however. Most of them gave the dirty young man a thumbs-up gesture, and many of them smiled, and called out, "Atta Boy, Duke!"

When the trucks passed us, we could see that "the Duke" had brought his wounded, and yes, his dead, with him. When those trucks passed, "the Duke" saluted.

When the last vehicle had passed, the dirty young man hoisted himself out of his turret, reached down and pulled a Garand from somewhere inside, and climbed down off the tank named "Ilse."

He had two days' growth of beard and nine days' road filth on him. He searched out our colonel and walked to him. When he got close, we could see a major's gold leaf on his fatigue jacket collar.

He saluted, a casual, almost insolent wave of his right hand in the vicinity of his eyes, not the snappy parade ground salute he'd given as the trucks with the wounded and dead had rolled past him.

"Major Lowell, sir," he said to our colonel. "With elements of the 73rd Heavy Tank."

We'd all heard about Lowell and his task force, how they had been ranging between the lines, raising havoc with the retreating North Korean army for nine days. I think we all expected someone older, someone more grizzled and battered than the dirty young man who stood before us.

At that moment our colonel got the word that the young soldier who had ignored his orders to hold fire and two others near him had been killed when one of Lowell's tanks had returned his fire. The death of any soldier upsets an officer, and it upset our colonel.

"If you had been where you were supposed to be, Major," our colonel said, "that wouldn't have happened!"

Young Major "Duke" Lowell looked at the colonel for a moment, and then he said, "What would you have us do, Colonel, go back?"

There shortly came a radio message for Major Duke Lowell, and he left his task force in Osan. He had been ordered to Tokyo, where General of the Army Douglas MacArthur was to personally pin the Distinguished Service Cross to his breast.

Greer wondered what Lowell would do with his guidon. Put it away probably and never look at it—even if he'd gotten more than a little shaken up when Jiggs gave it to him.

The needles were in the green. Greer depressed the stick-mounted mike switch as he picked it up.

"Light on the skids with the Bird," he said. He dropped the nose to pick up speed and then picked the Big Bad Bird up to get over the tops of the pine trees.

"Viper," Colonel Brandon's voice came over the FM radio. "This is Viper Base. How do you read?"

"Loud and clear," Greer said.

"All right, Viper, I have you in sight," Colonel Brandon said.

Giving in to a perverse impulse, Greer dropped the Bird below the treeline so that PIO asshole couldn't see him. Then, when he was sure Brandon was searching for him, he pulled the cyclic and picked up a quick 500 feet.

"Viper," Colonel Brandon said, "what I want you to do is make one low level, low speed pass past the camera platform."

Greer complied.

"All right, Viper, very nice, thank you. What we're going to do now is do it. Take your position."

Greer flew a half mile away. Downrange he could see the T34.

"Start the T34," Brandon ordered.

"T34 ready to roll," a voice came back immediately.

"Move the T34," Colonel Brandon ordered. Greer couldn't detect any movement of the tank at first, but he saw a man hoist himself out of the driver's seat and leap off the T34 over the left track. Then he could see that the tank was moving. He saw the man run toward the jeep which would carry him off the range.

"Viper," Colonel Brandon ordered, "hold your position!"

Greer amused himself by doing precisely that, holding his position, a motionless hover 500 feet off the ground, the most difficult of all rotary wing flight maneuvers.

"Stand by, Viper!" Colonel Brandon ordered.

Greer did not bother to reply.

Thirty seconds later, Colonel Brandon gave the order.

"OK, Viper, kill it!"

"Jesus Christ!" Greer said, to himself. He dropped the nose, gave it the juice, and felt the forces of acceleration against his back.

When he was 300 yards from the tank, he depressed the trigger of the rocket firing mechanism for the right-side canister.

The fifty-four rockets had been manufactured at the Red River Arsenal in Texas. For facility of manufacture, the stabilizing fins at the rear of the rocket were about the last step of the manufacturing process. It had been determined that it was easier and, more important, safer, to save this step for last. All it involved was the positioning of three wedge-shaped pieces of aluminum—like the feathers of an arrow—into slots already in position at the rear of the rocket's cylindrical body.

Each stabilizing fin was held in place with three rivets. The fins, the slots for them, and the rivets were aluminum, which does not spark. The automatic riveting machine was powered by compressed air. There was no danger of a spark there, either.

The worker who installed the stabilizing fins was required

by her job description to inspect each rivet on each fin. The automatic riveting machine was a fine machine and seldom failed to do what it was designed to do. Inevitably, the riveters found the three rivets in place where they were supposed to be. Inevitably, particularly at the end of a long day, the machine operators didn't look quite as closely as they should.

The fourth 3.5 rocket in the right-hand system on Greer's Bird had only one rivet, the most rearward one. The near perfect machine had run out of rivets.

The single rivet had been sufficient to hold the stabilizing fin rigidly in place during shipment and while passing through the bin into the chute when CWO (W4) Dutch Cramer had loaded the ordnance.

But the blast of firing the first three rockets in Greer's first firing run had been sufficient to loosen the stabilizing fin. When it was fired, the fin's nose came loose. The strength of the rivet fastening the fin to the cylinder was strong enough to keep the fin from separating from the cylinder, however. What it did was hold the fin sideward against what had now become the rocket's slipstream. Obeying the laws of aerodynamics, Ed Greer's fourth rocket, instead of moving horizontally toward the T34, raised its nose almost vertically.

The odds were that in such an event the rocket would pass harmlessly through the rotor arc. There were only three rotor blades, each only sixteen inches wide.

The odds went against Ed Greer and the Bird.

One of the rotor blades struck the impact fuse of the rocket 0.75 second later, and the firing mechanism detonated the explosive charge. The force blew off three-quarters of the blade and a half second later shattered the windshield of the Bird.

The Bird lost its aerodynamic lift and was simultaneously subjected to enormous out-of-balance dynamic pressures, as the engine whirled two intact rotor blades and the stump of the third.

The Bird crashed to the ground nose-first, striking it at 105 miles per hour and with sufficient force to detonate the explosive heads of the forty-seven, forty-eight, or forty-nine rockets still in the system. The precise number remaining at ground impact was never determined. There was not much left of the Big Bad Bird, nor of First Lieutenant Edward C. Greer.

(Two)
Quarters No. 1
Fort Rucker, Alabama
26 December 1958

Master Sergeant Wesley, in his dress blues, knocked at the door of the guest room (actually two rooms and a bath) of Quarters No. 1.

"Come," General E. Z. Black said.

"That PIO colonel's out here, General," Master Sergeant Wesley said.

"Get the sonofabitch in here, Wes," General Black said. The general was bending over the bed, fixing his ribbons to his tunic.

"Zeke!" Mrs. Black said. "That's not going to change anything." Mrs. Black was adjusting her hat before a mirror.

Sergeant Wesley stepped out in the hall.

"The general'll see you now, Colonel," he said. He held the door open for him, and then followed him into the room.

When General Black straightened up, Master Sergeant Wesley busied himself with the ribbons of the general's tunic.

"I sent for you an hour ago," General Black began. "I am not in the custom of being made to wait."

"I was on the horn to Washington, sir," Colonel Brandon said.

"Talking to the Chief of Staff, were you?" General Black inquired.

"No, sir. To the Chief of Information, trying to salvage as much as we can from this."

"The next time I send for you," General Black said, "you put everybody but the Chief of Staff in second place."

"Yes, sir," Colonel Brandon said.

"For your general information, Colonel," Black went on, "I have spoken with the Chief of Staff. Two items on our agenda affect you."

"Yes, sir."

"One, I have been charged by the Chief of Staff with handling this situation," General Black said. "Two, the Chief of Staff has approval for the immediate posthumous award of the Distinguished Flying Cross to Lieutenant Greer."

"That's very nice, sir," Colonel Brandon said. "It fits right in with what I've discussed with the Chief of Information."

General Black looked as if he were going to say something, but then he was distracted by Master Sergeant Wesley, who was holding out the general's tunic. He slipped his arms into it.

"Mrs. Black, Sergeant Wesley, and myself are about to pay our respects to Mrs. Greer," General Black said. "You can ride with us and tell me what you have discussed with the Chief of Information."

There were four Chevrolet sedans sitting half on the grass along the driveway, an MP patrol car in front. With his hand on her arm, General Black led his wife to the car immediately behind the MP car.

"I'll drive," Master Sergeant Wesley said to the sergeant first class who held the door open. He got behind the wheel. General and Mrs. Black got in the back seat. Colonel Brandon got in front with Wesley.

Three of General Black's four aides-de-camp got in the car behind his, and four burly young men in civilian clothes got in the last car. The MP car started moving.

"Who are the guys in civvies?" General Black asked.

"CIC, sir," Colonel Brandon said. "Just in case."

"Don't do that again, Brandon," Black said. "Is there a radio in this thing, Wes?"

"The CIC is gone, General," Sergeant Wesley replied, picking up the microphone.

"I am paying a personal visit to the widow of a friend of mine, Colonel," General Black said. "Can you get that straight in your mind?"

"I was thinking of the press, sir," Brandon said. "They're sure to be at the house."

"Fuck the goddamn press!" Black said.

"Zeke, for God's sake, get control of yourself," Mrs. Black said.

He exhaled audibly.

"Let me have the benefit of your thinking, Colonel," General Black said. "Your's and the Chief of Information's."

"Yes, sir."

Colonel Brandon spoke reasonably, assuredly, and almost steadily during the fifteen minute ride off the post down Rucker Boulevard to Ozark and then up Broad Street to the plantation-style residence of Mayor and Mrs. Howard F. Dutton.

The major points he made were these:

(1) The networks were in town, and they were going to come up with some sort of a story, and the only option the army had was to make that story as little embarrassing under the circumstances as possible.

(2) The air force had already begun to "take shots" at them in Washington, the gist of their argument being that the "tragedy" would not have occurred if (a) the army had only asked for air force expertise in aerial rocket fire and (b) by implication, if the army had lived up to the 1948 Key West Agreement not to arm their helicopters.

(3) The national television media was going to want visuals. It was Colonel Brandon's judgment that they had no choice but to turn over the film the army film crew had shot of what was to have been the dress rehearsal. In response to General Black's inquiry, "how gory is it?" Colonel Brandon replied that it wasn't "really gory." It was "heart stopping." The explosion had been "spectacular" rather than "gory."

(4) Since the network TV crews *were* here, they could probably be talked into taking additional material. Colonel Brandon suggested that a full military funeral, with an aircraft flyover, would probably receive "good coverage." Greer's posthumous award of the DFC would "tie in nicely" there, particularly if Mrs. Greer could receive it from the hands of General Black.

(5) There was nothing the army could really do about getting caught in violation of the Key West Agreement of 1948 but plead excessive enthusiasm, as had been previously decided. A short announcement by General Black (Colonel Brandon handed him "Proposed Remarks *vis à vis* The Viper") could, if properly handled, take care of that nicely. In essence, what he would say was that the idea of rocket-armed helicopters was a good one, and one which, after joint air force-army development, was surely going to become an important weapon in the arsenal which guaranteed the peace. The implication, Colonel Brandon explained, was that all the army had done was

investigate the feasibility of the idea. Now that they were convinced the idea had merit, they would of course, in keeping with the spirit of the Key West Agreement of 1948, turn responsibility for technical development over to the air force.

General Black grunted once or twice during Colonel Brandon's presentation. It was his only reaction to it.

There was a large crowd of people gathered on the sidewalk in front of Howard and Prissy Dutton's plantation-style mansion. There were half a dozen Ozark city policemen, as many Dale County deputy sheriffs, and even two Alabama state troopers. Only known personal friends of the Duttons were permitted to walk up the sidewalk to the porch of the house.

The state troopers waved the little convoy to the curb.

"Stay in the car, please, Colonel," General Black said. "I will give you my decision shortly."

Colonel Brandon was surprised to see that Sergeant Wesley marched into the house with the general.

They were greeted by Prissy Dutton, who looked as if she were dazed on tranquilizers. She announced that "the mayor's taken to his bed."

The sliding doors between the parlor and the dining room of the Dutton house had been opened. A buffet had been set up on the dining room table. There were thirty people munching in the dining room, as many standing around the parlor, and about as many filling folding chairs which lined the walls of both rooms.

Mrs. Edward C. Greer, in a black dress, a single strand of pearls around her neck, sat on a red plush couch resisting attempts from a black woman standing behind her to take the baby, who was sleeping on his mother's shoulders.

"Wes," General Black said, "close that door and get these people out of here."

Master Sergeant Wesley first closed the sliding doors, and then started easing people out of the room. The room emptied with surprising speed, until only three couples remained: Colonel and Mrs. Robert F. Bellmon; Major and Mrs. Rudolph G. MacMillan, and Major and Mrs. Sanford T. Felter.

"I said everybody, and I meant everybody," General Black said. "That includes you and Wes," he added to his wife. He looked at Melody Dutton Greer. "You want to give the baby to one of the women?" he asked.

"Is that a command, General?" Melody asked.

He took her meaning. He waited until the black woman, very reluctantly, had allowed herself to be ushered out of the room by a firmly gentle Master Sergeant Wesley, and then he closed the door after her.

He walked to where Melody sat and sat beside her.

"Let me hold him," he said. "Your shoulder will go to sleep."

"Why not?" Melody said, bitterly, and passed the sleeping infant to him. The child stirred, but did not wake.

"You been drinking?"

"Sure," Melody said.

"You want another drink?"

"No," she said.

"I just learned that Ed's being given the DFC," General Black said.

"You know what you can do with your goddamned medal," Melody said. "Is that what you're doing here? To tell me they're coming up with a medal?"

"No," he said. "I came to tell you I'm sorry."

"Thank you," she said. "Now, can my friends come back in?"

"Not just yet," he said.

"Why not?"

"Because I'm the one you want to see," he said.

"Is that so?"

"Yeah, I'm the one you want," he said.

"I don't know what the hell you're talking about," Melody said. "And forgive me, General, but I really don't much give a damn, either."

"Aside from the expected, ritual expressions of sympathy, let me tell you why the others feel bad," General Black said.

"Be my guest," Melody said, sarcastically.

"Felter feels guilty because Ed kept him alive when they walked out of the jungle at Dien Bien Phu," General Black said. "And because if Felter had not arranged for Ed to go to Algiers, he would not have ultimately wound up flying the Bird."

"Fascinating," Melody said.

"MacMillan feels guilty because it was Ed flying the Bird and not him. The Indo-China business, too, to a lesser degree. But primarily because he knew how to fly the Bird and wasn't flying it when it crashed."

"I'm getting just a little bored with this conversation," Melody said. She got up and walked to the door, and for a moment it looked as if she was going to open it. Instead, she went to a table with bottles on it and splashed whiskey in two glasses. She walked back to General Black and handed him one. Then she sat down, drained hers at a gulp, and leaned back against the couch so far that her face was looking up at the ceiling. She sighed audibly.

"Shitshitshitshit," she said.

"Bob Bellmon," General Black went on and then stopped himself. "As of today, by the way, Brigadier General Bellmon. He doesn't know yet."

"Whoopee!" Melody Dutton Greer cried, raising her empty glass gaily.

"General Bellmon's feelings of guilt are somewhat more intellectual. He was the one who came to me and asked for permission to build the Bird. And he was the one who had to order your husband to fly it."

"He didn't have to order Ed," Melody objected. "My late husband was just as crazy as the rest of you. The ultimate volunteer: 'Look, Ma, no hands!'"

"But they're all wrong," Black said. "I'm the sonofabitch responsible."

"What are you on, General, some kind of a guilt trip? What the hell did you have to do with it?"

"I'm the one who sent him to helicopter school," Black said. "That's at the low end, the personal end. I didn't want him to go. But I fixed it so that he could go. At the other end of the guilt spectrum, I'm the one who made the decision to go ahead with the Bird. Statistically, there was no question that someone would be killed during the testing. All I could do was hope it would be somebody I never heard of. Not Ed. It didn't work out that way. So if you're looking for somebody to blame, Melody, here I am."

She looked at him for a moment, shook her head, and then

leaned back again so that she was looking at the ceiling.

"Which leaves us where?" she asked.

"Has Major Lowell been to see you?" General Black asked.

"No, he hasn't. Every other uniformed sonofabitch and his brother has, but now that you mention it, I have *not* been honored with the condolences of the *legendary* Major Lowell."

"Lowell is the only practical one of us," General Black said. "He understands that when you really have nothing to say, the thing to do is to say nothing."

Melody looked at him again.

"Hey," she said, "I appreciate your coming here. I really do." She rested a hand momentarily on his arm. "It took, as Ed would say, 'balls.'"

He didn't reply.

"But, at the risk of repeating myself, where does all of this leave all of us."

"With him," General Black said, indicating the child.

"Don't worry about him," Melody said. "Not only is my father—who at the moment, by the way, is drunk out of his mind—rich, but that baby is now eligible for all sorts of benefits from a grateful government. There was a guy here already just bubbling over with facts and figures."

"He will not have his father," Black said.

"No fooling? Jesus!"

"You're a young and attractive woman," Black said. "You'll probably remarry, and the boy will have a man around. And I'm sure that Mac and Felter and Bellmon and his other friends will maintain their interest. But the boy will never know his father."

"What the hell are you up to now? Are you trying to make me cry? To make me start screaming and pulling my hair out? Is this some new kind of new console-the-widow therapy?"

"He'll never know what kind of a man his father was," Black said.

"He'll have that goddamned medal you talk about," Melody said. "He can look at that and say, 'My daddy was a hero; here's ten bucks worth of silver-plated metal to prove it.'"

"He can have more than that, if you're up to it," Black said.

"I don't have the faintest idea what you're talking about," Melody said.

"There are circumstances which make a very elaborate military funeral possible for Ed," General Black said.

"You can stick your elaborate military funeral up where you put the medal," Melody said.

"Bands, flags flying, troops marching, a . . . whatever they call it when they fly airplanes overhead . . . and a four-star general, the Vice Chief of Staff of the U.S. Army, pinning his medal on his widow."

"Maybe I am getting a little drunk," Melody said. "Because you sound just about as impressed with that bullshit as I am."

"It doesn't mean a thing to you, but to a kid in his impressionable years and older, looking at a movie of how the army buried his father, that just might make him think his father was something special."

She looked at him.

"Ed *was* something *special*," General Black said, barely audibly. After a moment, Melody Dutton Greer said: "Hey! Come on. For Christ's sake, what if somebody saw you? You're supposed to be a general. Stop crying."

XVIII

(One)
Fort Rucker, Alabama
28 December 1958

The main post chapel was a temporary building, thrown up as quickly as possible with the other temporary buildings in 1941, designed to last six years. But when Rucker reopened, it had been painted and there had been a "rehabilitation allocation" from the Office of the Chief of Chaplains which had provided for interior refurbishment, for a red carpet for the aisles, an electric organ, and the other accoutrements of a church.

It was full now. Admission had been by invitation only, and more invitations had been issued than there were seats.

The remains of Lieutenant Edward C. Greer in a government-issue gray steel casket, covered with an American flag, rested on a black cloth-covered stand in the center of the aisle.

There were three clergymen. The Dutton family clergyman was a Presbyterian. He was there. The post chaplain was a Baptist. He was there. And so was the Third Army chaplain.

Ed and Melody had been married by an Anglican priest, and Melody had requested—the only thing she had asked for—an Episcopal funeral ceremony. An L-23 had been dispatched to Third Army headquarters in Atlanta to get the ranking Episcopal chaplain.

Sitting in the first pew on the left was the widow, holding Howard Dutton Greer on her lap, her parents (General Paul, Jiggs wondered (a) how they had managed to sober up Howard Dutton and (b) if he was going to make it through the ceremony), and the black woman who had raised Melody and was now seeing her baby through this.

Across the aisle were the pallbearers. The pallbearers were the Bird People, plus Brigadier General Robert F. Bellmon, less Major Craig W. Lowell and CWO (W4) Dutch Cramer. Major Lowell and Dutch Cramer had declined the honor of serving as pallbearers. Jiggs knew where they were. They were either in Annex 1 of the officer's open mess or in Dutch Cramer's BOQ paying their last respects to a lost buddy by drinking themselves into oblivion. Dutch Cramer was taking Greer's accident personally and hard. It was his ordnance that had gone off at the wrong time.

The service was being filmed. Unobstrusive windows had been cut in the wall between the chaplain's and the choir's vesting rooms in the front of the church (permitting the camera to shoot the audience from that angle) and in the wall of the chaplain's office by the vestibule. These cameras, and the accompaning sound equipment, were manned by the army photo team. General Black had personally denied the television crews access to the chapel; the film the army shot would be made available to them.

The TV crews were outside the chapel. An army six-by-six truck would carry one crew during the procession from the chapel to Parade Ground No. 2 so that it could film the procession in process, and other crews were in place along the route the funeral procession would follow and at the parade ground itself.

An enormous amount of preparation had gone into Lieutenant Greer's final rites. The "Plan for the Memorial Services for Major General Angus Laird" had been taken from the file and used as the starting point. General Jiggs had been somewhat surprised at how far General Black had gone along with Colonel Tim F. Brandon. He had accepted most (but by no means all) of Brandon's suggestions. General Jiggs had been even more surprised at General Black's willingness to make himself available to keep the TV networks happy.

A tour of the WOC battalion, Colonel Brandon had pointed out, was not really news. A tour of the WOC battalion by the Vice Chief of Staff of the United States Army was news, worth forty-five seconds on the six o'clock news. The general had permitted himself to be trailed all over the post, out to Laird Field to the Aviation Board, anywhere Colonel Brandon had suggested. He had even (and this really had surprised General Jiggs) permitted himself to be taken for a ride in the white H-13H by General Jiggs. All they had done was take off and fly out of sight and then return to Pad No. 1, but it had given the network TV people a "shot" of general officers in flight, and Black had gone along.

And there had been, as there inevitably are when large numbers of people are involved in something solemn, elements of high comedy.

It had been decided and accepted without question that Lieutenant Greer's casket would be carried on a tank from the main post chapel to Parade Ground No. 2, where Mrs. Greer would receive her husband's Distinguished Flying Cross. There were no tanks at Rucker, so two M48s had been ordered down from Fort Benning. Someone had then realized (1) that not having been ordered to provide tank crews, Benning had not sent any and (2) there was no place on a tank where a casket could be carried.

Both of those problems had been solved by the Red Army maneuver troops from Fort Riley, the ones who had brought the Russian T34s down. They, of course, were qualified tank crewmen who could drive the M48s, and they quickly welded a platform to support the casket over the engine compartment.

Platforms. Both tanks had been so modified, in case something should go wrong with one of them. As the Red Army tank crews had brought six T34s from Riley to make sure three would be available, there were two M48s where one was going to be needed. There were two public address systems in place where one would be needed. There were four extra jeeps standing by in case something should go wrong with the four jeeps which would be used as flower cars. The term was redundancy.

There would be, of course, a riderless horse with reversed boots in the stirrups to be led in the procession behind the tank with Greer's casket. In the dry run, the first time the horse heard the tank engine start, he voided his bowels and then jerked loose from his handler and galloped wildly away with half a dozen field-grade officers in hot pursuit.

A second horse had been acquired, who was not terrified at the sound of a tank engine.

In the middle of all this, there had been grand theft, helicopter.

More than a little chagrined, the commanding officer of Rotary Wing Training had sought audience with General Jiggs. An H-19C was missing, and the colonel was absolutely convinced that it had been stolen. He wanted the FBI notified and a bulletin sent to all airfields within 350 miles of Rucker asking that they report any H-19C that had landed at their field.

General Jiggs had not been willing to go along with that. He didn't doubt that an H-19C was missing, but the idea that anyone would steal one was absurd. If someone had reported an H-34B was missing or an H-37 or one of the new YH-40s, Jiggs would have been concerned. An H-34B could be flown somewhere and stripped for parts, for the Sikorsky was now in wide civilian use. It was conceivable, though unlikely, that the Russians might want to grab a YH-40, so they could study it. But a worn-out, ancient H-19C? Absurd!

What would you do with it? To whom could it be sold? He concluded, and so informed the commanding officer of Rotary Wing Training, that one of two things had happened to the "stolen" H-19C:

(1) It had simply been misplaced; that is, someone had taken the wrong H-19C when making an authorized flight. The thing to do, General Jiggs told him, was to conduct an inventory and see if anybody had an *extra* H-19C, which would be the case if someone had taken the wrong one off someplace.

(2) A practical joker was at work, someone who thought

more of a good belly laugh than of his career and had taken the machine and hidden it somewhere on the reservation in the sure and certain knowledge that a lot of people would be running around like headless chickens when it was discovered missing. If this scenario were valid, the thing to do was look for the missing H-19C in places where someone so inclined would be likely to hide it.

None of this, however, affected the people or the proceedings in the chapel. On the right side of the chapel immediately behind the pallbearers, sat the brass: General and Mrs. E. Z. Black; Lieutenant General and Mrs. Richard D. Hoit (General Hoit commanded Third Army, in whose area Rucker was located. He had not known Lieutenant Greer, but if the Vice Chief of Staff was going to his funeral, so was he); Major General and Mrs. Paul Jiggs, and Mrs. Robert F. Bellmon.

Behind the family (on the left) and the brass (on the right) were the other distinguished guests and friends. An area of the lawn outside had been set aside for distinguished guests and friends who had invitations, but for whom there was no room inside. Loudspeakers would carry the ceremony to them.

The Third Army chaplain raised his hand in blessing.

"The peace of God, which passeth all understanding, be with you and yours," he said.

The pallbearers (Brigadier General Robert F. Bellmon; Major Rudolph G. MacMillan; WOJG William B. Franklin; Master Sergeant Wallace Horn; Staff Sergeant Jerry P. Davis and Corporal Sampson P. Killian) rose and took their places around the casket. The organ began to play "Nearer My God to Thee." On the fourth bar, the organ was joined by the 77th U.S. Army Band outside.

The casket was carried down the aisle.

The widow and her family followed it out and then the brass. By the time they were outside, the casket had been installed on the rack on the back of the M48. A line of soldiers moving quickly, but *not* running, carried the floral tributes from the chapel to waiting jeeps. The floral tributes included one from the French government, who had also ordered their consul general from New Orleans to pay final respects to a holder of the Croix de geurre. The decision to send the consul may have been based more on the fact that network TV crews were going to be on hand than on Greer's service to France, but the point was that he was there, and his Citroen with the CD tags and his purple ribbon of office worn diagonally across his chest gave Colonel Brandon another good shot.

As soon as the widow and her baby and the black lady had gotten into the first of two limousines, the driver of the M48 started his engine. A cloud of acrid diesel smoke was blown down the line of cars and the people waiting to get in them.

There was a second Cadillac limousine carrying Mayor and Mrs. Dutton, and then General Black's staff car, and then (as protocol demanded, since a consul general of a friendly power ranks a three-star general) the Citroen with the CD tags, then General Hoit's and General Jiggs's staff cars. Mrs. Bellmon rode with General and Mrs. Jiggs.

Preceding the M48 were a company of the WOC battalion; the color guard; the staff car carrying the three clergy; and the four jeeps carrying the floral tributes.

Following General Jiggs's staff car were the 77th U.S. Army Band; a company of troops from the Aviation Center; the officers and men of the U.S. Army Aviation Combat Developments Agency; the officers and men of the U.S. Army Aviation Board; and then the other distinguished guests and friends.

The funeral parade moved slowly away from the main post chapel, down the winding street past the officer's open mess golf course, down Third Avenue, and finally to Parade Ground No. 2.

There were permanent bleachers erected on Parade Ground No. 2, and they were filled with people. Military personnel, except for essential operating personnel, had been ordered to be present. Civilian employees had been encouraged to be present.

The Cadillac hearse and a matching flower car which would take the casket from the post to Memory Gardens in Ozark following the award of the DFC were waiting behind the bleachers. Interment would be private.

When General Jiggs got out of his staff car, he saw, circling a mile or so away, the aircraft which would make the flyover, the final item on the agenda. When he got to the VIP stand, he saw something that was not on the schedule of events.

Drawn up at the end of the parade ground, just at the crest of the hill beyond which were the old artillery range impact areas, were the Russian T34s. They were parked in a line, twenty yards apart. Five of them. There had been, he recalled, six, but Greer had blown one of them away just before he went in.

He wondered if that was another of Colonel Tim F. Brandon's bullshit ideas or whether it had been the idea of the T34 tank crews, a tribute on their part. Well, no matter. It was too late to do anything about them now. There they sat, red stars and all.

The troops and the band had formed on the parade ground. The band was playing what the schedule of events called "appropriate music" (at the moment, "For in Her Hair, She Wore a Yellow Ribbon" in a mournful tempo) while people found their seats.

The M48 with Greer's casket was parked directly in front of the bleachers, equidistant between the troops and the bleachers. The color guard was standing next to it, facing the bleachers. They would serve as a background for the shot in which General Black would award the DFC to the widow.

When all but a few stragglers had found their seats, the band began to play "The Washington Post March." The troop units marched past the bleachers and then back where they had been.

General Black and party marched out onto the field. The post adjutant would read the orders awarding the DFC posthumously to First Lieutenant Edward C. Greer. General Black would then walk to where the widow sat in the bleachers and pin the decoration to her dress. He would then turn and make his "final remarks," during which he would apologize to the air force for violating the Key West Agreement of 1948. Then the flyover would take place, an empty slot in the final "V" formation representing the lost pilot.

When that was over, the pallbearers would carry the casket from the M48 to the hearse, and that would be the end of it.

It had been arranged for whatever was said over the microphones to be transmitted to the aircraft circling a mile or so away, so their flight over the parade ground would be when it was required sequentially, rather than at a specific time. It had been realized by the planners that it would be next to impossible to run the operation by the clock.

And, as always, there was one sonofabitch who hadn't gotten the word. In addition to the steady drone of the aircraft engines orbiting a mile or so away at 3,500 feet, there came the sound of one chopper, much lower and much closer. Heads turned to locate it.

The ground control officer behind the bleachers went on the air, repeating over and over, changing frequencies to make sure the dumb sonofabitch finally heard him, "Chopper operating in vicinity of Parade Ground No. 2, immediately leave this area. Chopper operating in vicinity of Parade Ground No. 2, immediately leave this area."

The pilot apparently wasn't listening to his radio, or more likely, the ground control officer decided, he was listening to the adjutant reading the general order awarding Greer his DFC. Whatever the reason, the sound of his engine didn't go away, and when they finished reading the order, it even grew louder.

And then as General Black walked across the field to present the DFC to Melody Dutton Greer, the machine came in view. It popped up behind a row of barracks behind the massed troops, and then a moment later dropped out of sight again. They could hear the engine, but they couldn't see it. The next time they saw it, it was behind them, and people just had time to turn their heads and spot it and identify it as an H-19C before it dropped out of sight again.

The ground controller ran from his portable radio to the VIP section of the bleachers and to the microphone General Black would use for his remarks. He grabbed it.

"Helicopter operating in vicinity of Parade Ground No. 2, leave the area immediately. Leave the area immediately."

If the dumb bastard was listening to the speeches, he would hear the order.

The chopper appeared a third time, this time to the left of Parade Ground No. 2. It popped up, but this time it did not immediately drop back down again. This time, the cyclic obviously in full up position, the engine obviously being called upon to deliver full emergency military power, it rose nearly straight up to maybe 2,500 feet. Then the nose dropped, and the sound of the rotors changed pitch. The chopper pilot made a full-bore, high-speed run down the center of the parade ground, coming so low that he actually had to pick the chopper up to get over the M48 with the flagged-draped casket on it.

One of the network TV cameramen, spinning rapidly to keep the chopper in his viewfinder, fell off the camera platform. In desperation, he grabbed for the camera and pulled it off the platform with him.

That meant, Colonel Brandon thought, that only two networks would be able to telecast the antics of this idiot. Then he realized that this was wishful thinking. The media stuck together. One of the two who had got the shot would make it available to the moron who fell off the platform. This whole thing would be on the six o'clock news, although not exactly in the way Colonel Brandon had intended.

When the pilot got to the tanks, he pulled the chopper up again and stood it on its side, then passed over the troops in ranks. Still banking, he turned back over the parade ground, slowing up, straightening out, until he was in an "out of ground effect hover" directly over the M48.

The downblast from the rotors blew dust thirty feet in the air. Hats flew. Major MacMillan and WOJG Franklin jumped up on the M48 to lie on the casket, to keep the flapping flag from being blown off.

The helicopter could be clearly seen now. The fuselage had been painted black. On the fuselage, between the trailing end of the door and the tail boom, was a white outline sketch of Woody Woodpecker. Woody was pictured leering with joy as he threw beer bottles.

Above him, in clear, legible letters was the legend: Big Bad Bird II.

There were strange-looking objects, which very few people had ever seen before, mounted on the landing wheel struts. Exactly fifteen seconds after Big Bad Bird II had come to a hover over the M48 carrying Ed Greer's casket, there was a dull rumbling noise from the helicopter. A stream of 3.5 inch rockets came from the left canister, twenty-seven in all in 7.5

seconds. Then in another 7.5 seconds, twenty-seven more from the right canister.

In fifteen seconds, fifty-four rockets. In fifteen seconds, five perfectly functioning T34 tanks were turned into so many tons of twisted, useless metal.

Big Bad Bird II dropped its nose and flew slowly down the parade ground through the clouds of dense black diesel smoke rising from the blown-away T34s and disappeared.

The TV cameras made an arty shot. They followed the dense cloud of smoke from the burning T34s as it rose up into the sky.

Melody Dutton Greer looked up at General E. Z. Black.

"Is that what Ed was working on?" she asked.

"That's it," General Black said.

"You really put on a show for me, didn't you?" Melody asked.

"I had nothing to do with it, honey," General Black said. "That was the 'legendary Major Lowell' paying his condolences."

General Black then delivered his final remarks. He departed from his prepared text. He made no reference whatever to the air force—or to the Key West Agreement of 1948.

Major General Paul Jiggs had concluded who was responsible long before General Black had. He had suspected who was responsible when he'd seen the spectacular climb the pilot had made before he made the high-speed run. When he'd returned to hover over the casket, there had been no doubt. Jiggs couldn't see the pilot, but the right-side window had had something taped to it: the soiled and somewhat frayed guidon that was once the property of the 73rd Heavy Battalion. General Jiggs had even been able to read the grease-pencil lettering which spelled out "T/F LOWELL."

He called over the provost marshal.

"Get me Major Craig W. Lowell," he said. "He's probably going to try to take off from Laird in the next couple of minutes in a civilian Aero Commander. But I don't care where he is. You get him for me."

* * *

(Two)
Laird Army Airfield
Fort Rucker, Alabama
28 December 1958

General E. Z. Black walked into the VIP lounge where Major Lowell was being detained. An MP captain and the airfield commander called "atten-hut" almost in unison.

"Thank you, gentlemen," General Black said. "That will be all." He waited until they had left before speaking.

"Fascinating demonstration, Major," he said, finally.

"L'audace, l'audace, toujours l'audace, mon général," Lowell replied.

"What I really would like to know, Lowell," General Black said, "is whether that was audacity or stupidity, and more importantly, whether you know the difference."

"I didn't want the Big Bad Bird going down the toilet, General," Lowell said.

"That's it. That's the bottom line?"

"Yes, sir."

"Where did you get the other firing mechanisms?" Black asked.

"Redundancy, General," Lowell said. "I learned all about redundancy when I was a young officer."

"And you got Cramer to help you?"

"I assume full responsibility, General."

"And besides, 'what the hell, they won't court-martial me anyhow; I'm being thrown out of the army anyway, and a court-martial would be embarrassing'?"

"That did occur to me, General," Major Lowell said.

General Black went to the window and pushed the curtain aside. An air force Grumman, a VIP transport, was waiting for him. He had been down here too long as it was.

"You have an interesting ally, Major," General Black said. "Actually, it's ironic."

"I'm afraid I don't quite understand you, sir," Lowell said.

"Brandon," General Black said. "That horse's ass actually tried to save your ass, Major. He lost no time in pointing out to me that socking it to you would not be in the best interests of the army."

"He's a horse ass," Lowell said. "But you need people like that."

"The army needs all kinds of strange people, Lowell. Horse's asses like Brandon, and even people like you."

"Sir?"

"Let me tell you what happened, Lowell," Black said. "I was so goddamned mad when that asshole came and said we should handle your case with what he called 'delicacy,' I almost kicked his ass. Literally, not figuratively. I had a nearly uncontrollable impulse to open the car door and kick his fat ass out."

He looked at Lowell to make sure Lowell understood he was telling the truth. "A long time ago, I learned something about myself," he went on. "It might be useful to you. Whenever you *really* lose your temper, there is a very good possibility that you're wrong about whatever pissed you off."

He paused again. "Phrased very simply, when you break a shoelace, that's your fault for not noticing the shoelace was worn and should have been replaced. You understand?"

"I don't get your point," Lowell said, simply.

"What really pissed me off about you, Lowell, had nothing to do with your screwing the senator's wife. What enraged me was that I had personally given you an order, and you had disobeyed me."

"You mean about staying away from Felter?"

"That's right. Here you are, a miserable major, with a well-deserved reputation for being, on occasion, a colossal fuck-up, and you get an order from the Vice Chief of Staff and you disobey it."

"I'm guilty of that, sir."

"And I'm guilty of violating a principle of command that I learned when I was a second lieutenant," General Black said. "Never give an order you know will not be obeyed."

"You had the right to expect me to obey your order, sir," Lowell said.

"The right, sure; but considering the personality, no reasonable expectation that you would."

Lowell looked at him and said nothing.

"I didn't think it through," Black said. "There was no way,

no way, that you were going to sever your relationship with a man who had saved your ass in Greece, who had buried your wife when you were off at war, simply because some old fart who can't pour piss out of a boot tells you to."

"I don't think of you that way, General," Lowell said.

"OK. Put it this way. You decided the order made no sense, so fuck it."

"Yes, sir. That's pretty close."

"OK. Now I'll explain point two of this little lecture. Once I got pissed off at you, it was easy to keep pouring gas on the flames. Whatsername, the senator's horny wife, for example. And then I found the real excuse to get mad at you."

"What was that?"

"'How dare that young sonofabitch, with a brain like his, with a proven capability of combat command, fuck up his own career the way he has? I'll fix his ass: I'll throw his ass out of the army.'"

He stopped and lit a cigarette, and then looked into Lowell's eyes.

"Am I getting through to you, Major?"

"I understand what you're saying, General Black, and I'm grateful for the explanation," Lowell replied. "But I don't understand the point of it."

"I dared entertain the hope," Black said, sarcastically, "that a few words of a philosophical nature might be of value to you in your later career, when you might lose your temper and make a bad decision."

"They make decisions by committee in the banking business, General," Lowell said.

"You missed my most important point, Lowell. Perhaps I should have spelled it out."

"Sir?"

"When you know you've made a mistake, you bust your ass to correct it. Even if it means you are going to have one hell of an argument with the Chief of Staff."

"I don't want to sound stupid," Lowell said, "but the only interpretation I can put on that is that you have changed your mind about throwing me out of the army. And I'm afraid to hope for that."

"As of 1 January 1959, you are relieved from DCSLOG and assigned here for duty with the Army Aviation Board as project officer for the rocket-armed helicopter."

"Thank you, sir," Lowell said.

"Don't make me regret it, Major," Black said. He met Lowell's eyes for a moment, and then he pushed open the glass door from the VIP lounge and walked out to the Grumman VIP transport.

They had not, Lowell realized, exchanged salutes. He pushed open the glass door and went out on the taxiway. The door to the Grumman was already closed, and the pilot was in the process of starting the port engine. The Grumman started to taxi.

Major Lowell raised his hand in salute and held it, even when there was no response from inside the airplane, until the Grumman had turned onto the runway and started the takeoff roll.

Bestselling War Fiction and Non-Fiction

☐ Bat 21	William C Anderson	£2.50
☐ Royal Navy and the Falklands War	David Brown	£8.99
☐ The Cocaine Wars	Paul Eddy	£3.99
☐ China Seas	John Harris	£3.99
☐ Passage to Mutiny	Alexander Kent	£3.50
☐ Colours Aloft	Alexander Kent	£2.99
☐ The Hour of the Lily	John Kruse	£3.50
☐ The Bombers	Norman Longmate	£4.99
☐ Convoy	Dudley Pope	£3.50
☐ Winged Escort	Douglas Reeman	£2.99
☐ Typhoon Pilot	Desmond Scott	£2.99
☐ The Spoils of War	Douglas Scott	£2.99
☐ Johnny Gurkha	E D Smith	£2.95
☐ Duel in the Dark	Peter Townsend	£3.95

Prices and other details are liable to change

ARROW BOOKS, BOOKSERVICE BY POST, PO BOX 29, DOUGLAS, ISLE OF MAN, BRITISH ISLES

NAME..

ADDRESS...

....

....

Please enclose a cheque or postal order made out to Arrow Books Ltd. for the amount due and allow the following for postage and packing.

U.K. CUSTOMERS: Please allow 22p per book to a maximum of £3.00.

B.F.P.O. & EIRE: Please allow 22p per book to a maximum of £3.00.

OVERSEAS CUSTOMERS: Please allow 22p per book.

Whilst every effort is made to keep prices low it is sometimes necessary to increase cover prices at short notice. Arrow Books reserve the right to show new retail prices on covers which may differ from those previously advertised in the text or elsewhere.